Falling for Owen

Also by Jennifer Ryan

The Return of Brody McBride
Chasing Morgan
The Right Bride
Lucky Like Us
Saved by the Rancher

Short Stories
"Waiting For You"
(appears in *Confessions of a Secret Admirer*)
"Can't Wait"
(appears in *All I Want for Christmas Is a Cowboy*)

Falling for Owen

Book Two: The McBrides

JENNIFER RYAN

EPub Edition APRIL 2014 ISBN: 9780062306081

Print Edition ISBN: 9780062306104

JV 10 9 8 7 6 5

Chapter One

DALE HID BETWEEN two buildings, watching his wife and her cocky lawyer walk down the steps from his office. One of the upstairs rooms in the converted two-story home probably had a freshly rumpled bed. No way the guy got away with stealing his wife, convincing her to divorce him, and sleeping with her right under his nose.

Not his fault she pushed him too far. She knew better than to cross the line, especially when he was drunk and not in control. They'd done this kind of thing often enough.

He'd left her pissed off and knocked a few back at what used to be Roxy's bar. The McBrides owned it now. He'd driven home half in the bag and discovered a bunch of pigs in his yard, red and blue lights flashing. Maybe he'd had a few too many and said things he shouldn't have when the cops approached him. Definitely shouldn't have hit the cop and gone for his gun in some mad dash to get to his wife and make her take back all the lies spilling from her cunning lips.

Still, he'd gone to jail and the no-good lawyer across the street took advantage of his wife, convincing Shannon to press assault charges and file for divorce. While he sat rotting in a cell for more than a year, that man took what belonged to him. Well, Shannon would come back. She always did.

And he'd make the lawyer pay.

Chapter Two

Claire woke out of a sound sleep with a gasp and held her breath, trying to figure out what startled her. She listened to the quiet night. Nothing but crickets and the breeze rustling the trees outside. A twig snapped on the ground below her window. Her heart hammered faster and she sucked in a breath, trying not to panic. Living in the country lent itself to overactive imaginings about things that go bump in the dark night. The noise could be anything from a stray dog or cat to a raccoon on a midnight raid of her garbage cans—even an opossum looking for a little action.

Settled back into her pillow and the thick blankets, she closed her eyes, but opened them wide when something big brushed against the side of the house. Freaked out, she slipped out of bed and went to the window. She pulled the curtain back with one finger and peeked through the crack, scanning the moonlit yard below for wayward critters. Not so easy to see with the quarter moon, but she watched the shadows for anything suspicious. Nothing moved.

Not satisfied, and certainly not able to sleep without a more thorough investigation, she padded down the scarred wood stairs to the living room. She skirted packing boxes and the sofa and went to the window overlooking the front yard. Nothing moved. Still not satisfied, she walked to the dining room, opened the blinds, and stared out into the cold night. Something banged one flower pot into another on the back patio, drawing her away from the dining room, through the kitchen, and to the counter. She grabbed the phone off the charger, went around the island, and skimmed along the breakfast bar to the sliding glass door. She peeked out, hiding most of her body by the wall and ducking her head out to see if someone was trying to break into her house. Like she thought, the small pot filled with marigolds had been knocked over and broken against the pot of geraniums beside it. Upset her pretty pots and flowers were ruined, she stepped out from the wall and stood in the center of the glass door to get a better look.

With her gaze cast down on the pots, she didn't see the man step out from the other side of the patio until his shadow fell over her. His eyes went as wide as hers.

"You're not him," he said, stumbling back, knocking over a larger potted pink miniature rose bush and falling on his ass, breaking the pot and the bush with his legs. She hoped he got stuck a dozen times, but the tiny thorns probably wouldn't go through his dirt-smudged jeans.

In a rage, she opened the door, but held tight to the

handle so she could close it again if he came too close. She yelled, "What the hell are you doing?"

"I'll get him for this and for sleeping with my wife," the guy slurred. Drunk and ranting, he gained his feet but stumbled again. "Where is he?" The man turned every which way, looking past her and into her dark house.

"Who?"

"Your lying, cheating, no-good husband."

"How the hell should I know. I haven't seen or heard from him in six months."

"Liar. I saw him drive this way tonight after he fucked my wife at his office and filled her head with more bullshit lies."

"Listen, I'm sorry if my *ex* is messing with your wife. I left him almost two years ago for cheating on me. Believe me, I know how you feel, but he doesn't live here."

"You're lying. He drove his truck this way and stopped just outside."

"He doesn't drive a truck."

"Stop lying, bitch."

"I'm not. You have the wrong person."

"You tell that no-good McBride he better stop seeing my wife. If he thinks a bunch of papers will ever set her free of me, he don't know what I'm capable of, what we have. He'll be one sorry son of a bitch. She's mine. I keep what's mine."

"You don't understand."

"No. You don't understand," he said almost like a whining child. "You tell him, or I'll make him pay with what's his." He pointed an ominous finger at her. "You tell him if he doesn't leave my wife alone and let her come back to me like she wants, I'm going to hurt you before I go after him."

Pissed off he'd just threatened her life for no good reason, she fumed. "Listen mister, I don't know the man you're talking about. He doesn't live here."

"Bullshit. Don't lie to me, bitch." He grabbed one of her patio chairs and threw it at the sliding glass door. She dashed sideways along the patio and the house wall, narrowly avoiding getting hit. The glass door shattered into a million tiny bits of glass beside her.

"That's it. I'm calling the cops." She dialed 911.

He ran to her and knocked the phone out of her hand into a pile of dirt and torn marigold roots.

"Help me!" She hoped the call went through and someone heard her.

The man pushed past her, knocking her down. She cut her bare foot on a broken shard of pottery. The man disappeared around the corner of the house. A car engine started out front. She ran the other way, down the shorter side to cut him off and, hopefully, get his license plate number to give to the cops. She ran for the driveway, but he pulled out of the trees to her left. The engine revved, and he clipped her on the side, sending her crashing to the pavement, scraping her knee and elbow before she twisted and cracked the back of her head on the driveway. Stars burst on the inside of her eyelids. She lifted her head and opened her eyes, only to see his red haloed taillights fade and disappear around the corner and onto the main road.

Bleary eyed and dizzy, she tried to plant her hands on

the ground and raise herself up. She fell flat again. The world spun and shadows swam, making her close her eyes, only to open them and see nothing but blurry shapes.

Her eyes closed, her face hit the cement, and everything went black.

CLAIRE WOKE TO chaos. Two men hovered over her. She threw up her hands to push them away, but they grabbed hold and pushed her arms to her sides.

"You're okay, Miss Walsh. We're the paramedics. The police are here."

"How did you guys get here?"

"The 911 dispatcher got your address from your phone number. She heard you call out for help," someone out of her line of sight explained.

She stopped struggling and tried to concentrate on what they said. She didn't know how she got on her back. She didn't care. She squeezed her eyes closed and prayed for the pounding in her head to end.

Right guy pressed a gauze pad to the back of her head. Left guy took her blood pressure. A cop came into her line of sight at her feet.

"Miss Walsh, do you know who did this to you?"

"No. I heard something outside and came down to investigate." That's when she remembered the skimpy T-shirt that only hit mid-thigh, but was rucked up to her hips. She tried to pull it down, but left guy held her arm, checking the blooming bruise on her shoulder where she hit the cement. He'd cut her shirt to investigate.

"What did you see, Miss Walsh?"

"Please call me Claire. Uh, nothing at first. I heard something knock over the pots on the patio. I thought maybe an opossum or raccoon strolled over for a midnight snack. I checked out the glass door and someone came out of the shadows and scared me half to death. My hip and feet hurt."

"You've got a nasty bruise on your hip and several nicks and cuts on your feet. Two, maybe three need stitches," right man said, dabbing antiseptic on the cut on her jaw, making her hiss in pain.

"Miss Walsh, Claire, did you see the man who did this to you?" the officer asked.

"It was dark, but he was about four inches taller than me with dark hair. He wore jeans and a dark flannel shirt. Drunk, maybe on something. He kept talking about his wife sleeping with some guy named McBride."

"Well, I'm Sheriff McBride, and I can tell you it wasn't me, so which infamous McBride? Brody or Owen?" another officer asked, walking out of her house and making his way down the path from the porch.

Infamous? There had to be a story there.

"You've got me. I don't know either of them, though we share the mail slots out on the road. Our mail gets mixed up because the addresses are so close. He said something about McBride helping his wife leave him."

"Got to be Owen. He's a lawyer now. I'll call him, see if he can give us a name."

Now? As in he'd been on the other side of the law at one time? Interesting.

Chapter Three

The pounding on the door frightened Shannon, bringing her off the couch, her hands pressed to her thrashing heart. She stared wide eyed and held her breath, resigning herself to the inevitable, knowing who was on the other side.

"Open up, Shannon. Damnit, woman, let me in."

Her ex-husband's familiar, ominous voice didn't make her feel any better. She moved to the door, making sure she'd remembered to not only throw the locks, but put the chain on the door, too.

"Shannon," Dale snapped, making her jump.

"Go away. You can't be here. I have a restraining order."

"If you think a piece of paper will keep me away, you're stupider than even I thought."

The comment stung, but he'd said a lot worse to her over the years. His words slurred, telling her he'd been out drinking, which made him all the more volatile. Drinking tended to make Dale forget his actions had consequences. Oh, he'd spout off apologies after he sobered up, but they were empty words she'd heard too many times.

"I'll call the cops."

"You do, and you'll regret it. Just like that lawyer you're fucking is going to regret stealing my wife."

The threat made her frown. Owen had been nothing but good and kind to her. He'd made her see that she deserved better than Dale. She deserved a man like Owen, who could provide for her in a way Dale never had.

"Owen didn't have anything to do with me leaving you."

"He filled your head with nonsense and lies. He'll think twice now that I got him good."

She recognized that tone and the threat behind it. "What did you do, Dale?"

"You think he's something special, but he's stringing you along while he's got another woman on the side."

"You don't know what you're talking about." She gripped her hands together, trying not to think of him with someone else. Her feelings for him had grown over the last months. They'd grown closer as friends, and she hoped something more.

"He's got a woman living in his house, keeping his bed warm, while you're nothing but a cheap afternoon fuck."

"That's not true." Owen took care of her like Dale never did.

"Sure is. Now open this fucking door."

His fists pounded so hard, he rattled the door in its frame and the chain clinked against the wood. She pressed both hands to it, holding it closed. When he got like this, there was no telling him to stop, or detouring him from whatever he got into his head.

"I'm calling the police," she screamed. "Go away."

He pounded the door with one more thwack of his fist against the outside and all went quiet. She waited. Nothing.

She turned, her knees buckled, and she slid to the floor, her back against the door. All of a sudden, he pounded five more times, rattling her spine along with the door.

"This isn't over."

With those ominous words, everything went quiet again. Deep in her soul, she knew he meant those words. This would never end. He'd never stop. Unless someone stopped him.

At one time, she'd appreciated his single-minded need for her. She'd cultivated it. Not anymore. She needed something more.

She needed Owen.

Chapter Four

OWEN WOKE OUT of a restless sleep the second the phone rang. The clock read twelve forty-seven. Good news never came this late at night. He hoped this didn't have anything to do with Shannon, his trouble-prone client. He wished he knew why women stayed in bad situations instead of walking away and never looking back. Shannon had a tendency to waffle under pressure. She'd given her husband far too many chances to prove he wasn't worth a single one of them.

He hoped she hadn't listened to whatever sob story Dale conjured to elicit her sympathy, only to draw her in close again. Close enough to hurt her.

Owen grabbed the phone on the second ring. "McBride."

"Owen, are you okay? He said he hurt you. You have to be all right. I don't know what I'd do if I lost you."

The last part set off an alarm in his head. Wasn't the first time she'd set it off either.

"Shannon, slow down. What are you talking about? I'm fine."

"Dale. He came by, drunk and belligerent as always. Yelling about seeing us together and you taking me away from him."

Owen raked his fingers through his hair and sat up on the side of the bed, naked and frustrated. Mostly because his bed was empty, but also because his client's never-ending saga with her ex-husband continued to drag him into her life. He cared about all his clients in some respect, but she'd taken the job he did and the protection it provided her and made it into something more. She'd never quite crossed the line and pushed him for anything, but her reliance on him grew more and more each time they met. He needed some space.

"Where is he now?"

"He left when I refused to open the door and threatened to call the cops."

Well, at least she'd gotten that part right this time. In the past, she had opened the door and gotten yelled at and worse. She'd seen the inside of an emergency room more times than he'd like to count because of her ex.

"Good job. Never open the door to him. He disobeyed the restraining order. I'll contact the police and let them know."

"So, he didn't hurt your girlfriend?"

"I don't have a girlfriend."

Her audible exhale of relief sent up another red flag. Still, he didn't know what the hell she was talking about. He hadn't dated anyone in nearly a year. God, had it been that long? His many restless nights confirmed the unhappy truth.

Another call came in on his line. "Hold on, Shannon. I've got another call."

"Um, okay."

He clicked the talk button to switch lines. "McBride."

"Owen, it's Dylan."

His cousin had moved back to town recently with his adopted son and took over as sheriff. The late-night call probably meant more trouble.

"Hey man. What's up?"

"I'm looking for a guy about five-eleven says you slept with his wife. Know who I'm talking about?"

Owen swore. "Dale Monoghan. Released from prison about a month ago. Spent those weeks of freedom stalking and harassing my *client*. Skipped out on the halfway house two days after moving in and has been MIA ever since. My client is on the other line. Dale just left her place spouting off about hurting me and my girlfriend, though I'm not seeing anyone. I'd appreciate it if you sent someone to her place to make sure he's left and she's in one piece."

"I'll send an officer right away. We've got a problem with your name on it at the Walsh place down the road from you. Miss Walsh confronted a trespasser. Your guy is up for a hit and run charge and some other misdemeanors. Can you come down and answer some questions?"

"Is Claire all right?"

"Banged up, but nothing major."

Owen swore and raked his hand through his hair again. The thought of someone hurting the quiet, beautiful woman whose property adjoined his pissed him off. His stomach tied in knots. His mind conjured one terrible image after another. He hated to think of her hurt and frightened.

He'd never formally met his long-distance neighbor, but he'd seen her several times in her yard when he stopped near her place to get his mail. He took his nieces into her store in town once in a while. They loved it. He liked looking at her. He might have asked her out, but she'd always had this off-limits vibe about her, even if she did stare at him sometimes with this odd look about her.

Looks like he'd at least get an introduction tonight, though he didn't think she'd be happy to meet him if his client's ex caused her trouble and hurt her. Damn the drunk asshole.

"On my way." Owen put action to words and grabbed his jeans. "Send a deputy over to 214 Walnut Road. I'll let my client know they'll be there soon."

He switched lines and slid his legs into the jeans. He grabbed a long-sleeve shirt out of the dresser.

"Shannon, I've asked the police to come and check on you. Dale harassed a woman and hit her with his car. If he comes back before they get there, do not open the door."

"Oh my God. Is the woman okay?"

"I don't know. I have to go see. Do not open the door to anyone but the cops. I'll speak to you later."

He hung up and tossed the phone on his rumpled bed. Socks on, he grabbed his boots and stuffed his feet inside and ran down the stairs, grabbing his keys as he headed out the door to his truck. He jumped inside, started it up, and punched the gas, nervous and anxious to get to his neighbor's place.

Owen's truck slid to a stop in the driveway behind two sheriff cars and the ambulance. The paramedics' presence sent an ominous chill up his back. He had no idea how badly the woman had been hurt, but the thought of even one mark on her sent a shaft of guilt through his system. He should have done more to keep Dale behind bars longer.

The headlights and porch lights lit his way around the ambulance to the walkway where the paramedics kneeled next to a blonde, her head bent to her chest as they worked on her feet. Propped on a gurney, her feet bled from multiple cuts. Owen ignored the looks from the deputy and his cousin, Dylan, and went directly to the woman. Kneeling beside her, he cupped her cheek in his palm and asked, "Are you okay?"

Like slow motion, her face rose up and her eyes met his and he fell into the green depths and felt something shift inside his chest. The taut band that took hold of him with the call pulled tighter and stopped his breath. Her eyes filled with unshed tears. She shook and trembled under his hand, but she didn't speak.

"Hey now, you're okay. It's going to be fine. Don't you worry. I'll take care of everything."

"We need to talk," Dylan said.

Owen smiled at Claire, despite the circumstances.

"Wish you could slap the cuffs on *me* this time?" he asked his cousin.

"It'd be fun. For me. Why, feeling nostalgic?"

"No. What happened?" Reluctantly, he stood and faced Dylan and this mess head on. He stayed right beside the woman. Drawn to her, the urge to protect her kept him rooted to his spot beside her. He wanted to touch her again, offer up some kind of comfort, but refrained, willing himself to be calm and act rationally and not touch a stranger like she was his best friend. And more.

"Claire—"

Pretty name.

"—heard a noise outside and came down to investigate. A man, five-eleven with dark hair, appeared at the back door, where he'd broken several flower pots and fell over drunk. She went out to investigate. They exchanged words, and he threw a chair through the glass doors." Dylan indicated he look through the open front door, straight back to the chair lying on its side on the dining table.

"The description fits Dale, but how did you know this has to do with me?"

"The guy, Dale, threatened to hurt her to make you pay for sleeping with his wife."

"I am not, nor have I ever slept with his wife. She's a client. Let's get that straight right now. I represented her in the divorce and helped put him behind bars for hurting her."

He didn't know why he felt the need to defend himself so vehemently. He didn't want Dylan thinking he slept with his clients. On second thought, he didn't give a shit what Dylan thought. He didn't want Claire thinking he would do something like that, or that he was dating anyone.

Why did it matter so much? He knew her name, but didn't know her. Still, something compelled him to make the clarification.

Which is probably why he looked her right in the eye when he made the statement. He shot Dylan a cold glare. His cousin hid a smirk that set off Owen's temper even more.

"How long have you known Claire?" Dylan asked, a note of suspicion in the simple question.

"I don't. Not really. I've seen her in passing from the road when I grab my mail and at her shop in town."

"He brings the girls in sometimes," Claire said from beside him. Hearing her voice, so soft and timid, made his gut tighten.

"How is Rain?" Dylan asked.

"She's great."

"And happy Brody is back in town. I haven't seen them since that shit went down with Roxy. I'll have to stop by and catch up. He's another reformed troublemaker."

Dylan had the luxury of growing up with a father who loved him and did right by him. Owen and Brody's uncle wasn't a drunk. No, he lived a good life with his wife and son and worked hard. They were well off, while Owen and Brody scraped by all their lives with their alcoholic father.

Where Dylan grew up the high school all star, he and Brody had been the outcast troublemakers. Well, things changed.

"We're not cocky punks anymore. Aside from growing up, we took our lumps and learned our lessons. It's been a long time since I trespassed on Ms. Firths's property to fish in her pond." One of his many smaller transgressions. "Now, tell me why Dale attacked Claire for no good reason."

"He thinks you're having an affair with his wife," Claire explained, drawing his attention once again.

He bent next to her and gave her his full attention. "What did he say to you?"

"He wanted to know where my husband is. I told him my ex doesn't live here, and he said he saw him drive by in his truck. I knew at that point he didn't mean my ex, but you. I tried to tell him he had the wrong person, but he swore he'd get back at you and he'd hurt me to do it."

She drifted off for a moment, so he brushed his fingers up and down her arm to draw her attention.

"My head hurts," she whispered, her eyes going soft and distant again.

"She hit her head on the pavement after he hit her with the car," Dylan explained. "Knocked her out for at least a couple of minutes."

"Honey, you need to go to the hospital. You probably have a concussion."

"We're taking her for stitches and to get her head examined in a few minutes," the paramedics confirmed.

"I'll come with you."

"Why?" Claire asked.

"I'll drive you home. You're in no condition to be left on your own."

"I don't need your help."

"You've got it all the same. In some roundabout way, this is partially my fault. The least I can do is make sure you're tended to at the hospital and you're safe when you return."

Claire considered the shambles of her dining room and patio. The glass scattered on the floor and the giant hole in the sliding glass door. Her mind spun out with all she needed to do to put things right: Call the insurance company and a glass repair service. Clean the floor and board up the window. There went her kitchen budget. The trip to the hospital would probably wipe it out.

"No new refrigerator, I guess."

"Dinosaurs aren't as old as that thing you've got in your kitchen," Dylan teased.

Owen's laugh and smile were sure to pull any woman in the vicinity under his enigmatic spell.

She couldn't help herself; she laughed with them. If it held a note of hysteria, oh well. She hurt everywhere, her muscles ached, and she felt like crying, but the tears didn't come.

"The man who did this really hates you," she said.

"I can handle him. He's not a nice guy. He beat and mistreated his wife for years. She finally had enough and pressed charges. I convinced her to leave him for good."

The frustration in his voice spoke of a lot more to the story. "You don't think she'll stay away from him?"

"I know he won't stay away from her. We'll find him and make sure he pays for hurting you."

"You think he'll come back."

"If he thinks you're tied to me, he might."

She appreciated his honesty and ran her shaking hand through her hair and brought it back down to her lap. He took it into his warm, rough hands and held it. Their eyes met again and she fell into the blue depths and his earnest gaze.

"You'll be okay. I promise."

Unable to answer, she gave him a nod. She wanted to believe him, but she'd learned over the past few years not to rely on anyone but herself for everything. She'd worked hard to rebuild her life and find a direction that made her feel self-assured and accomplished. She thought she'd put fear behind her and embraced this new life and living alone.

She'd find her center again, once the initial terror wore off and she had her home back to rights. She'd take on a project in the house, maybe finish the master bath. She'd already bought all the supplies. She imagined how it would look once complete and sighed. God, how she'd like to sink into a warm bath, close her eyes, and forget this day ever happened.

"Time to go," the paramedic said.

Owen stood and backed away, giving her space, but she wanted to call him back. The reassuring feeling she'd had when he held her hand disappeared under the rush of pain and fear she couldn't escape.

Her head spun and she reached up and put her hand to her aching head and the lemon-size knot at the back. The paramedics had cleaned off the blood. Right guy gave her an ice pack and she leaned back on it, closing her eyes.

"I'll be right behind you, Claire. I'll catch up to you once the doctor sees you," Owen promised.

"You're very kind, Mr. McBride, but it's not necessary. I'm sure I can find my own way home."

"My name is Owen. Use it," he pressed gently. "Get used to me hanging around. Until they find and lock up Dale, I'm not taking any chances he comes back and hurts you again. Besides, someone needs to help you clean up this place."

"I'll take care of it."

"You don't have to do it alone. Get her in the ambulance," he ordered the paramedics, not giving her a chance to argue further. Funny, she didn't want to argue with him. She liked the idea of him hanging around. Who wouldn't want a gorgeous man to help her out and protect her from the bad guy? Besides, she just liked looking at him. Tall, blond, eyes the color of a summer sky that went soft when his gaze fell on her. Every flex of his muscles revealed beneath the shirt that fit tight across his chest and over his well-defined arms. All that strength muted when he touched her softly. Her skin still tingled where he'd brushed his hand up and down her arm. She wondered if he'd make the rest of her feel that good if he kept touching her. Everywhere.

Maybe she really did need her head examined.

Chapter Five

HOURS LATER, TIRED and hurting, Claire sat on the bed behind the curtain in the ER. She'd been poked and prodded, had her head and cognitive and motor skills evaluated and her feet stitched in three different places. Luckily, none of the cuts on the bottom of her feet were too bad. She'd be able to walk, once the swelling went down. The sides of her feet hadn't fared as well. Some of those cuts went deep.

She had a new, not-so-cute pair of flip-flops. Still, they looked better than her bloodstained shirt. The blue fabric had faded long ago. Tight across her breasts, the fabric dropped to mid-thigh. She plucked at the unraveling thread at the hem. Time to throw it out.

With her head bent, she stared at the pair of dark brown cowboy boots that appeared on the floor just past her feet. She looked up and nearly laughed when Owen made a point to look her right in the eye, instead of dipping his gaze to the deep V in her shirt and her nearly completely exposed breasts, thanks to the paramedic cutting it open to check her bruised and scraped shoulder. She appreciated his good manners, and the way he seemed to ignore her state of undress for her benefit. Mostly. He shifted from one foot to the other, signaling his discomfort. The intensity of his stare made her feel like she held his complete attention. She liked it. It filled her with a warmth she'd never felt and wanted to keep, but she'd fallen for a handsome man once before and found nothing but heartache and anger when his need for every female's attention overshadowed every promise he'd made to her. Never again. Still, it didn't hurt to look. And dream.

"Ready to go? The doctor signed you out."

She could get used to that deep, husky voice. "Sure."

He didn't make a move to leave, so she stared at him and tried to lighten the mood and his intense study of her. "I don't think pink's your color."

"Huh?"

"Is that my robe you're holding on to?"

He'd walked in with it over his shoulder. He held it in his hand and brushed his fingers over the soft material. She bought it for the same reason. She'd never felt anything so soft against her skin. A tactile person, she loved to buy soft, luxurious-feeling things because sometimes all you had to hug was a blanket.

Judging by the muscles stretching the cotton shirt Owen wore, there wasn't much soft about him. She liked that, too. Sometimes wrapping yourself in strength gave another kind of comfort. One she hadn't allowed herself in a long time. Tonight, after the ordeal she'd been through, she wouldn't mind having those strong arms wrapped around her and pressing her cheek to his hard chest.

Maybe the doctor could give her a pill to counteract the stupidity part of her brain. This man had children with a beautiful woman she didn't know. Their relationship seemed more like friends, and she'd put him and the kids' mother in the divorced or never married and separated category. Either way, he wasn't for her.

Owen pulled the robe off his shoulder and draped it over her back. She stuffed her right arm in with ease, but her left shoulder hurt like hell where she landed and skidded on the driveway. The nurse had placed an ice pack over it and wrapped her shoulder with an elastic bandage to hold it in place. Cold, her nipples stood out against the T-shirt's thin fabric. The nurse left ten minutes ago to get her a blanket, but must have gotten sidetracked with a more important task.

"Let me help you. That shoulder doesn't look so good."

"It's not so bad."

"Now that it's numb, right?"

She giggled. "Right."

"Nice shoes."

She stared down at her bandaged feet in the flip-flops. "Yeah. Want to go dancing?" she teased.

"Any time you want." His voice didn't hold a teasing tone, but she let it go, remembering him with his girls and the woman he may or may not be together with now, but still had a commitment to because of those beautiful little ones. She thought fleetingly again about what she'd wanted out of her marriage and how all her dreams crashed and burned along with the vows her ex made to her.

The nurse walked in with a wheelchair, saving her from having to comment. Owen took her arm to help her off the bed. That same zing of heat and awareness rippled through her at his touch. His smoldering blue gaze met hers, but she settled into the chair, avoiding the look and what it told her. He may be interested, but she refused to be the other woman in his life.

Owen took over for the nurse and wheeled Claire out the double doors of the ER and straight to his truck parked at the curb. He set the brake and took her hand to help her up. He liked touching her. Something strange came over him that he liked so much he felt compelled to do it again and again.

Her condition made climbing into the truck difficult, so he put his hands on her tiny waist and lifted her up and into the seat. Her hands grabbed hold of his shoulders and for a second he stared at her with his hands on her and her hands on him, a wonderful electricity circling through him to her and back. Connected. He'd never felt this way about any other woman he'd touched.

Again, she broke free of the spell first and scooted further onto the seat. He let her go. She'd been through a lot tonight. Tired, she let out a yawn and settled back in the seat. He took both her feet, knocking off the flip-flops, and placed both her feet on the dashboard. He brushed his fingers over her pretty pink painted nails, smiling because she had really cute toes.

"All set?"

"Uh, yeah, I'm fine."

He grabbed the seat belt and wrapped it around her, leaning in close. She didn't move. Held her breath. He hid a smile, knowing he affected her as much as she stirred him.

Yeah, he'd dance to any tune she played. An unsettling thought for a man who'd spent his life enjoying women, never really taking the time to get to know them. Not really. He had a million questions he wanted to ask Claire. Well after three in the morning, he'd have to wait. A perfect excuse to see her again. Not that he needed a reason.

He'd seen her a dozen times over the last year and half, but he'd never introduced himself, even though he'd wanted to. Of course, most of the times he'd had his nieces with him, so hitting on a woman with them present—not cool.

"You know, we've never actually met. I'm Owen McBride." He held out his hand to her.

She took it and shook. "Claire Walsh. You come into my shop with your girls."

"They love your place. Whenever I steal them from their mother, they ask to go to your café and bookstore. I think they like making a rough guy like me play tea party."

"You always seem to enjoy yourself. You're really good with them."

"I love those girls to death. They have such a fresh and unspoiled view of the world. They remind me not to be so serious. I have so much fun with them."

Claire's soft smile turned into another big yawn. "I'd really like to go home."

"Okay."

"Are we leaving soon?" she asked when he didn't move to get in the car and drive them home.

"As soon as you give me back my hand."

This time, he smiled when she looked down at their joined hands she held in her lap. She released him and squirmed in her seat. Yeah, he wasn't the only one who felt the heat between them.

He closed her door, skirted the front of the truck, and jumped in behind the wheel. He held the key, but didn't turn it and start the engine. Instead, he cocked his head and stared at her one more time, from her pretty toes to her disheveled golden hair. Nervous, she grabbed the long strands, brought the bundle over her shoulder, and draped it over her breasts. The mass waved softly down to nearly her waist. His eyes followed the line to her legs, outstretched to the dashboard. She tugged at the hem of her short robe.

Claire seemed oblivious to her appeal. Of course, she'd had a hell of a night. Still, she looked better than great, even with the gash along her jaw, the ice pack wrapped around her shoulder, and her feet wrapped up in bandages. He liked her rumpled hair and clothes. It made her seem more approachable, where her put-together, business-casual-slacks-and-blouses appearance at her shop made her seem less so because she was so appealing.

"With all that happened tonight, I forgot to ask if you'd like me to contact someone for you. Your parents? A friend? A boyfriend maybe?"

"I'm not seeing anyone."

"Glad to hear it."

"Isn't your wife waiting for you to get home?"

He turned in his seat and faced her. "Do you really think I'd say something like that if I had a wife?"

"A wedding ring doesn't always stop a man from flirting."

"I'm not wearing a wedding ring."

"They slip off as easily as clothes when a man wants another woman."

"I'm going to chalk up the insults to my character to the fact that you've had a crappy night and you're exhausted."

"Oh come on. You come in with your girls all the time. It's only natural I'd think you actually married their mother, though I don't see you with all of them often."

"While I love and adore Rain, she belongs to my brother, Brody. And so do the girls."

"Huh?"

"I love them like they're mine, but the girls are my nieces," he said, shifting back in his seat and starting the engine. "That ex you referred to earlier must have been a real piece of work. Someone should kick his ass."

"Well, after hearing you with the sheriff . . ."

"Right. I got arrested a couple of times for drunk and disorderly, started a couple of bar fights back in the day, so

I must be a deadbeat dad who knocked up some woman and never married her. No matter what I may have done in the past, I never hurt a woman or treated her bad. So we're clear, I don't sleep with my clients either, despite what that asshole, Dale, said to you tonight."

"I was going to say you've obviously changed, moved to the right side of the law as an attorney, helping women escape their deadbeat and abusive husbands, and I'm sorry for jumping to conclusions about the girls. You come into the shop with them. They kind of look like you, so yeah, I thought they were your daughters. I've even seen you play softball with them."

"Don't worry about it. With a past like mine, I'm used to people thinking the worst."

Her hand settled on his arm and he tried not to notice the way she softly rubbed her hand over his bicep.

"It's very sweet you have tea parties with your nieces and play ball with them. You look especially fetching in the pink boa and golden crown." She held back the smile, but underneath she was laughing at him.

He relaxed and felt his own smile. "Is it your secret way of torturing men, keeping all those dress-up clothes in the shop?"

"Kids love to play pretend. When little girls can get the big, strapping men in their lives to be silly with them, it builds their confidence and endears the men to them even more."

"Yeah, well, I'd do anything for Dawn and Autumn."

"When they grow up, they won't settle for a man who'd do anything less. You're really good with them."

"How'd you end up with a guy who'd be stupid enough to cheat on you and lose you?"

"How do you know he did?"

"You thought Dale was looking for your ex, who supposedly slept with his wife."

"Right. Well, Mike is one of those people who can stare you right in the eyes, smile oh so charmingly, and lie like the devil without a care. In the beginning, I can honestly say he really wanted me. I didn't make it easy."

"He liked the chase."

"Apparently, his favorite part."

"So when he caught you, he needed that chase again."

"He lives for it. It didn't happen right away. We were happy. For a while. But I wanted something too permanent for his liking."

"A faithful husband isn't something you should have to want for; it should just be when you commit to someone and say vows."

"One would think. He tried, but in the end, it's just not who he is. It's taken some time to get to the point where I can look back and know I didn't push him out the door. He had one foot out the whole time."

"What finally made you walk away?"

"I'd been thinking of leaving for a few months. I wanted kids, and judging by the age of the girl who showed up at my house demanding I give my husband the divorce he told her he wanted, so did he."

Owen laughed, but tried to smother it in the end. "Sorry. That's funny."

"Didn't seem like it at the time, but yeah, it's funny."

"He's a dick who doesn't deserve you. Anyone stupid enough to lose a great woman like you should be shot just for being an idiot."

"You barely know me, how do you know I'm not some shrew of a wife?"

"Your shop and the way you are with the kids who come in there. You love what you do. You put your whole heart into it. I have no doubt you did the same with your marriage. Any man who'd give that up doesn't deserve to live."

Some part of him had been paying close attention to this woman. He'd never really thought about her like this. Yes, he'd been drawn to her, but he'd kept his distance. Well, he'd been a busy man, taking care of Rain and the girls in his brother's absence and building his law practice. Sure, business was booming, but that didn't mean his personal life should suffer.

Maybe all he'd been waiting for was a chance to meet Claire outside her shop. When he wasn't dressed up like some overgrown wannabe drag queen in a crown and boa.

He'd never seen enough interest from her to prod him to make the introduction sooner. Probably because she'd always thought he belonged to someone else. Now she knew better, and some of the looks she cast him on the drive home made him hot and ache with a need he hadn't felt in a long time.

"You passed my driveway."

He stomped on the brakes and glanced in the rearview mirror. Sure enough, he'd gone right past her place, headed home. Some kind of late-night unconscious slip, or is that really where he wanted to take her?

"Sorry. Autopilot, I guess."

Too tired to analyze things now, he put the truck in reverse, backed up, and pulled into her driveway. Dylan and his deputies left right after Owen followed her to the hospital, but they'd left the lights on inside the house and at the porch.

He slid out of the truck and went around to her door. She already had it open, so he took her hand and held her steady while she slid out. She winced when she put weight on her feet. Without a thought, he scooped her into his arms, closed the truck door with his hip, and carried her up to the front door.

"You can set me down. I can walk. The worst of the cuts are on the side of my feet."

"I don't mind," he said, leaning down so she could put the key in the lock.

He stepped into the living room and stopped short, seeing the broken glass door and shambles in the dining room.

"Damn, I'm really sorry this happened."

"Not your fault. Really, you can put me down."

"This is the best part of my night."

She smacked him on the shoulder, but he set her on her feet and held her by the arms to steady her.

"Okay."

"Yeah. Um, thanks for bringing me home. I appreciate you staying with me at the hospital."

"Dismissing me already." He frowned and shook his

head. "Well, I'm not leaving until that window is boarded up and this place is cleaned." He glanced at the boxes stacked around them. "You've lived here for quite some time. Why haven't you unpacked?"

"It's a process."

"Too busy working on the shop to do the house."

"No money to do the house after I set up the shop. My ex left me with a lot of bills and crap credit."

"Asshole."

"And then some, but thanks. It's nice someone else sees him like I do."

"Your family didn't support you in the divorce?"

"They did, but they blamed me for not sticking it out, trying to make it work. Like I did something to drive him into those other women's arms. I didn't deny him my heart or my bed, but when he cheated, they still thought I made him do it."

He cupped her face. "He's an asshole. You're better off without him. Let's never speak of him again."

She laughed. "Sorry. I'm tired and that guy demanding to find my husband because he was sleeping with his wife brought it all up for me again."

"You were hit by a car, you had your past thrown in your face, it's late, and you're tired. Why don't you go change, and I'll sweep up the glass and take care of boarding up the window. If you give me your insurance information, I'll call them first thing in the morning and start your claim and have a new sliding door put in as soon as possible."

"You don't have to do all that."

"I want to. This wouldn't have happened if not for my client. Let me do this. It's the least I can do."

"You'll find the information in my office." She pointed to the closed door off the living room. "Bottom drawer of the desk in the file marked insurance."

He smiled to lighten things and teased, "An organized woman. Dangerous creatures."

"Yes, well, stay out of the other stuff. There be dragons with sharp teeth who'll burn your ass for snooping through my papers."

He laughed. "Not the trusting sort, are you?"

"I've been burned already."

"I'm not out to hurt you, honey. Just help you."

"You can't be that good looking and not have some flaws." Her cheeks blazed red.

He laughed again. "I've got plenty of flaws, but none that will bite you on the ass. Unless you want me to," he teased. "Because it's a fine ass, and I wouldn't mind."

Her eyes went wide. Maybe a spark of interest crossed them before she spun around and fled for the stairs. Well, limped to the stairs due to her injured and severely bruised hip. The doctor told him she'd been lucky not to break it.

"I'll be down to help you clean up in a minute," she mumbled, not looking back.

"I'll be here." Meaning he wasn't going anywhere anytime soon. He liked her.

He stared at the broken door, the glass on the floor, and toppled chair and knickknacks. Dale came here and hurt her because of some perceived rivalry. Well, Owen wasn't going to stand by and let him follow through on his threats to hurt Claire to get to him.

He may not have really known her before tonight, but if someone did hurt her, it would affect him. She had a hold on him. For the first time, he didn't feel the need to shake a woman off and put some distance between them. No, he wanted to draw Claire in and keep her close. To what end, he didn't know. But he definitely wanted to explore the possibilities racing through his head.

Chapter Six

CLAIRE ENTERED HER room, saw her rumpled bed, and sighed. She wanted to crawl in and sleep the day away. Not going to happen. Things needed to be done. She had a strange man in her house. Okay, not so strange. Handsome. Gorgeous. Funny. Nice.

She stopped that line of thinking and headed for the bathroom, pulling her robe off and tossing it in the hamper. It took some doing to get the bandage holding the ice pack on her shoulder off, but once she did, she winced at the throbbing ache. She checked the bruise in the mirror, but couldn't see the scraped, raw skin under the bandage. Not so bad now, but in another day it would bloom into a vivid display of color about four inches in diameter.

Careful as she moved her arm, she pulled her bloody shirt off and tossed it in the trash. She turned on the cold water, cupped her hands, and doused her face, staving off the tears that threatened whenever she thought about what happened tonight. The fear came back, knotting her stomach and making her hands tremble.

She'd worked so hard to create this life on her own. Now, being alone terrified her.

She dried her face on a towel and grabbed her brush, pulling her hair up and into a ponytail. She couldn't believe she'd spent the last few hours in the presence of Owen and the cops looking like she'd been struck in a lightning storm, her hair a mass of frizz and tangles.

Refreshed, she walked into her room naked and went to the dresser. A truck engine idled outside. Maybe Owen finished cleaning and was getting ready to go home. As much as she'd like this long night to end, she didn't want to be alone.

She pulled on a clean pair of white pajama bottoms with tiny purple violets and a matching purple tank top. She didn't know what to do about the sliding door. She'd have to call someone first thing in the morning. At least the insurance would cover a new door. One less thing for her to pay for to upgrade the older home. She'd gotten the place cheap because it needed a lot of work and upgrades. Over time, she knew she could make the place her own. She liked home-improvement shows and trying her hand at new projects. So far, the upgrades to her bathroom had turned out wonderfully. Still, the insurance deductible would set her back.

Dressed and feeling fatigued, she went downstairs, careful of every step she took on her sore feet. The living room lights were still on, but she veered to the kitchen to make a cup of tea to calm her nerves and help her sleep. Maybe she'd splurge and make a cup of her favorite hot chocolate. There might even be a can of whip cream in the fridge.

The glass had been cleaned up. Her broom and dustpan sat next to the stainless steel garbage can. She turned to the cupboard to take down the hot chocolate when she realized she didn't hear the truck any longer. Owen must have left. Her stomach tightened and her heart sank. Despite not knowing him well, she'd hoped he'd stay, or at least say goodbye.

She found the hot chocolate and turned to get a mug from the other cabinet.

"Hey," a deep unfamiliar voice said from behind her. Every nerve went on alert. Her heart pounded with fear. Instinct told her to run, but how far could she go with him so close? She grabbed a knife from the butcher block beside her and spun around, hurting her sore feet but not really feeling the pain.

"Stay where you are. Don't come any closer."

Somewhere in her muddled mind he looked familiar, but the fear stole her rational thoughts. Her hands shook and she backed up into the counter, looking everywhere for an escape that seemed impossible.

"Hey now, you're okay. I'm not going to hurt you."

Tears filled her eyes. Too much to take in one night, she stammered, "Get out. Leave me alone." The stranger took a step toward her, and she took one toward him. "Get out, or I'll gut you where you stand."

One side of his mouth cocked up in a slanted grin. His eyes flashed with admiration, confusing her.

"I'm not going to hurt you. I'm looking for Owen."

"He doesn't live here. Why does everyone think he lives here?" she yelled.

A flash of movement came from her left; she swung to face the new danger and inhaled when Owen rushed her, pushing the knife out of his way and pulling her close. She immediately dropped it and grabbed hold of him as he kept his back to the stranger, her back to the counter, and his big body protecting her.

"You're okay, sweetheart. That's my brother, Brody. He came to help me board up the glass door." He hugged her closer when she grabbed fistfuls of his shirt and held him tighter, crying all over the front of his shirt, her face buried in his chest, her bravado from a moment ago drained away, overwhelmed by her fear. Owen was here, holding her, keeping her safe. She needed him and refused to let go, even when he tried to back away.

"Brody, man, you want to give us a minute."

"Sure. I just wanted to let her know I'm here. She's got a lot of guts, facing off with me with that knife. I like her."

"Yeah, I like her, too." Owen brushed his hand over her head and settled into her, holding her tight and close.

Brody left with a chuckle and an "I bet you do."

All of a sudden she felt foolish, but it didn't stop her from staying in Owen's arms. She shifted on her feet, and he slid his big hands down her back to her waist, hoisting her up onto the counter. His warm hands settled on her thighs, spreading them wide so he could stand between them. Close. Intimate. Their eyes met, and he reached up and swiped his thumbs across both her cheeks, taking away the tears.

She got hold of herself enough to say, "Your brother is huge."

"You just faced off with an ex–Army Ranger. He could take you out with one lethal smile."

"He wasn't smiling."

"He doesn't much, since he got home. Unless he's with Rain. She's bringing him back to himself, but it's a long and slow process when you've seen and done the kinds of things he has during the war."

"You admire him."

"He's a tough guy with a big heart. He suffers from PTSD, so wielding a knife in front of him, or sneaking up on him—not a good idea, sweetheart, if you want to live."

"You really were protecting me."

"I don't think he'd hurt you, definitely not on purpose, but you never know what will set him off. He gets lost in flashbacks. He may not have seen you, but an enemy his mind is still fighting. I didn't want to take a chance. Like I said, he's better now that he's back with Rain and the girls."

"What if that other man comes back?" Tears clogged her throat and made her words stilted and shaky.

Owen cupped her face. Their gazes locked. They held their breath. She thought he'd kiss her, but he never moved. Despite standing between her thighs, he maintained a protective yet safe distance. He didn't crowd her, or press into her like a lover. No, he stayed on that side of the boundary of comfort versus intimacy.

"It's late," she mumbled to break the lengthening silence.

He didn't move away, but the ready-to-pounce muscles relaxed and an ease came over him. She wondered how he held himself back like that, when all she wanted to do is leap into him and every hot encounter his eyes promised.

"Yeah, too late to pretend I don't want you, and you don't want me."

"I don't even know you."

"Yeah, you do, or you wouldn't have let me back into your house tonight. We'll get to the details over time."

"You're not a man who takes no for an answer."

"Sweetheart, you never said no, either with words or actions, judging by the way you're holding tight to me right now."

She unfisted her hands from his shirt, like she'd been holding on to a snake. He wanted her back. Bad.

"Sorry."

"Don't be. I'm not. Get used to me hanging around, because I'll be watching out for you until they find Dale and lock him up for hurting you."

"You don't have to do that."

"He threatened your life. I take that very seriously, especially from a guy like him, who is willing to come here and nearly run you over with his car in the dead of night."

"Bad choice of words."

"Sorry."

"He was looking for you."

"Yeah, drunk and stupid he showed up to take me on with nothing but his bad attitude. Sweetheart, I'd have demolished him if I was here. When he sobers up, he'll realize that, and next time he might not be so stupid and come better prepared."

"You really think he'll be back."

"If he wises up, no. But Dale has yet to prove he uses his brain for more than basic survival."

"Great." She leaned her head to his shoulder and sighed heavily.

"See, you're already getting used to having me around."

She bolted upright again and glared at him, making him laugh. He'd pushed far enough and gave her some space, taking the mug beside her and going to the ancient fridge and filling it with milk. He put the mug in the microwave and set the timer.

"What are you doing?"

"Taking care of you. You'll get used to that, too."

"Owen."

"Claire, relax. Take a breath. It's been a long night. The sun will be up in about two hours. I feel guilty as hell about what happened and you getting hurt. Let me do this for you."

She planted her hands on the counter and let her head fall between her shoulders. She didn't so much acquiesce as she didn't argue further, which gave him an opening to get to know her better.

He stirred chocolate mix into the mug of hot milk, grabbed the whip-cream can from the fridge, and squirted a generous mound on top. Just for fun, he squirted a heap into his mouth and ate it up, smiling. She smiled back and took the mug, licking the sweet cloud and sighing.

"Better?" he asked.

"Getting there. Thanks."

"Stay put. Let me help Brody with the door. It shouldn't take but a couple of minutes, and I'll be right back."

"I don't have any wood."

"He's renovating the cabin up at Clear Water Ranch. He brought some with him."

"Well, ask him what I owe for the wood and his help. I'm happy to pay."

"Claire, relax. I'll take care of everything."

"But . . ."

He stared her down until she relented and took a sip of her hot chocolate. He left her sitting on the counter, cup in hand, a resigned look on her face, but not a trace of fear. Not anymore, but it would come again when she tried to sleep. He'd stay and chase away the ghosts if they intruded again tonight. This morning? God, he needed some sleep. If he hurried, maybe he'd get to bed by five, sleep until eight. He'd pulled all-nighters before, he could do it again.

"Got your girl squared away?" Brody asked when he stepped out onto the back patio.

"She's not my girl. I just met her. Besides, after what happened tonight, she'll probably kick me out of her life for good."

"Don't bet on it. She's been checking you out for the last few minutes from the kitchen window."

Owen wanted to turn and look, but stayed put. His

cocky smile gave away too much, and Brody laughed at him.

"You two looked real cozy in the kitchen. She's a little banged up and on edge, but she's got fight and heart. She's a beautiful woman. Why aren't you seeing her?"

Owen laughed. "Because up until a couple months ago I was taking care of your soon-to-be fiancée and children." Everyone knew Brody and Rain were getting married, but his thick-headed brother had yet to ask her officially, making it a running gag between them.

"Don't put your lack of a love life on me. Rain can take care of those girls, herself, and an army all on her own. While I thank you for all you did while I was gone, you're the one who didn't put yourself out there. I'm just saying, she seems like a nice woman. You should take her to dinner."

"Yes, I'll take her to dinner, and she'll completely forget that bastard attacked her because of me."

"You take on too much for your clients. You're not to blame for what happened. Don't feel guilty for something that you didn't do and couldn't have prevented. Do everything you can to find that guy and put him where he belongs, but don't blame yourself that she got hurt."

"I like her," Owen admitted.

Brody had a piece of plywood at his feet and a tape measure stretched across it. He marked a spot and grabbed the skill saw. He tossed the extension cord to him. Owen stepped back into the dining room and plugged it in on the side wall. He walked back out to help Brody hold the wood while he cut it.

"What if he comes after her again?"

"Do what you can legally to keep him away. If that doesn't work, put him down."

"Rain hasn't smoothed out all your rough edges, I see."

"You woke me up in the middle of the night, took me out of Rain's bed, and your girl pulled a knife on me. Sorry if I'm not more agreeable."

"I appreciate you coming over to help me out."

"I'm just giving you a hard time. You knew I'd come. I owe you for taking care of my girls. Did she nick you?" Brody cocked his head to indicate the three-inch gash in his shirt.

"She missed, thank God. I don't think she realized she took a swipe at me."

"Adrenaline. She's going to have a hard crash. Soon."

"Yeah, so let's get this done so we can both get some sleep."

"You're staying with her tonight."

"I just can't take a chance Dale gets a bug up his ass and comes back."

"Is Dylan trying to track him down?"

"Yeah, but who knows where Dale went after he harassed Shannon at her place."

"If you need my help keeping an eye on Claire, say the word and I'm there."

"Thanks. I'm going to keep my eye on her until this thing is resolved."

"As good excuse as any to spend time with her."

Owen ignored Brody's knowing smile and hefted the heavy board and took it over to the door. Brody brought the drill and screws. They made quick work of the task.

"That should work for now." Owen stood back and surveyed their work, satisfied. "I'll call her insurance company and get the door replaced tomorrow first thing."

"You need to talk to your client. If this guy is fixated on you and her and now Claire, you need to warn your client about saying something that could make this worse."

"I'm afraid she may have already said something about us."

Brody's eyes narrowed on him.

"Nothing is going on with my client," Owen defended. "Well, on my part anyway. I've stood between her and the ex and helped her get away from him. She's grateful and sees me as her protector. She's started to rely on me and pushed for me to help her with things outside my scope of lawyerly duties."

"Put a stop to it now. Set her straight."

"I've tried to gently nudge her to do things on her own."

"Give her a shove. You don't need her life dragging yours down."

"I will. I'm also going to make damn sure nothing else happens to Claire. She didn't deserve this."

"No, she didn't, but it's not your fault."

"You said that already."

"Apparently you need to hear it again because I can see the guilt written all over your face."

"Thanks for your help. Go home."

"I'm headed that way." Brody stopped in the middle of rolling up the extension cord around his hand and arm. "Owen, don't ever think you don't deserve what I've found with Rain and the girls. Whatever we did in our past, that doesn't mean we can't make something good for our future."

"We aren't who we used to be. We've changed." Owen spoke the words, but deep down he wasn't so sure that dark part of himself didn't still exist, just waiting to come out and screw everything up in his life like he'd done so many times.

"We have. Remember when we sat at Rain's kitchen table when I came back and you said Rain had let you be a part of a real family. It doesn't have to be the way we grew up with the old man swapping one woman for the next, using them up and tossing them out."

"I'm nothing like the old man. I don't use women for nothing but sex and treat them like shit."

"Never said you did. I'm just saying you can have what I have if you want it."

"I just met this woman. I'm not planning a wedding."

"I'm just saying change your perspective. Go into a relationship looking for forever, instead of just tonight, and you might find what you're really looking for. Don't be stubborn like me and waste years because you think you don't deserve it."

Owen didn't say anything. What could he say? He and Brody shared a past that they'd both had to work damn hard to overcome. At some point, they'd each decided to stop walking the road to destruction and take a new path toward something better. Law school and opening his own practice gave Owen a sense of satisfaction and accomplishment, but he still felt like he was missing something in his life. He'd found a piece of it being a part of Rain and the girl's lives. With Brody back, he still felt a part of their family, but he wanted his own. He loved spending time with Dawn and Autumn, but he envied his brother every time the girls called Brody "Dad."

"It's late. I'm out of here. Go put your girl to bed." Brody cocked his head toward the kitchen window. Claire still sat on the counter, her head down between her shoulders, eyes drooping.

Tonight—well, early morning now—he'd put her to bed and watch over her. Some things were inevitable. He wished she hadn't suffered that terrible scare, or her injuries, but Dale's reckless move brought him here tonight. Claire made him want to stay.

Chapter Seven

THE FRONT DOOR shut and the locks clicked into place. Claire tracked Owen's movements through the small house by his heavy footfalls on the wood floors. He kicked the box next to the sofa on his way to the dining room. She'd done the same thing a hundred times, always with a silent promise she'd get around to moving it. Owen took care of it for her. The box landed on another with a scrape of cardboard. It made her smile. Such a small thing, but it meant a lot to her.

Funny, she'd lived alone for a while now and thought she'd gotten used to it. Not so much. Having him moving around her house, her things, made her realize how lonely she'd been for company. How nice it was to share a space and find comfort in another's presence.

She hadn't moved since he'd set her on the counter and gone out to help his brother board up the sliding door. Their deep, muffled voices carried into the house, though she couldn't make out the words. The familiar, easy way they talked spoke of their close bond. She didn't have any siblings and wished many times for a sister or brother to lean on and confide in when times were tough. As close as she was to her parents, they sometimes didn't understand her need for independence. They too often wanted to fix her problems for her, instead of letting her do things her way.

The lights went out in the dining room and Owen entered the kitchen, stopping several feet away. She leaned on her hands, her head bent nearly to her chest. She could only see his feet and legs.

"Claire, you're exhausted. Why didn't you just go up to bed?"

"The meds kicked in. Too tired to move."

Unexpected and exciting, he plucked her right off the counter and settled her in his arms and against his broad, hard chest. Too tired to make a fuss and exert her independence, she gave in to something else entirely and snuggled closer, nestling her face in his neck and settling her head on his strong shoulder.

His chest rumbled with a laugh. "You're like a contented cat, snuggling in for the night."

"Deep down, I'm fine on my own. The meds have made me mushy and weak."

"Not weak. After the night you've had, you just need a hug."

He squeezed her to his chest. She tried to hide the wince of pain, but he felt her stiffen in his arms.

"Sorry, overstepped."

They reached the top of the stairs, and he stopped.

"No, you didn't. I didn't realize how banged up I got. I feel like I got hit by a car," she joked. "The meds are helping out considerably.

"My room's on the right."

Owen walked down the hall and entered her room, stopping just inside and looking around.

"Wow. It's like another house in here."

"I moved in over a year ago, but I spent all my time opening the shop and running it. A couple of months ago, I started on the house. I spend so much time at the shop, the most time I spend here is sleeping, so I redid the master bedroom first. I've upgraded the bathroom, but I still need to add the finishing touches."

"You added the flower pots on the back patio with the lounge and table set."

"I like to drink my coffee out there in the morning when the weather is nice."

"You spend a lot of time working, so spending the morning outside is relaxing."

"Yes. Sounds like the same is true for you, too."

He nodded. "I spend most evenings outside reading over briefs and preparing for court. I take care of the horses and barn cats. It gets me out of my head."

"You can put me down now."

"I knew you'd say that."

She laughed, and he set her on her bed.

"Can I get you anything?" he asked.

"I'll be fine. Thanks for helping clean up and taking care of the door. If you'll just lock up on your way out, I'd appreciate it."

"I'm not leaving. I'll crash on your couch for a couple of hours. I'll drive you to work. What time do you need to be there?"

"You don't need to do that."

"Yes, I do."

"Owen, it's not your fault that guy got the wrong address."

"It doesn't change the fact he threatened you and is still on the loose. Until they catch him, I'm keeping a close eye on you."

She opened her mouth to protest, but the determined look in his eyes settled her and made her stop. Tonight, she didn't want to be alone, and having him in the house while she slept made her feel better.

Settled into the pillow, she gave up the fight to stay awake and closed her eyes. "I need to be at the shop by ten thirty."

He pulled the blanket at the end of the bed over her and tucked her in. She sighed, content to have him close and in her space. After what her husband did to her, she'd kept men at a distance. Maybe she needed to stop putting all men in the same category as her ex.

Owen brushed his hand over her head. "Goodnight, Claire."

"There's a blanket in the hall closet," she mumbled.

"I'll find it."

"Leave the light on in the hall."

"You got it, sweetheart."

She peeked through her lashes, watching him walk to the door and turn back to look at her before he turned off the lights.

"Owen."

"Yeah."

"Thanks."

He closed the distance between them, planted both hands on the bed beside her shoulders, and leaned down and kissed her on the forehead. He pushed back up and leaned over her, his gaze locked with hers. Something intense vibrated around them and the moment stretched.

Without a word, he stood and walked out of the room, leaving her wanting to call after him to come back.

Chapter Eight

CLAIRE WOKE TO the smell of coffee and pancakes. Stiff and sore, especially her battered hip, she made her way to the bathroom for a quick shower. Clean, dry, and feeling a bit more limber, she dressed in simple black slacks with a turquoise top. She slid her re-bandaged feet into her sandals and went downstairs, amazed to see Owen at the stove, dressed in gray slacks, a crisp white dress shirt with a blue-and-gray tie draped around his neck, but not tied. He looked classy and elegant. Not like the man who'd been woken out of his sleep in the middle of the night and pulled on worn jeans and a Henley shirt. No, this Owen hid the ranch owner under a smooth varnish of class and sophistication.

He flipped pancakes with one hand and talked on his cell phone with the other.

"Yeah, the measurements I gave you should work. How long?

"Not good enough. I need you to put a rush on it."

Without missing a beat, he poured her a cup of coffee and handed it to her with a smile.

"Hey, the insurance is picking up the tab. Get it done. I've got to go. Give me a call when you're ready to install it." He hung up and stared at her.

The unexpected touch of his fingertip along her shoulder made her flinch.

"Still hurt?"

"No, not really. Maybe a little. I'm surprised you're still here."

"I ran up to my place about an hour ago and got ready for work. Called your insurance first thing. They'll cover your damages."

"Is it worth them paying, since I have to pay the deductible?"

"I paid the deductible."

"Owen . . ."

"Claire."

"But . . ."

"I also negotiated a better deal on your insurance. You'll get an updated bill and a small refund in a few days. Since Brody has a contractor working on his place, I called him. He'll have a new double-pane sliding glass door installed day after next. He'll even send the bill to the insurance company for you."

"Um, thanks."

"You're welcome. How do you feel this morning?"

"Achy and slow."

"Drink your coffee. It'll help wake you up. I think your pain meds are in your purse."

"I'll get them." She moved to the counter, out of his way, but not far enough that she didn't feel the pull between them. That weird sense of the morning after churned her stomach with nerves, but she didn't know why. It's not like anything really happened between them last night. He brought her home from the hospital. He took care of the broken window last night and this morning, saving her the trouble and money on her insurance. He stayed last night so she wouldn't be frightened, and he didn't comment on her childish need to keep the hall light on while she slept.

She let out a sigh, remembering the kiss he planted on her forehead and the intensity in the look he gave her last night. She snuck a peek over her shoulder. He plated up several pancakes, swiped a knife through the butter, and spread it over the stack. He grabbed the foil-covered pan on the back of the stove and spooned out steaming eggs. He caught her watching him and smiled.

"Something the matter?" he asked.

The butterflies in her gut and the voice in her head nudging her to kiss him.

"What are you doing here?"

"Making you breakfast." He handed her the plate of food and turned back to the stove and prepared another plate for himself.

"Why?"

"I thought you might be hungry. You shouldn't take those meds on an empty stomach."

"Did you hear from the police about Dale?"

"They're still looking for him."

"So, that is why you're here."

"Get used to me hanging around. I'm not taking any chances he comes back to make good on his threat."

"What if he sees you with me, it confirms his suspicions that I'm important to you, and he hurts me because of that?"

"I'm not going to let anything happen to you."

"You can't be with me every minute of the day. You have work. I have work. We hardly know each other."

"You'll get to know me. Besides, even if they caught Dale today, I'd still want to spend time with you. How about dinner tonight?"

"You're serious."

"We'll discuss it over breakfast. Come sit with me."

He walked out of her kitchen and into the dining room and took a seat at her table. She could count on one hand the number of times she'd eaten there with guests. Most of the time, she sat at the small breakfast table in the kitchen. Alone.

She sat next to him and took a bite of the buttery pancakes and closed her eyes with a sigh. "These are outstanding."

"Rain is the pancake maker in the family. The girls devour them most mornings. I paid attention. When you're a long-time bachelor who lives miles from town, learning to cook is a necessity.

"Come up to the ranch tonight. I'll barbeque up some steaks." He looked sideways, considering something, and said, "I'll take you out. We'll have a nice quiet dinner in town before I bring you home tonight."

"You don't quit, do you?"

"It's just dinner, Claire. We both need to eat. Besides, that smile you're trying to hide tells me you don't want me to quit."

She hated to admit having a gorgeous man interested in her, making plans to take her to dinner, or—even better—cook for her made her want to smile. She liked Owen and his easygoing way. She didn't feel pressured by his confident assertion that she'd fall in line with his meal plans. He somehow read in her that she'd like to spend the evening with him. Like he read her need not to be alone last night and stayed because she wanted him to.

Not ready for an intimate dinner with him at his home, she casually said, "How about Madeira's in town."

"I love Italian. It's a date."

Her stomach fluttered, and she gave in to the smile. "It's a date."

The first one she'd had in nearly a year. The last one she'd gone on because a friend set her up. What an awful experience that turned out to be. They had nothing in common, and the guy seemed to think dinner and drinks equaled sex in the front seat of his car.

Owen sat across from her casually eating his breakfast, making dinner plans, and glancing at her with that sexy gaze that told her how much he wanted her. She had no doubt he'd let her set the pace, but at no time would he back off. Something thrilling to look forward to and embrace if she dared.

After her husband's betrayal, she'd shied away from men and any hint at something intimate. She'd refused to trust any man with her heart, and all she'd done was put up a wall to keep everyone out and her alone. Not anymore.

She stared across the table and straight into Owen's amazing blue eyes. She read the challenge and accepted it.

"I have a feeling I'm going to be in desperate need of a glass of wine by the end of the day. I can't wait."

"Me either," he said in his casual way that wasn't casual at all. Owen reminded her of a predator stalking his prey, waiting for the perfect opportunity to strike. Funny, for the first time in years, she felt wanted in a way that went beyond sex. Though she knew he wanted that, something about the way he stared and studied her told her he wanted a hell of a lot more. She wanted to surrender to him all he silently asked, because Owen wasn't the type of man to demand what he wanted. Either she gave of herself freely, or he'd back off, because he didn't want anything she wasn't willing to give with her whole heart.

"Eat your food. We need to leave soon so I can get you to work on time."

"I'm so sorry, you must be late. I didn't think. You probably start work much earlier."

"It's no problem. My assistant is covering the office. I don't have to be in court until two."

"What kind of case are your working on?"

"I represent all kinds of people and cases, but today it's a shoplifting charge. One of my client's daughters is quite the klepto. She's been caught five times. God knows how many times she didn't get caught. So far, she hasn't had to serve jail time. Her father usually buys her way out of it, but this time she took a twelve-hundred-dollar sapphire ring."

"Her father can afford to buy her whatever she wants and doesn't understand her compulsion to steal," Claire guessed.

"Exactly, but he loves her and wants to see her get the help she needs. I'm trying to work out a plea deal. We'll see how it goes and if the judge will be lenient."

"You care about her."

"She's a sweet kid who doesn't deserve to sit in juvenile detention for three months because she can't control her impulses. She needs a psychiatrist and tools to help her fight her compulsion. She knows it's wrong, she just can't help herself."

"You'll do the best you can. If you talk to the prosecutor and explain her to him the way you did to me, he'll give you the deal."

"Thanks for the optimism, but the prosecutor on this case is looking for convictions, not necessarily what is best for the accused."

"You'll convince him. If not, you'll convince the judge."

"Maybe I should take you with me to court. One look at you, and they'll be putty in your hands."

"I doubt it."

"Why? I am."

"Hardly. You're just worried Dale will come back here."

"You know that's not the only reason I'm here."

"I'm still trying to figure you out."

"No. You're convinced I'm lying just because I'm talking. Take your ex-colored glasses off and see me. Don't judge me based on your asshole ex's actions. I'm not him. Listen to the words coming out of my mouth and know they are the truth. I won't lie or manipulate you to get what I want. That's not my way. At least, not anymore. Back in the day, when I was that guy my cousin, Dylan, talked about, yeah, I'd say anything to get a woman in my bed and out as quickly as possible. I'm not that guy anymore. I've seen what two people who love each other can share."

"Your brother, Brody, and Rain."

"Yes. They've had a hell of time getting to where they are now, but two things hold them together more than anything else. They love each other fiercely, and they are honest with each other always.

"Growing up with my old man, well, let's just say I learned what not to do when it comes to women and children. I've fought damn hard to break free of my past and realize my life isn't his life. I am not him. I am not your ex."

"I'm sorry if I made you think I don't trust you."

"You don't. Not yet. And that's okay. Just stop assuming I'm only out to hurt you, or take something you're not willing to give. If you're not interested, all you have to do is say so. I can't say I won't be disappointed, but I'll leave you alone if that's what you want."

"I am interested," she said more boldly than she actually felt. "Please understand, my caution comes from experience. You've already proven you're not like the asshole. I'm glad you came last night. I'm glad you're still here this morning."

"See, I'm not so hard to like," he teased, putting her at ease after the tense moments they'd just shared.

She thought about the years she'd spent with her ex and realized they'd never had such an honest conversation like this in their whole marriage.

"What's that face?"

"I like you a lot."

"The face you made says otherwise."

"Just thinking about the past and you and right now. I'm not the naïve girl I used to be."

"You're a beautiful woman."

She smiled because he meant the compliment, unlike her ex, who used to say such things to distract her from his lies and deceits.

Stop thinking about him and concentrate on the man in front of you.

She'd finally seen the light and decided to move on with her life instead of letting the asshole's actions keep her from doing so because she feared getting hurt again. Not anymore. She really did like Owen and wanted to get to know him better.

Owen held up his glass of orange juice. "To diving in with our eyes open."

She clinked her glass to his and gave him a genuine smile free of any trepidation. "I'll drink to that."

Chapter Nine

OWEN PARKED THE truck outside Claire's Café and Bookstore. He studied the storefront like he was seeing it for the first time. He'd never really noticed all the details. Cream walls with hunter-green trim lent a cottage feel to the small two-story building. Ladies sat at four of the six bistro tables out front, drinking coffee and tea. Some read books, others chatted with friends. All of them greeted Claire with a wave or hello as she stepped out of the truck with Owen and walked to the front door. Several leaned into their friends and whispered, their eyes darting from him to Claire. Yeah, the small-town grapevine was alive and well. By mid-afternoon, everyone in town would know he'd driven Claire to work. By evening, they'd set odds on how long until he proposed, would it be a May or June wedding, and how long before a little one was on the way.

Funny, none of it mattered to him. Even more disturbing was how much he wanted all those things. The thought of sharing them with Claire didn't stir any desire to flee, but to move closer and claim what he wanted.

They entered the store, announced by the bouncing silver bell over the door. The smell of coffee, pastries, and cinnamon filled the air. Despite breakfast this morning, his stomach rumbled and his mouth watered.

Several people occupied the tables inside. A couple of customer's stood at the back, perusing the bookcases and reading.

"Morning, Claire," Gayle called from behind the counter. Owen had been in her husband's geometry class in high school. It seemed a thousand years ago, but Gayle didn't look a day over forty, though she must be in her early fifties.

"Hi, Gayle."

Claire limped to the counter. Gayle saw the bandage on Claire's elbow and sticking out of her shirtsleeve. She rushed over and took Claire by the shoulders, making her wince. "What happened?"

"It's nothing, really."

"Are you okay?"

"I'm fine. Someone hit me with their car last night."

That drew stares from many of the customers. If people hadn't heard about Claire's visitor last night already, they would now. He didn't need to worry about leaving her at work. Once word spread, everyone would look out for her. Still, he hated to leave her here. He couldn't be with her every second of the day, but he needed to know she'd be safe.

"Did they catch the guy?"

"Not yet," Owen said. "I'd appreciate it if you made sure Claire isn't alone in the shop and doesn't go anywhere alone until they find this guy."

"You know Owen, right?" Claire asked.

"Sure do. Don't you worry. I won't let her out of my sight. Can I get you anything, Mr. McBride?"

"No, thanks. And your husband generously gave me a C minus in his class. Please, call me Owen."

Gayle smiled and her cheeks pinked. "He must have recognized your potential."

"I didn't make it easy on him." In fact, he'd lived up to the badass McBride name for too many years and wondered how many other people saw something better in him back in the day when he'd been nothing but self-centered and cocky for no good reason.

"I don't know any teen who makes anything easy."

"Yeah, well, I especially went out of my way to make life hard on myself and anyone around me."

"You landed on the right side of the law," Claire said from beside him. He appreciated her support.

"We got a new shipment of books, and the order from that boutique you love came in, too."

Claire's face lit up and her smile transformed her face. She'd smiled at him this morning, but not like this. He wanted to see that carefree, excited smile on her face more often.

"Wait here. I'll be right back," she said.

He had work to do, but if she wanted him to wait, he'd wait.

Man, you've got it bad.

His gaze on her pretty bottom as she rounded the counter confirmed his thoughts. Hell yes, he wanted her bad. Like no one he'd ever dated, he felt drawn to her. She made him feel like a horny teenager, but also like a man who'd found someone special. The first he understood. The second scared him, but not enough to back off. Hormones won out over self-preservation. If Claire figured out just what kind of power she held over him, God help him.

She stood by the espresso machine, making some coffee concoction, and glanced over at him with a shy smile.

Maybe if they were both nervous about this situation it wasn't all bad. They'd get through this awkward discovery period and find a rhythm and a comfortable companionship like his brother and Rain shared.

"Hey, can I borrow your phone?" he asked.

"It's in the right pocket of my purse."

He pulled the bag closer and found the phone, along with a pack of wintergreen mints, a dark brown hair band he hoped she never used to bind up the long mass of waves cascading nearly to her waist, and a chocolate mint protein bar.

He tapped from one screen to the next until he had her contacts list open. He added his name, address, and all his phone numbers: home, cell, office. He took his phone from his pocket and did the same, adding her home and work address and work phone number he took from the business card on the counter.

She set a tray with two cups in front of him and a white bakery bag.

"Here. Type in your home number and cell for me."

She took the phone without a word and did what he asked.

"What's all this?" he asked.

"Your assistant comes in on Saturday and orders a double-shot nonfat latté with an apple cinnamon muffin. Since you already had breakfast, I put a double fudge caramel brownie in the bag for you and"—she put her hand on the other cup—"this is an Americano. You'll love it.

"Thank you for everything you did last night and this morning."

Touched she remembered his favorite treat and made him a coffee, he took a sip of the drink and smiled. "It's good. Thanks."

"You'll score points with your assistant when you bring that in." He didn't say anything, so she cocked her head and studied him. "You won't tell her you got it for her. You'll tell her I sent it."

"See, you're getting to know me already. Stay off your feet as much as possible. You don't want to tear any of those stitches."

They stood together and the awkward moment stretched.

"I really want to kiss you goodbye," he whispered.

"But you won't because everyone is watching, even if they're pretending not to."

"Exactly. I'll see you tonight. What time do you get off?"

She cocked an eyebrow, but didn't comment on the

double meaning of that sentence. Still, her mind aligned with his, and she was thinking about sex. He wanted to make another suggestive remark about what time he'd get her off, but held back, waiting for that playful time they'd banter like that and fall into each other's arms.

"Since Gayle opened, I close at seven. What about you?"

"I'll get off whenever you do." He let that hang between them, because he'd love to see her writhing in passion. The thought made him hard and aching just thinking about it. "I'll pick you up for dinner. I'll make the reservation for seven thirty just in case you're running late. If we get there early, we'll grab a drink at the bar."

"See you tonight," she said with an easy smile, though her hands remained knotted together on the counter.

"Please don't go anywhere alone today. Call me if anything happens. Promise."

"I promise. I have no intention of making myself an easy target."

"You weren't an easy target last night. You frightened off Dale and pulled a knife on my brother."

"Don't remind me. He must think I'm nuts."

"Let's hope Dale thinks you are. My brother thought you were tough and brave. That's a lot said coming from a guy like him."

He gave in and put his hand over hers on the counter, giving them a quick squeeze before he turned and left, every eye in the place on his back. He didn't care what anyone said or thought.

He drove to his office, worried about her safety and missing her already.

Chapter Ten

OWEN PARKED HIS truck outside his office, got out, grabbed his suit jacket draped over the seat, and put it on. He grabbed the drinks and bag of goodies from Claire and walked up the steps to his office door.

Janine smiled when he entered, but he didn't get a word of hello out before someone slammed into his chest. Trying to avoid spilling the hot coffee and dumping his briefcase on the floor, he held his arms out wide, only allowing the dark-haired woman to burrow in close to his chest. Pressed down the length of him, he stood stock-still, trying to figure out what the hell was going on.

"You're okay," the woman sobbed.

"Mrs. Monoghan, turn him loose before you break him." Janine came around her desk and took the coffee tray, bakery bag, and his briefcase, leaving him with his arms in the air, wondering what to do with them now that he wasn't holding anything and his client had attached herself to him like an octopus.

Her arms had slipped inside his jacket and her hands gripped his shirt at his back. Her face pressed to his chest and he swore she snuggled up against him, despite the tears choking her words.

"I thought he did something to you. You didn't call me back last night, or this morning, and I thought the worst."

Owen's gaze met Janine's and she shook her head in dismay. "I told you he had other matters to attend to and nothing happened to him."

Finally coming to his senses, he gently took Shannon by the shoulders and tried to set her away from him, but she held tight, tilting her head up to meet his gaze.

"You're so hard."

Janine nearly choked on the laugh, but coughed to cover. He didn't find this one bit funny. Yeah, five minutes ago he'd been hard as stone, standing talking to Claire at her place, but not now. For the first time, he wanted to shove a woman away. Shannon had crossed the line, coming here and throwing herself at him like this.

Okay, maybe he was overreacting.

She worried about him, and rightfully so with Dale involved. He reined in his temper and used only as much force as he needed to make her release him and step away. When she did, he took another step back to add more space and give him room and time to think. She didn't deserve his anger. She didn't do anything wrong. Dale hurt Claire and his anger should be directed at him, not his client.

"Shannon, aren't you supposed to be working at the pet store?"

"My shift starts in twenty minutes. I needed to see you and make sure you were okay."

"I'm fine. Dale hurt my neighbor last night. Maybe you should be concerned about her."

"Oh, well, of course I am. It's just Dale threatened you and he thinks we're . . ." Her voice trailed off and her cheeks pinked with embarrassment.

Owen frowned, catching the mocking look from Janine.

"Come into my office. We need to talk."

He led her down the short hallway, past the library to the back room that had once been the dining room of the old house he converted several years ago. He purposefully stood behind his desk and waited for her to take the seat across from him before he sat. She did so, but gave him a confused look he ignored.

"Tell me what happened when Dale stopped by your house last night."

"Well, um, he pounded on the door and demanded to come in. I told him I had a restraining order and that I'd call the cops if he didn't leave."

"Okay. Then what?"

"He kept pounding, saying he got you good, and that you had a woman in your bed, and I was nothing but a cheap afternoon fuck for you." Her gaze fell away and the words came out soft, touched with her embarrassment. "You don't have a girlfriend, so he must have got it wrong."

"He did. He tried to run down the woman who lives down the road from me with his car. Luckily, he didn't hit her square, but grazed her. She's got some scrapes and bruises and a goose-egg knot on her head and a massive headache, but she's okay."

"Well, that's good."

"Is there any reason Dale would believe you and I are sleeping together other than the fact I'm your lawyer and he's seen us together at the courthouse?"

"Who knows why Dale gets something in his head? I can tell you this, once it's in there, he won't let it go. He's like that, coming at me all the time with the same old thing, true or not. Like a dog with a bone, he's not going to just give it up."

"When he left your place last night, did he still believe you and I are sleeping together and that woman is my girlfriend?"

"Nothing I say will convince him we haven't slept together."

Funny, he almost heard the word *yet* come after that sentence. She made it sound like they weren't right now, but the possibility lay in the future.

Not a chance.

He'd found something with Claire and he couldn't wait to see her tonight to explore it more deeply. And yet the nagging feeling that getting close to her would only feed into Dale's delusion that he was sleeping with Shannon, had a girlfriend, and that Dale could hurt Claire to get to him left him unsettled. He hated that Dale's assumption about Claire was right.

He'd work on making the girlfriend part true no matter what. He refused to give up Claire because of some asshole's twisted mind. He'd protect Claire and see Dale in prison for hurting her, but nothing and no one would keep him away from her.

"If he calls you, I want you to contact me. If he comes by your house or work, call the police immediately. Do not take the time to try to talk him down from whatever crazy thing he's got in his head. Promise me you won't take any chances."

She beamed him a huge smile. "I won't. I'll call you if I hear from him at all."

"And if he comes by, you'll call the police."

"Yes, of course. So, why didn't you call back last night?"

"I stayed with Claire at the hospital until they released her, then drove her home." Tired to the bone, he scrubbed his hands over his face. "I helped clean up her house after Dale broke a window, then I stayed with her to make sure Dale didn't come back."

"Oh," she said, not conveying a bit of sympathy. "Well, I guess she was grateful for your help. You've done so much for me, and if she needed you to help her, well, that's so nice of you."

He didn't know what to say, so he kept his mouth shut.

"So, Claire. Do you know her well?" she asked.

"Met her last night. Dropped her off at her shop down the street this morning."

He kept it vague. He didn't want anything getting back to Dale, and he certainly didn't want to discuss his personal life with a client. Especially when his client had a thing for him. Oh, he'd ignored it in the past, thinking she'd get over it once his involvement in her life waned. No such luck. The more Dale interfered in Shannon's life, the more his involvement with her.

"Shannon, one more thing. Our relationship is strictly professional. I hope you made that clear to Dale."

"Of course. We're friends."

Why did that of course sound like a placating statement that went with a wink? Like, *of course our relationship is strictly professional.* Wink. Wink.

He gave up. If she wanted to think there was some double meaning behind his words, what could he do? He told her the truth.

"If you'll excuse me, I have some work to do before court this afternoon."

"You had such a difficult night. Let me make it up to you and take you to dinner."

He opened his mouth to protest, but she cut him off before he said one word.

"If you're not up to going out, I could cook for you at my place. We'll have a nice relaxing evening."

"Shannon, I appreciate the offer, but I don't think it's appropriate. Besides"—he softened his refusal—"I have other plans."

"Oh, well, some other time. I'll leave you to your work. I'm off to the pet store," she said, cheerily refusing to hear what he said.

She held out her hand to shake. Not wanting to be rude, he took it and shook, but she didn't let him go. Instead, she took his hand in both of hers and held it.

"Thank you, Owen, for always looking out for me. It means so much that you would take such an interest in your client."

He pulled his hand free and stood to show her out, since she seemed inclined to dawdle. "You're welcome."

He led the way out of his office, feeling her eyes on his back. She hurried to catch up, but in the cramped hall with his wide frame she brushed up against him. He thought she'd give him some space, but she didn't and walked a few steps beside him. He shortened his stride and let her go ahead with a wave of his hand.

"You're such a gentleman."

The woman didn't see the obvious. He wondered if she'd missed all the bad vibes and signals from Dale and married him anyway, hoping he was the dream in her head. Maybe she'd believed she could change him. No such luck. People were who they were, and they didn't change unless they wanted to or had a compelling reason. Dale proved time and again he didn't want to change to keep Shannon. He thought of her as nothing more than a possession.

Janine sat at her desk, drinking her coffee and eating her muffin. She popped a bite into her mouth and gave him a huge smile.

"Thanks for stopping by, Shannon, I'll see you later." The words left his mouth, her eyes lit up, and he wondered why he said anything. Everything he said, she took the wrong way. He held back a groan and pretended to sort through the files on Janine's desk, his back to Shannon, dismissing her.

"I'll call you if I hear anything from Dale."

"K."

The door closed behind him and Janine winked. "Wouldn't surprise me if she encouraged Dale back into her life just to get your attention."

"She hasn't had a good life. Lord knows being Dale's wife only brought her pain and hardship. She's looking for kindness."

"She's found it in you and laps it up like a kitten at a bowl of milk."

"Once Dale is back in jail, she won't have a reason to come around. She'll feel safe again and fall back into her routine."

"She has a thing for you."

"She's my client. That's all. Why do I have to keep explaining that to people?"

"I never said she was anything more to you than a client. I'm just warning you that she's got tender feelings. She likes you and a harsh brush-off may not be the way to keep your distance. In fact, it may do the opposite and make her try harder to get your attention."

"I see your point, but after what happened and her showing up here today, I thought firmer words were needed."

"How did that work out for you?"

"She didn't hear anything I said the way I intended."

Janine laughed. "Well, as you said, she's been through a lot and doesn't want to give up the one person who has been kind to her. Stick with gentle but firm and eventually she'll hear you."

"Let's hope." He took his coffee and drank deeply. Even lukewarm, it tasted like heaven.

"Thanks for the coffee and muffin."

"You're welcome, but Claire is the one who sent them."

She gave him another knowing smile. "How is Claire?"

He had called Janine early this morning to give her a heads-up that he'd be in to work late.

"Tired and hurting, but at work, trying her best to put on a brave front."

He hired Janine after he fired his last assistant-slash-paralegal because she spent far too much time hitting on him and trying to get his attention. At sixty-two, Janine was looking for a steady job after going from one temp position to the next after a huge firm in Colorado Springs laid her off during the economic downturn that gave the firm an excuse to let go of many of their older staff members. Their loss, his gain. Janine was a whiz with a computer and an even better paralegal. She saved him hours of research and taught him something new every day they worked together. He wouldn't trade her for ten young, eager, fresh-out-of-school assistants.

"Do you think she's pretty?"

"No." He kept a straight face, took a sip of his coffee, pretended to think on the matter. "I think she's the most beautiful woman I've ever seen."

"Took you long enough to notice. How many times have you taken the girls to her shop?"

"I noticed. She didn't seem interested in more than serving me tea and cookies." He remembered his conversation with her last night. "Actually, she thought I was married or at least involved with Rain and that the girls were mine. I set her straight on that score."

"I'm sure you did."

He bet Janine gave up the fight not to laugh at him any second. "Do you know her?"

"As well as anyone in town knows her. She keeps to herself. We've exchanged small talk at her shop while she puts my order together. She's smart and kind. She loves children. You can see it in the way she talks to them and plays, the way she's set up the store to include them. While she sells some pretty knickknacks, nothing is ever hands-off for the little ones. If something breaks, she brushes it off like it's nothing.

"She's worked hard to get her shop up and running. She does a good business, though I think many of the men steer clear because they think it's all tea parties and ladies clubs. For the most part it is, but she makes some wonderful lunch specials. Her pastries and desserts are to die for."

"You got that right. I love her brownies."

"You should take your clients there for meetings. It's quiet and there's a private table in the back of the book section. It overlooks a small garden she planted out back to make the perfect sitting area."

"Really? I guess I never paid much attention."

"Well, two little girls can be very distracting."

"That's for sure."

"Next time you go in, take a look around. Everything in the shop is observed, down to the tiniest detail. As a whole, you don't notice all the little things about the shop, but look closer and there are surprises here and there. It's a treasure trove of things you don't know you need or want until you see them.

"I've been in the store a few times and discovered one gift or another that was just perfect for a friend's birthday, wedding, or a get-well present. At Christmas it's not uncommon to see ladies sipping tea and filling out their Christmas cards from the lovely selection of cards and handmade paper she sells."

"It isn't just one shop, it's several little ones tucked inside that building. She gives people a place to gather, talk, read, write a letter, buy a gift, and share a meal." Owen summed up Janine's observations and thought he understood Claire a bit better. She may have kept to herself over the last year, but she'd made a place for people to come and gather around her.

"Ask me, she's looking for friends. She keeps herself apart while drawing people to her. She still doesn't feel quite a part of this community, but she's getting there. Meeting you, being a part of your life and the vast number of people you know in this town will anchor her here even more, if that is what you want."

"She hasn't decided to stay. That's why she's quiet and distant. She's afraid people won't accept her."

"This town is growing, but it still has a small-town mentality. They don't know her people back to her great-greats. Word will spread about what happened last night and that you brought her home from the hospital. People will talk. If you start seeing her, they'll talk more."

"I dropped her off at work. You'd think I walked her down the aisle."

Janine laughed. "Small towns."

"I don't know what to do."

"Ask Brody. He's got a couple of little girls. I'm sure he can fill you in on the mechanics."

She said it with a straight face, which only made it all the more funny. He busted up laughing, realizing she'd done it on purpose to make him relax and stop being so serious. After the night he had, the lost hours of sleep, he needed the levity.

"Watch it, or I may just have to show you my moves to prove to you I know exactly what I'm doing."

"Not before I sue your ass for sexual harassment. I've seen the way you look at me," she teased.

"You'd lose. I've seen the way you stare at my ass every time I walk past your desk."

"You've got a great ass."

Unable to help himself, he laughed again. "I have work to do."

"I checked in with the sheriff's office. They still have no leads on Dale's whereabouts."

"He's probably holed up in some dive motel outside of town with a bottle and a prostitute."

"What Shannon ever saw in him."

"People aren't always who we think they are when we first meet them. Sometimes they change over time. Or maybe it's they can't hide who they truly are forever."

He thought of Claire's asshole ex.

"Let's hope Shannon has wised up."

"Keep checking in with the cops about Dale."

"I will. I'll check on Claire at lunch."

"Thanks. Do you have the number for Madeira's?"

She clicked a few keys on her keyboard and wrote the number on a sticky note. She held it up to him, but didn't let him take it. "Hot date."

"First date of many."

She handed him the slip of paper. "Good answer."

Chapter Eleven

CLAIRE WIPED THE counter down. Her last customer left ten minutes ago. The store hadn't been this busy since last Christmas. Gayle stayed an extra hour to help her with folks who came in for a light dinner or dessert and coffee. Many bought books. Others bought some of the new collectibles she'd ordered and stocked on the shelves this afternoon. Pleased with the day, she didn't see Owen on the other side of the glass door until she was about to lock him out. She smiled and laughed when he gave her a mocking frown.

"Trying to get rid of me already?"

"Not at all. I'm starving and you're buying."

"Ouch."

She laughed and put her hand on his jacket lapel. "Sorry. I'm happy to see you. I've been looking forward to a quiet dinner."

"With me."

"That's why I was looking forward to it," she admitted, trying not to squirm under his intense blue gaze. She snatched her hand back and grabbed hold of a lock of her hair, hanging over her shoulder. "Um, I need just a minute."

"Take your time."

Owen stuffed his hands in his pockets and sauntered to one of the display cases by the book shelves, glancing at this and that. She wondered what he was looking for, but scurried behind the counter and boxed up the last of the pastries and brownies from the extra batches she made that day to meet the demand of her many new customers, thanks to the gossip spreading far and wide about Owen dropping her off this morning and why. She hoped at least half came back on a regular basis. She might even be able to buy a new refrigerator for her house.

She set the bakery box on the counter and dashed to the back bathroom to check her makeup in the mirror. With a little water on her hands, she finger-combed her wavy hair over one shoulder to hang down to her waist. She loved the effect. She swiped on some tinted lip balm to accentuate her mouth and not make her look so pale and washed out.

She stepped back into the main part of the shop and didn't see Owen.

"Where are you?"

"Back here," he called.

She walked past the seven-foot-tall bookcases and found him standing by the back seating area. She loved this alcove the best. Tall windows made the spot bright in the day. In the evening, especially when it got dark earlier in the fall and winter, she had two lamps on side tables that cast a soft glow over the round wood coffee table, leather love seat, and two leather club chairs. Sky-blue and cream-colored pillows offset the deep brown sofa and chairs. A potted fern sat in the center of the coffee table, giving the space a real at-home feel.

"What are you doing?" she asked, wondering why he stood staring at the alcove.

"You're really smart."

"You're basing this on furniture?"

He laughed and turned to face her. "No. I've been in your shop little more than half a dozen times with the girls. I never really paid attention. They love it here."

"I'm glad."

"You've made a place for everything. Coffee with friends up front and outside. A quiet reading spot here to be alone or quiet with friends. Over on the other side, well away from this tucked-away corner, you've got an area for the children to sit and read, play games and dress-up that doesn't disturb others."

"Well, too much in a small store," she added.

"Yes. Books of all types to please a variety of tastes, just like your selection of treats and lunch items, not to mention the variety of knickknacks and collectibles carefully chosen and displayed."

"Um, thanks. This isn't your kind of store, but your summation pretty much hits the mark."

"All those things make this place unique and fun. It's the way you've set up the shop that draws people in and gives them a sense of comfort. It's why they keep coming back."

"I'm glad you like it. Shall we go?"

"Yes, if we spend any more time alone, I'm going to have to find out."

"Find out what?"

"What it's like to kiss you."

The anxious little butterflies in her stomach she'd been trying to tame all day thinking about their date tonight stirred into a whirlwind of flutters. She swallowed hard, staring up at him. Her gaze fell to his mouth and back to his smoldering eyes.

"Maybe if we get it out of the way, we can enjoy dinner without constantly thinking about it," she boldly suggested.

"Have you been thinking about kissing me?"

She didn't know what to say. Unable to look away, she stared up at him, mesmerized by his sky-blue eyes and the way he studied her.

"I've been thinking about you all day," he admitted, his voice soft and husky. "You make it impossible to concentrate on anything when I'm worried about your safety."

"So that's all you thought about? My safety. As you can see, I'm perfectly fine."

"Yes, you are, except for your aching feet, your hip that makes you favor that leg, and the throbbing headache that makes you squint in the bright light up front."

"Observant."

"Yes. I am. While I thought of your safety often today, I also couldn't help thinking about your beautiful green eyes and the arch of your upper lip and the fullness of the bottom one. I wondered if your eyes would fall closed when I kissed you and if your lips would fit to mine. I wondered how you'd taste and if after one kiss I'd be able to stop from sharing another." He took a step to her. "And another." One more step. "And another."

He closed the distance, standing so close his jacket brushed against her blouse, but their bodies remained a mere inch apart, her head tilted back to look at him. He never took his hands out of his pockets.

"We need to find out," he whispered, his head descending toward hers, his gaze dipped to her mouth.

She held her breath and their mouths met in a soft sweep of his lips to hers. Her eyes closed and she sighed. In that moment, his mouth settled over hers. She stood on tiptoe, meeting him with the same passion and tenderness.

Desperate to regain her balance and stop her spinning head, she ended the kiss, falling back onto her flat feet.

"I need to work on my imagination. That was far better than I thought," he said, smiling down at her.

"We should go to dinner."

"Okay."

"You're not moving," she said, still standing close to him.

"You're still holding on to me."

She let her gaze fall from his broad chest to her hands fisted in his shirt at his sides. She'd pulled most of the material out of his waistband.

"You're hands are still in your pockets," she said, wondering why it bothered her, besides the fact she wanted him to want her as desperately as she wanted him.

"That's because if I grab hold of you, the only place we're going is to the floor."

Her gaze flew up to meet his and she read the truth in his eyes. He did want her. Badly. It only took a second to realize as much as she'd like to give in to her desires, she'd done that with her ex and not seen who he really was. With Owen, she wanted to know the whole man, everything about him. The kiss proved they were compatible in one area, but she wanted more from him. She'd had a couple casual affairs in college based on nothing but lust and hot sex. While enjoyable—and she and Owen could certainly burn up the sheets—she wanted something real this time with a man who took the time to not only notice her, but the store she'd built and the heart and soul she'd put into it.

She spun on her heel, winced when she hurt one of the deeper-stitched cuts, and walked away from him to the front of the store. He chuckled behind her, but didn't protest her exit.

She grabbed a light-blue-and-green crystal-and-gold necklace from one of the displays on a shelf, another gold circle necklace draped around the lamp shade near the front windows, and pulled the tags off both. She put them over her head and arranged her hair, the necklaces dressing up her otherwise business-casual outfit.

"Those are really pretty."

"Thanks. Since you're in your suit, I thought I needed a little something extra for dinner."

"You don't need anything. You're beautiful just the way you are."

She stopped in the process of grabbing her purse and looked up at him. He smiled and waited for her to say something, but she couldn't. He meant those simple words and they melted her heart and endeared him to her even more.

I'm in so much trouble.

If she lost her heart to this man, she didn't know if she'd survive if things didn't work out, because with Owen it mattered more than it ever had with anyone else.

"Let's eat, I'm starving," he said.

The implied *for you* didn't go unnoticed. She grabbed the bakery box and held it out to him. "Your favorite brownies and a few other treats."

"You must be sweet on me if you're giving away your goods."

Not admitting to anything, she smiled sweetly and replied, "Well, they are leftovers. It's either toss them out or give them to you."

"Good choice. No sense wasting something this good."

"My thoughts exactly."

This time his eyes told her he understood she meant the two of them together, too.

Chapter Twelve

OWEN OPENED CLAIRE's door and helped her down from the truck. She took his hand without reservation, making him happy she accepted him so easily. After the kiss they shared, he didn't want to let go of her, but pull her closer. Aware of her hesitation to take things too quickly, he held her hand and escorted her into the restaurant without putting his arm around her and pulling her to his side.

The hostess recognized him immediately, and despite the many people waiting, she showed them right to a table near the window. Complete with candlelight and tall potted plants to shield them from the next table, it was intimate enough to give them privacy, but still not too secluded as to cut them off from the many other guests watching them.

Owen held Claire's chair and waited for her to take her seat before he took the one next to her rather than across. He even scooted a bit closer so they could talk, get to know each other better without having to raise their voices over the din of the other guests.

"Our specials tonight include a delicious salmon ravioli with white sauce, and Portobello mushroom with chicken and rigatoni in a white wine and fresh herb sauce." The waitress came to stand beside the hostess. "This is Anna, she'll take care of you this evening. Enjoy your meal."

"May I take your drink order? Mr. McBride, your usual?" Anna asked.

"Yes, please."

"And for the lady?"

"What are you having, Owen?"

"They have a really great Californian cab I love."

"We stock it especially for Mr. McBride," Anna added.

"I'll have what he's having," she said, smiling at him.

"In that case, bring the bottle."

"As you wish, Mr. McBride. Would you like an appetizer this evening?"

He looked to Claire and she smiled prettily at him, melting his insides.

"I'll defer to you again," she said, trusting him with the order, and he hoped a lot more.

"The antipasto platter and pancetta focaccia twists."

"Excellent choices. I'll leave you to the menu. The specials are listed inside as well. If there is anything you need, please don't hesitate to ask."

Owen spotted Rain and Brody heading in their direction. "Can you kick them out?" He indicated his brother with a nod in their direction.

Anna smiled and laughed. "Sorry, no. I'll be back with your order in a few minutes."

Owen dropped his napkin on the table and stood to greet his brother and Rain. She came around the table and hugged him close.

"Hello, beautiful."

"Hi. Fancy meeting you here." Rain cast a glance Brody's way and Owen caught the guilty look.

"What? I'm hungry, and we're celebrating," Brody defended showing up at the same restaurant, like Owen hadn't mentioned it when they talked earlier.

"Celebrating what?" Owen asked.

"Can I tell him now? It's been three months."

"You're pregnant," Owen guessed, crushing Rain to his chest. "Oh, honey, I'm so happy for you. Both of you. I know how much you want this."

"We're very happy. But we're being rude. Introduce me to your friend," Rain demanded.

"Oh God, Claire, I'm sorry. This is Rain. Rain, Claire."

"It's lovely to meet you," Rain said, reaching across him to shake Claire's hand. "I heard a lot about you this morning."

"I'm sure you did."

"You remember my brother, Brody, from last night."

"Keep the knives away from her," Brody teased.

Claire's face turned pink with embarrassment. Owen shot his brother a dirty look.

"I'm so sorry about that."

"No big deal. I'm not the one you nearly gutted last night." Brody nodded in Owen's direction.

Claire stared up at him with a question lighting her green eyes.

"You weren't thinking clearly and you tore my shirt before I took the knife from you."

All the color washed out of Claire's face. He took her hand and squeezed. "Sit down."

"Don't mind if we do," Brody said, seating Rain in the chair beside his.

"Brody, they're on a date," Rain scolded.

"Now, it's a double date."

Owen didn't care what they did. His sole focus remained on Claire. "Breathe. I'm fine. No harm done."

"I didn't know," she mumbled, worrying him.

"You didn't need to know. My brother needs to keep his big mouth shut. It's no big deal."

"I could have stabbed you."

"You didn't."

"I'm sorry."

"No need to be. Brody scared you after you'd been terrorized. It's only natural you'd fight."

Anna arrived with the wine and poured a small amount into his glass. He went through the ritual of smelling and tasting it, though he hardly paid attention. He gave Anna a nod that the wine was good, and she poured for the table.

Owen took Claire's hand from her lap and held it. "Take a drink. You'll feel better." When she did as he said, he stared across the table. "Nice work. Did you come here to purposefully ruin my date?"

"No. I promised Rain a nice dinner out. Messing with you is a bonus. But I am sorry I upset you, Claire. You didn't need that after last night's trouble. How are you feeling?"

"Fine, until you showed up."

She said it with a straight face and Brody frowned and leaned back in his seat, obviously dismayed by her statement. Owen wanted to groan and throw up his hands in defeat. The date had started off so well, now it had gone to shit. Claire would probably never want to see him again.

"I'm just kidding," she added, smiling and giggling nervously.

Brody sighed out his relief. "You look better. How's the head?"

"A few glasses of wine, and I'll be fine."

"That should be a slogan," Brody said.

"Here, have mine." Rain set her glass in front of Claire's place. "I can't have it anyway."

"Congratulations."

Owen caught the look of envy on Claire's face and remembered that she and the asshole broke up for more than his cheating. She'd wanted to have a family. Well, he liked the idea of having kids. Hell, he loved hanging out with his nieces.

"Your girls are wonderful. Always so full of joy and fun when they come into the shop," Claire said, engaging Rain in her favorite topic. Her girls.

"Always so full of sugar when they come home from your shop." Rain smiled, then gave Owen a frown because he was famous for taking them out, feeding them nothing but sugar, and dropping them home for Rain to deal with the inevitable sugar crash and cranky attitudes.

"I have no idea what you're talking about," Owen lied with a smile on his face, making Claire laugh beside him. Her distress from a moment ago forgotten, he hoped.

"They must be so excited about the baby," Claire said.

"They don't know," Brody answered.

"We haven't told anyone but you two. We wanted to wait until the first trimester was over to be sure everything is all right," Rain explained.

"You're okay?" Owen asked, concerned.

"She's perfect," Brody said, smiling and taking Rain's hand, kissing the back of it.

"You should bring the girls to the shop. I'll make pink and blue tea cakes. You can surprise them."

"What a wonderful idea. We'll do that Saturday after the softball game."

"I'm not wearing the pink boa," Brody announced.

"That one belongs to Owen," Claire teased, shooting him a mischievous smile.

Anna arrived with the appetizers and took their order. He didn't mind Brody and Rain's intrusion, not when Claire seemed fine and at ease with the group. If things went well, he hoped they'd spend a lot more time together.

"Owen tells me you were in the military, Brody. Have you been back long?"

"It's been several months now. I came back for Rain and discovered I had two little girls."

"You're fixing up the cabin on the family ranch?" Claire asked.

"Owen has the big house. I'm building Rain and the girls a house where the cabin used to be."

"It's going to be gorgeous if we ever finish it," Rain added.

"A couple more months. Then, we'll get married," Brody said, smiling at Rain.

Owen knew that smile didn't always come easy for his brother, but Rain brought it out more and more each day.

"You still haven't asked me."

"I will," Brody teased.

Owen leaned in to Claire, like he was telling her a secret. "This has been going on since these two got back together. Brody tells her they're getting married, but Rain isn't one to take orders, even from Brody, so she's waiting for her proposal."

"All he has to do is ask," Rain confirmed.

"Which Brody hasn't done, because he's stubborn and ornery," Owen added.

"Not true. Well, true," Brody said, laughing at himself. "You see, Claire, I did some bad things back in the day. Rain and the girls paid a high price. I owe her the perfect proposal."

"I don't need perfect, I just need you."

"You've got me. But like you said, we did everything else backward, this I need to do right."

"It's taking you long enough." Rain pouted.

"The best things in life aren't always fast or easy."

Claire raised her glass. "I'll drink to that."

They all clinked glasses. "You took over Roxy's bar and changed the name to McBride's, right?" Claire asked.

"Changing the name was the first order of business," Rain said, giving Brody a look.

"Owen helped us broker the deal. He's a great lawyer and negotiator. You ever need help, he's your guy," Brody said, choking Owen up that he thought so highly of him.

"Thanks, man, but I already got her to go on a date with me, you don't need to sell me on her."

"Doesn't hurt, especially when we crashed your party."

"I don't mind," Claire said, her tone and smile telling all of them she meant it. "I haven't had a chance to spend a lot of time with anyone in town. Most of the time it's chitchat while I put their order together. Until last night, I think the only thing Owen and I said to each other besides his order was, 'Have a nice day.'"

"Yeah, well, I'm an idiot for not asking you out sooner. Besides, you thought Dawn and Autumn were mine, so you weren't exactly sending out the 'I'm available' vibe to me."

"It's okay. I've spent every waking hour setting up the shop and making sure it runs smoothly. I probably wouldn't have been very receptive to a date."

"Which is why you still haven't unpacked your house," Owen pointed out.

"I'm working on it."

"You've only finished your bedroom."

"How do you know this?" Rain asked, planting her elbow on the table and dropping her chin into her hand, her total focus on him, and a knowing smile on her face.

Owen copied her posture. "I put her to bed last night."

"Do tell."

"Hardwood floors and a thick, deep green rug. Sage walls and oak furniture. A queen-size sleigh bed."

"Your feet will hang off the end."

"I don't care."

Claire slapped him on the back, but he kept going, knowing she didn't understand what he and Rain were really talking about.

"Please don't get her started," Brody pleaded.

"Cream-colored spread with the same color sheets and blanket. The sheets had green leaves on them."

Rain sighed. "Perfect."

"Antique crystal lamps on the nightstands, silver framed photos of her as a child and with friends at college on the dresser along with a collection of antique perfume bottles. Black-and-white photographs of Paris framed in silver on the walls."

Rained sighed again, her eyes going dreamy.

"A reading corner by the window with a crystal chandelier above a tan chenille chaise lounge. A round table beside it in distressed white with a green glass vase filled with white roses."

"So dreamy."

He chuckled. "You're so easy."

"Which is why I love her, but please don't get her started on decorating tonight. One meal without deciding the color of this room or that one, that's all I ask," Brody pleaded.

Claire laughed beside him. "I'm a closet decorator myself. I haven't finished the house because I like to have the whole plan in mind before I start. The master bedroom is done—"

"And sounds absolutely lovely," Rain interrupted.

"I'm about to finish the master bath. I've got the major items done. Sand-quartz countertops, the claw-foot tub has been refinished, thick white towels hang from brushed nickel towel bars. The walls are a soft sky blue." She turned to him. "Kind of like your eyes."

"You're just bragging now," Rain said, smiling.

"I need to add the finishing touches. I can't wait to finish."

"Yeah, well, I've got a whole house to do myself, and this one"—Rain cocked her head in Brody's direction—"is no help at all."

"I told you to do whatever you want to the house. All I wanted is to fill the rooms with the girls and however many more children you'll give me."

Rain smiled at Brody with a world of love in her eyes. "I'm working on the next one right now."

Brody kissed her hand again. "See, I did my part. Now you decorate his or her room."

"Yes, dear."

Brody looked at Claire. "She doesn't really mean that. So you two talk decorating, and Owen and I will talk horses and sports and everyone will be happy."

Claire laughed and looked across the table at Rain. "Did you see the latest issue of *Southern Living*? They featured a refurbished Louisiana mansion. You might be interested in seeing the master suite and living room. I fell in love with the kitchen countertops and tiles."

The next hour they spent talking with some, but not much, input from Owen and Brody. Rain and Claire covered decorating, swapping likes and dislikes, ideas for this room and that one. Over dinner, Rain asked Claire about her college experience, since Rain had missed out to raise the girls. Claire talked about her friends, classes, and even some funny anecdotes about working as a waitress at a local pub to pay for her books. She'd received a full academic scholarship. Owen had been right to call her smart.

To Brody's dismay, Rain told Claire about them growing up together until one day they looked at each other and being friends just wasn't enough anymore. Rain covered the basics of how they split up, how she got Autumn from Roxy, and how Brody came home to get them all back together as a family.

Claire opened up about her ex-husband and how she fell for a lie. He understood that someone as smart and capable as Claire would take her ex's betrayal as a personal insult to her intelligence. The thing was, when it came to matters of the heart, the mind may see, but the heart still wants until it doesn't.

Owen listened carefully to everything she said about the asshole and everything she didn't. In the end, she said the only thing he really needed to know.

"The marriage turned out bad, but not because I didn't put my heart into it. I still want the husband and kids and home, but next time I want it all with a man who wants them with me, too."

Rain and Brody shared a look. They had exactly what Claire was talking about and knew it.

Claire caught Owen staring at her.

"And that is the last thing I should have said on a first date. Or any date. Sorry, I'm out of practice."

"Never apologize for saying what you want," Owen said. "Makes it easier on us guys."

"How about some of that decadent double chocolate raspberry torte I saw on the menu?"

He laughed and gave her a nod. "Anything you want."

"You may regret saying that someday."

"I doubt it," he responded, feeling very much like indulging her every whim for the rest of his life. It shouldn't be like this. Not this fast. Not this easy. Not this complete. Then again, what did he know? He'd never felt this way about anyone.

"I'm so glad you said something because I'm dying for a piece of cheesecake with fresh strawberries and cream," Rain gushed.

"Craving. Really?" Brody asked, an indulgent grin on his face.

"Yes. Really."

"Like you need a reason to want cheesecake," Owen teased.

"The baby wants cheesecake. I'm just making sure he gets it."

"Now it's a he?" Brody asked.

"We'll find out in a few months when they do the ultrasound."

"Owen, are you hoping for another niece or a nephew?" Claire asked.

"If I can't have one of my own, whichever one she has will be my new little buddy."

"Why can't you have one of your own?" Claire sucked in a breath. "I'm sorry. That was rude and intrusive."

He laughed and Brody nearly choked on his coffee.

"I can have kids, but I don't have a wife, and Rain is already using her uterus for Brody's new McBride baby."

"Oh," Claire mumbled, her cheeks pink, making her even prettier and endearing.

"Get your own uterus," Brody teased.

He and Claire laughed and dessert arrived, distracting them from the baby topic.

"Brody, tell me the worst thing Owen ever did," Claire said out of the blue.

"Not a chance. Owen and I stick together. We don't rat on each other."

Claire turned to him and he nodded his confirmation of the truth in Brody's words.

"A real and true bro code."

"When you grow up with a father like ours, yeah, you learn to rely on each other," Owen confirmed.

She wanted to know about him. She could have asked him, but she'd asked Brody to get his view, because Brody had shown himself as direct and truthful to a fault. Brody didn't care what anyone thought of him; he spoke the truth even if you didn't want to hear it.

Owen would like to keep his darker side a mystery until she got to know who he was now better, but if she was going to see the whole picture of who he was, she needed to see the flaws.

A risk, but he gave Brody a look to go ahead and sat back and waited for Claire's reaction.

Brody looked him in the eye and said, "The bar fight."

"She asked for the worst thing I ever did."

Brody took a deep breath and sighed it out. "Owen and I used to party hard back in the day. We drank to excess and went from one woman to the next." Brody glanced at Rain. "Sorry."

"No sorry for telling the truth. Go on. Tell her what happened."

"Owen and this girl named Molly were seeing each other off and on for months."

"Tell her the whole truth," Owen coaxed.

"Owen and Molly used to have sex on a regular basis. He didn't care what she did. She didn't care what Owen did. They used each other for sex and nothing else."

Claire sat back in her seat, but kept her gaze on Brody as he told the tale.

"They ran hot and cold with each other, depending on the night and Owen's mood. Molly liked to have fun, so when Owen didn't want to play, she found someone else who would. Owen did the same. Molly found someone else less volatile than Owen was back then, and it seemed she had a good thing going for a couple of months.

"So, one night Owen and I are raising hell down at Roxy's, drinking and playing pool. Molly is at the bar with another girl. The friend leaves and this big dude comes up to Molly and starts yelling at her, causing a scene, but the music's too loud and Owen can't hear what they're saying. I didn't really give a shit and kept playing pool against this other guy.

"So the guy leaves Molly crying at the bar. Owen goes over to see what happened. The next thing I know, he's dragging the guy out the front door. I look back at the bar, and Molly's tears are all dried up, and she's got this smug smile on her face. Only one reason a woman looks like that: she's just played Owen. Her friend returns and says something. Molly says something back and the friend gets pissed and runs for the front door. I chased after her, but too late to stop Owen."

Brody sucked in another deep breath and sighed it out. Owen wished Claire hadn't asked. He hated going back to that night more than Brody hated telling the story.

"Owen confronted the guy in the parking lot. He accused the guy of hitting Molly in the stomach until she 'lost the baby.' The guy denied it, pissed off Owen would even suggest such a thing. Drunk and angry, he threw a punch at Owen, barely catching him when Owen ducked out of the way. Owen came up fighting and clocked the guy, breaking his jaw. Drunk, in a rage, Owen tackled the guy and beat the living hell out of him, until I caught up to him and pulled him off. Owen broke three bones in his hand, but the guy ended up in the ICU for a week and the hospital another five days."

Claire's gaze fell on him, but he couldn't look at her. He sat quietly contemplating the moisture dripping down his water glass, seeing nothing but his bloody hands and the guy's pulverized face.

"I make Owen take a seat on the curb. Molly's friend is screaming and cussing, leaning over the guy, crying, 'No, no, no.' She jumps to her feet and runs over to Owen, standing over him demanding to know why he'd beat the guy half to death when he'd done nothing wrong.

"Still pissed off, Owen jumps up and gets in her face, saying Molly told him what he did to her. The friend gasps, put both hands over her mouth, then explodes with a string of swear words I won't repeat in polite company, and tells Owen Molly is a lying bitch. She took Molly to the clinic a week before to abort the baby. The guy somehow found out and confronted Molly at the bar, pissed she got rid of his baby."

"He was a good guy who wanted his child, and I beat him half to death because that lying, cheating bitch played me," Owen spat out, still pissed about the whole damn thing.

Claire looked across the table at Rain and asked her, "Did you just hear the same story I heard?"

Rain smiled and nodded, knowing something Owen couldn't figure out by Claire's tone.

"Yes I did."

"I thought you were going to tell me the worst thing he ever did," she said to Brody.

"I just did."

"Let me get this straight. The worst thing he ever did was defend a woman he believed to be innocent by beating the shit out of some guy he thought hit her when she was pregnant with his baby."

"Yes, but it was a lie and the guy was innocent," Brody clarified.

"Yes, I get that, but Owen didn't know that. He didn't do it for no reason."

"It doesn't matter why I did it, the guy almost died," Owen snapped.

"I take it the cops came. What did they say?"

"The other guy threw the first punch. Owen got off on the fight, but they took him in for drunk and disorderly after he went to the hospital for a cast on his hand," Brody said.

"Still, it sounds to me like the worst thing you ever did shows your true character better than anything."

Owen scrubbed his hands over his face, wishing he never gave Brody permission to tell her the truth about him. He might have gone his whole relationship with Claire without her finding out his true character. He'd spent the last years earning his degree, defending his clients, and staying out of trouble.

"Your instinct is to protect the innocent and pummel the guilty. You only got it wrong because you were drunk and that girl lied to you."

"Yes, and six months later the guy died of a prescription drug overdose." Owen finished the story.

"That's not your fault," Claire said.

"If I hadn't fought with him, he'd have never ended up in the hospital and on those meds."

"If that bitch hadn't lied, none of it would have happened."

"Told you," Rain said.

"I hope she got hers," Claire said.

"Owen turned her in for dealing. The cops found over a pound of marijuana in her apartment stashed in the heating vent. She went away for eighteen months." Rain raised her glass of water. Claire clinked her glass of wine to it, toasting to their shared opinion of Molly.

"Not good enough, but I guess it will have to do for what she did to you," Claire said.

"She didn't do anything to me."

"She made you believe what you did was wrong even though you did it for all the right reasons. If you don't believe me, believe your brother and Rain. Neither of them thinks what you did is wrong."

"Brody just told you the worst thing I ever did."

"I told her the worst thing you think you did," Brody clarified. "I agree with Rain and Claire. Not your fault, man." Brody turned to Claire. "He's the older brother. He always protected me from our old man as a kid. His mother, too, until she left." Brody looked him dead in the eye. "Look how well you looked out for Rain and the girls when I was gone."

Owen sighed, not knowing what to say when Claire, Brody, and Rain all praised him for trying to do the right thing.

"Now, tell me the worst thing he ever did," Claire demanded of Brody.

"He stole a candy bar when he was ten from the grocery store. He felt so guilty about it, he went back the next day, confessed to the manager, and paid for the candy bar. He swept the store every day after school for two weeks."

Claire feigned a look of horror. "You didn't."

He couldn't help himself and laughed.

"Face it, Owen, underneath the bad-boy McBride rep, you're just a good guy," Claire said, squeezing his arm. He took her hand and kissed the back of it, feeling better that she saw him in a good light and made him rethink the events of that night. He'd always feel guilty for what he did, but it didn't hold the sting of shame it once did.

"Best thing he ever did?" Claire asked both Brody and Rain.

"Took care of Rain while I was gone and Rain was raising the girls on her own," Brody said.

"He's a loyal friend and an even better uncle," Rain added.

"Those things I already knew," Claire said. "Any guy who has tea parties with his nieces in public has to be a really great guy."

Owen still held her hand in his and gave it a squeeze. "How about you? Best and worst thing you ever did?"

"Best thing I ever did was spend my senior year of college taking care of my ailing grandmother. Best year of my life. She taught me to cook and sew and I got to know her better in that year than I did growing up. She lived an ordinary life filled with some extraordinary moments. I used to make her tell me the story about how she met my grandfather and married him against both their parents' wishes. They were married for fifty-two years and happily renewed their vows three times, the last one on their fiftieth wedding anniversary.

"Worst thing I ever did, not tell a friend her boyfriend hit on me and lied that I thought he was a great guy. She really liked him. A month after he grabbed my ass and kissed me, she found out he was cheating on her. Completely shocked, she told me what happened and must have read something on my face because she asked me if I knew. I told her what happened and that I thought the guy was a jerk, and she didn't need him. Too late. She was pissed I didn't tell her, blamed me for the whole incident, and said I was jealous. That was the end of a really good friendship.

"Oh, and I apparently tried to stab you last night."

Owen laughed, along with Brody and Rain.

"He probably deserved it," Rain teased.

"No, he took care of me last night and I appreciate it."

Claire yawned, reminding him neither of them got much sleep last night.

"I need to take you home. It's late and you need to get some rest."

He'd paid the check for the table during dessert, so everyone stood. Just because he needed to, he brushed his hand down her long hair, placing his hand at the small of her back to lead her out behind Brody and Rain. Despite Brody and Rain joining their date, he felt it went well, and he'd gotten to know Claire better. Maybe it hadn't been the intimate evening he wanted, but somehow this seemed better. He liked seeing her with Brody and Rain. The women hit it off.

Outside the restaurant, Claire stopped beside him. He shook hands with Brody and hugged Rain. "Bye, beautiful. I'll come by and see the girls soon."

"Any time you want. Bring Claire." She cocked her head in Claire's direction, then pulled her aside for their goodbye.

Rain and Claire stood together talking, so Brody pulled him aside. "Everything at her place is set up. The directions are on the table."

"Thanks."

"Sorry about crashing your date. I really didn't know you were coming here tonight, but I think it worked out."

"You stayed so Rain and Claire could get to know each other. Claire doesn't have many close friends in town and you knew they'd hit it off."

"Claire has a lot of Rain's finer qualities. I like her. I'm glad you like her. It's about time you made *me* an uncle."

Owen laughed. "If you keep showing up on all my dates, that's probably not going to happen."

"I'll back off. I was worried about her after last night. No word on Dale?"

"Nothing."

"Let me know if you need help with him. I've got your back."

"I've got yours."

Owen went to Claire, wrapped his arm around her back, put his hand on her hip, and drew her close. She leaned in to him. He wanted to believe it was only because she wanted to be close, but he felt her fatigue in the sigh she let out.

He looked down at her bandaged feet. "How are you feeling?"

"Tired. A little sore, but I had a great night."

He gave her a squeeze to his side. "Me too. We'll see you guys later. I'm taking her home."

Chapter Thirteen

CLAIRE SAT NEXT to Owen in his truck, tired from the long day, and at peace to be quiet with each other. She liked the comfortable silence. His hand settled over hers. She turned her hand to link fingers with his and gave him a squeeze. He returned it, briefly letting his gaze stray from the road ahead to settle on her and sweep down her body and back to the road. The look was enough to keep her warm, but the heater pumped out hot air to ward off the chill of the night. The stars glowed overhead. The lull of the engine relaxed her as much as Owen's presence.

"I had a really good time tonight."

He cast her a sideways glance; his charming smile made her insides turn over. "Even though my brother crashed our date."

"I like him. Rain is really great. Does Brody mind you calling her beautiful all the time?"

"Not at all. He knows how much I love Rain, and I'm

just being affectionate. Brody and I grew up wild on the ranch, the old man drinking himself into oblivion most every night. We never had a normal home life. When I came back to town to help Rain with the girls, she made me part of their family. I learned what a real mother is, and how to be a father figure the girls can look up to and respect. So, yeah, I call her beautiful, not because she is on the outside, but because she is on the inside where it counts the most."

"She means that much to you."

"She's my sister and the best friend I've ever had besides Brody."

"I always wanted a sister or brother," she admitted.

She had to admit his affection for Rain showed in the way he spoke to her and the obvious bond they shared. She understood his need to belong to a family, since his childhood sounded anything but ideal.

"Do you visit your parents in Briargate often?" he asked.

"I stayed in town after the separation and through the divorce. I needed to figure out what I wanted to do. I managed a restaurant and bakery. I wanted to find something similar, but less demanding of my time. I also needed a break from friends and family whispering and talking behind my back. If I heard one more 'It's too bad they couldn't make it work,' I seriously think I might have screamed until I lost my voice."

"So you moved here and opened the shop."

"Well, not exactly that straightforward, but yes. The asshole left me in debt up to my ears and ruined my credit. I lived with my parents for eight months and worked my regular job along with every part-time and odd job I could find to pay off the debt."

"I hate that asshole."

"Me too. He still owes me a hundred grand from the divorce settlement, which he refuses to pay."

"Can he pay?"

"Despite the crap he made of our marriage and finances, he makes a decent living as an account executive at an ad agency."

Owen glanced at her with a skeptical glare.

"You see why I trusted him to take care of our finances. He's accountable at work, but apparently hiding things from me was his favorite pastime."

"You should go back to court and make him pay."

"I could, but then I let him back into my life for another round of arguments and excuses."

"Good point, but you shouldn't let him get away with not paying you."

"He won't. I put a lien on his house."

"Smart."

"He taught me to cover my ass."

"It's a really nice ass."

She giggled. "Thanks."

They drove into her driveway and the outside porch and garage lights came on automatically. "Hey, how did that happen?"

"I asked Brody's contractor to send over an electrician to put the motion lights up. The back door is still boarded up, but the new door should be installed tomorrow."

"And the bill will come to me, right?"

"I took care of it."

"Owen, no. I can't let you do that."

"It's already done," he said, sliding out of the truck to come around and open her door for her. She had to admit, she liked his charm, generosity, and manners. She found it so rarely in other men these days.

He held his hand out to her and she took it. His warmth seeped into her skin and sent a zip of electricity up her arm. Their gazes locked in a shared moment of awareness. She'd forgotten how wonderful the beginning of a relationship felt. The quickening of her heart from just a look or simple touch of hands. The warmth that washed through her system when the connection between them intensified until all she wanted to do was reach out, wrap her arms around him, and draw him close. The way a kiss blanked out her mind and made her want to lose herself in the moment.

She stopped beside him on the porch and dug through her purse for her key, but Owen opened the door for her. She stared up at him and he smiled that smile she was getting used to seeing whenever he did something without her knowing.

"I took the spare key from the kitchen and came back this afternoon to let the electrician in."

Something beeped, filling the entry with the loud noise. She turned to the sound and found a keypad alarm panel on the wall. Owen punched in a four-digit code.

"That wasn't there when we left this morning."

"Did I mention the alarm company came by at the same time as the electrician?"

"Let me guess, you paid for that, too."

"Guilty."

"Not going to happen." She dumped half the contents of her purse on the side table by the sofa and found her checkbook and a pen. She held them in front of her and glared at Owen.

"How much do I owe you for everything?"

"How much do I owe you for bringing Dale into your life, the headache you've had since yesterday, the stitches in your feet, the busted-up door, and the loss of your sense of safety and security in your own house?"

"You didn't bring that guy into my life. It's his fault this happened, not yours."

"I don't feel that way, and you won't convince me of it." He reached out and traced her cheek, down her neck to her hurt shoulder. "I stayed last night to make you feel safe and because I needed to know you're safe. I can't spend every night on your couch until they find Dale. Not when I want you the way I do."

"Owen, you can't say things like that."

"Why? It's the truth. Although I hate what happened to you last night, I'm glad I met you. So, the security system is for your peace of mind and mine. Come over here and follow the instructions on the sticky note next to the keypad to reset the password."

She huffed out a sigh. "This isn't settled."

"Fine. Buy me lunch tomorrow, and we'll call it even."

"I'd have to buy you lunch for a year to pay you back for all of this."

"Deal. I'm fine with that."

She glanced over her shoulder and gave him a disgruntled look and a shake of her head. He smiled, which made her laugh. "Stubborn."

"Yes, I am when it comes to you and your safety."

"Dale probably realized he got the wrong house and you and I aren't a thing and won't be back at all and this is all for nothing."

"Let's hope, but I'm not taking any chances." He moved in behind her, and she felt the heat of him down her back, but he didn't touch her. He leaned his head in close to her ear. "We do have a thing." His deep voice sent a shiver through her body.

She wanted to lean back into him, but didn't. They barely knew each other.

His warm hands settled on her shoulders, his fingers gently massaging her tight muscles.

"Punch in the new code."

She did, trying not to sigh out her pleasure as his strong hands worked out the knots in her neck.

"The number is one, three, seven, nine."

"Why are you telling me that?"

She turned to face him, admitting what he'd already guessed earlier. "Just in case something happens."

"All you have to do is call—anytime—and I'll be here. If something happens—you hear a noise outside, you see something that isn't right, anything that scares you—hit the emergency button. The cops will come and the alarm company will call me. If the alarm is tripped for any reason, a break-in or even a fire, they'll dispatch help and contact me."

"You know, it took a while for me to settle in here

alone, a new town and business, living on my own really for the first time. Now, I'm nervous."

He reached for her, pulling her close and wrapping his strong arms around her. He settled his head against hers and just held her close.

"You did all that. You'll get through this. If you don't want to be alone, I'm happy to stay with you."

She wanted him to stay, but she couldn't let Dale win by taking away her independence and sense of security. "You're right. I'll be fine. You made sure I'll be okay."

"I've tried, but unless you're in my sight, I'll worry."

Owen let out a deep sigh and hugged her close. He leaned back and looked down at her. "Do you want me to take you to work tomorrow?"

"I'll drive myself. I don't want to put you out any more than I already have."

"I'm not put out in the least. It's my pleasure to spend time with you."

To prove it, he leaned in and kissed her. She thought nothing could compare to the kiss they shared at her shop, but she'd been wrong. This kiss was soft and slow, a melding of mouths and something more. His lips met hers again and again in light caresses. She sighed and he dove in, taking the kiss deeper and sliding his tongue inside to taste and tangle with hers. She gave herself over to the kiss, the moment, and him.

Everything felt right. She'd never been with anyone and let go, but with Owen she knew she could and he'd protect and treat her right. He had since the moment he walked into her home and life yesterday.

Owen ended the kiss, though she didn't want to stop. She wanted to hold on to him all night. His gaze swept her upturned face. His eyes smoldered, telling her he felt the same.

"I'll say goodnight." He traced his finger over the side of her face, drawing a lock of hair back behind her ear. "Take your meds and get some sleep, Claire."

He hesitated a moment before he let her go and opened the front door. She wanted to call him back, take him to her bed, and give in to the overwhelming need building inside of her every second she spent with him. Something held her back. Not only had they just met, but she wasn't sure she wanted him to stay just because she feared being alone in the house again. She didn't want to take that intimate step and discover her mixed-up, lust-laced feelings weren't the real thing.

"Owen." She hesitated, wanting to call him back into her arms to give her that sense of safety she'd felt moments ago. "I had a really great time tonight. Thank you. For everything."

"It was my pleasure. See you tomorrow at one thirty for lunch. Lock the door and set the alarm."

With that he left, making her laugh. She'd said she'd pay him back for everything he did with lunch. Apparently, he'd taken her up on the offer, and they had another date. She let out a soft squeal of delight as happiness and anticipation rippled through her whole system. She thought she'd never sleep, thinking Dale might come back to hurt her to get to Owen. Instead, Owen gave her something else to think about. Him.

Chapter Fourteen

DALE STOOD NEXT to the tree, the bark scraping against his arm, but he didn't care about the rough abrasion against his skin. He tipped the bottle to his lips and gulped down the last of the whiskey like a soda. The sting burned his throat and gut, but not as much as the sight of that damn lawyer walking the hot blonde up to the porch.

The motion lights surprised him. He'd come by earlier to scope out the situation. He might have gotten the wrong house last night, but he followed the lawyer to her shop this evening. If they didn't know each other before, they knew each other well now. It didn't take the lawyer long to make his move, kissing her in the store. Maybe the asshole learned his lesson last night and stopped seeing his wife and moved on.

He liked her long hair, the curve of her full breasts, and the sway of her hips. He hated the way she looked at the lawyer, her eyes going right to his handsome face. Dale wanted to punch in that smug smile. The lawyer thought he could have any damn woman he wanted. McBride had the blonde, he didn't need to go after Shannon, too.

Dale threw the empty bottle at his feet and stormed off into the night, thinking of a new plan. A better plan.

Chapter Fifteen

CLAIRE TAPPED THE last nail and hanger into the wall and grabbed the picture from the floor at her feet. She caught the wire on the metal hook and stood back, adjusting the frame just so. Perfect. The four sea scenes in pastel blues, purples, greens, and tans lined one wall of her sky-blue-colored master bath. They added to the tranquil feel she'd tried so hard to achieve with the muted walls, potted ferns, thick towels and rugs, and pretty light blue glass jars on the sand-colored granite countertops. She'd spent a small fortune to have the old-fashioned claw-foot tub refinished with the pretty silver feet. Totally worth it.

The rest of the house may have been old and in need of repairs, but she'd get to them in time. Right now, her priority had been the master bedroom and bath. She deserved the luxury here. She worked long hours, and since her finances had been in such a mess, the only luxury she had was a decent night's sleep in a soft bed.

Too bad last night she'd barely slept at all, thinking about Owen and all the things he'd done for her. All the things she wanted him to do to her in that bed.

She shook off the thoughts and studied her bathroom again. A few more sleepless nights and predawn decorating sessions and she might get the house in order. Finally.

She'd do the living room next. That way when Owen came over, they'd have someplace comfortable to sit.

She stopped in her tracks in the middle of her bedroom and considered that last thought and how easy it was to picture spending an evening on the couch watching a movie with Owen, cuddling together, and kissing. Definitely more kissing. The man knew how to make her knees go weak and her heart melt.

Still, another man had done the same, and he'd turned her life upside down. Not in a good way.

Owen didn't compare to her ex. Sure, they were both extremely handsome men, but Owen had a sincerity and charm that drew her in. Her ex pulled it off in the beginning, but then she'd seen right through him because he wasn't real. Everything he did always had an ulterior motive. Owen had a genuine goodness about him. She'd spent the first hour of dinner last night looking for any kind of hidden agenda behind his words and actions. After a while, she stopped looking for what wasn't there and settled into learning as much about him as possible.

The thought made her anxious to get to work and lunch with him. She stood a few feet from the dresser and stared at her image in the wall mirror. She slid her hands over her sides and the satin-and-lace nightie she'd slipped on last night rather than grabbing one of her favored old T-shirts or tank tops. Last night, thinking of Owen and feeling more like a woman than she had in a long time, she'd dug out the sexy lingerie her ex had barely noticed on her shortly after their marriage. Another red flag she should have noticed sooner.

She gave herself a critical look. Not bad. Her full breasts filled out the tight bodice that barely contained or covered her. Slim, her hips flared softly to fill out the skirt that ended at her thighs. For the first time in years, she felt sexy. Owen made her feel sexy. Just thinking about him made her breasts feel heavy, her nipples tighten, and she clamped her thighs tight as her mind wandered to images of him running his hands over her body and freeing her from the silky barrier so he could set his hands on a journey over her heated skin.

She sucked in a deep breath and shook off the erotic images. She needed to get to work. The sooner she did, the sooner she'd get to see Owen again.

Giddy and feeling an excitement she hadn't felt since dating in high school and college, she showered quickly and dressed in her favorite dark purple slacks and a cream-and-violet flower-print blouse. She'd have to be extra careful not to spill anything on it while she baked this morning. She even dug out her pretty lingerie. A lavender bra-and-panty set she'd bought to make her feel pretty and feminine when she'd felt anything but desirable after her marriage fell apart. Wearing it today made her feel sexy and naughty and daring.

She wished she could wear a pair of heels, but her feet still hurt and the stitches didn't come out for several more days. The sandals didn't exactly complete the outfit, but they'd do for now.

She walked downstairs, grabbed her purse, and went to the front door. She hesitated, looking out the windows, studying the front yard and driveway, looking for anything out of the ordinary. Everything seemed fine, but still she hesitated. Not even six in the morning, the sun hadn't quite cleared the hills, leaving most of her yard in dark gray shadows.

"Come on, Claire. You can't lock yourself away in the house forever."

She tapped in the code on the security panel, unlocked the door, stepped out onto the porch, and closed and locked the door again. She waited for the last beep on the alarm signaling it was armed and walked to her car, grateful to Owen for putting in the system and saving her sanity. She may not have slept well, but she hadn't stood guard listening for every little sound because she knew if someone got into the house, the alarm would sound and someone would call Owen.

She didn't like this need to know he'd come if something happened, but on the other hand, it felt good to know he thought enough to take care of her and wanted to know if something happened to her. It may have started as some misguided obligation because of his client's ex, but after last night, the kiss and evening they shared, she felt it had turned into a personal duty for him. Independent and able to stand on her own, that didn't mean she couldn't accept Owen's help without losing her pride.

She unlocked the car door and slid into the seat, rushing to relock the door. She put her hands on the steering wheel and tried to calm her racing heart with a few deep breaths. She hated feeling this way.

The drive to town helped to calm her, until she arrived at her shop, parked, and walked to the back door. The dark windows and empty, creepy alleyway sent another chill up her spine. She raced to unlock the door, rush inside, and slam the door behind her. She twisted the bolt into place and flicked on the lights. She spun around to sweep her gaze across the kitchen and office area, searching for Dale.

Alone and creeping herself out for no good reason, she tossed her purse on the desk in her small office and went to the ovens and turned them on. She pulled on her smock over her outfit, buttoned it, and pulled the ingredients from the cupboards and refrigerator to make muffins. By the time she finished the last batch of scones, brownies, and cookies, pulled the tray of triple-berry tarts from the oven, and took delivery of the bagels and breads, Gayle arrived just before seven to help her with the morning crowd. The shop smelled wonderful and her nerves dissipated. She fell into routine, busy with her customers and restocking the display case.

Most of her customers came in the morning. Though the lunch crowd was steady most days, the diner down the street got most of the business. People in town tended to opt for burgers and other hot meals over her sandwich, wrap, panini, and salad selection. Several different groups of ladies met at her place each week on different days for book clubs, "mommy meetings," and get-togethers with friends. She enjoyed watching the close-knit groups and envied their weekly lunches and the camaraderie they enjoyed.

She and Gayle were the best of friends, but the difference in their ages kept a distance between them. They were at different places in their lives. Still, she relied on Gayle's wisdom and motherly advice when she needed it.

"It's almost time for you to go. Don't want to be late for your date."

"It's not a date. I'm repaying him for a favor. That's all."

"Everyone in town knows about your dinner date last night."

"We had a good time, but it wasn't exactly a date. Brody and Rain joined us."

"Meeting his family already." Gayle gave her a knowing smile.

"Stop. It's not like that."

"It's not?"

"He wanted to do something nice for me because of what happened."

"Stop kidding yourself and talking yourself out of knowing he likes you and wants to get to know you better. If he didn't, why would he make a date with you for lunch today when he saw you last night?"

"I set myself up for that when I told him I needed to pay him back for the alarm system and lights he put up at my house."

"He's the most eligible bachelor in town. He's got a great job and makes better than decent money. He's also known for being generous whenever there's a need for a donation for one thing or another in this town. He probably could care less if you paid him back. He wants to see you. So go in the back, get yourself pretty, and I'll finish packing up the meal you spent twenty minutes preparing."

"It's too much," she admitted, self-conscious she'd gone to so much trouble to make the perfect lunch and presentation.

"It's perfect. He'll see you put a lot of effort into this date because it matters to you. You'll see, he'll appreciate it."

"I'm trying too hard. He'll think I'm desperate."

"If I had a gorgeous, kind man like him waiting for me, I'd be desperate to see him, too."

"You don't think this is moving too fast?"

"What? Dinner one night and lunch the next day. That's not fast, honey, that's getting-to-know-you time. So go. Get to know him better and enjoy the afternoon. This place will be quiet for the next few hours, so don't feel you have to rush back."

"It's lunch, not a weekend getaway."

"Well, if it turns into a weekend getaway, don't you worry about the store. I'll lock up tonight." Gayle smiled and tried to hold back a laugh when she scowled at her.

She wanted to grab the lunch basket she'd made and make a clean getaway, but she took Gayle's advice and went to the back bathroom and brushed out her long hair. She swiped on some tinted lip balm and pressed her lips together to even out the color. Nervous and giddy at the same time, she pressed both hands to her fluttering belly and studied her face in the mirror.

"It's just lunch. That's all."

Still, she hesitated. She squared her shoulders, spun on her heel, walked back to the front counter, and grabbed the basket Gayle had just finished packing with the last of the items she'd put together.

Without a word, she headed for the door.

"Have fun," Gayle called, and she sailed through the door.

With her nerves in a tangle, easier said than done.

Chapter Sixteen

OWEN CHECKED THE time on his laptop for the fifth time in two minutes. He should have asked to see her for breakfast. Or stayed at her place last night. Not that she'd asked him to, or indicated she wanted him to stay. She wasn't the sleep-with-a-guy-on-the-first-date kind of woman anyway. It had been one hell of a date too, despite Brody's interference. Still, Claire had a good time and made a friend in Rain, who'd called him this morning with some random question about whether he remembered the softball game this weekend. Of course he remembered, Rain just wanted to ask him about Claire. He told her the truth. He liked her. A lot.

The morning dragged into afternoon slower than the courts doled out justice for many of his cases. He checked in with Dylan to see if he had any leads on Dale, but they had nothing, and other cases took priority at this point. For all they knew, Dale skipped town and wouldn't be back. Owen didn't think so. Dale had a thing for Shannon that went beyond reason, which is why he'd fixated on Owen's involvement in what he believed was Owen taking away his wife.

His fingers flew across the keys, but his mind wasn't really on the notes he typed out for his upcoming court appearance. He needed to see her, to know she'd made it to work this morning and everything was fine. Hell, he just wanted to look at her again. Images of her kept him up half the night. Most of them had been sex-filled dreams of her tempting him into a passion he'd never felt and craved like nothing else. Tired beyond reason, he'd fallen into a deep sleep in the early morning hours and woken out of a nightmare where Dale had killed Claire and taunted him with mocking laughter that Owen would never have her.

Owen shook off the nightmare even now, telling himself she was fine. He tapped out another sentence and tried to concentrate on each point he needed to make on his client's behalf. All he wanted was for time to speed up and one thirty to arrive so he could spend time with Claire.

When was the last time he felt this anxious to see a woman? Never. Oh, there'd been women in his life he enjoyed spending time with and even looked forward to seeing again and again, but nothing like this. She was different. Seeing her with Brody and Rain last night, the way she fit in with them, with him, showed him that it might be possible for him to have what Brody and Rain shared. He didn't know if he'd have that same kind of deep love with Claire, but there was something there. Something he wanted to explore and build on until he knew for sure one way or the other. The thought of this turning into something lasting didn't faze him in the least. Hell, he welcomed it if he got to spend time with her.

"Hi." Her soft voice broke into his concentration. He stared at the jumble of nonsense on his screen and sighed. He should be thinking about his client and winning his case, instead of daydreaming about a woman, but he couldn't seem to help himself where she was concerned.

He looked up and his insides knotted. She leaned against the door frame, trying to look casual, but ended up looking sexy as hell with her head tipped just so and her long golden hair hanging over one shoulder and down her chest.

"Damn, you're more beautiful today than yesterday."

She smiled shyly and her gaze fell to the floor before coming back up to meet his. "I brought lunch."

All I want is you.

"I'm starved," he said instead of giving in to his baser needs and leaping up from his desk and diving for her.

"Shall we eat in here?"

He hit SAVE on his laptop, though he should have probably deleted just about all the rubbish he'd written over the last hour. Maybe he'd salvage some of it after lunch when he'd had his Claire fix and could hopefully think clearly again.

He stood and came around the desk. She smelled of flowers and baked goods. Musky and sweet and tempting. His mouth watered. He wanted to kiss her, but held back and tried to pull off "casual," even if he felt nervous. He wanted this to go well, so he could see her again.

"Let's go down the hall to my library. It's more comfortable in there."

"I hope you don't mind my coming back. Janine wasn't out front, so I let myself in."

"No problem. She took a late lunch, too."

"We're alone?"

"Yeah. Why? Does that bother you?"

"No." The word came too fast, but she smiled. "I just wondered if maybe you had an aunt or cousin joining us today."

He laughed. "It's just you and me. Thank God. I really did want to have dinner alone with you last night. I had no idea Brody and Rain would join us."

They walked down the hall and entered the library.

"It's fine. I'm just teasing. I liked them a lot, and I really did have a great time last night."

"I'm glad. We'll do it again soon."

"Double date with your brother?"

"Well, I meant go to dinner, but yeah, I guess it would be fun to double date with them again."

"I'd like that."

She gave him another of those shy smiles he liked so much. They stood in the archway to the library. An awkward silence settled between them as he stared down at her.

"All I want to do is kiss you."

"Maybe you should, so I can eat without thinking about it constantly."

He cupped her face and leaned in, though the basket she held in front of her kept him from getting too close. Probably better that way, or he'd have her sprawled beneath him on the floor.

He brushed his thumbs over her soft cheeks and stared down into her beautiful green eyes. His lips hovered over hers. "I don't think anything will stop me from thinking about you."

He remembered the taste of her, the way she made his blood run hot, but he'd forgotten the sweetness of her that made his heart stop and everything inside him want to protect and keep her safe forever. She touched something deep inside of him and drew out all the feelings and emotions he'd never known he possessed. He fought to keep the kiss gentle and light, despite some great warrior inside of him demanding to strip her bare, sink his hard cock inside of her, and claim her as his prize.

Maybe he'd do it anyway, because he liked feeling this way about her. Still, she probably didn't come today to be mauled by the guy who got her attacked just the other night. Shifting his thinking to match the kiss, he pressed his lips to hers and held it for a moment, letting her settle into him before he brushed his lips to hers again and stood back and looked down at her upturned face and the pretty flush of pink on her cheeks.

"See, it didn't work. I'm still thinking about kissing you," he teased.

"Maybe we should try that again."

To his surprise, she shifted the basket to her side, reached up and grabbed his tie, pulled him down, and planted her lips over his. He'd kept things light, but she took him under with one sweep of her tongue against his lips. Every thought fled his mind but one: *Closer.* He needed to be closer to her. His hand slipped under her silky hair to the back of her neck, careful not to hit the lump on her head. He held her close, his tongue tangling with hers until the hand wrapped around his tie turned and, palm to his chest, she gently pushed him away, their mouths separating at the very last second when he could no longer reach her. She held him at arm's length and inhaled deeply, letting it go on a sigh. Her heavy eyelids told him he'd affected her as much as she'd affected him.

"Want to try that one more time?" he asked, holding back a smile when she stared up at him and shook her head no.

"Not if we're ever going to eat."

He took her cue and held out his hand, indicating she should enter the room. She shifted the basket again. He took it from her. "Let's sit on the sofa."

"I love this room. It's not what I expected."

"It used to be the living room when this was somebody's house. I wanted to keep the feel of the place because it's got a history and it's part of the feel of this downtown area. In the winter, I like to light a fire in the old stone fireplace and sit in here working. That's why I have the couch and coffee table here in front and the conference table by the windows. This is sometimes a good place to sit and talk with clients. It's more casual and less intimidating, especially if the case involves something traumatic."

"You've got a lot of books. Are they all law books?"

He glanced over at the three towering bookcases that stretched floor to ceiling. "Most of them are current. I like to collect old law books. You never know when some obscure law that's still on the books, but no one really knows about, will come in handy."

"Smart."

Settling in to the casual conversation, he waited for her to sit on the sofa. He took the seat next to her and stayed close. The heat and pull between them drew him in and made him wish they were at his place or hers, alone, with no opportunity for anyone to catch them in a compromising position. He'd already taken a chance, kissing her when anyone could walk into the office. Janine left to give him some privacy for lunch, but that didn't mean a client wouldn't stop by, or someone else looking to hire a lawyer.

"I try my best to do everything I can for my clients." He didn't want to talk about work, so he changed the subject. "What did you bring for lunch? This looks great."

He liked the way she'd packed the rectangular basket. White dishes and linen napkins sat next to a pair of glasses and a bottle of chilled raspberry Italian soda. Two sandwiches were wrapped in white butcher paper. Two bags of his favorite potato chips. One of her amazing desserts hid in the Styrofoam container. He smelled chocolate and berries.

She took one of the plates and opened a sandwich, arranging it on the plate just so before she handed it to him with one of the napkins.

"I'm so glad it's not one of those tea sandwiches with cucumbers."

She laughed. The sound made his gut go tight.

"Those are for tea parties. This is for feeding a hungry man lunch."

Things between them seemed so easy and comfortable, so he reached out and wrapped his arm around her back, pulling her close. He kissed the side of her head. "You remembered I like roast beef with cheddar on sourdough."

"With pepperoncini's."

He took one from the sandwich and popped it into his mouth. "So good."

She giggled again and his gut did that thing and everything inside him settled.

"What are you having?"

"Turkey club on sourdough. No peppers."

"No, you've got those sprout things. Chick food."

"You got man food, I'll stick with this."

He rubbed his hand up and down her back. She gave him a smile over her shoulder, her hair falling down over his hand and arm. He grabbed a handful and gave it a playful tug. He loved the softness of it and wanted to feel it draped over his bare chest when they made love.

"You're the best." He meant it. He appreciated how much thought she'd put into lunch, making it personal and nice with all the added extra stuff. He leaned back into the sofa with his plate, draped his napkin over his shirt and tie, and settled in to eat and spend time with her.

"How was last night? Did you sleep well?" he asked.

"Not really. Why? Do I look that bad?"

"You don't need me to tell you how beautiful you are, but I will again if it makes you happy."

He thought she'd smile or laugh, but instead she turned serious.

"The alarm system helped ease the worst of my fears. I did get a few hours' sleep. I really appreciate that you did that for me."

"The police will find Dale and you won't have to worry. How are your feet and head?"

"Better. No headache and the stitched cuts don't hurt anymore. They look better. My hip still aches."

"How's the shoulder?"

"Still sore. I've got more range of motion today. Working it out while I mix up batter for the baked goods helps."

"Good."

"So, how has your morning been? What kind of cases are you working on today?"

"I'm helping a client with some business contracts, and I have two upcoming divorce cases."

"Are there any happy divorces?"

"None that I've seen, unless you count the person who gets the most. They seem to think they're happy, but really they're just alone again with a bunch of stuff."

"Not your favorite part of the job."

"No. That's why I don't handle very many of them. I mostly do it for clients I work with on other matters."

"So, Shannon was already a client."

"No. She and I went to high school together. I didn't know her well back then, but when things with Dale got really bad, she asked if I'd help get him out of jail. Instead, I convinced her she deserved better."

"She wanted you to help *him* after he hurt her."

"I'll never understand the psychology behind women who defend and go back to the men who hurt them. I'm happy Shannon decided to leave him. I just hope they find Dale soon and put him back behind bars where he belongs."

In need of a change of subject, he asked, "What are you doing this weekend?"

"Working."

"Don't you ever get time off?"

"The shop is closed Sunday and Monday. Tuesday Gayle and Mary Ann work."

"Mary Ann?"

"She's a stay-at-home mom. She comes in a few hours a couple of days a week to help out while her two boys are in preschool. It gets her out of the house and gives her family some extra income."

"So you have Sunday, Monday, and Tuesday off."

"Most of the time. Since I own the shop, I usually take that time to catch up on paperwork and inventory."

"So if I want to see you on the weekend, it has to be Saturday evening or Sunday. Darn, I wanted you to come to the softball game on Saturday afternoon."

"What time?"

"Eleven."

"At the sports park or the school?"

"The park. Will you come?"

"Sure. I'll ask Gayle to cover the shop for a couple of hours."

"I'll pick you up."

Finished with their sandwiches, she pulled the dessert carton out of the basket and opened the lid. He leaned forward to get a look.

"Chocolate raspberry torte. One of my favorites."

"You have it with the girls at your tea parties."

"I like to get them all hopped up on sugar and send them home to Rain. It's fun being the uncle."

She laughed. "I don't know if Rain appreciates that."

"She does. I get the girls out of her hair for a few hours and she gets some peace and quiet."

"Until you bring them home on a sugar high."

"It's not a perfect system, but it works for me." They shared a laugh at Owen's selfish behavior.

Owen took the fork from the basket and cut a piece of the cake and held it up for her to take a bite, since she'd only brought one piece.

She took the fork in her mouth and pulled back to scoop the cake off. Their eyes met and held for an intense second, both of them aware of the other and wanting something more than dessert.

"Owen."

He nearly dropped the fork when the woman's voice intruded on the intimate moment he shared with Claire. They both jumped and the spell broke.

He looked up, surprised to see Shannon staring at them from the library entrance, a frown on her face.

"Shannon. What are you doing here? Is everything okay?" He stood and drew her attention from Claire and walked over to her. She looked up at him and smiled warmly.

"I needed to see you. I'm sorry to interrupt your lunch meeting."

He didn't correct her outright, but wanted to make it clear this was his personal time. "Claire is a friend of mine. We were just finishing lunch. Did you and I have an appointment today?"

They didn't, which begged the question of why she showed up unannounced at his office. Again.

"Dale called me at work today. I hung up on him, but he keeps calling back. My boss is really mad. Dale keeps swearing and making threats if I don't talk to him. I don't know what to do, so I came to tell you."

"Did Dale say where he is?"

"No. As soon as I heard his voice, I hung up just like you told me to do. We're not married anymore. He doesn't have any reason to contact me. That's what you said." She wrapped her arms around her middle in a defensive gesture that told him how much Dale's threats scared her.

He reached for her and rubbed his hands up and down her arms by her shoulders to reassure her. "Yes. That's right. You don't need to talk to him."

She took a step closer, but he gently held her away. One thing to console a client. Quite another to make them think you were personally involved.

"We'll contact the police and let them know what's happened. If he calls again, maybe you can get him to tell you where he is, so the police can pick him up. The sooner, the better. I don't want him to come back and hurt you. You're being extra careful, right?"

She beamed him a smile. "Yes. My boss walks me to my car after work. When I get home, I make sure to lock everything up and set the alarm."

"Good. Keep your eyes open. If you even think you see something strange when you get home, don't get out of the car. Use your cell phone to call the police. Have them come and check the house for you."

"I just want this to be over."

"I know you do. So do I. In fact, I had an alarm system put in Claire's house, too, to be sure she's safe."

"Why?" The question sounded more like a demand for an answer.

"Claire is the woman Dale attacked the other night."

"Oh, so that's why she's here."

Claire frowned and looked to him to correct Shannon's assumption that this was a business lunch. He wasn't about to explain his personal life to a client. "The police need your help to find Dale. You're the only one he contacts. I don't want to scare you, but he's not going to stop until he has you back, or the police put him behind bars again."

"I'm not going back to him. Not this time. I did in the past, but I want something better." She bit her bottom lip and hugged herself close. Her words came out fast and shaky. "You helped me see that I can have something better." She touched his arm, and he took her hand and gave it a pat to reassure her again.

"Yes, you can, but we need to stop Dale."

Claire walked up beside him, her basket packed with the dishes and lunch wrappers. He immediately dropped Shannon's hand and turned to her.

"Where are you going?"

"Back to work. You need to take care of this."

"Give me a couple of minutes, and I'll walk you out to your car."

"No need. I walked over."

"Claire, if Dale is still intent on hurting you, it's not safe for you to be out walking alone."

"I'm not going to live my life hiding. It's a public street with lots of traffic. My shop is only four blocks down. I'll be fine."

"No. I'll walk you back."

"We need to contact the police," Shannon interrupted.

Claire touched his arm much the same way Shannon had moments ago. He'd brushed aside Shannon's gesture, but with Claire he couldn't ignore the immediate and intense need to touch her back.

"I'll be fine. You've got work to do."

He took her hand in his and held firm. He didn't want her to leave like this.

"We didn't finish our dessert."

"I left it for you on the coffee table." She gave his hand a squeeze and pulled free. "Bye."

He wanted to call her back, but Shannon grabbed his arm to get his attention and pull him back from taking another step in Claire's direction. He hadn't realized he'd moved to go after her.

Claire opened the door to leave and Janine walked in. They exchanged hellos and goodbyes with a smile, but Janine's smile faded when she spotted Owen with Shannon.

Janine drew closer and wrapped an arm around Shannon's shoulders. "Shannon, dear, you look upset. Let go of Owen before you wrinkle him all up. I'll get you a cup of tea."

"Dale called," Shannon explained her presence in his office.

Janine pulled Shannon down the hallway toward the kitchen. "Well, you'll report him to the police."

Their voices faded down the hall, but Owen didn't move. His gaze remained locked on the closed front door through which Claire had exited. He had a strange feeling they'd taken a step back in their relationship. He'd felt so close to her, sitting in the library, sharing a meal and conversation and just being together. Now, he felt a barrier between them, and he didn't like it one bit.

Owen wanted to go after Claire, but he turned down the hallway and went to the kitchen. Janine sat across from Shannon facing him. The soft look in her eyes told him she regretted his date ending this way. He didn't like it himself, but duty called. If he could get Shannon to calm down and maybe help them find Dale, the threat against both women would be over. He wanted Claire safe.

Shannon sat with her back to him and a mug of hot tea between her hands. She turned when Janine looked up at him and jumped up, nearly toppling the chair. She threw her arms around him and held tight. "You have to make him stop. He won't leave me alone. I'm so scared he's going to come after me again." Tears made her words come out stilted.

Stuck with her wrapped around him, he didn't know quite what to do but give her a pat on the back. She wiped her eyes but didn't let him go. She tipped her head up and her sad, tear-filled eyes made him cave. He didn't know what to do with a crying woman, so he hugged her close, pat her on the back some more, and reassured her. "It's going to be okay."

Janine stood and took Shannon by both shoulders and pulled her away from him and helped her back into the chair.

"Drink your tea, dear, while Owen goes to his office and contacts the police to report what's happened."

Owen mouthed, "Thank you," and took the opportunity to retreat.

A shy, sweet girl, Shannon hung out with the unpopular kids in high school who were most likely to become the geeks who ruled the world of electronics and science and put all the jocks and most of the popular kids to shame by the ten-year reunion. How she ended up married to Dale mystified him.

Maybe it came down to the attention Shannon so obviously needed. Even with him, she wanted his attention on her. He'd seen the stunned look on her face when she saw him with Claire. From what she'd told him about her marriage to Dale, he'd showered her with affection when they first got married, and she loved him for it. They had some hard times, Dale started drinking, lost one job after another, and affection turned into fights about money and his drinking. Some of those fights brought the police out to their house for domestic disturbances.

Eventually, Dale turned on Shannon when she got a job and started supporting them. A real blow to Dale's ego, which resulted in several trips to the emergency room for Shannon. Dale hated that Shannon earned the money in the family and sometimes forgot herself and let him know she could buy what she wanted, since she'd earned the money, and that didn't include keeping him in booze. Owen agreed with Shannon, but Dale took exception, using it as yet another excuse to hurt Shannon and convince her to do as he said.

Owen shook his head and fell into his chair at his desk and grabbed the phone and called the sheriff's office and left a message for Dylan. Nothing more he could do. He still didn't know where to find Dale.

Frustrated they still didn't have a lead on Dale's whereabouts and that his date with Claire ended so abruptly, he stared out his window and wondered what to do next. He needed to make things up to Claire. He also didn't like that she'd walked back to her shop alone.

He grabbed his cell phone and hit the screen for his "favorite" list and pushed Claire's name. She answered on the first ring, making him smile for the first time since she left.

"Hi, Owen."

He loved hearing his name from her. "Hi. You made it back to the shop without incident."

"It was a lovely walk back."

"I'd have made it better."

"Oh yeah? How?"

"I'd have kissed you goodbye."

"Then I'm sorry we got interrupted. I'd have liked you to walk me back."

"I wanted to, but Shannon . . ."

"Has a crazy ex-husband and a lawyer who cares about her feelings."

"Not more than I care about yours. I hate that our date got ruined."

She sighed, making him wonder if she'd changed her mind about seeing him again this Saturday for the softball game.

"Up until the end, I had a great time."

"But?"

"I wasn't ready for it to end," she admitted, her voice soft and earnest.

"I don't want it to end. I want to see you again."

"You will. We have a date this weekend."

"What about lunch every day for a year? You promised."

She laughed, making his gut unknot and his nerves unravel. "Are you really going to hold me to that?"

"Unfortunately, I have back to back meetings tomorrow and court, and I probably won't eat lunch at all. I even have a dinner with a client, and all I want to do is cancel everything and take you out for a quiet evening—just the two of us alone. No interruptions or distractions."

"I'd like that. We'll do it next week."

"Why does that seem so far away?"

"You'll see me Saturday at the game. I'll get to check out your mad softball skills."

"I'm coaching, not playing."

"Too bad. I bet you're something on a field."

"You'd be right. Brody and I both played baseball in high school. I played at college for a couple of years."

"I'll see you in a couple of days."

He hated to let her go, but he had calls to make, and he still needed to get Shannon back to work.

"I didn't get to kiss you goodbye."

"Looks like you owe me."

"I'll pay you back with interest."

"Now I'm really looking forward to seeing you."

"Not as much as I'm looking forward to seeing you."

The call started to sound more like two high school kids talking on the phone. He felt like he did back then, when speaking to a girl made him nervous and anxious all at the same time. When it was the right girl, it felt this thrilling and it turned his brain to mush and made him think crazy thoughts and say sappy things he'd never say otherwise.

Determined to save some of his dignity, he ended the call. "I'll see you soon, Claire."

THE DOORBELL RANG, startling Claire. She put her mug of tea on the mantel next to the photographs she'd just arranged. The pile of wadded newspapers on the floor at her feet scattered with her steps, making a bigger mess out of her living room. She'd emptied three boxes of books plus the box of framed photos. Once she cleaned up, the living room might actually look like someone lived here.

Nervous about someone stopping by this late at night, she peeked out the window and saw Owen's truck in the driveway, spotlighted by the new lights. Just to be sure, she didn't open the door, but asked, "Who is it?"

"Crazy stalker."

She laughed and punched in the code on the alarm, opening the door with a smile. "Just who I wanted to see."

Owen didn't come in, but leaned his shoulder against the door frame. "How are you?"

"Fine. Come in."

"I'm not staying. I just needed to see that you're okay."

"I am. I'm finally unpacking and putting the living room to rights."

"All you need is that couch. It's really comfortable."

"You're welcome to have a seat. We can find a movie on TV."

"I'd really like to, but I've got to get up to the house and feed the animals. I'm late as it is."

"What do you have up there?"

"Couple of horses and seven barn cats."

"Seven?"

"I rescued Mama and Papa."

"Of course you did," she said, because that was who Owen was.

He chuckled. "Papa got to Mama before I got Mama to the vet and now I have five kittens to add to the mix."

She smiled, loving how sweet he sounded talking about his pets. "Sounds like you've got quite a brood at home. Thanks for stopping by to check on me."

"That's not the only reason I stopped by."

"No. You just wanted to stand in my doorway staring at me."

"I like looking at you. But I came because I owe you something."

His eyes narrowed and he reached out, hooking his arm around her waist and drawing her close. A flash of heat shot through her system, and she leaned into him, their faces an inch apart. She loved the hard muscles in his chest pressed against her aching breasts. His hand splayed wide over her lower back. She thought he'd kiss her fast and hard, but he took his time and let his gaze roam over her face, studying her. The moment stretched, the anticipation built, and not until her body relaxed and melted against his did he slowly lower his head the last few inches to sweep his lips over hers. Eyes still open, he watched her. One soft kiss turned into another and another. He took his time touching his lips to hers to find the perfect fit and rhythm.

Her eyes closed and she fell into him. He took the kiss deeper, sliding his tongue along hers in a long sweep, never hurried or timid, but sure and confident and full of patience. Time stopped. The world around them disappeared. With her arms wrapped around his massive shoulders, she held him close. His arms banded around her. Held in the circle of all that strength, every kiss a moment stretched out to experience the passion building between them, she felt safe and protected and loved like she'd never felt. Maybe he wasn't *in* love with her, but the way he kissed and held her, took his time to explore and learn the way she liked to be touched, told her she meant something to him. This meant something to him.

His mouth moved from hers. He kissed her cheek and forehead, his arms tensing around her, pulling her closer for a hug she returned with as much strength and depth of emotion as she felt from him.

"I could get used to kissing you goodnight."

"I thought you owed me a kiss goodbye."

"I have this strange feeling it'll never be goodbye between us, Claire."

With those words hanging between them, he released her with a sweep of his hands down her back to her hips. He gently set her away and traced a finger over the side of her face.

"I'll see you soon." Owen turned and walked back to his truck. Before he got in, he turned and stared at her, smiled, and shook his head. "You're not what I expected."

He climbed into his truck, started the engine, and drove away.

In a daze, she closed the door, locked it, set the alarm, and turned to her messy living room.

"What the heck does that mean?"

Chapter Seventeen

CLAIRE PACKED THE bottles of vanilla cream soda, a sandwich, fruit salad, and Owen's favorite potato chips in the San Francisco Giants bucket. She added the bag of chocolate chip and peanut butter cookies. Her mind lingered on last night's kiss, and his odd statement. She still didn't know what he meant, but by the smile he gave her, it wasn't something bad.

"Lunch with Owen again?" Gayle asked, leaning over her shoulder to peek into the bucket.

"No. He's got back-to-back meetings, but I wanted to make sure he got a good meal." She tilted her head in Gayle's direction. "Do you think it's too much? Maybe it's presumptuous to leave him lunch at his office."

"It's not too anything. It's a nice gesture. He'll love it."

"He stopped by to check on me last night."

Gayle gave her a knowing smile. "Really?"

"Nothing happened."

Something in her expression gave herself away. Gayle smiled even bigger and bumped shoulders with her. "Nothing?"

"He didn't even step foot in my house."

Gayle's smile fell. "Oh. Well, something put that glow in your cheeks."

"He kissed me," she confessed, trying but failing to hide a smile.

"Ah, the first kiss. At this point, it's been so many years, I can't remember mine with Ray. Looks like Owen left quite an impression on you."

"It wasn't our first kiss. But I do think it was the start of something."

"The way that man looks at you." Gayle smiled and got this far-off look in her eye. "Yeah, there's definitely something there."

Claire hoped Gayle was right and she wasn't reading more into Owen's kiss goodnight than was really there. She'd let her imagination, hopes, and dreams run away with her once. She'd let her emotions lead her instead of using her head to see what was right in front of her. But that was a different man, and a different her. This time, she had her eyes open.

She took a moment to think about what she really wanted. It didn't take long to decide she wanted to see where things with Owen led, because she believed in love and happiness and finding someone to share her life.

"I'll be back in about half an hour."

"Unless he asks you to stay for lunch."

"He already told me his day is booked solid."

"You never know. Maybe he'll make time."

She'd like to think he would, but didn't put much hope into the thought. He had clients counting on him, and he wasn't the type of man to blow off work. Instead of staying with her last night, he'd gone home to see to his animals. Those two thoughts told her more about him than anything she'd tried to decipher already.

He's a good guy, who rescues cats. Stop looking for trouble.

"I don't expect him to make time. I'll drop this off with Janine and be back soon."

She picked up the bucket and went out the back door to her car. As much bluster as she'd had yesterday, telling Owen she didn't mind walking alone, the trip back to her shop made her more nervous than she cared to admit. Not that she thought Dale would be brazen enough to attack her on a public street in broad daylight. Still, she felt uneasy after what happened and wondered how long it would take before she didn't look over her shoulder every second of the day.

The drive only took a couple of minutes. She pulled into the small parking lot beside Owen's office and parked next to his truck. Surprised to find him at the office, she hoped to see him, but figured he'd probably be in a meeting with a client.

She entered the office with Owen's lunch tucked under her arm. Janine looked up from her computer and her startled gaze darted to the library doors and settled back on her. She walked to Janine's desk and set the bucket on the corner.

"I know he's in meetings all day, I just wanted to leave this for him."

Again, Janine's gaze went to the library door. She turned and spotted Owen sitting on the sofa, fast-food lunch sacks and soda cups spread out before him and the same woman who'd interrupted them last night sitting next to him, so close their thighs touched. Owen stared back at her, his blue eyes intense and filled with what she thought was regret, though she hated to think it may be guilt.

Her heart dropped into her stomach, and the hurt filled every cell in her body.

CLAIRE'S VOICE DRIFTED in from the front office and Owen winced, knowing how bad this looked. He'd tried to tell Shannon he didn't have time for lunch today, but she'd insisted. She'd gone out of her way to bring it to him, and he hated to disappoint her or make her feel unwelcome. He thought to spare twenty minutes, sit with her and stuff lunch down his throat, tell her gently that he appreciated her effort and the kind gesture, and send her on her way. Instead, she'd trapped him into lunch, talked nonstop for the past fifteen minutes, not letting him get a word in, and now he was behind schedule and Claire had walked in and given him that guarded look that tore at his heart and made him feel like a complete asshole.

"Please excuse me, Shannon, Claire just arrived for our meeting."

Owen ignored Shannon's pout, stood, and closed the

distance between him and Claire. She'd turned to leave, but he wrapped her in a light hug, despite the overwhelming desire he had to crush her to him.

"Claire, you made it. I'm so glad to see you," he said in a cheery tone for Shannon to hear. With his back to Shannon, he hoped she didn't notice him dip his head to Claire's ear and whisper, "I'll explain in a minute." He brushed his lips against the soft skin beneath her earlobe. Her body shivered under his hands. Her gaze met his, and he pleaded with his eyes for her to give him a minute to make this right.

He spotted the Giants bucket on Janine's desk and inspiration struck.

"So, this is your big idea. I have to say, you've got my attention. I love it." Claire looked at him like he was crazy. Janine raised an eyebrow as baffled as Claire. He smiled and went with it.

"Catering for parties and socials." He held up the bucket and examined it. "Party buckets for tailgating, or weekend get-togethers to watch the game. Nice.

"We've got a lot to talk about. A new business license, insurance if you make deliveries, so much to think about if you're going to take on this new project."

Claire's frown softened and she caught on to his game. "Well, I haven't made any decisions yet. It's a big expense, and I'm not sure it's worth it at this time."

He wondered if she was trying to tell him she hadn't made her mind up about him, and maybe he wasn't worth her time if every time she turned around Shannon and Dale got between them.

"It's definitely worth your consideration. Customers are going to love this. They'll be beating down your door to place orders."

"Maybe, but if it gets in the way of my shop, maybe it's better to focus on that rather than take on something new that could easily turn out to be a complete failure."

Yep, they were definitely talking about their relationship. No way he failed at this. He wanted her too much.

"Since you like the idea so much, maybe you should buy in," Janine suggested. "You know. Fifty-fifty."

The smile came easy, because he'd already anted up. Now all he had to do is hope he had the winning hand and stay in the game.

"Excellent idea. Claire, let's move this into my office. We'll discuss the project and terms."

"Like I said, I'm not convinced this is a worthwhile venture to pursue."

Stubborn woman. Well, she could make this as hard as she liked. He wasn't giving up.

"I'm willing to go over the details at length."

He turned to Shannon, who sat quietly staring at them. "I'm sorry to cut things short, but as I said, I've got a full schedule."

Shannon gathered up her lunch and stuffed it into one of the bags, leaving his untouched food on the table. She stood and gave him a soft smile.

"I'm so glad we had a few minutes alone together to talk." She placed her hand on his arm, stood on tiptoe and brushed a kiss on his cheek. "Thank you for taking the time for lunch."

Stunned by her actions and what she implied, he didn't respond, but watched her walk out the door.

Claire took a step to follow Shannon out, but he snagged her wrist and pulled her down the hall to his office.

"Owen, I need to get back to the shop."

He didn't say a word, just pulled her past his office door and slammed it behind them. He dropped the bucket on the corner of his desk and turned to her.

"It's not what it looked like."

Her eyes narrowed. *Shit.*

"I'm sorry. I didn't know she was coming. She just showed up."

One side of her mouth tilted in a *whatever* scowl.

"Claire, really, I . . . Fuck it." He pulled her into his arms and kissed her. She didn't respond at first. He didn't expect her to, so he convinced her with soft brushes of his mouth to hers, his hands gently kneading her lower back until she settled against him. He gave her the time she needed to feel how happy he was to see her.

She planted both hands on his chest and pushed him away, but only to arm's length and stared up at him.

"Let me make our previous conversation very clear," he began, interrupting her before she said even one word. "This thing between us is worth your time and effort. I am not playing games. I want you. Only you. Shannon is a client and a nice lady. I didn't want to upset her for no good reason when she's been through so much and showed up here with lunch to show her appreciation for everything I've done for her."

"She has a crush on you."

"She's my client and nothing more to me. You, on the other hand, have my full and undivided attention."

"Is that right?"

"Yes. Always. I may have been a real bastard in the past moving from one woman to the next, but they never overlapped."

"Except for Molly. You saw other people while you were seeing her."

"I fucked Molly on occasion. We did not have a relationship. That was as much her preference as mine." He ran his hand over his head and through his hair and let out a frustrated sigh. "I am seeing you exclusively. That will not change. Ever. No matter where this thing goes, I'd never do that to you, Claire."

She stood staring at him, giving him no indication she believed him. "What? Do you want it in writing? I can draw up a contract. We'll sign. You can state the terms. My balls in a jar if I ever cheat on you."

That brought a smile to her face. She closed the distance between them, wrapped her arms around his neck, and stood on tiptoe to hug him close. Her chin on his shoulder, she said, "This is my hang-up, and you didn't do anything wrong. I'm sorry for acting like a shrew."

"No apology necessary. I told you I didn't have time for anything today and you came here to bring me lunch and caught me with another woman."

She stepped back, and he let her have her space. "No. That isn't what happened at all. You were having lunch with a client and being the nice guy that you are. I'm sorry to keep you even longer. I'll let you get back to work. Enjoy your lunch."

Still not convinced. He needed to prove he meant what he said. "What did you bring me?"

"It's in the bucket. You'll see."

"Show me." He stood his ground in front of his office door, her escape route. No way she left this office before she truly believed in him and what they had together.

"It's just a sandwich, fruit, chips, cookies, and a couple of sodas."

"Yeah, what kind of sandwich?"

"A turkey club with Havarti. No sprouts."

That made him chuckle. "Sounds good. What kind of cookies?"

"Peanut butter, chocolate chip. Janine likes those, so share with her."

He smiled. "We talked about those at dinner. They're my favorite."

"I made them for you."

"Just for me." He closed the distance between them.

"Yes." The word came out breathy.

His proximity got to her. He reached for her, tracing his fingers over her cheek and down her neck. The pulse point jackhammered under his fingertips.

"I love the way you packed it up. The Giants are my favorite."

"I know."

"You know all those little things about me, but you still don't see what is right in front of you. You are my favorite, Claire. No one else." He kissed her on the forehead, turned, and sat on his desk. She turned to face him, and he dug through the bucket for a cookie, took a bite, and let out a satisfied groan when the sweet treat melted on his tongue. "God, these are so good. You spoil me."

That earned him a smile and a thoughtful look. "You spoiled me last night."

"I didn't do anything but stop by for my goodnight kiss."

"You stopped by for that and to make sure I was okay."

"I needed to know you were okay," he confirmed.

She stepped between his legs and pressed her hands gently to both sides of his face, staring at him, studying his eyes. "Yes, I believe you."

Not just for last night, but about Shannon too, he understood. "That's because I'm telling you the truth. I'll always tell you the truth."

She leaned in close and kissed his cheek. The side of her head pressed to his and she held him for a moment. He rubbed his hands up her back and down in long sweeps, letting her know how much he liked having her close and wishing they had more time.

As if on cue, Janine knocked on his door. "Mr. McBride . . ."

She used his last name, which meant his next client had arrived for their meeting, which he was not prepared for due to the interruptions and his aching arousal.

"Mr. Calloway is here to see you."

"I'll be right out."

"Have a good day," Claire said next to his ear, her lips brushing his cheek with another light kiss. He wanted much more, but she stepped out of his embrace, and he let her because he needed to cool off and get a handle on his raging desire for her.

"Any day I get to see you is a good day."

She smiled. This time, it didn't hold any hesitation.

"Please tell Janine I need five minutes."

"To eat your lunch?" she asked, pointing to the bucket of food.

"No, to stop thinking about you and sex."

Her gaze raked over him, stopping momentarily on the bulge in his slacks before shooting back up to his face.

"Run, while you still have a chance," he teased, though his voice held a deadly serious note.

"You'll only catch me, won't you?"

"Yes," he confirmed, telling her just how much he wanted her and nothing was going to stop him from getting her.

"I'll see you Saturday at the game."

He sighed. Saturday seemed so far away. He wanted to ditch the rest of his appointments, cancel dinner with his client, and go home with Claire and take her to bed. Not going to happen.

"I'd walk you out, but . . ." He shrugged and she giggled.

"Why don't you eat half your sandwich and think about baseball."

"I could try, but all I ever think about these days is you."

Chapter Eighteen

Claire left Owen's office with a shake of her head and a chuckle at his predicament. She had to admit, the thought of him hot and wanting her made her feel sexy and wanted in a way she hadn't felt for a long time. She liked that they could have a serious conversation one minute and laugh and tease the next. She especially appreciated his honesty. Not only about his lunch with Shannon and what it really meant, but about his feelings for her.

With a light heart and a smile on her face, she stopped by Janine's desk. "He's, ah, finishing up some paperwork for me. He'll need another five minutes."

Janine smiled up at her. "No problem. Did you settle the misunderstanding?"

"The partnership still stands."

Janine winked and nodded with satisfaction. "Wonderful. I'll see you at your next appointment."

"What does his Monday look like?"

Janine clicked a few keys on the computer and stared at the screen for several seconds. "Looks like he's in the office from eleven to one with no appointments. He'll probably work on paperwork and catch up on his casework."

"Thank you so much."

Claire turned to leave and spotted the older gentleman waiting in one of the chairs in the sitting area, his leather briefcase on the coffee table, a stack of papers in his lap. He glanced up at her.

"My apologies for cutting into your appointment time. I'm sure he'll be out in just a minute."

"I never mind waiting on a beautiful woman."

She beamed him a smile, and he returned to reading his papers.

She opened the front door and turned back to see Owen standing by Janine's desk, smiling at her.

"Goodbye, Claire, I'll see you soon."

That promise sent a shiver up her spine.

She stepped out, but before the door closed behind her she heard Owen's deep voice. "Sorry about the wait, Mr. Calloway."

"She was worth it."

"Yes, she is." His voice turned husky. "Come on back."

Claire went down the stairs, smiling like a lunatic. She rounded the corner to the small parking lot and dug her keys out of her bag. Ten feet from her car the smile died on her lips. She sucked in a breath and scanned the parking lot, turned and studied the street. Her heart pounded hard against her chest, the sound filling her ears. Nothing. No one.

Someone had slashed her tires.

Dale.

She couldn't escape him.

Hands shaking, she gripped the keys tighter, the car key sticking out between two fingers to use as a weapon if she needed it. She cautiously approached her car and walked around to the other side. Those tires were flat as pancakes, too.

"Damnit."

Furious. Scared. She sucked in a deep breath to calm her nerves and slow her racing heart. She squelched the overwhelming desire to run back into Owen's office and straight into his arms. She'd been on her own for too long to go cowering back inside to get Owen to help her out with yet another Dale-created mess.

You are a strong independent woman, she reminded herself. *Not Shannon, chasing after Owen to solve every little problem.*

She pulled out her cell phone and dialed 911, giving them her name and Owen's office address.

Someone touched her arm. She whirled around to confront her attacker, but stopped short with a gasp.

"What?" she asked, surprised to see the woman jogger standing behind her. She hadn't heard her approach.

"Sorry I scared you. Do you need some help?" she asked, her gaze straying to the flat tires.

"No. I'm on the phone with the police."

"Are you sure?"

"I'm fine. Thank you."

Claire tried a reassuring smile, but even she felt it fell short. The woman jogged off to finish her run, leaving Claire a mass of raw nerves.

"Yes, I'm sorry. Someone startled me. My tires have been slashed. I need to make a report," she told the dispatcher.

The rush of fear subsided to weariness. She pulled the tailgate down on Owen's truck and hopped up to wait for the police. Disheartened, she called for a tow truck, then she called Gayle.

"Claire's Café and Bookstore, this is Gayle."

"It's me. I'm going to be late getting back."

"Take your time. Told you Owen would want to have lunch with you."

"He's in a meeting. Someone slashed all my tires. I'm waiting for the cops and a tow truck."

"Are you okay? Do you need me to come and get you?"

"I'm fine," she said, despite her voice cracking on the last word.

"Does Owen know what happened? Why isn't he with you?"

"He's with his client. He'll know soon enough when his parking lot is overflowing with people and cars."

"Do you think this has to do with the other night?"

"I don't know for sure, but who else would slash my tires?"

"This guy has a serious fixation on you."

"He thinks hurting me will hurt Owen. The thing is, this just punishes me."

"I'm coming down there."

"No. Stay. I'm fine, just mad. And a little scared," Claire admitted.

"I don't like this, Claire."

"I'm not thrilled about it myself. I'll be back as soon as I can."

"Call me back if you need anything."

"I will. Thanks for covering for me."

"You need a break, Claire, some time to have some fun. You work too much."

"Yeah, well look what happens when I take an extra hour for lunch."

"This isn't your fault. Or Owen's."

"I know that. It's just . . ."

"It sucks. I know. Do what needs to be done. That's all you can do. Oh, and watch your back."

"I will. See you soon."

Claire held on to her phone and leaned against Owen's truck, staring at her flat tires. The police arrived and pulled into the lot. She breathed a huge sigh of relief and hoped she stopped jumping at every little sound.

OWEN SAT WITH Mr. Calloway and went over each section of the contracts, detailing what each meant and how it would affect Mr. Calloway's businesses. He made sure his client understood all the terms and conditions. Deep in thought, he didn't register the red and blue flashing lights sweeping across the wall until Mr. Calloway looked out the window and asked, "What's with all the police cars?"

"Claire." Owen didn't hesitate: he ran out of his office and sprinted out the front door and around the side to the parking lot. The cop car scared him, but not as much as not seeing Claire, until he moved further into the parking lot and spotted her beside his truck, in between her car and his. He rounded the tailgate, pushed past the policeman, and grabbed Claire by the shoulders, holding her at arm's length.

"Are you okay?" He scanned her face and her whole body, checking for any sign she'd been hurt. Aside from the bandages still on her feet, she looked fine, except for the trembling and her wide, scared eyes.

"I'm fine."

He pulled her into his arms and held her close, trying to calm his racing heart and assure himself she was safe and sound.

"Mr. McBride, someone slashed Miss Walsh's tires. She mentioned a client of yours may be involved."

Owen swore, but didn't let go of Claire. He couldn't. Not when everything in him wanted to keep her close and protect her from any and all threats. He didn't have time to contemplate the depth of his fear when he thought she'd been hurt and the overwhelming relief that replaced it when he found her safe and unharmed.

"Dale Monoghan. Shannon, his ex-wife, is a client. She was here earlier. He's been stalking her, though nothing I can prove substantially." Owen gave the officer the rundown on Claire's attack the other night.

Claire slipped from his grasp and leaned against his truck, arms wrapped around her middle, watching the other officer dust her car for prints. He hated to let her go, but understood how this latest incident pissed her off, and how some of that anger might be directed at him.

"So you think he saw Mrs. Monoghan here this afternoon. Saw Claire arrive to see you and slashed her tires to get back at you, through hurting her."

"That about sums it up." And put him in the category of "too dangerous to date" in Claire's book. He had to agree, but didn't want to end things with her. In fact, everything in him wanted to spend more time with her. He wanted to know her like no one else knew her. Right now, she wanted to be left alone. The wall of ice she'd erected around herself chilled him. He had to break through, because losing her and what they had together wasn't an option. It may be new and undeveloped, but that's what made him want to hold on with both hands. Because if it was this good now, what would it be like when they really did know each other better? What would it be like after they slept together? If kissing her made him burn, making love to her would be like touching the sun.

"We don't know if it was him," Claire commented, though she never took her eyes off the officer sweeping a small brush over her fender.

"It makes sense. Shannon visited earlier. You're here. I thought I saw something out the window when you and I were talking in my office, but I dismissed it as a bird or something disturbing the bushes. I think maybe Dale saw us together, confirmed you and I are seeing each other, and made good on his threat to hurt you to get to me."

"Why did he wreck my car and not your truck?" she asked, meeting his eyes for the first time. "Your truck is right here. Why not destroy your tires to piss you off?"

"I don't know, sweetheart, but I'll make this right."

"It's not for you to make right. You didn't do anything to me or my car. I'm upset and angry, but not at you."

"Then why are you over there and I'm over here?"

She bent at the waist and bounced off his truck to walk to him, but stopped two feet away and stared past him. "Tow truck is here."

"You called them already?"

"While I waited for the cops. I can't very well drive back to the shop."

"You're going back to work?"

"Owen, what do you want me to do? Go home, lock myself up in my house, and hide away?"

"Yes. Something like that. Stay here with me, where I can keep my eye on you."

"This happened on your property, twenty feet from your office window," she pointed out. "Last time, I was at home. Doesn't seem to matter where I am, he finds me."

"Claire . . ."

"We're all done with the car," the officer interrupted. "I'll check in with Sheriff McBride and update him on this latest incident." The officer handed him a copy of the incident report.

Claire grabbed it and stuffed it into her purse. "I'll need that for the insurance company."

"I'll call them and take care of everything," he offered, knowing by the set of her jaw she'd refuse.

"I've got it. You've done enough."

That one hit him right in the chest. He couldn't breathe around the noose tightening around his throat.

The officer gave him an apologetic look and went to his cruiser to leave. The tow truck moved into place to hook up Claire's car and pull it up onto the flatbed.

Claire walked up to him and let out a frustrated sigh. "I'm sorry. That came out all wrong. You've done everything you can to fix the damage at my house and help me feel safe when I'm there. I don't want you to keep fixing things for me because you think it's your mess to clean up. It's not."

"I just want to help you. If not for me . . ."

She pressed her fingertips to his lips. "Stop. We aren't going to keep going round and round about this. He wants me to get mad at you, leave you, so you'll know how he felt about his wife leaving him. Well, I'm not going to play right into his hands."

Her words penetrated and she tried to backtrack. "Well, I'm not your wife, and you don't feel . . ."

This time he stopped her with a kiss. He pressed his lips to hers and sank his fingers into her hair at the side of her head, tilting it to get just the right angle to make her fit to him perfectly. Surprised, she settled into the kiss and her eyes fluttered closed. He indulged his raging need for her, pulled her close, and dove in for more.

The kiss ended with both of them sighing out their frustration and holding each other close. He kissed the side of her head. "It kills me that he's hurting you. I want to stop him and everything that's going on, so that you and

I can be together without all this hanging over us. Don't think for one second that this doesn't bother me. It does."

She leaned her forehead to his chest and he rubbed his fingers through her hair to the knotted muscles in her neck.

"Pop, thanks for coming," Owen said, holding out his hand to shake.

Pop took it and gave him a solid pump before letting go. "Owen. This is some kind of trouble."

"Yes, it is. Claire, this is Rain's father, Eli. Pop, this is my very good friend, Claire. I'd appreciate it if you hooked her up with some new tires and got her back on the road."

"My pleasure." Eli gave him an approving nod. Normally, Owen would have smiled with pride for having Claire plastered to his side. In this case, he barely managed a halfhearted grin.

"If you'll sign here, we should have your new tires installed by close of business today."

"I really appreciate that, Eli. It's a pleasure to meet you. I enjoyed meeting Rain the other night at dinner. Your granddaughters are wonderful."

"Yes they are." Eli beamed.

Claire backed away from Owen, took Eli's clipboard, and signed the paper.

"I'll drive you to your shop," Owen offered.

Claire pointed to Janine, Mr. Calloway, and another couple, his next client meeting, standing at the end of the driveway, watching everything go down. "You've got your hands full today. I'll walk."

"I'm not letting you walk back alone."

"I can drop you," Eli offered.

"Thank you," Claire said, though she knew Owen would rather take her himself.

"Claire, I'll reschedule my appointments."

"Why? So you can babysit me? So he wins, because he's disrupted both our lives. Go back to work, Owen. We'll talk later."

Owen stuffed his hands in his pockets, hating that she scrambled up into the truck cab and leaned back, staring out the windshield lost in thought.

"I'll make sure she gets back safe." Eli gave his shoulder a squeeze and went around the truck, climbed in, and drove away.

Owen pulled out his phone and made a call, ensuring her safety until she got home.

CLAIRE'S HEAD SNAPPED up when the bell over the door rang out. Gayle squeezed her arm to reassure her everything was all right. Eli had dropped her off at the shop twenty minutes ago. She liked the older man and his no-nonsense, efficient way. He didn't mince words when he told her Owen was one of the best men he knew, and he hoped to see her again soon.

Her nerves were still shot, everything made her jump for no reason, and now she had a very large male to deal with.

She walked to Brody's table and glared. He ignored her and set up his laptop.

"Did Owen send you?"

"He's worried about you, and since you didn't want him here, I'm here."

She did want Owen here with her, but hated how much she wanted to rely on him. She needed to stand on her own. To know that she could, no matter the circumstances.

"You don't need to stay. I'm fine."

"You nearly jumped out of your skin when I walked in."

She didn't deny it. Her stomach remained tied in knots. "I'll settle down. Nothing is going to happen to me here."

"I bet you thought the same thing when you went to see Owen. I'm staying. I'll take you to pick up your car at Eli's garage and follow you home."

"Then what? Are you going to stay with me tonight? Tomorrow?"

"You should be safe at home with the alarm. The contractor installed your new door this morning. You'll be with us tomorrow at the game. Then, we'll see."

Right. How could they plan for something they couldn't see coming. Dale remained elusive. Even the police couldn't find him. At this rate, she may spend the rest of her life looking over her shoulder.

"Can I get you anything?"

"Coffee. Apple cinnamon muffin."

"What are you going to do?"

"Work," he said, booting up his computer and pulling out several files from his leather messenger bag.

"Okay." A man of few words, she didn't know what to think, so she went to get him his order. The bell over the door dinged and another customer came in. Brody glanced up, assessing the two women with one long sweep of his penetrating gaze before he turned back to his laptop screen. With his back to the wall, the room spread out before him, and with a clear view of the front door and the one leading to the back room and kitchen area, he'd picked a prime spot to watch over her. The muscles in her shoulders eased along with the knot in her stomach. She sighed and grabbed her cell phone. She hit the speed dial and waited. He answered on the first ring.

"Are you okay?" Owen's deep voice held a note of alarm.

"Thank you."

He sighed and she felt his relief through the phone. "You're welcome, sweetheart."

"Owen."

"Yeah?"

"I . . ." She didn't know quite what to say. The emotions welled up inside of her, but she couldn't put them into words. "I'll see you tomorrow."

"Count on it."

Chapter Nineteen

CLAIRE PACKED UP the basket and boxes for the girls' softball game, feeling a sense of déjà vu. She'd packed up yesterday and look what happened.

"Where did you go?" Gayle asked.

She snapped out of her space-case haze and focused on the box of cupcakes in front of her.

"Sorry. I'm tired."

"It's understandable you didn't sleep well last night."

"Every time I started to drift off, I thought I heard a noise, then I'd wait to see if the alarm went off. Of course, nothing happened."

"Did Owen stop by last night?"

"Brody followed me home, went in the house and checked every nook and cranny, then kissed me on the head, went back to his car, made a phone call—I'm sure to Owen—and left. Owen stopped by around ten after his business dinner, kissed me in the doorway like the other night, asked me if I wanted him to stay, and left when I told him I didn't need a babysitter. I heard his truck drive by early this morning, but he didn't stop off."

"Um, why did Brody kiss you?"

"Oh, I think it has to do with Owen kissing Rain all the time."

Gayle's eyebrows practically disappeared under her gray, sprinkled-brown bangs.

Claire laughed. "Owen and Rain are really good friends. They're close. The night we went to dinner together, he kissed her on the head in greeting and again when he said goodbye. It seemed a familiar gesture, so I assume Brody has adopted the same with me."

"So, it's so obvious that you and Owen are together and so close that his brother treats you like a sister. He even drops everything to sit sentry with you all afternoon."

The observation stunned Claire.

"Don't worry, honey. When it's right, it's right."

"I barely know him."

"You'll get there. Neither one of you is going anywhere. Plenty of time to learn all the details. You already know the most important thing."

"What's that?"

"He's a man worth getting to know."

Claire smiled, unable to deny that simple truth. "He is a great guy."

"Go have fun, honey."

Claire put the last of the items into the cooler at her

feet and took her end. Gayle grabbed the other side and helped her carry it out to her car.

The drive over to the ballpark gave her a few minutes to collect her thoughts and settle the butterflies in her stomach. Nervous about seeing Owen again, and that Dale might do something else to her, she had a hard time feeling like herself.

Parked next to Owen's truck, she swung out of her own car and came face-to-face with Brody, who'd been waiting in the parking lot for her.

"Guard duty resumes," she guessed.

"Anything happen at the shop today?"

"Lots, but nothing bad."

"Good." He kissed her on the forehead and gave her shoulder a reassuring squeeze.

"Will you help me with the cooler?"

"Sure thing." Brody lifted it out of her backseat like it weighed nothing. He stood and waited for her to lock the car, turn, and walk toward the baseball diamond.

Owen squatted behind home plate while one of the girls threw the ball from the pitcher's mound. He caught it easily and tossed it back.

"Dawn sure is quite the pitcher," she commented.

"Takes after her mother. Rain used to play in high school."

"What about Autumn?"

"She takes after me. The girl can ground balls like crazy. She's got agility and speed."

"You're really proud of them."

"They're my girls. I love them."

The two little girls rushed Owen at home plate and jumped into his arms. He caught them up and kissed both of them on the cheeks.

"Owen loves them, too," she said, smiling at the way he laughed and played with the girls.

"Yes, he does. He takes care of the people he loves."

She cocked her head to look up at Brody, who continued to stare at Owen with the girls, not giving anything away. He'd made his point.

OWEN DROPPED THE girls on their feet. "Go find your mom and get ready to play. I'm going to see Claire."

"She's really pretty," Dawn said.

"She makes really good brownies," Autumn added.

"Do you like her a lot?" Dawn asked.

"As much as Dad likes Mom?" Autumn asked.

"Yes, I like her a lot," he answered, giving both their ball caps a tug to cover their eyes and get them to stop asking so many questions. Ones he wasn't quite sure how to answer.

Did he like her enough to spend the rest of his life with her, like Brody and Rain had committed to do?

Well, he'd spent half the night convincing himself she was fine home alone, and the other half dreaming about making love to her. Even the cold shower this morning didn't cool his heated thoughts and unruly body.

"Is she coming to the family dinner next weekend?" Dawn asked, undeterred.

"We'll see." First, he needed to make sure yesterday's incident hadn't made her want to take a step back. She did show up today. He'd had his doubts since yesterday, but God, he was happy to see her.

He wanted to stop by her place this morning, but reined in his impulses and gave her some space. He'd given in last night and stopped to kiss her goodnight because he'd spent every meeting yesterday afternoon and dinner with his client last night trying desperately to focus on work and not her. He'd needed to see her like he needed his next breath. So he'd stopped by, barely said hello, and kissed her because he needed the closeness, and to know the bond they'd just begun to forge was still intact and not severed for good. The thought of the kiss they shared still rocked him. She'd given everything, letting him know despite everything she still responded to him on that level. Something to build on.

"You're staring at her," Autumn pointed out. "Daddy does that to Mom all the time."

"Both of you, go to your mother."

He left the little nymphs and headed for Claire and Brody, grateful to his brother for waiting in the parking lot to make sure Claire not only made it, but didn't run into any trouble. He'd been able to finish his work yesterday, barely, because he knew Brody was looking out for Claire for him.

"Brody," he said by way of greeting.

"I found your girl. I'll take this over to the benches."

Claire stopped in front of him and gave him a strange but appreciative appraisal from the top of his head down his body to his feet.

"You know, I never truly appreciated baseball until now. You look really good."

He chuckled. "I was wearing a suit yesterday." Which he thought she'd prefer to his backward baseball cap, T-shit, catcher's pads, sweat pants, and tennis shoes.

"Yes, and you were very handsome and professional. This . . . I don't know, you seem more approachable and fun."

"Well, by all means, approach and have fun. I'm all yours," he teased.

She laughed and smiled and it did his heart good because when she left his office yesterday, she'd looked angry and disillusioned. Last night, he'd left her dazed.

She walked right into his arms and wrapped her arms around his back, giving him a hug. Still laughing, she held tight and settled against him.

"Hi, sweetheart."

"Hi. I'm sorry about how I left things with you yesterday."

"I quite enjoyed our kiss goodnight. If you didn't, maybe I need to try harder." He leaned down and took her mouth and let his need for her rule. He forgot they were in public and there were a dozen families behind them. The last thing he wanted was for her to think her being upset and angry yesterday had tarnished anything between them.

She opened to him without any prompting from him. He dove in, slid his tongue along hers, drew her closer into his arms and held her tight. She matched his ferocity, driving his need higher and higher, until he wanted to drag her to the ground, strip her bare, and sink his aching cock into her wet heat and drive them both into oblivion.

"Owen, let's play ball," Rain called, saving them from making an even bigger spectacle of themselves.

Claire surprised him, breaking the kiss first and kissing his chin, his jaw, and down his neck until she went flat-footed again. She kept her hands on his chest and stared up at him with an open smile. He traced his finger over her forehead and down the side of her face, tucking a wayward strand of golden hair behind her ear. He touched the bruise on the back of her head under her hair. The swelling had subsided. The scrapes on her elbow looked better. He couldn't see the bruise and scrapes on her shoulder, but imagined they were healing too. These reminders spoke of what she'd endured the last few days.

"Don't frown. Go play ball with the girls."

"Can't."

"Why not?"

"Whenever I'm around you, I'm not fit to be seen by others." He gave her a cocky smile.

"Ah. Well, at least this time you've got the proper gear to hide your condition." She pointedly swept her gaze over the catcher's padding covering his chest that conveniently curved and dipped to hide his hard dick.

"One of these days, I'm not going to stop at kissing you and this won't be a problem."

"Well, let's hope we're alone when that happens." Her gaze shot past his shoulder to the many onlookers waiting for the game to start.

"Is it going to happen with us?"

Her gaze shot back to his. "Um, I don't know how to answer that."

"A simple yes will do." He smiled down at her, despite his serious tone.

She let out a nervous giggle and looked away. A pretty blush colored her cheeks.

"Claire, look at me." When she did, he gave her the honest truth. "If it's a yes, the when is, and will always be, up to you. No matter how much I want you, I'll never push you to give more than you're ready for."

"I think I knew the minute I met you it was just a matter of time."

"Then, take all the time you need. I'm not going anywhere."

"Except to play ball. Go. They're waiting for you."

"You'll be waiting when I'm done with a treat, right?"

"How do you know I brought you a treat?"

"You always bring me a treat."

"Maybe I didn't today."

"Sweetheart, just kissing you is a treat." He gave her a quick kiss, took her hand, and lead her toward the field. He kept her hand in his until she had to veer off to join Brody on the bleachers. She sat with him, and Owen kept an eye on her throughout the game, loving every smile she cast his way.

Chapter Twenty

CLAIRE CLAPPED FOR number twelve as she rounded third base and ran for home. So far, the Blue Jays were winning. This next run put them up by two. The girls cheered and Owen high-fived the little girl as she took off her batting helmet and made her way to her cheering friends in the dugout.

Owen got ready to take his place behind home plate again. The outfielders ran for their positions. Claire wanted to stay and watch, but she needed to pee. Hot from the bright sun and so much cheering, she needed a soda from the concession stand. She grabbed her purse and stood. Owen rose from his position, his eyes locked on her in question. Brody grabbed her arm and tugged.

"Where are you going?"

"Restroom and to get a soda. I'll be right back."

"I'll come with you."

"I'll be back in a minute. Stay and watch your girls. They're doing really great."

"Like you said, it'll only be a minute."

"He told you not to let me leave."

"Not alone."

She shot Owen a disgruntled look and spun on her heel to walk away, but Owen let out an ear piercing whistle. She turned back and he held both arms out wide in a questioning gesture. She rolled her eyes and pointed to the building across the tree belt. He gave her a nod, pulled his catcher's mask down, and went back to the game.

"A little overprotective, don't you think?" she asked Brody, who walked two steps behind her.

"No."

She laughed. Figured the two brothers were of like mind when it came to protecting the women in their lives. She stopped short and Brody grabbed her shoulders to avoid running over her.

"You okay?"

Was she? She'd seen the protective way Brody was around Rain. Before the game got started, he'd laid a protective hand over her still-flat belly and kissed her gently, giving her a look that told her to be careful, but he trusted her. When a ball flew past Rain on the third base line a little too closely, he'd risen to his feet and taken three long strides before he realized she didn't get hit. Rain, of course, rolled her eyes and waved him away to go sit down. He did, but that didn't stop him from watching her like a hawk.

"Claire. Are you okay?"

"Yes. Fine. Sorry. I, uh, zoned out."

Owen watched her with that same intensity. Even though he was involved in the game, he still noticed when she stood and tried to leave. He'd forgotten the game and parents watching and silently demanded to know where she was going.

He really did care about her.

She walked the rest of the way with a smile on her face and a warmth in her heart she'd been ignoring since she met Owen. Now, she couldn't pretend it wasn't real.

Business complete in the bathroom, she walked out shaking her wet hands. Brody stood waiting for her.

"Can I buy you a soda?" she asked.

"I could use some water."

"Coming right up." She stood in line behind a mother with a three-year-old boy wrapped around her middle, his chin on her shoulder and his eyes drooping with sleep. Something inside her softened at the sight of the little blond boy. She thought of Owen and a golden-haired son who looked like his daddy, playing ball on a Saturday just like today. She tucked that picture in her heart and hoped someday it might come true. She wanted a family more than anything. Maybe this time she'd found the right man to make the dream come true.

The mother and son moved away with their order, and she stepped up to the counter. Shannon looked up from her register, surprise widening her eyes.

"What are you doing here?"

"Owen invited me to the game."

"Oh, he's so nice."

Claire understood Shannon's attachment to Owen. He'd saved her from a bad marriage. She got the whole Prince-Charming, saving-the-damsel-in-distress thing Shannon saw in him. The same thing appealed to her, too.

"How are you, Shannon? You must have been very scared the other night when your ex-husband banged on your door."

"Not the first time. Won't be the last. He's like a dog with a bone."

"Yes, well, let's hope he comes to his senses and finds something else to amuse him."

"He's probably off drinking himself stupid."

"I don't know if you heard, but I think he slashed my tires yesterday at Owen's office."

"He probably followed me there and saw me with Owen. He can't stand to see me with another man. Owen is nothing like Dale."

"Dale must have been good to you sometimes."

"He was wild when we met, and I wanted to be wild with him. But things change. He changed. Owen helped me see that I deserve something better. I'm so lucky to have him on my side."

"He certainly does take very good care of his clients," she said diplomatically, reading between the lines. Shannon wanted to stake a claim, but Claire knew how he felt about her. She tamped down the immediate rush of jealousy and suspicion that something was going on between them.

"Owen is a very good friend."

"I'll have a medium Coke and a bottle of water, please." She changed the subject because they'd get nowhere going back and forth like this. Shannon didn't want to be friends and bond over their shared unhappy Dale experiences. No, she wanted to keep Owen all to herself. Who could blame her? After what she'd been through, Owen's kindness probably seemed like a true miracle in her life.

Shannon placed her order on the counter and rang up her total. Claire handed over the three dollars and grabbed the water and soda.

About to turn away, Shannon asked, "When will you start your new delivery business?"

Baffled by the questions, she cocked her head to the side. "I'm sorry, what?"

"The catering business you and Owen talked about starting."

Ah, the reason he'd cut his lunch with Shannon short to be with her. "It's still in the planning stage."

"Right," Shannon said, a note of disbelief in her voice.

"Have a good weekend," she said, and walked to meet Brody by the tree.

"What the hell was that all about?" he asked.

She didn't think Brody had been paying attention. She should remember his military background and the fact nothing got by him.

"Her ex-husband is the one causing all the trouble."

"I don't think she likes you much."

"She likes Owen," Claire said, handing over his bottle of water.

"Yeah, I got that."

"Owen is trying to keep a professional distance from her, but she relies on him."

"Maybe too much if her ex thinks she's having an affair with him."

"At least her taste has improved," she teased. They walked back to the ball field. Owen's gaze immediately shot to her, and she waved. His smile made her knees go weak.

"Yuck," Brody said from beside her. She cracked up laughing.

The game ended twenty minutes later with the Blue Jays still up by two. They circled around Rain and Owen with all their hands in the center. They pumped their hands up and down three times and shouted, "Blue Jays," waving their hands up in the air. They lined up to high-five the other team. Owen and Rain shook hands with the opposing coaches and the girls came running to her and Brody at the coolers. Rain and Brody brought the girls drinks. Claire had brought the snacks.

Owen didn't waste any time. He walked right up to her and gave her a kiss. "I missed you."

"You were right over there."

"Too far away from you, sweetheart. Did you enjoy the game?"

"I did. I saw Shannon at the concession stand."

Owen snagged a drink from the cooler and took a deep swallow. "I forgot she works here on the weekend."

The girls devoured the orange slices she'd spent her lunch break cutting up. Luckily, Brody remembered a bag to set on the ground by the cooler for the girls to toss in the peels.

"I thought you were bringing treats from your shop," Dawn said, disappointment laced in every word.

"I heard Mom say something about cupcakes," Autumn chimed in.

Claire smiled and opened the cooler, pulling out the two white bakery boxes. "Do you mean these cupcakes?"

All the girls cheered. Even Owen joined in with an exaggerated yell to match the girls, making her laugh and shake her head.

"See, I did bring you a treat."

"Does that mean I don't get to kiss you again?"

"Nothing stops you from kissing me."

"I like kissing you."

"I like you kissing me."

"Come here, sweetheart."

Caught up in the fun of the game, the excitement of seeing the girls win, and Owen's playful joking with the girls and her, she had no trouble walking into his arms, raising her head, and accepting the kiss he laid on her. Soft, sweet, nothing too racy in front of the children. He tasted of chocolate frosting and cake and the now-familiar taste of just him. He hooked his arm around her side and pulled her close. She leaned into him and settled into his side with a contented sigh. They watched the girls devour the cupcakes with an exuberance only children can display when cake is involved. She loved their chatter and squeals.

"You two look good together," Rain said, walking up beside them.

"Hey, beautiful, did you get a cupcake?" Owen asked, and this time the *beautiful* didn't bother her in the least.

"I need something more substantial before I start eating cupcakes. Besides, I don't think the girls left us any."

Claire stepped away from Owen, but he reached out and grabbed her arm. "Where are you going, sweetheart?"

"Well, I thought the game might end late and everyone might be hungry, so"—she opened the lid of the cooler and pulled out a couple of the Styrofoam takeout boxes—"I brought lunch. I thought we could have a picnic."

"You are the best girlfriend ever," Owen said, leaning in and kissing her while stealing a container from her.

Her eyes went wide and she stared up at him. Her stomach filled with fluttering butterflies. Excitement raced through her. The thrill of it made her lightheaded. Things were moving too fast. They needed to slow down, take a breath. No. Everything in her clung to the exhilaration, even if a small voice reminded her to remain cautious.

Owen leaned into her ear and whispered. "Breathe. Let it settle."

"Please tell me one of those is mine," Rain pleaded.

Claire shook off the shock and her conflicting emotions and handed over the container with Rain's name on it. She promptly opened the lid and sighed out her pleasure. "My favorite. Turkey and Havarti on sourdough. You remembered."

"I try to pay attention. You make it easy, because you order the same thing each time. Same with the girls."

"They're picky."

"Well, if you can get them off Brody's back, I've got lunch for them, too."

Rain called to the girls, rolling and playing with their father on the grass nearby, literally jumping all over him as he picked them up and tossed them around, wrestling them over his shoulders and tickling them unmercifully. Her gaze met Owen's and they shared a quietly tense moment. He smiled and she walked to him with her lunch container and sat down between his legs, leaned back into his chest, and held his arm when it banded around her middle, and he pulled her close and kissed her on the side of the head.

Yeah, you're his girlfriend.

The butterflies in her stomach made her giggle. He poked her in the ribs and made her laugh even more.

"What is so funny, sweetheart?"

"Nothing. This is a good day."

He kissed the side of her head again. "Yes, it is a very good day. Let's make it a better night. Come up to the ranch this evening. I'll make you dinner."

Chapter Twenty-One

CLAIRE DROVE DOWN the road to Owen's place, her stomach tied in knots. They'd had such a wonderful day together, she couldn't say no to his dinner invitation. Still, she didn't know exactly what to expect. She checked her face in the rearview mirror for the tenth time in half a mile. The light makeup job she'd done on her eyes with a faded violet shadow made the green stand out. Her lips were tinted a soft pink. She'd chosen her wardrobe carefully, changing from one blouse to another, until she finally settled on the simple soft pink tunic, black leggings, and ankle boots. She left her hair loose and draped over one shoulder down the front of her. She'd seen the way he looked at it and wanted to please him.

She had second thoughts about the matching pink lace bra and panties. They made her feel sexy, but this was just dinner. Right? She'd thought of nothing else but sleeping with him since . . . well, practically since she'd met him. He'd left the when up to her. Still, she didn't know if she was ready to take the next step. The hum in her gut and erotic thoughts in her head said otherwise.

She couldn't wait to see him again.

She'd never been to his place. The road to it was long and winding, following the fence line on her right. She passed the turnoff to Brody's place. Easy to spot the new construction, piles of lumber, and trailer sitting on the side of the property. She drove on and realized Owen's spread must be huge to cover so much land. He and Brody probably owned it together, but still. To think how much the land must be worth, and that they'd never sold it to be parceled off for land developments when others close to town had done the same.

The directions Owen gave her said to turn right on the second gravel road after Brody's place. She took the turnoff and followed the road around a bend. The two-story white house came into view and she gaped at the structure. She expected old and run-down, especially after some of the stories he and Brody told her about growing up here with their neglectful father, but the place looked well tended. The flowerbeds could have used some sprucing up, but the yard was clean, the bushes and trees trimmed. She loved the big red-and-white barn with the white fenced-in corrals and pastures. A beautiful dapple-gray horse pranced around a corral, shaking its massive head, having fun.

She parked behind Owen's truck and stepped out of her car. Halfway up the walkway to the porch steps, a loud catcall whistle rang out behind her. Unable to help the smile, she spun around and found Owen by the barn, leading a brown horse with a slightly swayed back. The horse might have caught her attention, but Owen held it. The hum in her gut intensified, rippling out waves of heat through her system. Dark brown boots, tight well-worn blue jeans, a white T-shirt plastered to his broad chest with splotches of water. His windblown blond hair swept backward with rake marks from his fingers. The man looked gorgeous in a suit, handsome and wholesome in baseball gear, and rough and rugged here on the ranch. His blue eyes squinted from the sun, but his gaze remained on her. As if he'd touched her, she felt the sweep of his gaze over her from head to toe. A shiver rippled over her skin.

She stopped several steps away, cocked her hip, and stared at him.

"I should have known you'd be early," he said, sighing and looking over his shoulder at his big friend.

She checked her watch. "I'm three minutes early."

He lifted his hand, but let it fall when he realized he didn't have his watch.

"Is it really that late?"

"I can come back later if you're busy."

"Hell no." Frustrated, he raked his hand through his hair. "I'm a mess. This guy decided to play in a mud puddle. I couldn't put him back in his stall covered in mud, so I had to wash him down. Give me five minutes."

"Take all the time you need," she said, her voice husky with the need to kiss him building the longer he stood there with that urgent look in his eyes.

"See something you like?" he asked, a half smile on his handsome face and a mischievous glint in his eyes.

"You are many different men."

"What?"

"I thought I liked the baseball look the best. Now, I'm thinking this is much better. I don't think I've ever seen a man look as good as you in everything he wears."

The glint in his eyes turned sultry and narrowed on her flushed face. "If you think I look good dressed, wait until I take it all off."

She swallowed hard. He'd unnerved her, but two could play that game. She let her gaze roam over him in a slow sweep. She took her time and savored every hard plane and rippling muscle outlined beneath his well-fitting clothes and revealed in his strong arms. She pointedly let her gaze settle on his waist and dip lower to his crotch. She swore his thick erection plastered to the front of his fly twitched beneath the barrier she wanted to rip away with her teeth, right after she tore off his shirt.

Yep, maybe the lace panties and bra started her mind down Dirty Road this evening, but she didn't need the frippery to want him the way she did. She just needed this man to look at her like that to make her nerves hum, her blood heat, and her body ache to have his hands on her.

"The anticipation is killing me, but right now I'm enjoying the dirty thoughts."

"Any one of them you want to act on, just say the word and I'm all yours."

The teasing tone didn't hide the fact he was dead serious, but she appreciated him keeping things light. Because of that, she walked to him. A step away, he took a quick step back.

"Don't touch me."

She raised her eyebrow, confused.

"I'm filthy. I don't want to mess up your pretty clothes. God, you smell like heaven."

She smiled at the compliment.

"You smell like a horse, but I'm going to kiss you anyway. Come down here, cowboy."

She didn't touch him, and he didn't touch her, but he did lean down and plant his mouth over hers in a sultry kiss made all the more intense because they both wanted to take things deeper, but held back from reaching for each other, pouring everything into the connection they made with only their lips.

The horse tugged on the rope, yanking him sideways, breaking the sweet kiss.

He held her gaze. "I'm sorry I'm running late."

"I'll wait."

"Come inside with me."

"Are you sure?" She eyed the giant beside him, nervous. She'd seen horses before, but never up close.

"This here is Luke. His buddy, Bo, is in the pasture."

"As in Bo and Luke Duke. *Dukes of Hazzard.*"

"I like you even more for knowing that. I'm totally picturing you in a pair of Daisy Dukes."

She laughed. "Not going to happen."

"Now I'm picturing you naked."

She smacked him on the arm, noticing how hard it

was beneath her hand. "Stop. Put your horse away. You promised me dinner."

"I've got most of it ready inside. Come with me. You can see the kittens," he practically sang in a teasing tone.

"Tempting me with furry fluff balls. Not fair." She followed him into the barn not expecting much, but quickly changed her opinion when she saw the neat, orderly, and clean interior. The pungent odor of manure she expected didn't exist. She smelled hay and horses, but the odor was rustic, even pleasant, not caustic. Owen took care of his animals, his things. He cared for them.

"I'll just be a minute brushing him down."

"Take your time."

A mewling kitten drew her attention to the stall on the right. "Go on, sweetheart. They're in there."

The kittens played on a blanket, tumbling over one another in a bundle of tan striped with black fur. All except the orange-and-white one attacking the mother's tail.

"Ah." She unlatched the gate and stepped in. Not frightened by her intrusion, the kittens bounded over on their tiny legs to attack her boots. One tried to climb up her. She settled on the floor and crossed her legs. Two tabbies bounded into her lap and pawed at each other in the circle of her legs. The redhead came over and she scooped him—no, her, she discovered with a quick look—up and hugged her close. "Hello, sweetheart."

She lost herself playing with the kittens, the redhead settled on her thigh to sleep. She pet her often, but used the feather on a plastic stick to tease and play with the others. The mother settled in for a nap beside her foot, keeping warm and enjoying the respite from the energetic babies.

One of the cats raised up on his hind legs, front arms outstretched, and pounced on the feather, grabbed hold with his tiny teeth, and shook his head like he was killing it. Claire giggled and tried to make him do it again.

"He's fierce," Owen said from the stall door.

She looked up and there he stood, arms crossed on the top of the door, his chin on his arm. He spoke of the kitten but stared at her.

"You're really beautiful when you laugh."

She didn't know what to do with such a compliment, delivered with so much honesty and charm. Her stomach fluttered and a shy smile stole across her face.

"This is playing dirty. I can't resist them. I'll have to come back to see them again."

"I'm not playing at anything, Claire, and you can come back any time you like. Maybe you'll even get used to the horses."

"They make me nervous."

"Do I make you nervous?"

"A little, but you're more predictable than they are."

"I'll have to work on that," he teased.

"No, you don't. I hate surprises."

"Some surprises are fun and make you happy. Like opening a Christmas present on Christmas Eve."

"My experiences say otherwise."

"I want to make you happy. Nothing I do will ever be designed to hurt you, Claire. I hope by now, you at least know that much about me and who I am."

She gently put the kittens crawling on her leg and shoulder on the blanket next to their mother. She took the sleeping redhead and tucked her next to a stuffed teddy bear. The toy made her smile, because Owen had bought it for the kittens to play with and cuddle. She rose and walked the few steps to him, his gaze always on her. She liked that about him, too. Whenever they were together, his focus always remained on her. Like at the baseball field when she stood to go to the concession stand. He'd known immediately, despite her being out of his line of sight.

Stopped in front of him, barred by the door between them, she stood with her face a few inches from his, since he leaned down on his forearms. She looked into his gorgeous blue eyes and studied him for a moment and thought about all she knew about him. All the things she wanted to know about him. Whatever this was between them, she wanted to hold on to it, explore it further. Know all there was to know about this fascinating man, who may have been a lawyer, a little-league softball coach, a rancher, but under it all was a kind and decent man who bought teddy bears for his kittens.

"I know who and what you are, Owen. I'd like to come back here, again and again, to see the kittens—but mostly to be with you."

That brought a smile to his handsome face. She put her hand to his jaw. His whiskers scraped against her smooth skin. She leaned in and gave him a soft kiss, keeping it light and poignant for the moment they shared. She leaned her forehead to his and sighed before opening her eyes.

"I like being with you," she admitted.

"Come up to the house and be with me."

"I'd like that," she said simply, knowing he meant for dinner, for company, for whatever else this night held for them.

Chapter Twenty-Two

OWEN WALKED UP the porch steps and stopped at the front door. Claire waited beside him, sneaking a peak at his ass while he leaned over and pried off his boots. He hid the smile, but enjoyed the thrill in his gut, the anticipation coursing through him that maybe tonight they'd take that next step. He wanted her more than he'd ever wanted any other woman. Kissing her made his head spin and his body hum. He could only imagine what making love to her would be like. Nothing compared to touching her. He needed to touch her and feel her body against his. This thing between them was different. Because it was so unique and new, it made it all the more fun to wait, because he wasn't looking to get it over with, scratch the itch and move on. No, this time making love to a woman, this woman, would make him want even more.

He craved her.

Everything about her appealed to him, right down to

her sweet smile and delightful laugh. With kittens crawling over her legs and one on her shoulder, she'd looked so happy and content. Just about weaned from their mother, he'd find homes for all of them, except the little redhead Claire so obviously adored.

He opened the door and let it swing wide, allowing Claire to go in ahead of him. He walked in behind her and stopped short when she paused in the wide entry. The empty living room to their left. Family room to the right. She looked from one to the other and glanced over her shoulder, one eyebrow raised in question.

"I've made all the needed repairs to the inside and outside of the house and barn, but I haven't had time to furnish and decorate all the rooms."

"Empty living room because you don't entertain here. Leather sofa, big-screen TV, wood tables in the family room. Guy comfort."

"Brody comes by to watch a game sometimes, but otherwise, I'm mostly alone out here. Why? You don't like it?"

"Actually, it looks rather comfortable. I like the simplicity of it. You need a rug to cover the hardwood floors and anchor everything. Maybe some colorful pillows to brighten things a bit, but I love the black wrought iron lamps with the amber glass shades."

"I saw them in a shop downtown. I wanted something that didn't seem so bright."

"I imagine after reading legal briefs and law books all day, the muted light helps with your tired eyes and helps you relax after a long day."

She paid attention. He liked her insight. The one thing he liked about living out here was the peace and quiet. His days were hectic and filled with meetings and court appearances. Here, he could relax.

Right about the rug, maybe some pillows, some kind of art on the walls in soft colors to brighten things but still keep it relaxed would round out the room. Maybe she'd help him out with those things.

Did he want her to help him decorate his house? He'd never really cared what anyone thought about his place. Yeah, he wanted her to like it here. He wanted her to want to be here with him.

"What's your favorite color?" he asked.

"Green. Blue. Purple."

He thought of the grassy fields outside. The blue sky he loved to sit on the porch and stare at for hours. The purple sunsets in spring. He liked her way of thinking. Or at least the way she made him think.

Yeah, those colors would work really well in here.

"Come on back to the kitchen. I'll get you set up before I take a quick shower."

Owen led the way down the short hall that opened into the wide kitchen with the windows off the back of the house. He loved this room and the way the light streamed in at dawn.

"Owen, this is beautiful. I love the white cabinets with the light sand-granite countertops. The pale green walls are bright and warm. I love the hardwood floors throughout. This place is really great."

"I'm glad you like it." He pulled the bottle of pinot

grigio from the fridge and grabbed the corkscrew from a drawer.

"Don't pour that for me."

He turned to her with a wine glass in his hand. "No?"

"White wine gives me a migraine."

"Really? But you drank the red the other night."

"Red doesn't have the same effect on me."

"I'll be darned. Okay, I have a bottle of the red. Would you like that instead?"

"Sounds great. So, what's for dinner?"

"I've got a couple of steaks in the fridge. I'll grill them up after I shower. I still need to make the salad and potatoes."

"I'll do that while you get cleaned up."

"Sit down. Relax. I won't be but a few minutes, and I'll take care of it."

"Don't be silly. I'll do it. Unless you don't want me rummaging through your cupboards."

"The house is yours. If you want to see the rest of the place, be my guest. Of course, the only room upstairs that's furnished is mine."

"You really did only do the rooms you needed."

"It's just me, rambling around this big house. Didn't seem necessary. There's a half bath past the stairs. The salad stuff is in the fridge. You'll find some bowls in the cabinet to the right of the stove. Potatoes are in the pantry. Whatever else you need or want is probably around here somewhere."

"Go. Clean up. I've got this. The kitchen is my domain."

He liked seeing her here, drinking wine, making

herself at home in his kitchen. She pulled out the tub of mixed greens, carrots, tomato, cucumber, and red onion from the fridge and set them on the counter. Her head came up and she stared at him.

"Really, I've got it."

"I see you do. It's just I wanted to do it for you, then the horse . . ."

"Owen, it's very sweet you wanted to make me dinner, but I don't mind. You got caught up taking care of your chores. No big deal."

"Claire."

She looked up from opening the bag of carrots.

"Thanks for making this easy."

"It is easy. No reason to make it hard because things didn't go exactly as you planned. How do you like your potatoes?"

"Cooked," he answered to make things easy for her.

"That I can do, no problem."

"If I wasn't a total mess, I'd hug you."

"Then you owe me when you come back."

"Deal."

Claire waited for Owen to leave the kitchen before she poked through his cabinets and pantry for what she needed. She fell in love with the kitchen. He may have gone bachelor bare in the living room, but he'd spared no expense in the kitchen, adding dividers in the drawers for utensils. They slid in and out and closed by themselves. She loved the huge refrigerator. He may not have very much in the way of actual food—beer took up one whole shelf—but the sheer size and newness of it made her jealous.

Her fridge didn't work nearly as well. The vegetable drawer froze her lettuce and anything on the door was barely above room temperature.

The contents of Owen's fridge implied he'd shopped for their meal, but not for much more. Maybe breakfast, judging by the two cartons of eggs.

The thought of staying and making Owen breakfast in the morning brought out another smile and made her belly glow warm. She couldn't remember ever smiling this much when thinking about a man. Oh, her ex had made her smile in the beginning, but they dimmed with suspicions of his ulterior motives. Owen wanted her in his bed, but that isn't all he wanted. He wanted to get to know her, to please her with this dinner date, and to protect her from any more trouble.

Settled into the kitchen and Owen's home, she went out the back door to the patio and smiled at the huge stainless steel grill. Such a guy thing. She liked the black wrought iron round table with chairs. The small puddles on the deck told her he'd spent some time washing things down before going to the barn to take care of other chores. A potted red geranium stood alone by the deck rail. The other pots were filled with dirt, but no plants. The backyard was nothing more than hacked-down weeds. The beauty of the yard came from the two towering trees on both sides of the patchy grass. Their thick branches sprawled high over the yard, deck, and house, shading everything. Dappled light filtered through the bright green leaves. She loved the peaceful cocoon they made over this lovely backyard spot.

She opened the lid of the grill, thinking to give it a clean and heat it for the potatoes, but didn't need to. The man kept a clean grill. She turned the knob and lit the burners. Lid closed, she turned to the pile of cushions by the back door. They still had the tags on them. He'd bought them for their date tonight. She tore off the tags and set the cushions on the chairs. Pleased with the dark green color against the black metal and the yard, she smiled.

In the house, she found a cylindrical clear glass vase and a tall pitcher. She went back into the pantry and grabbed a fat pillar candle and three thin taper candles. She put the pillar in the pitcher. She found a lighter in a drawer and lit one of the tapers and dripped wax into the base of the vase and placed each taper in the hot wax to keep them standing. She blew out the candle for now and took her makeshift candle holders out to the table along with the lighter. They'd dine by candlelight.

She went back into the house, pulled foil from another drawer and tore off a long sheet. Back in the pantry, she grabbed the bag of potatoes and an unopened jar of minced garlic. At the sink, she washed the potatoes and set them on the cutting board. She cubed them and dumped them into a bowl along with a tablespoon of the minced garlic. She sprinkled them with salt and pepper and a drizzle of olive oil. She mixed the whole lot and dumped the concoction onto the tin foil she'd laid out.

She tore off another sheet of foil and covered the potatoes, sealing the edges into a packet. She cleaned up the mess, wiping down the cutting board, and slid her potato packet onto the board to take out to the grill. She lifted the lid and slid the packet onto the rack and closed the lid.

Nearly done, she went back into the kitchen, chopped the mixed greens and put them in the large bowl. She added chopped carrots, tomato, cucumber, and red onion. She found a jar of sunflower nuts in the pantry and sprinkled them over the salad, along with the shredded cheddar cheese she pulled from the meat drawer in the fridge. She covered the pretty salad with plastic wrap and put it in the fridge to keep chilled.

Finished with those portions of the meal, she topped off her glass of wine, poured another for Owen, and took them both out to the table to wait for him.

Chapter Twenty-Three

OWEN STEPPED OUT of the lukewarm shower still mentally berating himself for botching his date with Claire so badly.

"You invited her here to impress her with dinner and be alone with her, and here you are, late for the date, smelling like horse shit when she arrives, and she's downstairs making dinner for you," he said to his wet mug in the mirror above the sink. "Just great."

In a hurry, he toweled himself off, swiped the towel back and forth over his dripping hair before dropping it to the floor and grabbing his brush. He ran it through his hair a couple of times to get it in order. He rubbed his hand over his scruffy face and thought about shaving, but didn't want to take the time.

"She's waiting for you. Hurry the hell up."

When did he start talking to himself? The woman was making him crazy, because all he wanted to do was rush downstairs to be with her.

Finished in the bathroom, he walked naked into his bedroom and swore at the unmade bed. His back to it, he grabbed a pair of boxer briefs from the dresser drawer and pulled them on. Going with Claire's casual style, he grabbed a dark blue long-sleeve Henley from the closet, put it on, and dragged on a clean pair of jeans. He dismissed socks and shoes and grabbed a pair of sheets from the linen closet in the hall to make the bed.

Wishful thinking? Maybe. But better to be prepared for anything. Especially when a woman like Claire was involved. She'd had this look about her earlier when she commented on the many ways he dressed. She wanted him. He didn't know if she'd give in to that need tonight or not, but God, he wanted to seduce her into his arms and into his bed. She'd already worked her way under his skin and into his head. He'd handed her the reins to that part of their relationship, and he wouldn't push her. He wanted to push and had to restrain himself from dragging her to his bed, but for the first time, it seemed important to take his time and allow her to do the same. They were building something here, something he wanted to last.

He threw the off-white quilt over the matching sheets and straightened it. He stuffed the pillows into their cases and tossed them on the top of the bed, pulling the cover over them. Finished, he scanned the room and swore. He picked up the dirty clothes from the floor and chair by the window, walking into the bathroom to toss them into the hamper along with his soggy towel. He pulled out two clean towels and hung them on the bars by the shower. He didn't know if he'd need both come morning.

Relatively at ease that everything was in order here, he left his room and pounded down the stairs, rushing into the kitchen to help her with the rest of the preparations. He stopped short in the clean, empty room. Unwarranted panic rushed through his system that she'd given up on him and tonight's date. He rushed to the back door and sighed his relief when he spotted her sitting at the table, her glass of wine in hand, her head resting on the seat as she stared up at the trees.

Beautifully relaxed, she drew him to her even with her back to him. Tempted beyond reason, he leaned over the back of her chair, registered her surprise in her wide eyes before they went soft with her smile, and kissed her. Spiderman had nothing on him and the upside-down kiss. He took his time and she relaxed into the cushion and him. Her hands came up and latched on to his biceps, sliding up to his shoulders and back down again. He took the kiss deeper, sliding his tongue past her sweet lips to tangle with hers. Those lovely hands of hers slid back up to his shoulders. He wanted to release the arms of the chair and cup her full breasts and mold them in his hands, but refrained, keeping to his promise to keep things light. Still, the woman tempted him into sin. He'd go willingly and with a smile.

Before things got out of hand, he kissed a trail from her lips, along her jaw, and down her neck. Since her head angled back, he had the perfect angle to nuzzle the soft skin under her chin. Her hands swept over his body to his neck and her fingers raked through his hair and she gripped on and held him tight.

"You smell so good."

"I think that's my line," he said against the spot where her neck met her collarbone. She smelled of sunshine and flowers. Sweet and heady. "You're just glad I don't smell like horseshit anymore."

She giggled and the vibration in her throat tickled his lips, drawing him in to press harder to the thundering pulse point. Her fingers glided through his damp hair, and she held on and pulled his face away so she could look at him.

"I put the potatoes on the barbeque. You need to get the steaks."

He needed to get her naked and underneath him. Too bad the good guy in him reminded him again to take things slow. The bad boy made him lean down and kiss the top of her rounded breast above her pretty pink sweater. He wondered if her nipples were the same pale pink, or a darker dusky color. He desperately wanted to find out.

He stood and walked around the chair to face her and give her some space. She reached out and took his hand and gave it a squeeze.

"You look great."

"Again, I think that's my line," he teased. "I'm clean and don't smell like a horse. A definite improvement. And now I can touch you without mucking you up. I'll get the steaks."

This time he gave her hand a squeeze and left her sipping her wine, a pretty blush on her cheeks after the kisses they'd shared. He pulled the platter of steaks from the fridge and unwrapped them. He snagged the steak rub from the counter by the stove and headed back outside. Claire stood in front of the barbeque, moving the foil packet over with a pair of tongs to the side to make room for the steaks. He set the steaks on the shelf at the side of the grill and leaned down and kissed her shoulder just above the sweater. Her long hair draped over her other shoulder and cascaded over her breast and down to her waist. He loved her golden hair. So bright and pretty in the dimming light.

"Sweetheart, sit down. Let me do this. You've done enough after I blew the setup of this date."

"Nonsense. I don't mind helping."

"You certainly did a better job with the salad. I wouldn't have thought to add the sunflower seeds and cheese. It looks really good."

"You're welcome. The potatoes are going to be even better."

"See, I would have just tossed them on to bake. What did you do?"

"Diced them, added some garlic, salt, and pepper, a little olive oil. They're going to be amazing."

"You're amazing." He gave her a quick kiss on the side of the head, stepped beside her, and grabbed the tongs to put the steaks on the grill. They sizzled when they hit the hot metal rack, and he closed the lid to let them cook.

"I love it back here," Claire said, a touch of nervousness in her voice he hoped to erase tonight. He wanted her to be comfortable with him all the time.

"While the house and barn are in good shape, despite the lack of furnishings in all the rooms, the yard still needs some work. I haven't had the time. Maybe you can help me out with that. I liked the planters and garden space you did at your shop."

"You could use some color back here. The trees provide a lot of shade and will help cut down on the amount of water you'll need. You could do some taller bushes along the back by the fence line and other pretty flowers along the sides and in front of the deck. They'd outline this space from the rest of the pastures."

"I'll have to hit the nursery soon, I guess. You could help me plant, and I'll cook for you again."

She gave him a sweet smile, but didn't quite commit. "Like I said, it's a pretty spot back here."

"Not as pretty as you." He loved it when she giggled like that. "I'll get the plates and silverware. How do you like your steak?"

"Medium rare."

"A girl after my own heart."

Her gaze met his and she said, "I believe I am," surprising him with her candor.

He waited for the nerves, the shackles of commitment clamping down, but nothing happened. Well, nothing but an easing in his chest he hadn't really been aware of until she confirmed she wanted something more. With her, he wanted more. But how much more? A relationship, yes. But did he want the whole deal, a wife and family? He wanted that, and hoped Claire wanted it, too. He'd have to wait and see if they could build it together.

Chapter Twenty-Four

CLAIRE PUSHED HER empty plate away, leaned down, and pulled off her boots, dropping them on the deck. If Owen went barefoot, no reason she couldn't make herself comfortable, too. She leaned back and rested her hand on her belly.

"That was a great steak."

"Can't go wrong with a thick filet and a beautiful woman for dinner."

She smiled, settling in and relaxing, her glass of wine in hand. She scooted her chair to face Owen and raised her feet and rested them on his chair between his spread legs. His warm hands settled over her toes and he rubbed, avoiding her wounds, his eyes locked on her face.

"I like that."

He scooted his chair closer, drawing her foot up to rest on his stomach and he continued to rub her toes and ankle, making the soreness dissipate. She straightened her other leg and rested it across his thigh.

"See, that wasn't so hard."

"What?" she asked.

"Getting comfortable with me."

"Tell me a funny story about you and your wicked past."

"You just want to see how many ways to Sunday I screwed up in my younger, wilder days."

"Well, you can leave off the stories about you and whatever girl you wanted that day."

"Then I've got nothing."

She laughed and nearly choked on her wine. He rose up and forward to pat her on the back as she coughed.

"Stop being funny."

"You said you wanted funny."

"Come on. This is the part where we get to know each other better."

"I thought we did that over dinner when we played Twenty Questions with each other. I still can't believe you've never gotten less than an A on a report card and only dated three guys your whole life."

"Well, if you think about it, how many girls did you actually date versus just sleeping with them?"

"Point taken, I'll shut up."

She smiled again at his easy way and the self-deprecation that didn't really bother him. He'd been honest with her about who he used to be and up front about how hard he'd worked to change his life. She'd learned a lot about him over dinner and simple conversation, least of which was that he didn't want to be the guy he was before, but didn't necessarily feel he had to apologize for living his life that way.

"Okay, there was this one time. Hot summer day, too much beer and time on my hands. I snuck onto Ms. Firths's property to fish in her pond."

"The trespassing incident."

"That was the time before, this happened later."

"Didn't learn your lesson."

"Not the first time, but the second time changed things."

"How so?"

"Let me tell the story," he teased.

She laughed. Because he made her laugh or because of the wine warming her belly—or maybe that was him, too. She tipped her nearly empty glass at him to continue.

"Okay, so drunk, hot . . ."

"Yes, you are."

He chuckled. "No more wine for you, you're tipsy. On second thought, definitely more wine."

He reached for the bottle, but she held up her hand to stop him. "I'm good."

"I'm counting on it," he teased, provocatively.

"Hot," she prompted.

"Burning." His deep voice made her conclude he meant for her. "So drunk as I am, I figure why not strip down and take a dip while I'm waiting on supper to take the bait. I take my swim, floating on my back in the pond, soaking up the sun, and riding my buzz unaware of anything around me. Next thing I know, I'm walking out of the pond to check my line, thinking I've probably got nothing, what with all my splashing and making noise, scaring all the fishes. So, I walk into the shallows buck naked and finally look up and see Ms. Firth standing right in front of me with her shotgun leveled at my gut."

"Uh oh."

"That's what I'm thinking, but then she smiles and her eyes glide down my bare-ass body. Now, I'm drunk and thinking this old woman can't possibly be thinking what I think she's thinking, so I make a smartass remark about her calling the cops and having me arrested for trespassing and indecent exposure. She shocks the drunk right out of me by saying, 'Nothing indecent about you, boy.'"

Claire gasped and giggle. "No, she didn't."

"Swear to God. I recover, figure I've got a way out of trouble, and laugh my ass off. Damn if I don't catch a fish at that moment. The pole starts bending and wiggling. She points to the pole with the shotgun and tells me to go ahead and grab it. I reel the catfish in and say, 'He's a big sucker.' She smiles, her gaze slides down to my dick, and she says, 'Yes, it is.'"

Claire busted up laughing. "You're lying. She did not."

"I'm telling you, she did. She must have been in her eighties and here she is flirting with me. I don't know what to do at that point, but she makes it easy and says if I want to fish in her pond I'll have to do it naked from now on, or she'll call the cops."

"What did you say?"

"'Yes, ma'am.'"

Claire laughed so hard she grabbed her stomach. "You are incorrigible."

"Maybe so," he laughed with her.

"So, you never trespassed or fished in her pond again."

"Hell no, she had the biggest catfish in the county in that pond. I fished there at least once a week."

"Did she call the cops on you again?"

"She kept her word and I kept mine."

"You fished naked." She gasped.

"Every time. Drunk or not."

"Did she come back to see you?"

"No idea. I never saw her, but I imagine she did come for a look now and again. She left me the acre of land the pond sits on that borders this property."

Claire shook her head, but couldn't help the smile. "I believe the widow Firth was sweet on you."

"Oh, she wanted me," Owen confirmed with a wicked grin.

"Yep, not a redeemable bone in your body."

"Hey, I'm faithful. I never fished naked at anyone else's pond."

That made her smile even more. "I like your stories. You've had a lot of fun in your life, but never at someone else's expense."

"Yes, and now I'm a boring lawyer, walking the straight and narrow. I only fish naked once or twice a month."

"Are you serious?"

"It's become a tradition of sorts for me." He chuckled and took a sip of wine, his eyes on her, his other hand and thumb rubbing circles on the bottom of her foot, hypnotizing her.

They settled into the quiet night together. After dinner and nearly two hours of talking, the stars and the candles burning on the table were the only light left. The flicker of candlelight played over his ruggedly handsome face. She wondered what it would feel like to have those strong hands move over her body. She wanted to feel his weight on her, to anchor her in this moment and to him.

Decision made, she pulled her feet off his lap and grabbed her shoes.

"Where are you going?" he asked, a look of reluctance and disappointment in his eyes.

"It's late. I'm heading up to bed." He frowned, but stood to see her out, missing the meaning of what she'd said. She clarified by asking, "Do I make a right or left at the top of the stairs?"

His gaze locked on hers, and he stood rigid and stunned three feet away. He closed the distance. All at once she found herself picked up off the ground, his arms banded around her and his mouth locked on hers in a fierce and passionate kiss that stole her breath. Her feet bounced against his shins as he walked into the house. She dropped her shoes with a thud on the kitchen floor in favor of sliding her fingers through his hair and pulling him close. Too awkward to be hanging down the front of him, she wrapped her legs around his waist and locked her feet to hold on. His big hands slid over her hips and cupped her bottom, pulling her snug against his thick erection.

He tore his mouth from hers, allowing her to take a ragged breath. The house was pitch black, but he kept walking toward the stairs. At the bottom of them, he halted and met her gaze despite the fact she could barely see him.

"Yes or no. Are you sure you want to do this now?"

"Yes. Now. Hurry up," she added to get him moving again.

He took her mouth again and the stairs two at a time. At the top, he turned left and entered a room several feet down the hallway. The light was only slightly better here, thanks to the windows facing the backyard and the three-quarter moon.

Owen's mouth left hers to trail kisses down her throat. He lifted her higher with his hands firmly planted on her ass, so he could kiss the swell of her breast. Hungry for her, he grunted out something incoherent and used one hand to pull the sweater over her head. Once gone, he unhooked her bra and pulled that barrier away. He didn't waste time or make her wait for what she really wanted: his mouth on her breast. He took possession. His lips clamped on to her hard nipple and he sucked hard. Heat pooled between her legs and she tightened her hold on his waist, increasing the friction between her leggings and the fly of his jeans. He clamped his hands on her hips and moved her up and down against his hard cock. His teeth raked across her nipple and his tongue swept over it. She sighed and let her head fall back as he sucked hard, grinded his cock against her clit, and she exploded in a white-hot orgasm.

She went lax in his arms, but he held her close, softly kissing his way up her throat to her ear and licking the lobe with his hot tongue.

"I'm not done with you, sweetheart."

"Ah, fuck me."

Something in him shifted and the hungry look in his eyes matched the way he urgently reached for her again. "I'm going to. Soon."

That *soon* turned her on and made her want. More. That became her mantra over the next several minutes as he laid her out on the bed and pulled her leggings and panties off in one long sweep of his hands down the side of her hips and legs. He pulled off one sock and kissed the inside of her ankle. Then he did the same with her other foot. Her gaze stayed locked on his and they communicated without words everything they wanted from each other in this way with a look and a touch.

Unwilling to simply lay docile waiting for him, she rose up on her knees at the edge of the bed and fisted his shirt in her hands, pulling him to her for a kiss. Owen came willingly and gave her what she wanted. He'd give her anything at this point. Responsive, open, no reservation in her moves or her kiss, he fell under her spell and let himself go. He didn't think, but acted on every desire she brought out in him.

Her hands slid up and under his shirt, pulling it high. Desperate to be skin-to-skin with her, he pulled the damn thing off himself and tossed it away. Her mouth roamed over his chest and he buried his hands in her long hair and slid his fingers through the silky strands, enjoying the play of her hands over his skin and the soft, wet kisses she trailed down to his belly, making the muscles go tight and his cock twitch and ache even more.

"I love all these hard muscles," she said, leaning back in his arms, her hands going to the button on his jeans.

"I have something else hard for . . ." *You* died on his lips when she slipped her hand down his pants and boxers and clamped her fingers around his dick. "Ah, God, sweetheart."

Her hand stroked up and down and back again. He lost himself in the rhythm and her lovely mouth. His hands found the bounty of her breasts and molded and shaped them at his whim. He caught her hard nipples between his fingers and squeezed. He loved the sighs and moans, telling him what she liked, how much she liked it, and eliciting his unwavering need to make her do it again.

Her hand dipped low again, fingers caressing him, nearly bringing him to his knees and to the point of no return. About to make her stop before he disgraced himself, she wrapped her fingers around his balls and squeezed. His cock jerked.

Beyond reason, he pulled her hand free and tore off the rest of his clothes. He pushed her back onto the bed and followed her down. She laughed and welcomed him with open arms. He lay between her thighs and she spread her legs wide to accommodate his much larger frame. He pressed her into the bed with his weight and her gaze met his. She must have seen the frenzy inside him reflected in his eyes. Her hands came up to his neck, her thumbs rubbed across his rough jaw with a scrape.

"We have all the time in the world."

Her being right didn't necessarily slow him down, but it did give him a moment to take a breath and tame his baser needs. Her hands sliding down his back and over his ass and gripping it tight only fueled his desire to bury himself deep inside her. Right now.

He leaned on his right arm and fumbled with the bedside drawer to grab a condom. Victory. He snagged one, despite the woman below him, kissing her way around his shoulder and down his side, while her hands roamed free over his chest and back.

He shifted and she moved, somehow, making him land on his back to avoid hitting her in the face. She settled on top of him with a bright smile, her legs straddling his thighs. She looked down at his hard cock and back at his face.

"You're a bit behind me. I owe you a little something extra for before."

"Honey . . ." He lost all thought when her lips pressed to his lower belly, her fingers locked around his dick, and she licked the tip of his penis, sending a shiver of need straight down his spine. He didn't know where this woman came from, how he'd gotten so lucky to have her in his bed, and he didn't care. When her mouth closed over his aching cock, he sank into the bed and savored every lick and stroke of her mouth over him. He tried to hold on, fisting his hands in the bedding, but that didn't stop the need from rising. He reached for her, sliding his hands over her shoulders and through her hair to drape it over one side so he could watch her mouth move up and down over him. That only made him hungrier for her. Unable to bear any more, he hooked his hands under her arms and dragged her up his body and kissed her hard and deep.

The tip of his penis pushed at her entrance, but she kept her head and broke the fierce kiss to sit atop him again. She pulled out the condom and sheathed him in it. She fell forward on her hands and dipped her head to kiss him. He grabbed her hips and brought her down on his hard cock in one long, fluid motion that stretched her and filled her. Taking care not to rush her, he let her settle atop him again. He exhaled, feeling her body wrapped around his. She looked down at him, and their gazes met. They shared the moment of connection with a soft exhale. They settled into each other, and then she moved and took him to heaven with one rock of her body over his. He let her set the pace, because where she went, he needed to follow.

He held on to her, because he didn't want to let her go—ever.

She leaned down and slid her tongue over his and softly bit his lower lip before she sat back up and moved over him to a rhythm all their own making. She pressed her knees into the bed and rolled her hips, then grinded against him. She loved the feel of his big hands wrapped around her waist, urging her on. She raked her fingers over the hard muscles in his chest. He moaned, liking the rough grab of her fingers over his heated skin and the wild way she made love.

His hands skimmed up her side to cup her breasts. She arched her back and offered them up to his attention. He slid his hands around her back and pulled her down. She leaned on her hands beside his head and his mouth clamped on to her taut nipple and he sucked hard, sending a shaft of heat straight to the place they were joined. He thrust deep and she grinded against him, sighing out her pleasure, her body tightening around his. His hot tongue swept over her breast, and he took her other breast into his mouth and licked and laved while their bodies pumped and grinded together.

His strength always surprised her in the nicest ways. She loved how he used it to maneuver her, but never hurt her. One large arm snaked around her, while he used his hand to push on her thigh to move her leg down his before he rolled and landed on top of her. She welcomed his weight and slid her hands up his back and around his neck, pulling him down for another hot kiss.

He leaned up on his arms, pulling out of her in a long, slow retreat that made her want to pull him back immediately to fill the emptiness he left behind.

"My turn," he said with a smile that was anything but nice and all about repaying her for the sweet torture she'd inflicted.

He pushed back into her in another of those long, slow strokes of his body into hers. She sighed.

"Spread your thighs wide. Make room for me."

She did as he asked without reservation, and Owen sank into her all the way to the hilt. He moved his hips in a slow circle, creating friction against her entrance without moving in or out. She shifted, tilting her hips to his and finding just the spot she wanted. He slowly went crazy inside, desperately trying to hold on and wait for her to join him in oblivion.

He pulled out and drove back into her, circling, riding her hard and deep, her breasts bouncing with the force of his thrust before he circled his hips again and she joined him, moving her hips to prolong the sweet friction that made her moan and tighten around him. Lost in this new dance, he kept the pace until both of them needed more. He gave it to her, hard and fast until she tightened around him. With one last deep thrust, he followed her over the edge.

Collapsed on top of her, his breaths came in sawing heaves that took him several minutes to slow before he realized she breathed as hard as he did, though not as well with his heavy weight on top of her.

He rolled to his side, gathered her close with one arm, and fell onto his back. She settled her head on his shoulder, her lovely breasts pressed to his ribs.

The quiet night settled around them. Their heated bodies cooled. She let out a soft sigh, her breath whispering over his skin. He held her closer.

"Stay," he coaxed, kissing the top of her head.

"I don't want to be anywhere but right here with you."

He smiled into the night. For the first time ever, he'd asked a woman to spend the night and began thinking about ways to get her to stay longer. Maybe even forever.

Chapter Twenty-Five

They sat in the circle of light cast by the candles on the table. They'd never see past that glow to the hiding spot behind one of the thick trees. They had long since finished the meal *he* cooked for her. That just riled.

Claire sat pretty as a picture, drinking her wine, her gaze always going to Owen, sweeping his body with a longing no one could mistake. Owen saw it, responded to it with smiles and smoldering looks that said only one thing: he wanted her in his bed tonight. Who could blame him, she was a beautiful woman.

Their conversation floated on the breeze in muted tones that gave no hint to the actual words said. The words weren't necessary when you watched the body language between the two of them. The way she tilted her head to listen. The way he touched her foot or leg, massaging her muscles, tempting her into more. He leaned in close, like he was telling her a secret. She smiled and laughed, giving him a playful smack on the arm.

Finally, Claire stood to leave, but turned back when Owen stood to walk her out. His charms weren't enough to make her stay, because he didn't really want her and she knew it. All he wanted from her, nothing more than a night in his bed.

Moving positions around the house after they went inside, the wait grew too long. Claire never came out the front door. Lights never went on in the house.

The anger came swift and hard.

So, she'd gone willingly to his bed.

Maybe she needed a stronger reason to leave. And if she didn't leave, maybe she didn't deserve to live.

Chapter Twenty-Six

CLAIRE WOKE UP by degrees. At first, the hand covering her breast seemed like just another cozy position to sleep next to Owen's big warm body. Then his tongue swept over her other breast, tightening her nipple. The hand over her breast caressed down her belly in soft, slow circles angling down until his fingers dipped low and one slipped into her slick core.

"You are always so hot a wet for me."

She smiled, thinking of last night and how he'd woken her a mere two hours after the first time they made love to do it all over again. The first time had been a combination of slow buildups and fast and hard lovemaking. The second time he'd taken her with a need that defied all logic or attempts to slow things down. He'd wanted her and had her in less than fifteen minutes, but she didn't mind when it was that explosive.

This was something altogether different. Just like

the man who looked like a lawyer one minute, a jock the next, and a rancher after that, Owen made love in much the same way. He had a way about him, depending on his mood. So far she loved the two he'd shown her. This slow, sweet, take-your-time Owen just might make her melt, when the others had simply demanded she play.

"More." She spoke the thought out loud. With him, she always wanted more.

"All you want and then some."

"I want you."

He planted a kiss on her stomach, his tongue sweeping out to taste. He did it again and again, sinking her deeper and deeper into his spell. His fingers worked in and out of her slick sheath, building the sweet tension coiling in her belly. He cupped her, rubbed his palm over that sweet spot he could find now with his eyes closed. She grinded her hips into his hand and his fingers stroked. She sighed, and he shifted up her body, planting more of those open-mouthed kisses until he got to her breast, where he took her into his mouth but kept things soft and light like a waking dream.

Nothing had ever felt like this. No one made her feel quite like this. Free. Loved. Special. Beautiful.

"Owen," she called to him, moving her hips, wanting more. Wanting him inside of her, filling her.

He shifted over her again, this time rubbing his whole body over the front of her as he rose up on his hands and nudged her entrance with the head of his cock. He pushed in languidly slow. She sighed out a long breath as he eased his way in until he was buried and softly grinding against her.

Owen buried his face in her neck and hair and whispered, "Good morning, my sweet Claire."

"It is now."

She meant it, and he liked her all the more because when he thought they might be awkward in the morning light, she surprised him and wrapped her legs around him and pulled him closer. No reservation. No hesitation. No shyness to her moves, or the way she wrapped her arms around his back and held him close as he moved in and out of her. He just wanted to be close to her, find the special moment they'd shared last night and know how real it was even in the light.

So he rocked his hips back into hers and lost himself in making love to her, kissing her neck, her lips, her shoulder as their bodies moved together. He stayed close to her, wrapping her up against him, needing the feel of her body moving against his.

She pulled her knees higher, and he sank deeper. Desperate to draw this out and show her he could be gentle. He tamped down his need to thrust harder and pick up the pace. Never passive, she grabbed his ass and pulled him to her, rolling her hips to create that delicious friction that always sent her over the edge when he pushed into her and circled his hips to increase her pleasure and his. Her wet core tightened around him, she gave him a soft bite on the shoulder and smoothed her tongue over the small hurt that sent a shaft of heat through his system. He kept the pace, but made his movements longer and harder. Her body tightened around him; she held him close and lost herself in the moment, pulling him with her into the depths of pleasure.

Spent, he lay on top of her, his arms banded around her in the same fashion as she had her arms and legs wrapped around him.

He felt like he should say something. His emotions felt heavy in his chest, but he couldn't find the words.

"I wish we could capture this moment somehow," she said.

He felt the same way. "Me too, but I have to get up and go feed the horses."

"It's barely morning."

"If I don't feed them at the same time each day, they get antsy and start beating down the gates."

"Is this your way of getting out of cuddling with me?"

He chuckled, liking the way she lightened the mood, but still kept things intimate between them.

"I'd like nothing better than to stay with you in bed all day, but I need to take care of this." He kissed her softly and rubbed his nose along her cheek to her ear. "Sleep. I'll be back."

"I'm counting on it."

That made him smile. He rolled off her and slid out of bed. He pulled the sheets up around her and she glanced at him briefly with a soft smile and a sigh before her eyes drooped closed again and she drifted back to sleep.

In the weak morning light, she looked ethereal with her golden hair spread over the white sheets. He liked seeing her in his bed. He liked it a lot. So much so that he wondered how he went about getting her to stay tonight, too.

It would make it easier to keep her safe. Then again, it might put a bigger target on her back. The thought sent a chill up his spine.

Chapter Twenty-Seven

Claire woke with a start, not knowing what made her uneasy until she saw a pair of jean-clad legs next to the bed she recognized.

"Don't you sleep?"

"Not when I have a beautiful woman in my bed," Owen teased.

She didn't want to think about the other women in his bed. He must have read her mind and added, "Of course, no other woman actually stayed the night here, or slept in my bed, so I guess it's just having you here."

That got her attention. "You've never had another woman to your house?"

"It's easier not to actually sleep with a woman if you don't have to make excuses to get them out of your house."

"So, are you standing there, trying to come up with a polite way to get me out of here?"

"Nope. I'm staring at your fine ass and hoping you'll roll over so I can stare at your beautiful breasts that make my mouth water."

"Well, saying things like that isn't going to get me out of your bed."

"I'm on the right track then."

She leaned up on her elbow, realizing the blankets were tangled at her waist, and he was in fact staring at her breasts.

"What exactly are you trying to do?"

"Decide if I'm going to make love to you again, or tell you I made you breakfast."

Her stomach rumbled at the mere mention of food. Her heart melted that he'd made her breakfast, which meant he really didn't want her out and fast. No, he wanted her to stay awhile.

"I guess that means you want the food."

She rose up on her knees in front of him and wrapped her arms around his neck, giving him a quick, sweet kiss. "I want you, too, but if you don't feed me and give me coffee, I won't have the strength to live up to the amazing sex we had last night and this morning."

"Well, come on, woman. Eat. I've got plans for you for later."

"Really?" she asked, wondering if this was real or just wishful thinking.

He traced a finger over her forehead and down the side of her face, tucking a lock of hair behind her ear, and unveiling even more of her breasts from behind the curtain of hair that fell over her chest when she got up.

"I was hoping you'd want to hang out here today. With me. It's Sunday. We don't have work. I'd like you to stay," he finished, a touch of hesitation in his voice.

"You mean that."

"That's why I said it."

"Okay."

"Okay, what?"

"I'll eat. I'll stay."

Since she was plastered to the front of him, she felt his exhale of relief all the way through her body. She hid the smile and gave him another quick kiss.

"Let me use the bathroom, and I'll be down in a minute. Can I borrow some toothpaste at least?"

"I found a spare toothbrush and left it on the counter for you."

"A toothbrush today. My clothes in the closet tomorrow. Before you know it, this might be a real relationship. You sure you wouldn't rather I run home, clean up, and come back later?"

She kept her tone teasing and light, but his eyes narrowed and his hands came up to cup her face.

"This is a real relationship. You and me and the possibility of forever. So brush your teeth. Put the toothbrush in the garbage can or in the holder, whatever makes you comfortable at this point, and come down and have breakfast with me."

She stopped him when he reached the door. Naked, sitting in the middle of his bed, she bared her soul. "Owen, do you know why I like being here with you?"

She expected a smartass remark like "Great sex," but he surprised her and asked in a solemn tone, "Why?"

"Because I know you want me here with you, and that scares me just a little bit."

"We understand each other then, because it scares me just a little bit how much I want you here. The thing is, you not being here scares me more."

She cocked her head and smiled, because she knew how hard it was for him to make that admission.

"If I had a camera, I'd take your picture right now. God, you're beautiful."

He walked back to the bed, planted his hands on the mattress, and leaned in for a kiss. She caught his face in her hands and held him in the kiss for a moment before touching her forehead to his, taking in the moment.

"Come down to breakfast when you're ready."

This time he did walk out the door, leaving her wondering about how fast this thing between them was moving. Where did she really want it to go?

She walked into the bathroom and stopped short at the sink, taking a step back when she saw what he left her. Not only did he find her a toothbrush, but he left her a towel, washcloth, a comb, and a hotel-size bottle of cucumber-melon lotion. She smiled and put her hand over her fluttering stomach.

"Damn the man makes it hard not to want to leap."

She turned on the shower taps and stepped into the hot spray to wash away the makeup she'd slept in. She used his soap and shampoo, wishing for more time to indulge in the huge white marble stall. She'd love to turn on the other shower across the way and have both of them work on her sore muscles. Owen had certainly given her a workout last night.

Finished in the shower, she used the towel he left her to dry off and squeeze as much water as she could out of her hair. She used the comb to get out the tangles and let it all fall down her back to air dry. She opened the bottle of lotion, smelled its sweet fragrance, and used some on her legs, arms, and hands. She grabbed Owen's toothpaste and used her new toothbrush to brush her teeth. She smiled at herself in the mirror when she automatically put the toothbrush in the holder on the sink without even thinking about it. She stared at the two of them together and shrugged the whole thing away.

"You never know. I might need it later."

Again, without any real thought, she opened the medicine cabinet and tucked the small bottle of lotion away. Done, she hung the damp towel on the empty bar next to his and walked back into the bedroom. She didn't have anything but her clothes from last night. Warm after her shower, she pulled on the tunic and left the room feeling sexy and flirtatious.

OWEN DIDN'T KNOW what had come over him this morning when he came back in from feeding the horses and saw her lying in his bed. He rushed through his chores because he wanted to be back in that bed with her. Instead of waking her with another round of morning sex, he'd showered and changed and rummaged through the cupboards to find her some supplies. He'd had to stop himself from grabbing her keys and going down the road to her place and packing her a bag.

The shower went off upstairs and he smiled, liking the fact she'd made herself at home and jumped in without even asking if he minded. Hell no, he didn't. That's why he left her the towel and supplies.

He cracked six eggs into the pan and scrambled them up with the spatula. He pushed the lever down on the toaster, added salt and pepper to the eggs, grabbed the shredded cheese from the fridge, noticed the bin of mixed greens, opened it, and pulled out a bunch of spinach to add to the eggs. He may not be a gourmet cook, but he could make her a decent meal. If she felt as ravenous as he did after last night, she needed the food as much as he did.

He folded the eggs and spinach over in the pan and added the cheese to the top. She walked up behind him, wrapped her arms around his middle, and looked over his shoulder, standing on her tiptoes. "That looks wonderful."

"You smell good."

"Thanks. I smell like you plus the lotion you left me. I used your soap and shampoo."

"Use whatever you like."

"Thanks, I knew you'd say that. I need coffee."

"I left you a mug by the pot."

She kissed his neck and walked over to the pot on the counter, giving him a nice view of her long, toned legs. He hadn't seen her walk in half-naked, but he sure did appreciate it.

"Honey, you've got the best looking legs."

She turned with the mug in both hands and blew on the steaming brew. She leaned back against the counter and crossed her ankles, completely at ease standing in his kitchen half-naked. God, he liked her.

"I like the way you go barefoot at home."

"Don't want to be walking through the house in my mucked-up boots."

"No, you wouldn't. You like things neat and tidy."

"Probably because my father lived a messy life, and Brody and I were always the ones to clean it up."

He dropped the subject and turned back to the eggs. He cut the omelet down the middle and slid each half onto a plate. The toast popped and he set the pan on a cool burner and grabbed the toast and buttered it. Claire opened the drawer behind him and pulled out silverware. He took the plates to the table and set hers next to his. He took the chair, and she sat in the padded cushion in the window seat. Before he took a bite, she leaned in and kissed his cheek.

"Thank you. This smells really good."

"You're welcome, sweetheart. Eat. You must be starved."

She giggled and took the first bite. "I am. Oh, man, that is so good," she said around the mouthful.

He laughed with her and dug into his own food. It didn't take either of them long to work their way through the meal with nothing but smiles and small talk.

Her phone buzzed and she rose to grab her purse off the counter and check it. She dug through her purse and pulled out a round plastic case, pulling a pill out of it and popping it in her mouth, chasing it with her coffee as she came back to the table. So, that answered the question about whether she was on birth control. Not that he hadn't protected her last night and this morning, but it was good to know they had backup.

Or was it?

He thought of his nieces, Dawn and Autumn, and the way they loved Brody. He wanted children of his own, but things with Claire were far too new to discuss having a family someday.

"Can I take your plate?" she asked, completely casual about everything this morning.

"I'll clean up."

"You cooked. I clean up. Finish your coffee. Relax. You got up a lot earlier than I did. Which I thank you for," she said, leaning down to kiss him.

"No sense both of us getting up on a weekend."

She brought the dishes to the sink, gathered the pot, spatula, and butter knife from the stove and put them all in the sink. Efficient as ever, she turned on the taps, soaked the dish cloth and drizzled soap over it, scrubbing the plates and all the rest, rinsing them, and setting them in the strainer.

He couldn't take his eyes off her.

Done with the chore, she leaned on the counter and stared out the window at the bright day. Sunlight caught the gold in her hair and brightened her softly pink cheeks. She used the back of her foot to rub a spot on her other leg and everything in him went tight at the sight of her long legs and the way the sweater barely covered her pretty bottom, exposing just the curve of her ass at her thighs, but only hinting at what lay beneath. Heaven.

"The asshole we're never to speak of was a complete idiot for ever leaving a good woman like you."

She turned her head to him and planted her chin in her palm. "I was never like I am with you with him. Last night, you weren't satisfied unless I was satisfied," she explained awkwardly. "Because you gave me the time and attention I needed, it made it easy for me to do the same for you."

"Are you telling me that asshole never gave you an orgasm?"

"Not never, but it was mostly up to me to hurry up before he got done. After a while, it wasn't worth trying to hurry up when he could care less if I was satisfied and happy."

"Are you shitting me?"

She didn't respond, telling him she told the God's-honest truth. "He should be shot. On second thought, let him live the rest of his life stupid and ignorant to what he gave up. You like sex."

She laughed and blushed but stayed where she was, looking oh so pretty and alluring because she didn't strike a pose, so much as she was comfortable with him now.

"I mean, you really like sex."

"I got it. But let's clarify. I like sex with you."

"That's what I mean. With a partner who matches you, reads you, you give and take and make love in a way I've never experienced."

That wiped the smile right off her face.

He rose and walked to her then, standing directly behind her. He pulled her hair away from her back and dropped it over her shoulder to puddle on the counter. She still didn't move, but let him move in behind her and press his hard cock to her backside. He clamped his hands on her shoulders and rubbed at the tense muscles, sliding his hands down her back. One hand raised the sweater and held it in the middle of her back. He got a lovely view of her heart-shaped bottom. She stopped breathing and he rubbed his other hand over one side of her bottom and dipped it lower, sliding one finger, then two into her already-wet core.

"I'm not an idiot. I know what I want. You. Happy. Always."

"I am whenever I'm with you."

That last sentence sent him over the edge. He unzipped his jeans, pushed them to his knees, and took her from behind in one hard thrust that made her gasp. Hands planted on the counter for balance, she spread her legs wide and let him take her. Born from some need to convince her she belonged with him, it took him a minute to realize if she didn't feel that way after everything they'd shared, nothing he said or did would make her. But she did feel that way. Why else would she give herself this way and all the ways she did last night.

He shifted his thinking and the way he made love to her and slowed things down. He pulled her sweater over her head and trailed his fingers lightly down her back. She glanced over her shoulder, and he leaned over her, pushing his cock deep, and kissed her gently once, twice, three times. He saw the question in her eyes. Things started out one way, but he'd changed things up and she adjusted to his mood with a sigh that sent her bottom brushing against his hips. She rotated her hips and he thrust again, pulled out slow, and thrust hard, staying seated in her heat. She responded to the contrasting moves, and he gave her more, sliding his hands around her ribs to cup her breasts and squeeze her hard nipples. She arched her back, offering up her breasts to his roaming hands and making her rump push against him even more. She moaned and he slid one hand down her belly to the spot they were joined. He rubbed the soft nub and thrust into her hard and fast. She let go in an intense orgasm that had her body squeezing every last drop out of him as he came in a blinding white-hot orgasm. He collapsed on her back as she lay braced on her arms in front of him. He rolled his forehead on her spine between her shoulders and sighed.

"Well, you certainly make me happy," he teased.

She laughed, easing the tension.

He backed away from her long enough to pull up his jeans and zip them. She put on her sweater again and turned to face him, her back against the counter.

"Claire, I'm sorry, the way that started . . ."

"Was your way of trying to prove something. I get it. It's a guy thing. I'm happy and you're happy. So we're good, but let's get one more thing straight."

"What's that? Never do that to you again."

"No. Please do that to me again."

"You're too good to be true." He let out a pent-up breath and waited for her to finish.

"Owen, there is no comparison between you and the asshole. Maybe at first I was looking for them, but now, I just see you. You are who I want to be with. You are the one who makes me happy. You are not an asshole."

He couldn't help himself; he laughed. "Thanks." He wrapped his arm around her neck and drew her close. "How about another shower, and then we crash on the couch and watch the new Bond movie."

"Daniel Craig. Now that's a plan I can get behind," she teased, making him laugh even more.

"Way too good to be true."

Chapter Twenty-Eight

OWEN DROVE THE road out of town toward home with Claire snuggled against his side. He rested his arm around her shoulders and held her hand, her fingers twined with his at her shoulder. He loved the way she leaned her head against him.

Late Thursday night, he couldn't wait to spend another weekend with her at his place. It had become their habit over the last month, ever since that first Saturday she came for dinner and stayed until he took her home early Monday morning on his way to work.

"You're late feeding the horses."

"I asked Brody to go by and take care of it, so I could take you out to dinner."

"You're spoiling me."

"Not possible."

He hugged her closer to his side, thinking of all they'd been through the last five weeks. God, had it only been that long? He'd known her longer than that, but not this way. Not with this much feeling and depth filling him up every time he saw her. They had a late lunch every day at his office. They spent most nights either at his place or hers. He hated the nights he slept alone.

More and more, his worry for her grew. Especially when she wasn't with him. After the incident with her slashed tires came the vandalism at her shop. Someone spray-painted the word BITCH on the wall at the back of the shop where she parked. Things remained quiet for a few days, until she came home one night to find her house egged. Tonight, they left the restaurant and found the passenger side of his truck keyed, the paint scratched and gouged. Again, they called the cops to report the vandalism. Frustrated, Claire went quiet on him. The cops remained vigilant, thanks to his sheriff cousin, Dylan, sending cars by Claire's shop and home on a regular basis. Nothing they did yielded any results, pissing him off. How hard could it be to find one man? Even more strange, the acts themselves seemed juvenile. If he didn't know better, he'd think a bunch of teenage hoodlums were harassing them, and not some hothead wife beater.

His stomach tied in knots thinking about everything. He rolled his head to alleviate some of the ache in his tense muscles.

The original attack seemed more in line with Dale's MO. Not this petty crap. If his goal had been to keep him from seeing Shannon, by now he should know he and Claire spent all their free time together. Why the fuck didn't he leave them alone?

Still, he'd seen Shannon several times over the last weeks. She'd called the cops to her house three times to say Dale had come by, banging on the door, trying to get her to let him in. Her nearest neighbor lived a hundred yards away. In her seventies, she wore hearing aids and listened to the TV turned up to max volume. Not a great witness to tell them where Dale went and if he'd changed vehicles, making it that much harder to find him.

Shannon remained on the fringes of his life, asking him to help renew the expired restraining order. Like any judge would deny the threat against her or Claire. He'd gone through the motions and filed the papers, presenting his case. Still, it did nothing, because Dale remained elusive.

Owen wanted to tear the guy to shreds for tormenting Claire and Shannon. He hated the fear and hesitation in Claire every time she went to work or came home. The two places she should feel safe. Dale had taken that from her. Owen would make him pay.

If Dylan didn't find him and arrest him, Owen would hunt him down and beat it into Dale that you do not hurt and terrorize women.

His cell phone rang. The dashboard clock read ten fourteen. Still about five miles from home, he pulled the phone from his pocket and handed it to Claire. He drove, and she swiped the screen.

"Please tell me it's Brody or Rain calling."

"It's Dylan."

"Of course it is."

Claire tapped the screen to accept the call and hit the SPEAKER button.

"Tell me you have him in custody." Owen waited for the inevitable bad news. Because he knew they weren't going to make it home, he pulled off the road onto the dirt shoulder and threw the truck into park.

"Shannon's been assaulted," Dylan said. "She's banged up, but okay."

"And you have Dale in custody, right?"

"He was gone before we got here. He came in through the back door."

"How is that possible? She's vigilant about locking up."

"She took the garbage out, came back in, and forgot to lock the door. She switched the lights off in the kitchen and headed off to bed. By the time she remembered the door, she went back to the kitchen to lock it, and Dale caught her in the living room. She begged him to leave. They got into an argument."

"He hit her. How bad?"

Owen gave Claire a look and she nodded her agreement. On the same page, he turned the truck around and headed back to town to check on Shannon in person. He needed to see her, talk to her, and find out as much information as he could about Dale. This had to end. Even the smallest clue could lead them to Dale. That's all he needed, that one thing that would be Dale's downfall.

"EMTs took her to the hospital. She's got some bruises and cuts on her forehead. Dale slammed her face into the tile counter. I've got officers checking local bars and other places he's known to frequent. We've checked with known associates and his family. No one has heard or seen him. Wherever he's been holed up, it's not in this county."

"Then try surrounding counties. Find the bastard before he kills someone." Owen spoke his worst fear. The words thickened the silence in the truck. Claire sat straight and rigid six inches away from him, staring out the windshield. His chilling demand made her turn away.

"We're working on it."

"It's been weeks. He's got to be close enough to slip into town and out to Claire's house easily and still get away. He's not a fucking brainiac. He's a drunk hothead. How the hell does he keep getting away with this shit?"

"You know how things go. He went into the joint a criminal and came out a better criminal. Either he's got someone helping him, or he's learned a few things about evading. His perfect timing can't hold up forever. He's going to make a mistake. We'll get him."

"You better fucking get him before I do."

Claire's hand settled on his thigh and squeezed. He put his hand over hers and took a deep breath to calm down.

"You know better than to make threats, counselor. Let me do my job."

"Do it better." Owen hit the END CALL button on his phone. "Fuck." He slammed the heel of his hand down on the steering wheel. Claire didn't remove her hand, but rubbed it up and down his leg, coaxing him to relax. Well, damnit, he didn't want to relax. He wanted to punch something. Preferably Dale's fucking face.

"It's not Dylan's fault," Claire said.

He sucked in another deep breath and let it out. "I know that. I'm just so damn frustrated. He hurt her again."

This time she did take her hand away and everything inside him went cold. She scooted away another few inches and his heart clenched, tightening his chest until he could barely breathe.

"You care about her a lot. I've seen the way you are with her. She's attached to you because you're good to her when the man who was supposed to be kind, her best friend, someone who loved her above all others, let her down and hurt her."

Owen pulled the truck over again and slammed the gear shift into park. He turned to face her, trying his level best not to yell.

"I am all those things to you that Dale should have been for Shannon."

Oh hell, he just told her he loves her. Did he? Yes. He did love her.

Not exactly the right time to tell her outright.

When he thought of the rest of his life, she was by his side. If something went well in his day, he wanted to share it with her. When things didn't go his way, he liked talking to her about it. Somehow, it made him feel better to share it with her. The good things became better. The bad seemed less significant. But she remained integral to his happiness.

Maybe he needed to think about it some more? Nope. Everything in him believed in that statement and what she'd said a man should be to his wife. He'd gone with instinct. Maybe it was too soon, too fast, too much to think about at a time like this, but he'd said it, and he'd let it hang for now.

When the timing was better, he'd say those three words he'd barely spoken at all in his life.

"I know you're pissed off that those two keep coming between us. When you're angry, I'm angry. When you're hurt, I'm hurt. When you pull away from me because of what that asshole did, it makes me even angrier. You and me, we're a team. If you want to go home, I'll turn the truck around and we'll go home."

"You want to check on her."

"I do, because she's my client and a friend. Nothing more. You are and will always be my priority. So if you want to go home together, I'm with you. Lord knows I'd like to forget any of this happened."

She scooted back across the seat and wrapped her arms around him, burying her face in his neck.

"I'm tired. I'm sorry she got hurt. I do want to go and see her and make sure she's okay. I just want this whole mess to be over. I know it's not your fault. I just don't understand why all this is happening to us."

Owen held her tight and felt the depth and weight of the sigh she let out. "I wish I could explain it."

Claire settled in next to him again, her head resting on his shoulder. He pulled back onto the two-lane road and headed for town once again. The silence gave him too much time to think. Her too, so he blurted out, "It's true, you know."

"You can't even say it."

He smiled, because he heard the teasing lilt to her voice. Oh yeah, she'd understood exactly what he'd said to her earlier.

"I will."

"Uh huh."

The quiet surrounded them again, nothing but the hum of the motor and tires spinning over the pavement. The town lights glowed up ahead. Claire shifted and looked up at him.

"It goes both ways, you know."

He bent and kissed her on the forehead. "I know."

She settled into his side, her left arm under his right, her hand on his thigh, his on hers, her right hand on his bicep. She held on tight and he gave her leg a squeeze to reassure her. This is how things should always be between them. Close. Connected. Easy.

These moments they shared were always short lived. They would be until the cops caught Dale and threw his ass in jail.

CLAIRE WALKED INTO the emergency room with Owen. She didn't really have a choice, since he'd taken her hand helping her from the truck and never let it go. She didn't mind. She loved it that he wanted to keep her close.

She still couldn't believe what he'd said—well, almost said. He meant it though. It took her off guard and made her think about how she really felt. Was it wishful thinking that he truly loved her? No. Owen wasn't the kind of man to say something like that and not mean it. Still, she'd hesitated to say it back. Probably because he'd held back from saying it outright himself. Of course, the moment hadn't been the best for something like that. It should be special. Not another moment ruined by Dale and Shannon and their continuing drama.

"I'm here to see Shannon Monoghan. I'm her lawyer."

"Mr. McBride, yes, I was just about to call you. She said you might drive her home."

"Um, of course," Owen said, giving Claire an apologetic look.

"It's fine. She needs a ride." She kissed his cheek to reassure him she meant it. "You're sweet."

"On you. Yes."

That made her smile and feel lighter.

He gave her hand a squeeze, but didn't let go. To the nurse he said, "Where is she?"

"Cubicle three, just over there." The nurse pointed them in the right direction and Owen led her across the crowded waiting room. So many people sick and in need of help at such an hour. Most of them looked tired and impatient. Claire could relate.

"Shannon," Owen called through the curtain.

"Owen. Oh, thank God, you're here."

They stepped past the blue drape. Shannon lay on her back on the gurney, her face about as white as the pillowcase she rested her head on. A large bruise spread over the right side of her face from her forehead down to her cheek. The impact injury to her forehead looked to be the worst of the damage, resulting in not only the ugly purple splotch, but a small nasty cut that had been stitched closed.

Since Owen let her enter first, Claire took Shannon's hand and held it for comfort. "How are you feeling?"

"Better now," Shannon answered, though her gaze remained locked on Owen, who stepped up to stand directly behind Claire. Shannon slipped her hand free of hers and grabbed for Owen's and held tight.

Claire restrained the jealous urge to rap Shannon's knuckles and say, "Hands off. He's mine."

"Did they find him?" Shannon asked, her voice breathy and desperate.

"No. No, they didn't. What happened?"

"I was doing some chores around the house. I took out the garbage, came back in, went to get ready for bed and remembered I didn't lock the door. I rushed back to lock it, but it was too late. He was already in the house."

"The police said you fought. He slammed your face into the kitchen counter." Claire prompted her to go on. The more information they had, the better their chance of finding him.

"It was nothing. The same old stuff we always fought about. He wanted me to forgive him and go back to him. I refused. He accused me of sleeping with you."

Owen slid his hand around Claire's side and rested it on her hip, his arm across her back. She took comfort in the simple gesture and leaned into him. Shannon caught the move but never took her gaze off Owen.

"By now he should know that I'm with Claire."

"I told him that, but he didn't believe me that you

aren't seeing the both of us. He said he's seen us together at your office, when you came to the house to help me with the security stuff, and when we met for coffee in the park."

What? Claire didn't know anything about any of this. Well, except for the meetings at his office for the restraining order and to catch up on the latest developments—though there weren't any—on tracking down Dale.

Owen didn't explain or look at her, but his hand tightened on her waist, holding her in place. She tried to break free, but short of ripping his hand away and storming off in a jealous-girlfriend huff, she couldn't break his hold. His silent way of telling her they'd discuss it later. Yeah, they would, and she'd give him what-for for keeping secrets.

Shannon must have seen her surprise and tried to explain herself.

"Oh, it was nothing but Owen being kind to me. Like he always is, seeing to this and that to help me out. He cares so much. I do so appreciate all the little things he does for me. Going above and beyond, well, that's what makes him such a good and successful lawyer. It's what makes him such a good friend."

The way Shannon said *friend* rankled. Claire would bet her store Shannon wanted something more with Owen. Maybe she did have reason to be concerned about the amount of time these two spent together.

It wasn't anything she did or said outright, but there was something there under the surface. The heat of rage built in her gut, but she tamped it down. She didn't want to show how much it hurt to think that she'd given everything of herself to this relationship and trusted Owen to see how hard that was for her to do. But she'd done it because she cared deeply for Owen. The only way to make a relationship work was to put her whole heart into it and trust that Owen didn't stomp on it.

Maybe you're making something out of nothing because of what the asshole did to you. His cheating and hurting you are clouding your judgment. You're letting Shannon's troubles and the way she relies on Owen during these hard times make you see things that aren't really there. Owen is a good and decent man. That's why you love him.

There, she'd said it. Or thought it. Whatever. The point is, he cares about people and doing the right thing. He'd never cheat on her.

Didn't he just not-in-so-many-words say he loves you? Yes. So stop looking for more trouble and be a friend to Shannon like Owen is.

She tried to refocus her wayward thoughts and smothered the unwarranted jealous-girlfriend bit.

"Owen is the best," she said, meaning it wholeheartedly.

"Shannon, did Dale say where he's been staying?"

"He didn't say much of anything besides yelling at me about how he's going to get back at you for doing the divorce and locking him up."

"He's completely out of his mind. I may have helped you with the divorce, but you wanted it."

"I guess he thought I'd stay with him like all the other

times. I probably would have if you hadn't convinced me that I deserve better."

"You do. We all deserve better than Dale," Claire added.

"Ah, he's not so bad when he's sober. Still, it's been a long time since he put the bottle down for any length of time. He's got demons."

"Yes, he does, and he keeps unleashing them on you and Claire. Did he say why he keeps going after Claire?"

"She's in the way," Shannon answered matter-of-factly.

Owen glared and gripped Claire's hip tighter. "What does that mean?"

"Oh, uh, I'm not real sure. Maybe he wants you to be alone because you took me from him."

"I didn't take you from him. You wanted to leave him for a chance at a better life."

"And I'll have it, too. They'll find Dale, and he'll get what he deserves. They'll lock him up for a long time for all the bad he's done, and the way he ruined my life. I could have gone to college and been something. Now, I cashier at the pet store and work odd jobs to make ends meet. What kind of life is that? I deserve a good husband. I'm going to have one, too."

"Well, I'm glad to see you've kept your resolve to stay clear of Dale," Owen said, giving Shannon's hand a squeeze. "Dale is in a lot of trouble. You don't need any more of that in your life."

"That's right. You'll make sure the police find Dale and punish him." Shannon gave Owen a soft smile that made him smile at her, too.

"Let's get you out of here and home. Do you have someone who can stay with you tonight?" Claire asked.

"Um, well, no. I'd finally gotten used to living on my own, then Dale gets out of jail and starts terrorizing me. Now, I don't feel safe there anymore."

"I know just how you feel." Claire put her hand on Shannon's arm for reassurance.

Shannon pulled her hand from Owen's and away from her and crossed them over her chest in a kind of hug. "I really don't want to be alone tonight," she admitted. "But I don't have anyone to call."

"I'll call your cousin, Trevor, to come and stay with you," Owen offered. "He's only a half hour away, and if Dale comes back, he can handle him."

"Trevor is away on one of his hunting trips. I'll be fine. Really."

"I could put you up . . ."

"Would you? I'd love to stay with you. Dale is sure to leave me alone then. No way he goes after you. You'd never let him get close to me. You'd kill him."

Claire stiffened at the thought of Shannon spending the night in Owen's home. With them.

Owen quickly adjusted Shannon's crazy way of thinking. "Shannon, that's not what I was saying. I could put you up in a motel for tonight."

"Oh, well, um, I thought . . ."

Claire glared. Yeah, she thought Owen would take care of her. Well, he would, but not in the same way he cared for her. Shannon better get that straight and soon, or she'd have to set her straight. This third-wheel shit was getting old.

"I don't have any of my things," Shannon said. "We'd have to go to my place anyway. You can't always be with me. On second thought, I'm sure I'll be fine there alone."

Damn right. Oh, the drama.

Still, the last word held so much loneliness, even Claire sympathized.

"If you're sure, I'll call the police and have an officer patrol your area tonight. We could call one of your friends to stay with you."

"I hate to bother them with my troubles."

"If they are your friends, they won't mind," Owen coaxed.

"No. Really. Dale is probably off drinking himself into oblivion. He won't be back tonight."

Claire wished she shared Shannon's definitive attitude. Then again, she knew Dale and his ways.

"If Dale is so angry with Owen, why wouldn't he confront him? After all, that's what he came to my house to do the first time he attacked me."

Shannon stared blankly and offered no answer for a good fifteen seconds. "Well, um, he was probably drunk that night and feeling like he could do anything. Now he sees that pestering you and me is an easier way to rile Owen."

Owen sympathized with Shannon, but it annoyed the hell out of him that her life kept crashing into his. He wanted to get her home so he could finish this night with Claire in his arms. He'd tried so hard to give Claire a carefree night out filled with good food and wine. A night to take her mind off things, but again things had turned ugly. Not Shannon's fault, but still, he'd had plans for himself and Claire at home alone. Again he had to put things on hold with Claire to deal with this mess with Shannon.

"You're probably right," Owen said. "I'll get the nurse and see if the doctor has discharged you."

Owen gave Claire a quick kiss on the head and left back through the drape.

"So, um, you two are seeing each other all the time now?" Shannon asked.

"Yes, since the night Dale came to my house."

"He was supposed to be my future," she said sadly.

Maybe at one time Shannon believed Dale was her future, but after all that happened, why not be happy to be rid of him? Well, hard to move on when he kept coming back and wreaking havoc in her life.

"I know what it's like to start over. You'll find someone new. Someone who is kind and loves you the way you deserve to be loved."

Owen drew the curtain back and allowed the nurse to roll the wheelchair to Shannon's bed. Her smile bloomed at the sight of Owen. Claire wanted to shake her head. Shannon thought of Owen as her white knight. Well, she could think it all she wanted, but in reality, Owen loved Claire. She held tight to that thought, even when Owen helped Shannon from the bed and into the wheelchair and Shannon held fast to Owen's hand all the way out to the truck he'd moved to the ER entrance.

Somehow Shannon ended up in the middle seat next to Owen. When he climbed in the truck behind the wheel, he looked over at Claire and gave her a surprised but resigned look, like he didn't know how that happened. She had to admit, Shannon sure did seem like a lost puppy, running after Owen like he was her everything. Claire understood her need to hold on to something good, but she'd have to learn to let go now that Claire was in the picture. Boundaries needed to be respected when a man was seeing someone. Shannon should understand that and adhere to them. If she didn't, Claire intended to remind her. Nicely, of course, but she wasn't going to sit back and watch another woman flirt with her . . . boyfriend. Wow, that sounded so strange. He seemed like so much more than that simple, youthful term in her life.

They really did have something special.

Settled, she let out a sigh, propped her elbow on the window, and watched the road disappear beneath the truck. The silence stirred her from her thoughts. She glanced at Owen. He leaned against the door. Shannon had fallen asleep and leaned against his shoulder. He glanced over at her and Claire gave him a smile to let him know it didn't bother her. He frowned and shook his head, not liking the situation or her so far away. She smiled even more, making him frown deeper.

She went back to watching the road and the houses that got fewer and far between as they left town. They didn't go too far before a large white house appeared on the right. Owen took the drive and passed it, slowing on the rutted, dirt road. The truck bounced and jolted. Shannon remained asleep, despite being thrown into Owen's side by a particularly deep rut.

"I don't know how she makes it down this road in her little car."

"Unlike your hulking truck, her little car can maneuver around these craters."

That earned her the first laugh she'd heard from him in hours. The laughs had dwindled over the last few weeks with the Dale storm cloud gathering overhead, threatening a hurricane any time things started to get back to normal.

Owen pulled up in front of a small cabin with four stairs leading up to a wide porch. A single bare bulb cast an eerie glow over the dark exterior. The place couldn't have been more than eight hundred square feet. A dead juniper stood on each side of the stairs. The rest of the yard was nothing but overgrown weeds and bare patches of dirt. A large flattop rock sat beneath an old oak. She'd have planted some pretty flowers and used the rock as a bench to sit and admire the yard. The dark brown cabin could use a lighter touch of trim. A bright white or softer cream. Right now, the windows stood as black eyes in a darker face that didn't welcome but made you leery.

Home should be a comfort, not something that caused intimidation and foreboding. Claire's spirit dropped thinking of Shannon out here alone.

Owen gently patted Shannon's knee to wake her. Her head rolled and she came awake with a start. "Huh. What?"

"Hey, sleepyhead. You're home." Owen kept his voice low and calm.

"This place is a dump. I'd love to move into town, or at

least a bigger, prettier house. Like yours," she added. "It's so big and bright and cheerful."

Claire couldn't argue, she loved Owen's place. It had great bones, and slowly but surely Owen was fixing it up. He even asked her opinion for projects he'd like to do in the future. Several items of her clothing hung in his closet. She'd left some spare makeup and toiletries in his bathroom. He'd done the same at her house. Over the last weeks, they spent more nights together than they did apart. Of course, Owen had to be home at certain times to feed and care for his beloved horses and cats.

"You didn't leave the outside lights on," Owen said.

"Someone must have turned off the switch."

"The motion lights are good protection. If Dale tries to come to the door, the lights might scare him off, or at least alert you that someone is near the house."

"Did they go on when Dale showed up earlier?" Claire asked.

"I-I'm not sure. Everything happened so fast, I didn't get a chance to see."

"You should get a dog. Living out here alone, a dog would alert you if someone came to the house." Owen had made the same suggestion before, but Shannon never considered it. For someone who worked at a pet shop, she didn't seem inclined to wanting a pet.

"I'd have to feed and walk the dog. I just don't have the time. My work schedule is erratic."

"Think about it," Owen said. "You'd have someone to come home to and you'd have a friend and companion for times like these."

"I have friends. I just don't want them to know my business. It's bad enough Dale hits me, I don't need everyone's pity and thinking I'm weak. I'm not weak."

"No one said you are." Claire rested her hand on Shannon's arm. She pulled it away, not wanting her comfort. "You're caught in a bad situation. Once Dale is apprehended, things will go back to normal. You won't have to be scared or worried again. You can live your life and be happy."

"I can't wait for that day to finally come."

Owen slid from the truck seat and offered his hand to Shannon to exit on his side. She slid across the bench seat and stepped down and fell right into Owen's chest.

"Sorry. I'm not very steady after the meds they gave me at the hospital. I'm sleepy and fuzzy."

Owen held her arm to steady her. Claire stayed in the truck. Tired of this whole situation, she'd let Owen take Shannon inside and get her settled.

"Claire, honey, come with us. I don't want to leave you alone out here."

"I'll be fine. I'll lock up the truck if it makes you feel better."

"You with me will make me feel better." His adamant tone caught her attention and made her exit the truck to follow him into the house.

Even worse than the outside, the furnishings were thrift-store castoffs in dark browns and blue-and-cream plaids. The coffee table had various size nicks and gouges to go with the overlaid water-ring stains.

The small kitchen didn't look much better, with its

cream tiles and dark brown grout. The cabinets needed either a coat of paint or a good grease fire to burn them to ashes. Either would be an improvement.

Shannon kept things neat and tidy, but everything looked old and shabby. She didn't have the know-how or the extra money to make over some of the better pieces or buy something new. It was sad. The whole place felt sad.

Claire wanted to go home, curl up in her soft and comfortable bed, surround herself with her pretty and bright things, and make love to Owen, the best thing in her life. Everything inside of her wanted to hold on to him. If she had nothing else but him, she'd have everything.

"Owen, honey, we need to go," she said.

She'd never called him by a sweet name, and it got his attention. He stared at her, his eyes going dark with a predatory stare, trying to read her How could she explain to him everything she was feeling? It just wasn't possible. She'd show him. In her bed or his, didn't matter.

She needed him.

Owen reached up and cupped her face, his eyes going soft. He leaned in and kissed her on the forehead. That's all. Just the simple touch of his lips to her skin, but she felt the extra second he took and the way his fingers softly caressed her cheek when he released her.

Yeah, he understood her need for him. She felt the same thing from him.

"Thank you for driving me home." Shannon's voice intruded on the moment Claire and Owen shared with her standing next to them.

"I'll just be a minute, sweetheart. Let me check the back door lock and make sure the motion lights are on."

Claire nodded. Since the place was so small, it was easy to watch him go to the back door and check the deadbolt and the slide lock. He hit the switch for the lights and they came on, a bright glare against the window over the sink. Not much to see at the back of the house but more weeds and pastureland beyond.

"Thanks for being such a good sport tonight, Claire. I guess I messed up your date."

"Date?" Claire asked, confused.

"Dinner with Owen."

"Oh, yeah. We had a great time. But how did you . . ."

"Owen mentioned it."

"Mentioned what?" Owen asked from the living room window. He checked the lock and the stick in the frame preventing it from sliding open for added protection.

"Our dinner date," Claire said, wondering why he'd mention it to Shannon at all.

"Dinner was good. The rest of tonight, not so much. I'm so sorry that son of a bitch hasn't been caught yet." Owen checked out the window by the front door and smiled. "Cops are here. A car will sit out front tonight. They'll do regular patrols out this way until Dale is caught and locked up, so if you see a car approaching, don't panic. Be vigilant, but don't automatically assume it's Dale."

Shannon walked to Owen and grabbed his forearm, looking up at him. "Thank you so much for everything."

"No thanks necessary." He gave her shoulder a friendly squeeze. "You should put some ice on that eye. Get the prescription filled tomorrow for the pain meds if you need them. Call me if anything else happens."

"I will."

Owen held out his hand to Claire and she took it, happy to leave.

"Lock up behind us. You should sleep easy tonight with the cops outside and the pain meds you took at the hospital."

"I'll try. Thank you again," Shannon called from the porch.

Claire and Owen waved back at her, but Owen didn't climb into the truck until Shannon closed the door and they heard the snick of the locks slide into place.

"Those are some bright motion lights."

"I got them cheap at the hardware store. They do the job."

"If she remembers to turn them on."

"They should stay on all the time if she leaves the switch in the house on. I don't know why she turned it off," he said, frustrated.

"Maybe the police turned it off by accident."

"I doubt it," he said, turning the truck onto the rutted road once again.

They hit the main road and Owen kept the speed slow, so he could talk to her. "I'm really sorry about tonight."

"You have no reason to be sorry. You did a good thing, picking her up from the hospital and seeing her home."

"I wish this whole business was over and you and I could move on with our lives."

She wrapped herself around his arm and snuggled

close to him. "I think things between us are moving in the right direction. I'm not going to let anything derail us or make me second-guess you. I've done that too much already."

"You saved me tonight."

"You didn't want to go in her house alone with her."

"She tends to be touchy-feely. After the comment about coming to stay with me, I didn't want to endure any more awkward moments. I've tried to make it clear she's my client. Nothing more. I want to help her, but . . ."

"She makes things weird and awkward," Claire finished for him.

"And she does stupid things like turning off the security lights."

"And forgetting to lock the back door when she knows Dale is still a threat to her."

Owen glanced at her and frowned. "See, it's not just me. Things with those two just don't add up to normal. Her growing need to have me intervene and protect her is getting uncomfortable and it's interfering with you and me."

"She's enamored with you because you saved her. Once things settle down and your interactions with her taper off, she'll find her bearings and someone else to shower with her affections."

"I certainly feel like I need a shower. I don't like what's happening with Dale, or her. This whole thing has me on edge. I feel like I'm missing something. Nothing adds up."

"He has to know the police are looking for him after the attack on me and all the vandalism. Why would he take a chance and come back here? What does he want to do, run away with her in some grand romantic gesture to get her back? He has to know he'll go to jail and they'll be apart again."

"Exactly. I'm glad I'm not the only one thinking he's crazy for pulling this shit." Owen rubbed his hand over his head. "If he's pissed at me, why not come after me like the first time? What purpose does it serve to go after you? All it's done is draw us closer together and piss me off even more."

"Maybe he's gearing up for some kind of showdown with you."

"Again, to what end? Picking a fight with me is not going to make Shannon go back to him."

"Maybe it's all just a guy thing. He thinks you slept with his wife and he wants retribution."

"When you see us together, would you think we're sleeping together?"

Claire hid a smile and enlightened him to some of Shannon's tactics to gain his attention. "Anyone who sees the two of you together is immediately drawn to Shannon and the way she looks at you."

"What are you talking about?" Owen pulled the truck into his driveway and cut the engine.

"She looks at you like you're dessert, and she can't wait to take a bite."

"She does not." He smiled and chuckled, uncomfortable. Probably because he knew she was right, but didn't want to admit it to her.

"Yes, she does. Take the scene at the hospital. She

clung to you." Claire opened the truck door and got out, but turned back to Owen before he exited. "She invited herself to stay with you."

Owen met her at the front of the truck and took her hand. "The only woman staying with me is you." He rushed her, bending at the waist and hitting her middle with his shoulder. She reflexively fell over his back and he stood tall, smacking her on the bottom. She hung down his back and smacked him on the ass.

"Put me down."

"I will. In our bed."

Our bed. Not his bed. Their bed.

It took some doing with her up and over his shoulder, but he got the door opened and slammed it shut with his foot. Two steps away from the door, he turned back to flick the locks.

"I can't even take my woman to bed without making sure the doors are locked up first," he grumbled, taking the stairs without any hesitation due to her added weight.

"Do you have any idea how sexy it is that you can carry me up these stairs without even breathing hard."

"Oh, honey, you'll have me breathing hard soon."

She laughed and rubbed both hands down his ass and thighs and raked her fingers back up. He retaliated, placing one big hand over her rump and squeezing. He slid his hand over her and his thumb traced the seam of her jeans down between her legs. He pressed, then circled his thumb over her center, finding that spot that made her sigh and melt. Two could play that game. Despite being upside down with her hair hanging to his feet, she slid her hands around his hips to the fly of his slacks, finding the rigid length of him. She worked both her hands over his hard cock.

"Ah, God, sweetheart, I want you so damn bad."

She laughed. "Then why are you just standing next to the bed? Put me down."

"Promise not to stop touching me."

"Put me down and find out."

She expected it, but when he flipped her over and she landed on the bed with a bounce, she gasped and laughed at the same time. He landed on top of her before the bed even stopped moving. His mouth took possession of hers, his tongue diving deep. She loved it when he was like this. All possession, demand, and heat.

Clothes disappeared in a hurried peeling of layers that resulted in tangled arms and legs and mouths tasting and licking and nipping at exposed skin.

Everything about Owen changed the second he thrust into her hard and deep. She expected the urgent pace he'd set to continue until they were both panting and rocketing into the stars. Instead, he went still in her arms and stared down at her. With a gentle swipe of his finger over her forehead, he pushed her hair from her face and met her gaze.

"I mean it."

No explanation needed. He loved her. Saying it didn't come easy for him. Maybe that's why she believed him, even without the actual words. Anyone could say it. People said it all the time without really feeling it. Owen had expressed how much he felt in those three words. When he gave her the other three words, they'd be forever.

"I believe you."

He needed to hear her say it. It set him off. Their lovemaking was wild. All grappling hands and a desperate need to be close. Skin to skin. He couldn't get enough of her. He demanded she give him everything. She gave it willingly, knowing exactly how he felt, because there'd been a moment in that little cabin where she'd needed to feel him and the love they shared and know that nothing would ever take this feeling away.

He rolled her over the bed and she ended up on top of him. She straddled his hips and rose above him on her hands, her hips grinding into his as he thrust up and deep. His mouth clamped on to her breast. His tongue swept over her hard nipple and he sucked hard. His hands gripped her hips, urging her to move with him. He dipped one hand between them, his finger circling the slick nub where they were joined. Her body tensed and tightened around him, and he thrust deep, spilling himself inside of her. The heat he'd built inside of her exploded. His hands gripped her thighs and squeezed as aftershocks rocked both their bodies. She collapsed on top of him, their breaths sawing in and out.

Owen wrapped his arms around her and held her tight to his chest. He buried his face in her neck and hair.

"Hey, honey, I'm not going anywhere," she reassured him.

"I don't want anything bad to happen to you."

"Nothing is going to happen to me."

"I wish I believed that."

Chapter Twenty-Nine

CLAIRE WORKED IN the barn, feeding Bo and Luke, dumping the old water from their buckets and replacing it with fresh. She'd grown to love the horses, though she remained cautious around them. In her head, she called them "the two old coots." They lumbered in and out of their stalls and to the pastures at their own pace. When Owen tried to get them to move faster, the crotchety pair stopped in their tracks until Owen stopped pulling on them. Watching him with them made her smile. He had such affection for them. They reminded him of the good times in his youth. Free. Wild. Riding the wind on their backs with Brody, escaping whatever hell their father had in store for them if they stayed home.

Finished brushing down Luke, she gave him a pat on the shoulder and rubbed behind his left ear the way he liked.

"All right, old man. You're all set. Eat your lunch, and

I'll let you out into the pasture when I finish with your brother."

She ducked under the rope at the stall entrance and went across the aisle to Bo's stall. He stood in the entrance, watching her with Luke.

"Jealous, big guy? Don't you worry. I'll brush you down, too."

Bo nickered and scuffed his foot in the straw. He leaned his head over the rope barricade and looked over at the cupboard next to his stall.

Claire smiled. "You're so smart. Yes, I'll get your favorite brush. Spoiled," she told him, rubbing the white diamond on his forehead. She peeled a spearmint from the roll on the counter and handed it over to the eager horse.

She ducked under the rope and grabbed the huge blue bucket from the corner of the stall, hauling it out to the yard to dump the remaining water. She dragged the bucket back to Bo's stall and drew the hose over. Bo nibbled at her hair while she filled it. He never actually ate or pulled it. Just played with the long strands.

Bucket full, she pushed on Bo's side to get him to move out of her way. Easygoing and amicable most of the time, he stepped back so she could get his food bucket off the holder on the wall. She tossed in a flake of mixed grass and hay and a scoop of crushed oats just like she'd seen Owen do so many times over the last weeks. She hung the bucket back up, and Bo snorted his thanks and lumbered over for lunch.

Careful when moving around his backside, she didn't

see the rake and stepped on it. The handle shot up and cracked her in the face over her right eye. Instinct kicked in, and she grabbed the handle to keep it from hitting her again or falling to the ground where Bo could step on it and hurt himself. The horse shied at the quick movement and hit her on the side with his hip, sending her backward off balance. She hit her head on the stall wall and caught the outside of her shoulder on a nail, ripping her T-shirt and skin in a long line. Blood dripped down her arm, but she ignored it, trying to move with the rake in her hand and Bo stomping and shifting to see where she'd gone. Nervous, the horse huffed and stomped his front foot.

Adrenaline gave her the strength to stand up and move to the front of the stall. She jumped back a step when she saw someone standing in the entrance.

"Shannon? What are you doing here?"

"I came to see Owen. I heard the ruckus and thought he was in here. Are you okay?"

"Fine," she said automatically.

"You shouldn't leave rakes lying around like that. Someone could get hurt."

The thing is, Claire hadn't used the rake. In fact, she didn't know what it was doing in Bo's stall. Owen was meticulous about the care and feeding of his horses. He'd never be so careless as to leave a rake on the floor in the stall. In fact, she hadn't seen it in the straw when she watered and fed Bo. Maybe she was too distracted with the horses and her remaining trepidation around them, but she didn't think so. Something seemed off. Owen didn't normally use a rake to clean out the stall. He used some red fork thing with many tines to scoop and pitch the straw into the wheelbarrow.

"Your eye looks bad. It's going to bruise. Did you break your brow bone?"

Claire raised a shaking hand to her face and felt the welt rising under her eyebrow. "No. I don't think so. It stings and throbs, though."

"I know." Shannon touched her forehead and the fading bruise from Dale's attack last weekend. The stitches were gone, but the small scar remained. Claire imagined the internal scars would never fade.

"Owen is up at the house on a call. One of his clients," Claire explained. Shaken, she rambled and stopped herself. She set the rake outside the stall door and turned to check on Bo. He lazily ate his food, keeping watch on her after every bite. She went to him and gave him a pat on the shoulder. As much to reassure him everything was all right as to make herself do it and not be afraid of him. He'd done nothing wrong. She'd spooked him.

"I'll come back and brush you in a little while."

She needed a few minutes to gather her wits and tend to the wound on her shoulder. She ducked under the rope at the door and checked both ways down the aisle. Shannon had left to go up to the house. Of course. No sense waiting for Claire when she really wanted to see Owen.

Claire stepped out of the barn and into the bright sunshine. Only about twenty paces behind Shannon, the woman hustled up the porch steps and rapped on the front door. Owen answered with a confused look on his face. He looked past Shannon and caught her eye. Still talking on the phone, he held up a finger to Shannon to wait. It surprised Claire to see him step out of the house and close the door behind him. He stood on the porch with Shannon, but turned his back on her and finished his call.

By the time she reached the stairs, he said, "I'll call you back, Tom. Something came up and I need a few minutes to deal with it." The clipped tone made Shannon wince. Claire wondered at his annoyance, too.

"Oh my God, Claire. What happened to you, sweetheart?" Owen took her face in his hands and tilted her head so he could get a good look at her eye and forehead.

"Did you leave a rake in Bo's stall?"

"Hell, no. Why, what happened?"

"I stepped on it and the handle whacked me in the head."

"What the hell? Was it the pitchfork I use to clean the stalls? Maybe I . . . no, I put it away. I'm sure of it."

"No, this was a metal rake."

"The one for the pasture?"

"I guess."

"What happened to your arm?" His fingers left her face to gently trace the cut and pull her shirt away from the wound. "That looks nasty."

"It hurts. Bo got spooked and hit me. I stumbled and fell to the floor and hit my head and shoulder on the stall wall. A loose nail caught me. You need to hammer it back in or pull it out. You don't want it to catch Bo's leg."

"You're worried about my horse. Look at you, honey. Come inside, so I can get you some ice to put on that."

"I'll be fine."

"How the hell did the rake end up in Bo's stall? He could have been hurt."

"I don't know. All I did was feed him and Luke and give them new water."

"You did all that?"

"Well, you were on the phone so long. I know how you hate to feed them late. They get so upset when you don't make it down to the barn to see them on time."

"Look at you, sweetheart, you're becoming a real ranch hand." He scanned her from her face down her white T-shirt and jeans to her feet. "You're wearing my boots."

She giggled and glanced down at her feet stuffed into his dark brown cowboy boots. The ones he wore to tend to the horses. "I didn't want to get my shoes dirty, so I borrowed yours. I have to kind of shuffle to keep them on. You've got some big feet, cowboy."

Owen smiled and for the first time acknowledged Shannon, standing next to them waiting. "What are you doing here?" he asked, surprised to see her.

"This place is amazing, Owen. I love the house and barn."

"Thanks, but why are you here?"

"Um, well, I tried to call your office because I know the calls forward to your cell."

"Yes, which is how my clients contact me in an emergency. So, what's up?"

"Ah, could we discuss this in private."

"Is this business or personal?"

Shannon gave Owen a brilliant smile. "I wish it were personal, but I need your help with a legal matter."

"Is this about Dale?"

"In a way, but I'd rather discuss it privately." Shannon glanced in Claire's direction.

"Can't this wait until business hours on Monday?"

"It's important. I'm here. Won't you help me?"

"I need to see to Claire's head and arm first."

"Honey, I'm fine," she assured him.

"No, you aren't. You're bleeding."

"I'll go in and wash up."

"If you feel dizzy, or . . ."

"Honey, I'm fine," she said, placing her hand on his chest. He covered it with his and held her close with his other arm.

"You're sure?"

"Help Shannon. I'll see you inside when you're done."

"Brody called and invited us to dinner tonight."

"Sounds great. What did the girls ask us to bring?"

He smiled and shook his head. "They want your double chocolate-chunk brownies."

She laughed and some of the tension in his gut let loose.

"Of course they do. We'll have to stop by my place to make them. I don't think your pantry has everything I'll need."

"Check. You made the last batch here, so we may have everything."

"I'll check." She walked right out of his boots at the door. He had to pry them off, but her little feet barely filled them. He couldn't explain the thrill in his gut at seeing her wearing his things. He loved finding her in the kitchen in the morning in nothing but one of his T-shirts or dress shirts. She said she liked the smell of him. Well, he loved everything about her. He needed to tell her. Soon.

Things between them moved so fast. Why the hell was he waiting? It wasn't some big secret she didn't know. They'd skirted the subject several times. He knew she loved him. She knew he loved her. So why the hell didn't they say it to each other?

Because then it would be real, and they'd have to deal with it. Well, he didn't think it required any great change in his life. He'd tell her. She'd stay with him. They'd build a life together.

Shit. They'd build a life together, which meant they'd get married. Is that what he really wanted? Hell yes. He hated the nights they spent apart. The best thing in his life was going to bed with her in his arms and waking up to her smiling face in the morning. He didn't want to lose that. He wanted it every day and night. As it was, she barely spent any time at her place. Half her stuff was still in boxes. All they had to do was move them here and unpack them.

"Owen, I'm waiting," Shannon said, letting her impatience show in her eyes and frown.

Owen shook off his thoughts of joining his life with Claire's. Well, his life was already tied to hers in a profound way if the sight of her bleeding made him this upset and angry. He'd like to know how that rake got in Bo's stall, but pushed those thoughts aside and focused on Shannon now that Claire had escaped into the house.

"Can we go inside and talk?"

"Let's take a seat on the porch." He held out his hand to indicate she precede him down the porch to the two rocking chairs set up by the windows with a table between. Normally, he'd have offered a glass of iced tea to a guest, but this was business and he intended to keep it that way. Here, on the porch, and not in his house that he now shared with Claire.

Like a gentleman, he waited for Shannon to take her seat before he took his own. He set his cell phone on his thigh and settled back to listen to whatever she found so important she'd come all the way out here looking for him.

"Tell me what's going on, Shannon."

"I'm being evicted." She dug out a folded stack of papers from her denim tote bag.

He took the papers and read through the first letter from her landlord and the attached lease Dale signed and renewed each year.

"You've got thirty days to vacate. The lease is up and it is within the landlord's right to ask you to leave without renewing the lease."

"I see that, but she says it's because of all the trouble Dale has caused. He's gone now. I tried to tell her, but she won't listen to me."

"Let me ask you something. Do you really want to stay in that house after everything that's happened? You could get an apartment in town, be closer to work and your friends. You'd save money on gas and probably pay less in rent each month."

"Well, to tell you the truth, I hadn't really thought of that. It would be expensive to move. I don't have the first and last deposit."

"According to this agreement, you'd get part if not all of the deposit back if the house is still in good shape and doesn't need any repairs."

"Well, Dale put a hole in the bedroom wall and busted the door handle on a couple of the other doors. I could probably patch the wall. There's some leftover paint in the shed I could use to paint the bedroom. I could buy a couple of new doorknobs at the hardware store. Maybe you could help me put them in."

A ripple of suspicion washed through him. She wanted to draw closer to him, but he wanted distance so he and Claire could live their life together free of all this drama and meddling. That's why he didn't want her in their house. This was their place, where they could be together, alone and happy. He didn't like having Shannon intrude on their time together.

Where Dale was concerned, he'd help Shannon any way possible, but for this kind of stuff, she needed to learn to do things for herself. "The doorknobs come with simple instructions. All you'd need is a screwdriver. You can do it yourself," he encouraged.

"Oh, well, I could probably do that."

"Of course you can. A smart woman like you can do anything. You might even have fun, picking out a new place to live, finding something that suits you without having to consider anyone else's opinion. If you move, maybe Dale won't find you so easily."

"He knows where I work. He could just follow me home."

"Always be vigilant. Never stop looking over your shoulder. You don't want him to catch you off guard."

"I'm so tired of being afraid."

"I know you are. I'm afraid Claire feels the same when she's not with me."

"Yes, well, she has you and I don't. I'm alone."

"No, you aren't. I'll help you any way I can. As your attorney," he added to make things clear. "A change might be just what you need to close the chapter on Dale and start fresh."

"I planned to start something new, but this isn't what I'd thought to do. Still, it makes sense, and really, what choice do I have. She's kicking me out."

"Maybe you should look at this as an opportunity to change your life for the better."

"Better is definitely what I want. You're right. I'll have to speed up my plans, but this could work. I'll have to start planning what to do over the next couple of weeks to get ready to move into my new place."

"Sounds like you've got some place in mind."

"I do. I thought it'd be a little while longer before I could make it happen, but I'll just have to adjust and make it happen sooner."

"That's the spirit. Make things happen. Don't just sit back and let them. That's a great way to think."

"As always, thank you for your help. I'm sorry to bother you on a Sunday. What with you and Claire off to a family dinner and all."

"I'm glad I could help. Now, if you'll excuse me, I need to check on Claire and call my other client back."

"Of course. Again, sorry to barge in on you."

"Go home and start making those plans. Make sure you can afford your new place. Let me know if you need me to talk to your landlady about the deposit."

He stood with her. Before he knew what she intended, she wrapped her arms around his middle and hugged him.

"Thank you for always helping me."

"You're welcome."

She leaned up to kiss him—on the lips or cheek, he couldn't be sure—but he took her shoulders and set her away.

"I'm with Claire," he said, gently reminding her and making it clear nothing was going to happen between them.

"I know. But friends can kiss goodbye, especially after everything we've been through together."

"I don't kiss my friends."

"You kiss Rain," she pointed out, not letting this go.

"Rain is closer to me than a friend. She's family. While I appreciate your friendship, you are still my client."

"Right. Need to keep a professional distance. I get it. Still, once they lock up Dale, I won't need a lawyer anymore, and we can just be friends."

The hug and almost kiss told him she wanted much more than friendship. He'd made it clear telling her he and Claire were a couple. He didn't want to hurt her feelings by being any more direct that he didn't want her. If she persisted, he'd make himself clear with a blunt refusal. If need be, he'd tell her to find another lawyer, too.

He put his hand to the small of her back to escort her off the porch and to her car. She leaned back into his hand, so he took it away and stopped at the bottom of the stairs.

"Drive safe. If you hear from Dale, call me and the police immediately."

"I will. Have a nice evening."

"You too."

Owen didn't wait for her to get to her car. Not when she'd invited herself to his home on the weekend with something that could so obviously have waited until Monday's business hours. He'd given her enough of his time. Besides, he needed to check on Claire and see for himself that she was okay.

Chapter Thirty

Owen found Claire sitting on the toilet in the bathroom, her shirt off, hair draped over her right shoulder, and Pumpkin sitting on her back, watching Claire clean the long gash on her arm.

"Honey, are you okay?"

She looked up at him, but didn't smile. "Can you take the cat? She won't leave me alone."

Owen grabbed the redheaded beast and held her up. "Stop making a fuss. She'll be okay." He set the cat on the counter, but she jumped onto Claire's back again. Luckily, she kept her claws sheathed, or Claire would have more cuts to contend with.

Pumpkin hissed at the cotton ball and head-bumped Claire.

"Yes, baby, you're sweet and this stuff stings like hell. I don't like it either."

Owen grabbed the cat and set her in Claire's lap. He

took the cotton ball, wet with witch hazel, and cleaned the cut out for her.

"This will take down the swelling and help keep this from getting infected," Owen said, dabbing at the cut and blowing on it to take away the sting.

"What did she want?"

"She's being evicted."

"Maybe that's a good thing. She can start fresh somewhere else."

"That's what I told her."

"She didn't need to come here on a Sunday and speak to you privately about that."

"No. She didn't. I think she was embarrassed to say anything in front of you."

"She wanted to be alone with you."

He didn't deny it. Over the last week, she'd shown up more than once out of the blue. At the grocery store. When he walked back to his office after going to Claire's shop to see her in the afternoon. At the pet store, she'd trailed after him, supposedly to help him gather what he needed, but it wasn't necessary. She didn't do that for anyone else who came in to pick up supplies.

"I still don't understand how this happened."

"Neither do I. I'd already been into the stall to feed and water Bo."

"Which I appreciate, by the way."

"I never saw the rake. It's not the one you use to clean the stalls. On my way back up to the house, I saw that one hanging in the tool area. You keep everything so neat and orderly. I don't know how it got there."

"Was Shannon there when it happened?"

"She'd just come in, looking for you. To her disappointment, she found me."

He gave her neck a squeeze. "No one could be disappointed to find you, sweetheart."

"Right."

She handed him a gauze pad. He pressed it to her arm and took the strip of tape she tore for him, securing the pad at the top and again at the bottom with the other piece of tape she handed him. Finished, he kissed her shoulder above the bandage.

He scanned her face and grabbed another cotton ball and wet it with the witch hazel. He dabbed at the bruise and small cut.

"This hurt?"

"Yeah."

"How's your vision?"

"You're still the most handsome man I've ever seen."

He smiled and gave her a kiss. "This doesn't need a bandage, though people are going to think I beat you."

"No one would ever think that of you, honey." She pet Pumpkin and sighed. "I'm tired. I think I'll lay down for a little while. I'll make the brownies later."

"You sure you're okay?"

"Fine. You kept me up late last night again. You woke me early when you left to feed the horses. Oh, you need to brush Bo. I didn't get a chance to do it."

"He'll wait until tonight. I'm worried about you."

"Don't you have to call Tom back?"

"Trying to get rid of me isn't going to change the fact I know something is upsetting you. Is it Shannon?"

"It's the whole thing. When is it going to be just you and me?"

"It's you and me right now. It's going to be me and you always. I promise. I was thinking earlier about us and how we've been going back and forth between your place and mine. Maybe it doesn't need to be like that."

"I don't understand. You don't want me to stay here?"

"No. I want you to stay here all the time."

"What are you saying?"

"Move in with me. Half your stuff is still in boxes. The rest we'll toss in my truck and bring here."

"You want me to give up my house?"

"Not if you don't want to. I just thought you might want to be here with me."

"I do."

Well, that took a load off and made his thrashing heart slow down again. "It's too soon for you. I get it. Forget I asked."

"It's just that I worked so hard to buy that place. It's mine."

"I get it. You've worked really hard to bounce back after what that asshole did to you. You don't have to sell the place. Keep it, but move in with me. You could rent it and make some extra cash."

"You really want me to move in with you."

"I really do. The best part of my day is being with you." He brushed his fingertips over her cheek and gave her a soft kiss. "You're tired. Take a nap. Sleep on it. You don't have to give me an answer right this minute. In fact, don't answer me until it's a yes."

She laughed, stood, and cupped his face, bringing him down for a kiss. She held him off an inch from her face. "Yes."

He crushed her to his chest and kissed her long and deep. Overwhelmed, he smoothed his hands down her bare back to her hips and over her bottom, pulling her closer, snug against him. His hard cock pressed to her belly. She went up on tiptoe and held him close, her arms locked around his neck. He slid his hands up her back and undid her bra, swiping his fingertips up her spine and making her arch into him. He put his hands under her arms and lifted her off her feet, breaking the kiss they shared in favor of trailing kisses down her neck to her breasts when he raised her high enough. She wrapped her legs around his waist and held tight, giving him the perfect opportunity to walk her back into the bedroom, put one knee on the bed, and lay her out beneath him.

She reached over his back and pulled his shirt up and right over his head. He let go of her long enough to work his arms free and slide her bra off her arms.

"You know, it really works in my favor when you're half-naked when I come up to see you."

She laughed, then gasped when he took her nipple into his mouth and sucked hard, just the way she liked it. He cupped her other breast in his palm and molded it to his hand. He wanted more and trailed kisses down her flat belly. He circled her navel with his tongue and over her soft skin along the hem of her jeans. A quick tug on the button and zipper and he had them undone and his lips pressed to the new patch of exposed skin above her purple lace panties.

"I so love your taste in lingerie. Like a present to unwrap, I love the pretty packaging, but what lays beneath is what I truly want."

He slid off the bed, taking her jeans and panties right off her long, toned legs. She smiled up at him and laughed when he reached down, spread his fingers wide, and traced a path from her ribs down her belly and deeper until he turned his hand and slid one finger into her slick heat.

"Owen."

Just that, his name on her lips and he was lost. He'd do anything for her, and right now he wanted to hear her moan and feel her come apart at his lips. He leaned down to her and settled between her widespread legs. He kissed his way up her thigh to her hip and detoured to her center, his finger working in and out of her core. He slid his finger deep and licked the wet nub, and she went wild, tilting her hips to his marauding mouth. He liked her this way. So open and giving and lost in the moment with him. He liked it even more when he was riding that high with her, so he licked and laved and took her to the brink.

Ready for him. He was more than ready for her. He shoved his jeans and boxers down and kicked them off. He rose above her and entered her hard and fast. She shattered beneath him on a deep moan, arching off the bed, her breasts pressed to his chest. He kissed her, long and deep, seated in her heat, her body clenched around his. He held perfectly still, desperately trying to wait her out. His tongue swept over hers, and she melted back into the bed. He moved, pulling out and thrusting deep, taking her up again, but this time he'd reach paradise with her.

Their bodies moved against each other, and Claire mapped Owen's back with her hands down to his hips. She gripped tight and pulled him to her. She loved him like this. Fierce and loving, he filled her and loved her until she couldn't think of anything but him. His breath came hard and fast against her neck. She moved her feet, digging her heels into the mattress and tilting her hips toward him. He sank deeper and ground his hips to hers, creating the most wonderful friction. He pulled out, nearly leaving her altogether before sinking into her again. She felt the tingle, and he grinded his hips to hers again. Finding that sweet spot, she rode the waves of pleasure. He caught her movement, did it again, and sent her flying over the edge. He thrust hard and deep and threw his head back, spilling himself inside of her.

She expected him to fall on top of her and crush her into the bed the way he always did and she loved so much. Instead, he held himself up on his forearms and pressed his forehead to hers. She opened her eyes and stared into his serious blue ones.

"What is it, honey?" she asked.

"I love you."

Everything in her went still. She forgot to breathe. She knew how he felt about her, but hearing him say it made everything inside her align and feel right. Her heart swelled and a smile bloomed on her lips without her thinking a single thought except, *He loves me*!

"I love you," she whispered, because the moment seemed so poignant.

"I want more than just you moving in here."

He wanted her to be his wife, but just like telling her he loved her without actually saying it, he made his point, so she made a point of her own. "I don't want it to just be you and me in this big house."

His eyes went wide with surprise, but then softened with the mischievous smile he gave her. "We'll work on that."

"That's my favorite part."

"Mine, too."

He settled on the bed beside her on his side and pulled her to him so she lay with her back to his chest. With his arm draped over her, his hand cupping her breast, she held his hand to her and closed her eyes.

Pumpkin jumped up on the bed and snuggled up next to her legs with a contented purr.

"Are you sure you're okay? Maybe I should take you to the hospital and a doctor can check you out to be sure."

"I'm fine. The wound hurts, but more like a deep bruise than anything else."

"You're sure."

"Don't you have to call your client Tom back?" she asked to distract him from worrying about her.

He kissed her shoulder and then her head next to the two wounds. "I'll stay with you until you fall asleep. You're more important than any client."

Chapter Thirty-One

Owen hung up the phone and wiped his hands over his face, rubbing his tired eyes. He closed the files on his desk and stacked them. He grabbed his briefcase from the floor and stuffed the pile inside. Despite harping on Shannon about coming to his house for business on a Sunday, he'd spent the last few hours on the phone with another client, going over the material for a fraud case going to court this coming week.

He grabbed his pen, made a few more notes on his legal pad and stuffed it into his briefcase, too. The smell of chocolate caught him by surprise. He glanced at the clock on his computer and swore. He'd lost track of time and forgot to go up and wake Claire. Well, she'd gotten up on her own. He hoped she'd slept well after they made love. She worked so hard, made love with him nearly every night, woke up early because he did, made him most of his meals, and did a hundred other things in her day.

She agreed to move in. In not so many words, she'd agreed to a hell of a lot more. He smiled, thinking of her as his wife, a couple of kids running wild on the ranch. Brody and Rain living just a hill away with their girls and a baby on the way. They'd be a family.

A shopping trip loomed. He'd never bought a woman jewelry. He tried to think of what Claire might like for an engagement and wedding ring. She usually wore round peridot earrings in the same shade as her eyes, or a pair of gold hoops the size of dimes. She had a gold chain with a heart pendant her parents gave her on her sixteenth birthday, and a gold band on her thumb that was her grandfather's wedding ring. Her grandparents had been married for fifty-two years. She said she wore it all the time to remind her that some men stick. Well, he'd show her he was the sticking kind.

A thought occurred to him. Brody still hadn't asked Rain to marry him. Maybe they could pick out rings together. That made him smile. They'd gone barhopping and picked out women together—separate women for each of them, of course. This time they'd pick out rings to keep the women they loved more than life itself.

He and Brody had turned into the staying kind.

Plans formed in his mind. None of them gave him pause. Not the ring, the commitment, the babies she wanted to fill this house with. Finally, everything in his life felt right. Now all he had to do is ask her to marry him. They'd spend their lives together happy on the ranch as a family. They'd fill this house with love and laughter, something it had sorely lacked during his childhood. He'd have it all with her.

A dark thought crept into his mind. Only one thing threatened his future with Claire. Dale. The man needed to be stopped. Frustrated, he stood and walked out of his home office to go find the one person sure to change his bad mood back to good.

He found Claire in the kitchen, standing by the counter, pulling cupcakes out of the hot tin tray she'd cooked them in and setting them on a wire rack. He leaned down and kissed her neck, stealing a cupcake while he distracted her.

"I saw that."

"I thought you were making brownies for the girls."

"I did." She pointed to the pan on the stovetop. "Rain likes vanilla cupcakes with chocolate frosting."

"You didn't have to make so much."

"It's no big deal. She's making dinner, the least I can do is bring her something she likes."

"She loves the brownies."

"So do her girls and Brody. They always eat them all. This way, she's got her own treat. She's pregnant. She deserves something special."

"I'll remind you when I'm spoiling you that you said that."

She stopped what she was doing and bowed her head, her chin nearly to her chest. "Do you mean that?"

"Hell yes, I'll spoil you when you're pregnant with my baby."

"I mean, do you really want to have a baby?"

He reached for her then and turned her to face him. She refused to look at him, so he touched his finger to her chin and made her look up.

"Is this one of those times where you confuse me with the asshole?"

"Do you really want a baby, or are you just saying that because you think it's what I want to hear?"

He planted both hands on the counter behind her on both sides of her and leaned in, so they stood eye to eye. Locked in between his hands, she stilled, her gaze locked on his.

"There is nothing in this world I want more than you and however many children we have together. I want you. I want to have children with you. I want to grow old with you on this ranch and watch our children grow and make us grandparents someday. If that's not clear enough, I'm prepared to take you upstairs and keep you in bed until you are pregnant. It's a sacrifice, but I'm willing to make it to prove to you how much I love you and want to have a family with you."

The smile finally came and she laughed, making his tight chest ease and the worry she wouldn't believe him and in him fall away.

"I love you," she said simply.

"Good. Because I love you, too, and everything I said is the truth."

"I'm sorry."

"Nothing to be sorry about. You asked me a question, I gave you the answer. There is nothing you can't say to me. Anything you want to know, you ask me, and I will always tell you the truth."

"It goes both ways."

"I know it does. Sometimes you need reminding."

This time the smile came easily. "I do, huh?"

"You're stubborn."

She poked him in the ribs. "I am not."

"Sometimes, you are." He closed the distance and kissed the disgruntled look right off her face.

Her hands came up to cup his jaw. The kiss ended when she leaned her forehead to his. "I really want to have your baby."

He took her hand and held it up in front of her, so she could see her grandfather's wedding ring. "We've got a few things to do first, but they shouldn't take too long if you're as serious as I am about this." He tapped the gold band with his finger. "Want to give me a hint, or be surprised?"

"Surprised. Round. Yellow gold. Six and a half."

Surprise her with the ring. Round diamonds in a gold setting to match her grandfather's ring and her size. "Got it. We'll work on the baby later tonight."

"I'm still on the pill."

"You don't have to be."

She opened her mouth to say something, but closed it.

"Okay, maybe we need to talk about this some more," he suggested when she hesitated.

"You changed your mind. You don't want to have a baby."

"Shush. Listen. We do a lot of talking without really spelling things out. So here's the deal. I love you. Someday soon, I'll ask you to marry me. You will say yes."

She laughed, but he kept talking.

"We'll get married. I'll leave most of the planning

of that to you, except one thing. It has to be soon, as in the next six months. Keep taking the pill, don't take it. I'm leaving that up to you. You decide when the time is right, because whenever you're ready, I'm ready to do it with you."

"You're always ready to do it with me," she teased.

He needed her to know he was serious, so he smiled but repeated, "I'm ready when you're ready."

OWEN SAT ON the couch in Rain's living room with Brody beside him in a chair. They watched the girls in the kitchen. All of them, Rain, Claire, Dawn and Autumn. They cleared the table, loaded the dishwasher, and put out dessert, all the while chatting and laughing and having fun.

"She fits in," Owen commented.

"She and Rain have gotten close over the last two months."

"Rain loves anyone who brings her cupcakes."

"Rain likes her. I like her."

"I love her," Owen confessed.

"I can see that you do. What are you going to do about it?"

"Marry her."

"Did you ask her?"

"Kinda. I guess we have that in common. I told her we're getting married, but I haven't asked her, yet."

Brody gave him one of his elusive smiles. "It must be a McBride thing."

"Yeah, well, I'm not taking as long as you to ask. I plan on buying her a ring this week. Want to come along?"

"You're serious."

"She wants to be my wife and have a baby."

"Are you ready for that?" Brody asked.

"With her. Yes. She doesn't want to wait on the baby. I've been thinking about it for a long time, since taking care of Rain and your girls. I think of the past and I see our future in that kitchen and I want to hold on to it with both hands."

"What about all this business with Dale and Shannon?"

"Nothing and no one is going to stop me from being with her and giving her everything she wants, because everything she wants, I want. As for Dale, one way or another, I'm going to stop him from ever hurting her again, even if that means I have to put him in the ground to do it."

"I'm free on Wednesday."

"To kill Dale?" Owen eyed Brody with one eyebrow cocked up.

Brody gave him one of those not-so-nice smiles. "I have your back, brother. Any time you need me, I'm there."

Owen believed him. He'd never had to worry about facing anything alone. Not when he had Brody around to back him up.

"I meant to get the rings."

"Oh, that should work. I have court in the morning through the afternoon, but I'll probably be done by four."

"I'll meet you at four thirty at your office."

"When are you going to ask Rain?"

"Soon. The baby is on the way. I hope to do it when the house is finished in a couple of weeks. New house. Fresh start. Me and her, the girls, our baby, and forever."

"I hear you, man." Owen clinked the neck of his beer bottle to Brody's, and they drank to the girls in their lives.

Chapter Thirty-Two

Owen clasped Claire's hand and stopped the truck in the driveway.

"I need to feed the horses again. I'll be back in about half an hour."

"Okay. Tonight was fun. You've got a really great family."

"Yeah. So, when do I meet yours?"

She smiled and let loose a nervous laugh. "We'll have to go for a visit."

"Invite them here."

"No way. If we go there, we can escape." He laughed with her. "I love my parents, but they can be a little much. They'll be supportive. They'll love you. But . . ."

"They're your parents and will grill you about how we met, what's been going on, and whether or not I'm the best choice for you."

"Yes. Exactly. See, you get it. When are you going to tell your mother?"

"Oh, that's not going to happen until the last minute. You don't want my mother showing up here, taking over . . . everything. She's a force unto herself."

"You like her."

"I do, in small doses. She's got the best of intentions, but she's a steamroller."

"She's in Florida with her podiatrist husband. He has magic hands." She laughed at his screwed-up face. "Brody said you make that exact face whenever you talk to her."

"As bad as things were with my dad, my mom is a whole other kind of crazy. But yes, I love her, despite the fact she drives me nuts."

"Let's wait on both fronts then. I'm happy to keep things quiet and simple as long as possible."

"Things haven't been easy."

"No, but that's not your fault," she reassured him.

He wondered how this had gotten so out of control, but put those thoughts out of his mind for tonight. Though nothing was official, she'd agreed to marry him.

He brought her hand to his lips and kissed her palm.

She pressed her hand to his jaw, and he held it there.

"I'll see you soon."

He slid from the truck and she dropped down next to him. He gave her a quick kiss on the forehead. She headed into the house, and he walked down to the barn. Something disturbed him. The barn door was left slightly ajar. Maybe Claire forgot to close it all the way. Maybe the latch hadn't caught and the wind blew it open.

Still, something else bothered him as he reached

the door. The horses didn't nicker and whinny like they always did when they heard the truck at this hour. They'd expect him to come and feed them.

He entered the open door and still heard nothing but the wind blowing through another open door. Bo and Luke didn't come to their stall doors to greet him. He rushed to Luke's open stall and looked in. The rope had been left down, the straw disturbed, Luke's lunch still in the bucket. He hadn't eaten.

Owen checked Bo's stall and found the same scene, except the door leading out to the paddock was open. He raced out, thinking the two horses were out in the paddock, though he'd have seen them when he drove up. He didn't find them, but one of the gates to the open pastureland stood open.

Nothing added up. Did someone come and steal his horses? Not likely anyone would want the two old guys. He didn't even ride them anymore and had left them to their retirement. Worried about their health and safety, he ran back into the barn and checked the tack. None of the saddles were missing, but two bridles and lead ropes were gone. Someone had definitely come in here and taken the horses. But why?

He didn't know, but he had to find them.

He ran up to the house and burst through the door, scaring Claire, who rushed out of the kitchen to see what happened.

"Owen?"

"Did you leave the barn door open after you fed the horses?"

"No. You said it sticks sometimes, so I made sure it shut."

"Did you open the outside door to Bo's stall?"

"I left him inside to eat. Why? What's happened? Are they all right?"

"They're gone."

"Gone? But how can that be? I swear, Owen, I took care of them just like you taught me."

He drew her close and held her. "I know you did, sweetheart. I'm not blaming you. I'm just trying to figure out what happened. It looks like someone set them free, but they put a bridle and rope on them, so maybe they rode them bareback out of here. Neither Bo or Luke is used to being ridden, so I'm not sure how the riders accomplished that without getting thrown, but either way, I need to find them and make sure they're safe."

"Yes. Of course, but how are you going to do that?"

"I'll run up the road to my friend Grant's place and borrow a horse and ride out."

"Call Brody. Have him help you. Don't go alone. Maybe Dale is trying to draw you out, so he can do something to you."

"Or maybe he's trying to draw me away, so he can do something to you."

The tremble that shot through her echoed in him. He rubbed her back and tried to think.

"I'll ask Brody to come and stay with you. I'll go find the horses."

"Should I call the police?"

"And tell them what? Someone let the horses out?" he snapped, pissed off this was happening.

"Owen, honey, I didn't . . ."

"I know you didn't. I'm just mad as hell this is yet another of Dale's stupid attempts to rile me for something I didn't even do."

"Well, it's working."

He held her close by the neck and rubbed his fingers under her soft hair. "Yes. It is. I wanted to come home and make love to you and hold you and dream about our future together. Instead, I'm chasing after horses, worrying about whether something is going to happen to you."

He kissed her, then pulled out his phone and hit the speed dial for Brody.

"It's me. I need you to come to the house and guard Claire." He explained to Brody about the horses, though it wasn't necessary. If he called, Brody would come.

"Give her your gun, go get the horses. Tell her not to shoot me when I get there," Brody teased, trying to lighten Owen's mood. Not working, but Owen appreciated the effort.

"Will do. Hurry up. I don't want her alone longer than necessary."

"On my way." Brody hung up. No doubt he'd be here in the next twenty minutes.

Owen went into his office and pulled the gun out of his desk drawer. He checked the weapon, assured all was as he left it after he cleaned it last, and made sure the safety was on. He found Claire in the kitchen, making a cup of tea.

"Here. Take this."

"I don't want that."

"You may not want it, but you may need it. So come here and take it."

She frowned, but drew closer and took the gun from his hand, holding it away from both of them. He smiled, appreciating the fact she respected the weapon.

He grabbed her hand and turned it so that she held the gun out to her side, ready to shoot. He pointed to the safety.

"Green dot. The gun is safe and can't be fired." He switched the small lever. "Red dot. The gun is ready to fire."

"Red. As in, warning, you're dead."

"Yes. Brody is on the way. I need to get going. Night is closing in fast and I'm losing the light to find those wayward beasts."

"Don't horses know their way home?"

"In most cases, yeah, they probably would have found their way back to their stalls, but if something scared them bad enough, they might have run and gotten themselves lost."

"The property is really big."

"Over fifteen thousand acres."

"How will you find them?"

"I've got a pretty good idea which direction they went. I'll do my best to find them tonight, otherwise I'll have to keep searching in the morning when there's more light."

"It's getting colder at night."

"Another reason to find them. They're spoiled old goats, used to being pampered. It's been a long time since they were left to their own devices out in the pastures. They'll need food and water. They'll crop grass, but water is more scarce on the property.

"Keep the gun and phone close. There's another handgun in the nightstand drawer upstairs if you need it. Anything happens, lock yourself in our room, call the cops, and anyone comes through that door, you shoot. Don't hesitate. Shoot and keep shooting until they're down. Promise me."

"Owen, I don't know if I can."

"If this is a setup and Dale is coming here to hurt you, you must. I can't live without you, sweetheart." He kissed her long and deep and held her close, praying nothing happened to her. "Brody will be here soon."

"What about you? Don't you need a gun?"

"I'm taking the shotgun and another handgun with me. Lock up behind me."

"You're like a one-man army with all these weapons in the house."

"I'm a country boy, darlin'. Horses and shooting are what we do." He led her back into his office and opened the gun safe in the closet and pulled out the guns he needed.

"Soon, you won't be able to leave guns out everywhere."

"I always lock them up when Dawn and Autumn are here. Safety first," he told her, smiling because it was so easy for them to talk about having a family.

He kissed her at the door, but waited to leave until he heard the snick of the deadbolt sliding into place.

CLAIRE SETTLED IN the living room with her cup of tea, the gun at her side, and the quiet. She listened to every little sound, her nerves on edge, her mind conjuring one horrendous fate after another for Owen and her.

She thought back to this afternoon, her time in the barn, feeding the horses and tending to their needs. She went over everything she did and couldn't remember ever going near the back door of Bo's stall.

She went through the scene with the rake and Shannon showing up. She couldn't believe Shannon had anything to do with what happened, but maybe Dale had followed her here. After she and Owen left, he let the horses out as a prank to rile Owen.

If he'd followed Shannon, maybe she was in danger. With that thought in mind, she went into Owen's office and clicked on his computer screen. She found Shannon's file and opened her contact information. She dialed Shannon's number and waited for her answer.

"Shannon, it's Claire. Are you okay?"

"I'm fine. Why do you ask?"

"I think Dale might have followed you here today. Someone let out the horses. Owen's gone after them, but I thought if Dale had been here to cause trouble, he might have gone to see you again, too."

"It's quiet here. I haven't seen or heard from him."

"Okay, well, I just thought I should check on you."

"It's tiring, isn't it? Always being on guard, reacting to every little thing he does, waiting for the other shoe to drop. Makes you just want to run away and leave it all behind."

Claire didn't know what to say. She did feel that way sometimes, but then she thought about Owen and her life with him and it gave her the strength to stand and fight for them. No one was going to take him away from her, or the life they were building together.

"Be careful, Shannon."

"You too." Shannon hung up on her.

Claire left the office in favor of the living room sofa to wait for Brody. She thought he'd be here by now. The clock on the mantel ticked off the time. Every second she worried more about Owen. She wanted to call and check on him, but he'd have no cell service out in the hills.

Someone tapped on the glass by the front door. She held the gun tight and launched herself off the couch, staring at the dark figure past the glass.

"Brody. Thank God."

She rushed to the front door and unlocked the handle and deadbolt, swinging the door wide.

"Give me that, sweetheart," he said, taking the gun out of her hand and tucking it down the back of his jeans.

She looked past him at the empty driveway. "Where's your truck? How did you get here?"

"I parked it at your place and walked up the road. I've checked the perimeter. We're alone. There's no one out there."

"Are you sure?"

He gave her a deadly look that made her take a step back.

"I'm sure. Got anymore brownies or cupcakes?"

"I kept a couple of cupcakes here. You want one?"

"Sure do. I didn't eat any of Rain's cupcakes. She loves them, and I hate to take them from her, even though they are really good. Mind if I watch the game?"

"Uh, no. Go ahead. I'll get you the cupcake and something to drink."

"I'll take a cup of that tea you're drinking." He pointed to her cup on the coffee table.

"Really?" she asked, surprised he'd want that and not a beer.

"What? I like tea."

"Okay. Make yourself at home."

They settled on the sofa together. It made her smile to see the huge man enjoying his tea and cupcake like nothing in the world spoke to the absurdity of him enjoying it with a gun at his side in easy reach while he watched a baseball game. He kept the sound low, no doubt aware of everything around them. She remained on edge despite Brody's outward show of ease. He projected no worries, but that didn't stop her from jumping six hours later when he patted her leg and said, "Owen's back."

She didn't hear anything for thirty seconds and then she caught the sound of an engine coming up the drive. She didn't know how Brody heard it that far away and over the sound of the late-night comedy show.

She jumped off the couch and ran for the door. Brody grabbed her hand and pulled her back.

"Not so fast, sweetheart. Let's make sure he's alone and all's clear."

"But it's Owen."

"Better safe than sorry."

They watched Owen slide from the truck, looking tired and haggard. He let out a loud, odd whistle at Brody and gave him a wave.

"All clear, sweetheart."

"Did you two work out some kind of signal?"

"Goes back to when we were kids and gave each other the 'all clear' if it was a good time to be home or not."

"That's sad," she said.

"That's the past. Go get him. Looks like he needs to see you right about now."

Owen stood in the pool of light cast by the porch and security lights. She ran down the steps and flew straight into his open arms. Dirty, sweaty, he hugged her close and she didn't care what he smelled like or how dirty she got. He was in one piece.

"Are you okay?" she asked, holding him close, her feet off the ground.

"I am now. How about you?"

"It's been quiet here."

"Thank God for that."

Claire leaned back and cocked her head in the direction of the horse trailer. Brody opened the back gate.

"You found them."

"It took a while, but with the full moon and some help from my friend, yeah, we tracked them down. They're exhausted, thirsty, and hungry, but none the worse for wear."

"Why are you such a mess?"

"I said we found them, I didn't say it was easy to catch them. I need a hot shower and you. It's been a long time since I've been in the saddle for hours on end."

"Go get cleaned up. Brody and I can handle the horses."

"No. I need to check them over in the light. Make sure they aren't hurt, brush them down, get them fed and watered and settled for the night."

"Owen, you're exhausted."

"I am, but I'm better, knowing you're safe and sound." He crushed her to his chest again. "You don't know how worried I was, even with Brody here to protect you."

"I felt ten times worse thinking of you out there alone."

Brody backed out Luke from the borrowed trailer. Owen kissed her on the side of the head, released her, and went to help.

"You look like shit," Brody said.

"I feel like it," Owen answered.

Guy talk. She shook her head and followed Brody and Luke into the barn. Owen came in behind with Bo. They worked in the quiet, settling the horses in their stalls. Owen and Brody worked them over, checking for any cuts, sprains, or other injuries. Luckily, the horses hadn't suffered anything but a scare and exhaustion.

Two hours later, the horses settled, the gates and doors secured, they made their way back up to the house.

Owen shook Brody's hand and pulled him in for a quick guy hug, complete with a slap on the back. "Thanks for coming, man."

"No problem."

"I'll drive you down to my house where you left your truck," she offered.

"Not necessary. I'll walk."

"You're going to check the property again before you leave."

"Just a precaution. Sleep good. I'll see you both soon."

Brody walked into the darkness and disappeared. "Shouldn't we wait to be sure he gets back okay?"

"No need. I'd be more worried about anyone he finds out there. Then again, if Dale is out there, good riddance if he tries to go after Brody."

"Do you think Brody would do something?"

"No doubt. If I get my hands on Dale, you can expect the same." He took her hand and led her up the stairs and into the house. "We both need a shower now." He pulled her up the stairs. "I might just have enough energy to make love to you before I crash."

"Owen, you need to sleep."

"I will. After."

True to his word, he stripped her bare in the bathroom. She took her time doing the same to him, rubbing his sore muscles as she peeled off his shirt. The knotted muscles in his back relaxed as she kneaded and rubbed and he let out a heavy sigh. She pulled his jeans down his thighs and rubbed her hands up and down the corded muscles, making him moan. She smiled and stood; leaning in close, she pressed her naked body to his and reached around to grab his ass and massage. His thick erection pressed to her belly. He stood in her arms, his shoulders sagging, his eyes closed. He enjoyed all the attention, and because he needed it, she gave him more, working her hands up his spine to his tense shoulders.

"I am so lucky to have you in my life," he whispered.

Held loosely in his arms, she laid her head on his chest and listened to the steady beat of his heart. "So am I."

She led him into the shower and turned on the spray, turning him so it beat on his head and back. She grabbed the shampoo and washed his hair for him.

He smiled and shook his head. "I'm not that tired."

"I don't see you stopping me."

"From touching me. Never."

He pulled her under the spray with him. Soap and water cascaded over both of them as he took her mouth and kissed her deep. She held on to him, rubbing her hands over his body, made all the more easy to massage him with the water making his skin slippery. He loved it and in turn loved her, slow and sweet until the water cooled and their bodies exploded with an intense orgasm that had both of them breathing hard and clinging to each other.

"Told you I could do it," he boasted. "Nothing and no one is going to keep me from loving you."

She hoped he was right, but her worries stayed with her even when they fell into bed exhausted. She couldn't sleep for listening to every sound, knowing danger was just a breath away with Dale out there somewhere, plotting to hurt them.

Chapter Thirty-Three

THE LARGE BUSH at the edge of the park provided cover to spy on Owen. He and Claire had drawn ever closer, despite the many pitfalls in their way. Nothing worked to break them apart. Claire refused to leave him. Owen's need to protect her, kept him close to her side, making it that much harder to cause them more trouble and pull them apart.

Time was running out. Something had to be done to show Owen the way.

Owen entered the jewelry store with Brody by his side. Everyone knew Brody and Rain were back together and headed down the aisle. They had to be there to buy Rain a ring.

Owen better not get any ideas about asking Claire to marry him. They barely knew each other. No, he wouldn't do that. Would he?

Time dragged on. How long could it take for Brody

to pick out a ring? Three customers went in the store. Two came out. Impatience and frustration only made the waiting more unbearable.

The door finally opened again. An hour after they entered the shop, Owen and Brody stepped out. Both carried the distinct black and gold bags with the shop's name and logo. They exchanged words and happy smiles, touching the bags together in some kind of salute, or toast. They parted ways, Owen walking back to his office, and Brody to his truck.

No way in hell did Owen give Claire a ring, ask her to marry him, and the two of them lived happily ever after.

No fucking way.

Subtle hadn't worked. This time, something permanent needed to be done.

Chapter Thirty-Four

Owen held the diamond engagement ring between his index finger and thumb. The diamond caught the light and shot rainbows of sparkles everywhere. He picked up the matching wedding band and held them together, imagining them on Claire's finger every day for the rest of their lives.

"You sure about this?" Brody asked.

Owen smiled, glanced at the rings in Brody's fingers, and said, "As sure as you are about that."

Because there was nothing more sure and real than Brody and Rain together. Owen had found that kind of long and lasting love with Claire. They may not have Brody and Rain's history, but they'd forged a deep and lasting bond over the last couple months, dealing with Dale. He'd brought them together, despite his best efforts to tear them apart.

The saleswoman stood before them, a knowing smile

on her face. "The lucky ladies are going to love them. Classic. Elegant. Just enough over-the-top to be spectacular, but not ostentatious."

Brody picked out Rain's first. After Owen saw the rings he'd chosen, nothing else in the case compared. The saleswoman gave him a nod and disappeared into the back room and came out with a tray of rings that stunned the senses. "Brilliant and bright" didn't begin to describe the array of rings. Brody took a look and reevaluated his first choice. He'd traded up and Owen picked out his set with Claire's specification in mind.

He had no doubt she was going to love it.

He didn't even care about the cost, just pulled out his wallet and handed over his credit card. Brody did the same. The saleswoman packaged the rings in red velvet boxes lined in white satin. Elegant and pretty. Claire would like that, too. She paid attention to such details at her shop. She'd appreciate it in this.

Bags in hand and several thousand dollars poorer, he and Brody exited the shop, excited and anxious.

"When are you going to do it?" Brody asked, standing on the sidewalk with him.

"I'm not sure. I need time to plan. I want to do it right and make it special. Something she'll always remember."

"What did Dylan say?"

"Nothing, as usual. They can't find Dale anywhere. He hasn't gotten a parking ticket or used his credit card. It's like he's disappeared and turned into some ghost who keeps haunting my life."

"What are you going to do now?"

"Hire a private investigator. I've done it for a few of my cases. He's like a dog with a bone on a case, he won't let it go until the job is done and done right. I wanted to hire him weeks ago, but Dylan assured me they were on it and they'd get Dale. I'm tired of waiting on them to find him. I'm tired of waiting for the next bad thing to happen."

"Get it done," Brody said.

"I will. For good this time. No more fucking around."

"I've got your back."

"I've got yours," Owen said with a smile. "Can you believe we're doing this? Us. The bad-boy McBride brothers are getting married."

"About damn time if you ask me," Brody said, smiling.

"Damn right. Family. We always wanted it. Now we have it."

They tapped bags.

"Catch you later, man."

"See ya," Brody said, turning to head back to his truck.

Owen tucked the bag under his arm and headed back to his office, smiling like an idiot. He took the stairs two at a time and entered the office happy to see Jeanine at her desk, typing away.

"Hey, pretty lady, wanna see what I just bought?" He pulled the ring box from the bag and held it up in front of her.

"Owen . . ."

He flipped the lid open, and her eyes went wide. "Oh. My. God. That is beautiful."

"Yes, it is," Shannon said, stepping out of the library.

"I tried to tell you. Shannon stopped by for an update on Dale."

Owen clicked the box shut and stuffed it back in the bag. "I'm glad you stopped by, Shannon. I wanted to tell you I'm hiring a private investigator to locate Dale. If the police can't do it, my guy will. He won't be distracted by other more pressing cases. His sole focus will be to locate and detain Dale until the police can pick him up and arrest him."

"Are you serious?"

"Yes. I don't like the way things have escalated. Dale is a loose cannon. There's no telling what he'll do next. Claire's safety and happiness are my top priority."

"Yes, I can see that," she said, her eyes going to the bag he set on Jeanine's desk.

"I'm doing this for you, too, Shannon. He's hurt you for the last time."

"Yes, it's time this ended for good." She cast him a sideways glance. "How long do you think it will take the investigator to find Dale?"

"Depends on where he is. Someone knows where he is, or is helping him hide. He has to have some place to stay, some way of getting money, since he hasn't used his credit card. The investigator will start with his last known whereabouts, his family and friends, and work from there. I expect with his single-minded determination we should have some good solid leads within a few days. Hopefully, Dale will be behind bars soon after.

"The investigator will probably contact you first. His name is Kevin Mehr. Tell him what you know. I'll ask the police to show him Dale's file. The more information we give him, the sooner he'll find Dale."

"All right. Um, I better get going. I'm looking at a new apartment today."

"That's great," he said, meaning it. "I'm glad to see you're moving forward."

"Yes. Soon, I'll have everything I ever wanted."

"Me too," Owen said, picking up the jewelry store bag. "I'll contact you once I have any information. Talk to Kevin. You'll like him. He's nice. He can help us finally end this."

"Yes. That's all I want, to end this."

Owen gave her a nod and walked down the hall to his office. He picked up the phone and made the call to Kevin to get the ball rolling. Twenty minutes later, Jeanine walked in with two bottles of his favorite beer. He'd explained the whole situation to Kevin and ended the call with, "Whatever it takes, man, find this bastard. I want him behind bars yesterday."

"I'll contact Dylan, get a copy of his file, and work with him to bring this to a close. I should be up to speed and off running by tomorrow morning."

"I appreciate it. You find this guy and stop him, I'll owe you."

"I've gotten more referral jobs from you than anyone else. The favor is mine to repay."

"You're the best and that's what I need right now. Call when you have something."

"I will. Bye."

Owen hung up and accepted the bottle of beer. He

twisted off the top and handed it back to Jeanine, taking the other bottle and twisting the top off that one.

"Congratulations."

He clinked his bottle to hers and downed a quarter of the contents in one long swallow. "Thanks. I needed that."

"You've got a lot to celebrate. Tom is happy you won the fraud case. That's some big-time billing coming in. Nothing traumatic has happened to you or Claire in four days. You've set Kevin on Dale's trail, and it looks like there's a wedding in your future. That was one gorgeous ring."

Owen pulled it out and looked at it again. "You think she'll like it?"

"If she doesn't, I'll take it," she teased. "She's going to love it, Owen. I am so happy for you both."

"I still have to ask her. I have no idea how I'm going to do that. Any ideas?"

"You'll figure it out. Make it personal. However you do it, I'm sure she'll love it."

"And say yes."

"You know she'll say yes. She loves you. Anyone can see that."

"Yes, so why does Dale keep harassing us when it's so obvious I'm with Claire and not Shannon?"

"Who knows why any deranged man does what he does. It'll all come clear when Kevin finds him."

"Do you think he will?"

"He's never failed to uncover whatever you sent him after. Why so skeptical?"

"I'm not. It just seems so convenient that Dale disappears after each incident. He's not a career criminal. He's only ever been in trouble for drunk and disorderly, domestic disturbances, and spousal abuse. The vandalism isn't his style. Letting out the horses . . . what purpose does that serve?"

"It pissed you off."

"Yeah, it all pisses me off, but how is that any kind of payback for me sleeping with his wife? Most of the things that have happened have been to Claire. Again, how does that pay me back? If he hoped she'd leave me because of it, it's only drawn us closer. And why would he want her to leave me? If I'm with her, I'm not with his wife. Why go after Shannon again and hurt her? That just draws me back into Shannon's life. None of it makes sense."

"Only one person is happy about you being in Shannon's life and that's Shannon."

"Yeah, she's not exactly Claire's biggest fan either, but let's face it, she wouldn't go after Claire this way. She's too quiet and submissive. Look how Dale has manipulated her all these years."

"That woman is enamored with you. I can't see her thinking that harassing you and Claire would put her in your good graces."

"Exactly, so we're back to Dale and his twisted mind."

Jeanine took a sip from her beer and tilted the bottle in his direction. "You know what I say, focus on your future with Claire. Let Kevin and Dylan do their thing and find Dale. Don't let him come between you two. Ask that girl to marry you, make pretty blond babies, and live a happy life. You deserve it."

He smiled and held up his beer in salute, then drank deeply. "I've got some paperwork to finish up. Thanks for the drink. Go on home to your husband. I'll see you tomorrow."

"You sure?"

"Yeah, now that the fraud case is done, we've got some breathing room on other cases. Might as well take advantage."

"Why don't you go home and start planning how you're going to ask your girl to marry you?"

Owen smiled and leaned back in his chair. "Great idea. I'll head out soon after you."

"Let me know when I can congratulate Claire."

"I will. Until then, let's keep this between us."

"I hope Shannon doesn't say anything."

"Why would she?"

"You never know what a jealous woman will do."

Chapter Thirty-Five

CLAIRE DROVE UP to her shop early Friday morning to bake before she opened for the day. She parked out front, because Owen warned her about parking in the back alley where there was less traffic and a better chance someone could take her by surprise. She didn't recognize the black Porsche, but the man waiting at the front door sent a flood of memories through her mind. She didn't know why her ex was here, but she wanted him gone.

She exited the car, phone in her hand, and sent off the text, not giving Mike, the asshole, her attention until she got to the door and he blocked her path.

"What are you doing here?" she asked.

"I need to talk to you. I've called a dozen times and you refuse to call me back."

"I have nothing to say to you. Move."

"Claire, honey, can't we talk, for old time's sake."

Funny, those old times seemed so far removed from

her life now. The hurt and righteous indignation she'd held on to had disappeared. She just didn't care about Mike or anything he did or wanted anymore. "Everything you ever said to me during those old times was a lie."

"Not everything. I did love you."

"Bullshit. Now move, or I'll call the police and have them move you."

He moved out of her way, but followed her inside her shop.

"This is lovely, Claire. It suits your eclectic style and flare."

"You'd know, since you kept several of the pieces I'd bought and wanted to keep."

"You didn't do so bad in the divorce."

"Not if you don't count the ruined credit, loss of a place to live, the debt I owed because of your whoring ways," she said with a sweetness to her voice she neither meant or felt for this man.

How could she be so stupid and naïve to ever think she loved him? Even more stupid and foolish was the notion that having a family with him would be the dream she'd wanted.

No, that dream would only be a beautiful reality with the man who walked in the door next. He gave Mike a once-over in one long sweep of his gaze and gave her a look that said he found him lacking. She cocked a brow and tilted her mouth and gave him a look that said so clearly, "You're right, and I was stupid once, but not anymore."

"Good morning, sweetheart. I've missed you."

"You saw me twenty minutes ago when I kissed you goodbye."

"So he's the reason you refuse to answer any of my calls," Mike said, sizing Owen up much the same way Owen had done to him moments ago.

Owen walked right up to her and gave her a kiss. She accepted it without hesitation. "Why is he calling you?"

"Don't know. Don't care. I have nothing to say to him. He's an asshole."

"Nice, Claire. I see you're still the bitter bitch. I came here to have a civil conversation with you." Mike took a calming breath and blurted out, "I'm getting married."

Nothing. That news didn't faze her in the least. She wanted him to move on and stay out of her life. She had someone better. Someone who really did love her. "My condolences to your bride."

"Damnit, Claire, why can't you make anything easy?"

"You certainly were, along with every woman you fucked while you were married to me." Okay, maybe that was a bit bitter, but he'd earned that shot.

"Can't you let the past go and listen to me now?"

"Why are you here now? What do you want?"

"I need you to remove the lien on the house, so I can sell it. My fiancé doesn't want to live there."

"Pay me the money you owe me, since you refused to sell the house during the divorce, and the lien will be removed."

"You know why I didn't sell the house. With the housing market in the tank, it would have taken months, and we'd have lost a fortune on it."

"I didn't care then, and I don't care now. If you'd sold

the house at a loss then, the debt would have been a hell of a lot less than I ended up owing to pay off all the other bills. But you didn't care about that, or how I'd pay those debts. You got what you wanted. Live with it."

"She's pregnant. I need to sell the house quickly and get another place before the baby comes."

Claire took a step back and put a hand over the knot in her stomach. This man had denied her the one thing she'd wanted more than anything. He'd done it by spending his time in other women's beds, instead of the one they vowed to share for the rest of their lives. To hear him ask her for a favor because he was going to be a father with another woman who didn't want to live in the house they'd shared rankled.

"Let me get this straight. You are engaged to be married. She's pregnant and doesn't want to live in the house you and I shared, so she asked you to sell it and buy her a new one and here you are asking me for a favor."

"I'll pay you the money after I sell the house."

"Sell the house and the lien will be paid out of the proceeds."

"In this market, I can't get enough out of the house to pay you and buy the house we've put an offer on."

She laughed outright and smiled, but not in a nice way. "So you want me to remove the lien so you can sell the house, buy your pregnant bride-to-be a new house, and I get shafted on the money you owe me."

"I earned the money to buy that house."

"I didn't earn what you did to me, or the debt I had to pay for it."

"I'll keep the house and never sell it. You'll never get your money."

"And your bride will never get the house of her dreams. You can't afford to keep the house and buy a new one. If you rent the house, I get half the rent until the debt is paid.

"Are you even sure the baby is yours? I mean, in ten months of marriage, I never got pregnant. With the amount of women you took to bed, not one of them showed up pregnant, until now. With the women you pick, you sure she's not cheating on you, the way you're probably cheating on her?"

His eyes narrowed, and he looked away, thinking about it. She'd hit the mark and made her point. He'd played her for a fool too many times for her to let him get away with trying to do it again.

"Claire," he said in that placating tone she'd grown to hate, because it meant he thought she was stupid enough to fall for it. She had many times, but not anymore. "She's my boss's daughter. I have to do this right, or I risk losing everything."

"Not. My. Problem."

He grabbed her arm to keep her from walking away. Owen stepped between them, and Mike let her go.

"Touch her again, and I'll lay you out on the floor."

"Who the hell are you?"

Owen tilted his head and gave Mike a smile that hinted at danger. "Claire, sweetheart, give me a dollar."

Claire pulled a dollar out of her purse and slapped it into his hand. She held it there with Owen's fingers wrapped around hers and glanced at Mike. "He's my very smart and handsome attorney."

"Claire, we don't need to involve attorneys."

"They are very expensive. Mine works for a dollar. How much will yours charge?"

"I should have known you wouldn't be reasonable. Even your parents said you've been acting strange lately. Now I see why. Your involvement with him has obviously changed you."

"Yes, it has. I now know what a real man acts like when he loves the woman he's with. I know what it feels like to be important to someone above all else. I know what it is to be loved so completely and without any expectation of getting something in return. I know the joy of loving someone who accepts me without wanting me to be anything but who and what I am.

"He loves me. I love him. Because of that, I'm a better me. I will not allow you to cheat me out of what is rightfully mine. You took everything from me without remorse. You stand here, asking me to accept even more loss and offer no words of apology for what you did, or what you ask of me today. While it's so obvious to you that I've changed, it is so blatantly clear you have not. So, no. I won't take the lien off the house. I won't let you be who you are with me anymore, because you think you can get away with it with a smile and an empty promise that you'll pay me back. I hope my denying you this makes you be a better husband and father. I hope you finally realize that sometimes you have to sacrifice and work really hard to get what you want and to make the ones you love happy, because their happiness is more important to you than your own."

"Claire, please. I need you to do this for me."

"You heard her. She said no," Owen interjected.

"You don't understand. Once I marry her, I'll have the money to pay you back."

Claire shook her head. "Of course. She's got money and has no idea that you owe me. She has no idea what she's getting herself into with you and your finances. Another relationship built on lies and doomed to fail. I really hope you go back to her and tell her the truth. If you love her, and she loves you, you'll find a way to work it out. It's not the money standing between you, it's the pile of lies you've told to get her to marry you."

"You don't know what you're talking about."

She laughed outright at him. "No? It pisses you off that I know exactly what I'm talking about. I lived it, remember?"

Owen wrapped his arm around her waist and held her close. He took a business card out of his suit jacket and handed it over to Mike.

"Have your attorney contact me with a real settlement offer, and we'll let you know."

Mike grabbed the card and stormed out of the shop. He revved the Porsche's engine and gunned it out of the parking spot out front.

"Good riddance."

"What an asshole," Owen said, kissing her on the side of the head.

"Some attorney you are. Why did you tell him I'd take

a settlement? He drives a Porsche. I drive a ten-year-old Honda."

Owen took her by the shoulders and turned her to face him. "First, thank you for texting me and asking me to come down here to help you out with this."

"Turns out, I didn't really need your help. I did like the way you stood there intimidating him."

Owen tilted up one side of his mouth. "He's a douche bag."

"You're sweet. Thank you for letting me handle that on my own."

"You needed to stand up to him. You showed him who you are and what he's missing out on for being such a douche-bag asshole. Isn't that the best revenge on an ex? Showing them that you're not pining away for them and that you've moved on and are happier without them. He hoped to find you here, waiting for him to help you out by giving you the money he was willing to offer as a settlement. Now, he knows you don't need it that bad and you've moved on. With me. Your better-looking, stronger, smarter attorney-soon-to-be-fiancé."

"You forgot arrogant and cocky."

"Ah, that hurts." He put a hand over his heart like she'd wounded him.

"No it doesn't. Besides, you do arrogant and cocky well."

"Thank you, honey. I aim to please. You."

"He hasn't changed. It makes me wonder what I ever saw in him."

"You saw what he wanted you to see, until you saw

through him to the truth and left him. Don't fault yourself for wanting to be in love and have a family. Those are good things, and he turned them against you."

"Yes, well, as you said, now I have you."

"Yes, you do. Always. Arrogant. Cocky . . ."

She wrapped her arms around his neck and went up on tiptoe to look him in the eye. "Handsome. Sexy. Sweet. Funny. Loving."

"Stop, you'll ruin my carefully crafted reputation as a tough attorney."

"You are tough and strong and fierce when you need to be. The one thing you are not is mean or hurtful. I really appreciate everything you are."

"Thank you, sweetheart. That means a lot. I feel the same about you. Maybe that's why we are so good together."

"We're good together because I'm hot for your body."

"Well, who isn't," he teased.

"But you're all mine."

"For months now. Last night. This morning. Right now if you want."

She laughed and laid her forehead to his chest. "You always know just what to say and do to keep me from dwelling on the bad things that happen."

He rubbed his hands down her back and settled them on her hips and gave her a squeeze. "That's why I offered the possibility of a settlement. If you stand your ground, he'll continue to be a part of your life, even if it is on the periphery. If you take a settlement, that's the end. He'll have no reason to ever contact you again."

"I didn't refuse when you made the offer for the same reason. But it better be a damn good offer. I'm not taking any more half-ass attempts to make me bend to his will."

"I think he's realized that under all that beauty and grace lies a steel disposition. He'll make a fair offer. If he doesn't, we'll counter, and he'll accept because there is no way in hell he comes clean to his fiancé before the wedding is done and over and all parties have signed on the dotted line and he has access to her money."

"You think that's what he's doing?"

"I know it is, and so do you. You saw it the minute you suggested the baby isn't his. He knows she hasn't been faithful, but for whatever ulterior motives they have, they're going to get married. He'll get the promotion at work from his father-in-law and access to the money. She'll get whatever it is she wants from him. Maybe he's found someone who wants what he wants, to be able to see other people and still have the illusion of what everyone else has for appearances' sake."

"That's just sad. Their child will be stuck in the middle of all that muck."

"It never ceases to amaze me what people are capable of doing to others. I see it all the time in my practice. We've seen it in dealing with Dale and Shannon."

"Ugh! I don't want to talk about them. This morning has been ruined enough."

"You're right." He traced his fingers down the side of her face. "I have to go to work."

"Thanks for coming when I called."

"You knew I would."

"That's why I sent the text."

That made him smile. "How about you repay me with one of those awesome coffees you always make me."

She laughed. "I told you you'd like it. Coming right up."

"Got anything sweet back there, besides you?"

"Why Owen McBride, are you flirting with me?"

"Just starting tonight's seduction a bit early is all."

"You have never had to seduce me into your bed."

"No, you come willingly—and often."

She let out a full belly laugh and turned to him, her cheeks heating with embarrassment.

"You're beautiful when you blush."

She closed the short distance between them and wrapped her arms around his neck. "I like this. You and me. The way you make me feel right now."

"Will you marry me?"

"What? No ring? No getting down on one knee, you just ask?"

"Yes. You and me and the way you make me feel right now."

"Yes, I'll marry you."

He crushed her to his chest, kissed her, and swung her around, making them both dizzy.

Owen never meant to ask her here. Now. He'd meant to plan something special. Dinner on the back patio like their first date. Candles. Moonlight. Soft music so he could hold her close and dance with her. None of that seemed to matter when they were right here. Right now. Together and sharing a moment of complete closeness and connection.

He'd put the ring in his pocket this morning for no reason, except he didn't want her to find it in the house. He could have put it in the office safe. Fate.

He let her loose and fell to one knee in front of her in the middle of her empty store.

"Marry me and I'll love you every day for the rest of your life and mine. We'll build a life together and raise a family. I will spend my whole life making sure you never regret saying yes. I love you, Claire. Be my wife and love me the rest of my days, and I'll die the happiest man on earth."

He held the ring up to her. Tears streamed down her cheeks. Her gaze never left him. "I will love you the rest of your life and mine. Yes, Owen, nothing in this world would make me happier than being your wife."

He rose and took her in his arms for another long kiss.

"Don't you want your ring?"

"I just want you."

"Well, I come with a ring, two horses, a bunch of cats, including your Pumpkin, a brother and some other family, a best friend, two nieces, and a bunch of other stuff. None of it matters as much as you do to me."

"I'll take it all and be happy with it, because I have you."

He slid the ring on her finger, and this time she looked at it. Her eyes went wide, and she gasped. "Owen."

"Do you like it?"

"I love it. Thank you. It's beautiful."

"Just like you asked. A brilliant round diamond that sparkles half as much as your eyes when we make love."

"You make everything in my life shine."

He held her close and pressed her head to his chest. He leaned his cheek to her golden hair and sighed, more happy and content than he could ever remember feeling in his life.

"That goes both ways, sweetheart."

Chapter Thirty-Six

OWEN WALKED INTO his office, coffee in hand, unable to stop smiling, and a determination to make his future wife happy every day for the rest of their lives. In order to do that, he needed to put a stop to Dale's vindictive harassment.

"I know you like those coffees Claire makes you, but that's not what put that smile on your face," Janine said, standing beside her desk, a stack of files in her arm.

"I asked Claire to marry me. She said yes."

Janine squealed, dropped the folders on her desk, and held up her hands in the air. "Of course she said yes." She wrapped her arms around his neck and pulled him down to peck his cheek. "Oh. Oh. I'm so happy for you. I can't wait to see her and congratulate her. Did you tell your brother and cousin?"

"Not yet. I just asked her twenty minutes ago." He'd wanted to stay and make love to her, but making love to her in the shop's kitchen wasn't quite the way he wanted to celebrate their engagement. No, he'd leave work early, buy her flowers, make her dinner at his place, and they'd share a quiet evening at home. No. Maybe he should take her out to dinner at Madeira's.

First, he wanted to deliver an engagement gift. Dale behind bars.

"I'm heading over to see Dylan now. I just wanted to check on things here before I left."

"Go. Talk to Dylan, put a stop to this mess, so you and Claire can enjoy this time and plan your wedding without worry."

Owen hugged Jeanine in a rare show of affection for his employee, who'd become a really good friend.

In his truck on the drive over to the sheriff's office, Owen called Rain's house, trying to catch Brody before he took the girls to school.

"Brody," his brother answered.

"I'm getting married."

"About fucking time," Brody said, completely serious.

Owen laughed. "Well, I have known her for less than three months. I don't know what's taken me so long."

Brody laughed and called to Rain, "Owen's getting married."

She squealed so loud Owen had to hold the phone away from his ear. She came on the line. "I am so happy for you. Did you get her a ring?"

"Gave it to her this morning right after I got her to promise to marry me. Soon."

"So, you asked her and gave her a ring and she said yes."

"Yes," he answered, knowing exactly where this was going.

"See, Brody, your brother knows how to do it. Why don't you?"

Brody came back on the line. "Congrats, man."

"You better hurry up and ask Rain to marry you before she decides to say no for spite."

"She won't say no. She loves me," he called loudly, obviously yelling at Rain. "She's taking the girls to school. What are you doing?"

"On my way to see Dylan. Didn't want to tell him the good news before I told you."

"I appreciate it. Any word on Dale?"

"That's what I want to talk to him about. I need to end this. Now. I don't want to marry her with this hanging over our heads."

"Let me know if you need me for anything."

"Let's hope it doesn't come to that."

"If it does, I've got your back."

"You always do. I'll catch you later."

"Owen?"

"Yeah?"

"I hope you and Claire are as happy as Rain and I are."

"We are. As the best man, start planning the bachelor party, because I'm not waiting to marry her."

"Who says I'm the best man? You never asked me."

"You're my fucking brother. Of course you're the best man. Get it done."

"I started planning it a week ago," Brody confessed with a definite hint of a laugh in his voice.

"Good. At this rate, I'll be married before you and Rain."

"You've got your way. I've got mine."

"Doesn't matter how it happens, so long as they're with us."

"Exactly." Brody acknowledged the simple truth.

They both felt the same way and had finally found what they'd wanted their whole lives. Love. Family.

Owen ended the call and parked outside the sheriff's office. He walked in and caught the little boy midair. He held Dylan's son, Will, aloft and swung him around before he drew him close and hugged him. He'd seen the boy several times since Dylan came home. It hadn't taken the little guy long to warm to him and the rest of the family.

"Hey, buddy. How are you?"

"No school. Stay with Daddy and play cops and robbers."

"That's exactly why I came to see your dad," Owen said, patting the little boy's back. "Dylan." He greeted his cousin with a handshake.

"I'm glad you're here. I was going to drop this one off at school and come see you."

"You've got news."

"I've been working with your PI. I went north and east. He went south and west on the hunt to find Dale outside of Colorado. Talked to him ten minutes ago. He found him. Dale's in custody."

Owen held back the swear words for the boy's benefit and let out a huge sigh of relief. "Tell me everything."

"Not yet. I need to get this one squared away."

Owen waited while Dylan said goodbye to Will. His assistant, Lynn, left with Will to drop him off at preschool, and Dylan called his mother to pick up Will later today.

"How are your mom and dad?"

"Same as they ever were. Dad is buried in work. Mom rules the house and us."

"Still interfering in your life, huh?"

"It never ends. She loves Will, though."

"He's a great kid. Can't wait to have one of my own."

"Trust me on this, get married first. It's not easy being a single parent."

"About that. I asked Claire to marry me this morning."

Dylan slapped him on the shoulder and grabbed hold. "I am so happy for you, man. That's great. Really great."

"Brody's planning the bachelor party. I'm sure that means we'll relive some of my youthful indiscretions. Seems to me, you left town just when you were getting old enough to do something interesting."

"I wish I'd stayed," Dylan said, a touch of sadness in his voice that Owen hated putting there, reminding Dylan of the girl he'd loved and lost so long ago.

"Have you found any proof to substantiate the rumors Jessie's dead?"

"Nothing."

"Did you talk to her old man, see if he cops to anything in one of his drunken outbursts?"

"Tried. Twice. Didn't get more than five steps onto the property when he came out and shouted for me to leave or show him a warrant. I pushed, but he refused to speak to me. Claims Jessie left one night and never came back."

"You don't believe it."

"Oh, he said it with enough conviction, but the haunted look in his eye says there's a hell of a lot more to the story."

"You don't think she left that house alive."

"I don't know what to believe."

Which really meant Dylan didn't want to believe the rumors her father killed her.

"She had every reason to leave. I hope she did, and she's out there somewhere," Dylan said, a hopeful note to his voice if not in his eyes.

"What's her brother, Brian, got to say about her disappearance?"

"Brian is like his old man, wasting away at the bottom of a bottle. Every time I see him, he beelines it in the opposite direction."

"Do you think he knows what happened and is hiding something?"

"I have no idea, and I've been too busy getting up to speed as the new sheriff to find out. I gather up rumors every chance I get, but no one has any concrete evidence she either left, or that bastard killed her. Soon, I'll corner her cagey brother and get the answers I need."

"I hope you get the answer you want."

"Me too."

Dylan led him back to his office and took a seat behind his desk. Owen sat in front of it and tried to rein in his impatience.

Dylan met his steady gaze. "I'm sorry this took so long. It's not that it wasn't a priority for me . . ."

"I get it, man. You've got a job to do, and prioritizing cases isn't always easy."

"I appreciate the understanding. This is a family matter, and I wanted it resolved quickly, but it's been damn hard to find this guy. Here's the thing. Dale is in some dinky town outside of Farmington."

"That's in New Mexico and more than four hours away."

"He's got a second cousin out there. The reason he didn't use his credit cards or bank account in the last few months is that the cousin's place is off the grid in the middle of nowhere."

"Okay, so how did you find him?"

"Your PI started with Dale's relatives outside the state, since I've had no luck finding him in Colorado. Anyway, local law enforcement in Farmington picked him up for drunk driving and resisting arrest. From the way things sound, they've had him in custody for a while."

"What's a while? A few days? Weeks?"

"I don't know exactly. The person your PI spoke with didn't have the information. They requested someone from my department come and pick him up. They're a small town, next to nothing in the way of resources."

"When will he be here?"

"Not until this evening. It's going to take all day to get him here. My officer just left about ten minutes before you arrived."

"So, he's been staying with the cousin and coming back here to harass Claire and Shannon? That doesn't make any sense. Especially since you didn't get any hits on his credit card. How's he paying for gas?"

"That's what I want to ask him. Why the hell would he go so far away, only to come back and cause trouble and go all the way back there? That's one determined son of a bitch if you ask me."

"I guess we'll find out when he gets here. Keep me posted. I want to know the minute he arrives. I want to question him and find out what the fuck his problem is, and why he can't leave Claire the hell alone."

"Listen, man, we've got to do this by the book. Don't make me arrest you."

"You'd love that, wouldn't you?"

"Hell yes, but I want this guy to pay for everything he's done, and I want the information he gives us to be legit."

"I got it. I just want to know why. It's so obvious to everyone but him that Claire and I are together. He can't possibly still think I'm sleeping with Shannon."

"Maybe he's just fixated on you."

"That's the thing. All of this has been way out of his normal behavior. You've seen his rap sheet. It's all domestic disturbances and drunk and disorderly charges. If he doesn't like someone, he punches them. It's what he's done to Shannon. How he solves every drunken fight in a bar when he feels invincible. He tried to run down Claire with his car. These are violent acts, meant to hurt someone. So, why go from that to vandalism?"

"I don't know, man. Maybe taking you head-to-head was just too much for him."

"Then why didn't he drink himself brave and come after me?"

"Maybe he's not as stupid as he acts."

"I don't fucking know what to think anymore. Everything I know about Dale says this is out of his normal behavior."

"We'll figure it out when he gets here, and we question him."

"I mean it, Dylan, something isn't right."

Chapter Thirty-Seven

Claire held up her hand for the hundredth time in the last hour to stare at the sparkling diamond ring.

"You'll blind yourself and everyone else if you keep holding that up to the light like that," Gayle teased.

She smiled and put her hand on the counter. Startled by the gasp behind her, she spun around and found Shannon standing in line behind Gayle's customer on the other side of the glass display case.

"Shannon. I didn't see you there. Are you okay?"

"That's some engagement ring," she said, gaze locked on the diamond solitaire.

"Owen asked me to marry him," Claire said, trying to break the news gently. Shannon had never been able to hide her attraction to Owen. Claire didn't want to rub it in her face by showing the true extent of her excitement.

"He really did it."

"Yes, he did." She couldn't hide her smile. She and Owen would move in together like they planned and soon they'd get married and have a baby. This time, she'd live the dream, not wish for it anymore.

Shannon gathered herself with a shake of her head. She smiled brightly and gave Claire's hand a pat. "Wow, that's wonderful. And fast. I mean, you've only been seeing each other a couple of months."

"When you know, you know," Gayle said, giving Claire's shoulder a squeeze. "You can see how much they love each other every time they're together. It's just there. I think it's romantic that he didn't wait, but asked you when the moment was right."

"The whole thing surprised me after the morning we had with my ex showing up here."

"Your ex wants you back?" Shannon asked.

"No. He wanted me to do him a favor. I made it clear he is my past and Owen is my future."

"How did he take that? I mean, Dale never takes no for an answer. He thinks he owns me."

"Mike didn't have a choice. I've moved on. Like you're doing," Claire pointed out to help Shannon see that she had and could continue to stand firm against Dale.

"Yes, I want something better. Someone better."

"Dale is determined to put himself in both our paths and ruin our plans, isn't he?"

"Yes, he is. They'll catch him though. He's too stupid not to get caught for everything he's done."

"I hope it's soon. Owen and I want to get married right away," Claire said, letting some of her excitement show.

Now that it was sinking in, she realized she didn't want to wait to make all her dreams come true. She wanted Owen and the life they dreamed together. She wanted it now.

"Doesn't it take a long time to plan a big, fancy wedding?"

"Owen and I don't need anything fancy. I think he'd like to keep things simple. Family, close friends, maybe out at the ranch in the backyard. We've talked about redoing the garden. It would be beautiful under the big trees."

"Yeah, he'd probably like that," Shannon said, shifting from one foot to the other and back again, her voice unusually high.

"I'm sorry, Shannon, can I get you something?"

"Just a small coffee and one pumpkin cobbler. It looks really good."

"How about some whip cream on that?"

"I'd love it. Thank you."

The contrast in Shannon's behavior always surprised Claire. One minute she was shy and reserved, sticking to Owen for support and protection, then she seemed shocked and despondent by the engagement news, only to put on her happy face and order coffee and cobbler.

Claire didn't want to upset the fragile woman, so she put her order together and handed it to her. "On the house," she said.

"Really? You're so kind."

Why did that sound mildly sarcastic? Well, what did Claire expect? Shannon had a crush on Owen. Claire had overlooked Shannon's possessive behavior up to now.

She'd do so again in hopes that Shannon realized Owen truly had picked her with no possibility of changing his mind. Not now. Not ever. He loved Claire and had proven that by asking her to marry him.

Shannon took her order and two steps to the door, but turned back before exiting the shop. "I'll see you soon."

A cold chill raced up Claire's spine. She had the overwhelming desire to find Owen and tell him what happened. But what would she say? Shannon came in for coffee and cobbler, acted like her usual erratic self, and left with an ominous but innocuous statement.

"What do you know about her?" she asked Gayle.

"Not much. Shy. Quiet. Smart from what I remember. It surprised a lot of people when she hooked up with Dale. They seemed an odd pairing. Then, he adored her, and she him. The odd pairing seemed to work for them for a while, until it didn't. Oh, they had their spats early on, but nothing like what it progressed to as the years went by." Gayle's gaze lost focus. "You know. I remember this one time she picked a fight with Dale in front of everyone at a summer festival. Boy, they got into it."

"She picked the fight?"

"Yes. Why?"

"You'd think someone who knows how volatile Dale is would know better than to pick a fight with him."

"Come to think of it, the madder he got, the more she pushed, but in a cunning, backhanded sort of way. I wasn't the only one to notice."

"Strange. And interesting. I'll have to mention it to Owen and see what he thinks."

"He'd know better than anyone about the cops showing up at fights. They'd have a report."

"I'll ask."

She meant to, but the day wore on and the shop got busy. Owen had meetings all afternoon and wasn't available for lunch. She missed him and couldn't wait to go home with him and celebrate their engagement.

The phone rang around six o'clock. Claire pulled the last wrapped crystal vase from the box and set it on the table with the others. She grabbed her cell phone and smiled. "Hi, honey, I was waiting for your call."

"Now, I like the sound of that," Owen said, a distinct smile in his voice.

"What do you want to do for dinner tonight?"

"I don't care about dinner, I just want dessert."

The innuendo wasn't lost on her. She'd spent the better part of the day thinking about him.

"Where are you? I'm craving something hot and spicy," she teased, dropping her voice an octave.

"Ah, honey, I hate to disappoint you, but I've got to go down to the sheriff's office."

"Did Dylan find Dale?"

"Yes and no. The PI I hired tracked him down in New Mexico, where he'd been arrested. One of Dylan's guys went to pick him up. Dylan just called, they'll be at the office in about ten minutes. I want to be there when they bring him in and question him."

"I'm coming, too."

"I don't want you there."

"He came after me. I want to hear what he has to say."

"I know you do, but you're also the victim. Dylan and I both want to do this by the book."

"Why do you get to be there and not me?"

"Because I'm your and Shannon's attorney."

"Oh, yeah, I forgot about that."

"I much prefer you think of me as your husband."

"Soon, you'll be just that, won't you?"

"Not soon enough for me. Go home. I'll meet you there after the meeting, and I'll tell you everything."

"You promise?"

"Yes."

"If you're going to be a while, I'll go to my place and work on packing up some of my stuff to move to your place."

"I like the sound of that. I'll be home as soon as I can. We've got a lot to celebrate. You're going to be my wife, and Dale will remain behind bars for a long time to come."

"I love you, Owen."

"I love you too. It's over, sweetheart."

Chapter Thirty-Eight

OWEN WALKED INTO the sheriff's office and stopped, stunned to see Dale in handcuffs, standing beside an officer, looking gaunt and haggard. Owen expected cocky, and Dale delivered.

"I just asked to see my lawyer. Have you finally switched sides and come to my rescue?" Dale asked.

"After what you've done, not a chance," Owen said, keeping his cool and assuming his lawyer nonchalance. He'd stick with the facts and make sure Dale paid.

Dylan stepped out of his office, looking mean.

"Mr. Monoghan, my deputy informed me you'd like a lawyer. I thought perhaps you could clear up a few matters, but if you're not willing to talk to us without your attorney present, I'm happy to put you in a cell until he gets here."

"You already know what happened when I went after him and his woman." Dale cocked his head in Owen's direction.

"Yeah, you tried to run her down with your car, even after she told you we didn't know each other."

"I didn't mean to hit her. That was a total accident. I swear. You took the turnoff on the road and stopped at her place. How was I to know you lived further on up the road. I didn't stick around, so you could catch me watching her place."

"No, but you stuck around to slash her tires outside my office."

Dale's eyes went wide with surprise, but then he smiled. "Did she run into more trouble after I left?"

"You know she did. You punctured her tires, spray-painted her shop, tore up the side garden, and keyed my truck. You drove the horses out of my barn and nearly ran them to death, you son of a bitch."

"Sounds like someone's got it out for you. I can say it makes me happy to see you get yours for stealing my wife away from me, but"—Dale pressed his lips together and shook his head side to side—"I had nothing to do with any of that business and no one can say different."

"I know you did it," Owen snapped.

"You've got nothing on me," Dale said, taking the seat in front of one of the deputy's desks, leaning back, and propping his ankle on his knee, like he had not a care in the world.

Dylan smacked his hand down on Owen's shoulder and turned him to face him. "I need to speak to you in private."

"Dylan, he's lying. He did it."

"Let's go into my office for a minute. He's asked for his lawyer, so we can't question him."

"Don't you worry, I'll be waiting right here," Dale said, leaning back with his fingers laced behind his head, elbows out, shackles jangling on his wrists. "Hey Sheriff, might I get a soda or something. It's been a long drive. I'm parched," he said, like some dainty lady out for tea.

"Get him a damn soda and keep an eye on him. He makes a move, you toss him in a cell," Dylan ordered, walking away, leaving Owen to follow.

Dylan shut the door behind him and moved around his desk to take a seat.

"What the hell, Dylan? He's guilty as hell."

"Of getting the wrong house and hitting Claire that first night. Yes. I agree. He just admitted as much. But . . ."

"No but. That's it. He did it. He's terrorized Claire."

"No, he hasn't. Not according to the police report I received when Dale arrived. According to this"— Dylan tapped his finger to the open folder and papers on his desk—"Dale arrived at his cousin's place two days after he attacked Claire. Three days later, he got cited for indecent exposure for pissing in an alley outside a bar. Drunk and stupid, the report says his cousin took him home after he slept it off in the drunk tank overnight. The day someone slashed Claire's tires, Dale and his cousin, along with three other men, were on a weeklong hunting trip. The police down there confirmed his alibi with all parties.

"Dale was in jail for DUI and resisting arrest when someone vandalized Claire's shop, keyed your car, and let the horses out of the barn. He didn't do it.

"So, Owen, who else has motive to go after you and Claire? No matter how you look at it, Dale couldn't have done these things, because he was too busy being stupid drunk."

"It doesn't make sense."

"It does if you look at this from another angle. Who was there when Claire's tires got slashed?"

"No one. We were at my office . . . Shit."

"That's right. Shannon came to your office that day," Dylan pointed out.

"She was at my house the day the horses got out. Fuck me. Claire got hurt that day. Someone left a rake in the stall. She stepped on it and whacked herself in the head and cut her arm open. She said Shannon appeared out of nowhere."

"Or so it seemed," Dylan pointed out.

"She never came after me. She went after Claire to get her out of my life."

"She keyed your truck and let out the horses."

"She keyed the passenger door. The side Claire sits on. The horses I think were to try to instigate a fight between me and Claire. Everyone knows I've had those horses since I was a teen. If anything happened to them, I'd be upset. She thought I'd blame Claire, and we'd break up."

"There's something else I found interesting in the reports."

"What?" Owen asked, despite the fact he didn't really want to know.

"The night Shannon claims Dale snuck into her house, got in a fight with her, and slammed her head into the counter—"

"He was in fucking jail," Owen finished for Dylan.

"Makes you wonder how many other times Dale swore he never touched her, and she had a bruise or worse when the cops showed up."

"Do you really think that shy, quiet woman bashed her head that bad on purpose?"

"I went back and reread the domestic disturbance calls again. I see a clear pattern to most of them. They got into an argument, which in most cases both parties agreed she started. The argument escalated, and when it got physical, the cops arrived."

"How many times did she call, or someone else?" Owen asked, thinking of everything in a whole new light.

"Most of the calls came in from her. Usually, when Dale got out of control and hit her too hard. The other times, when someone else called, her injuries were minor, or unremarkable. The officers I spoke to insinuated she relished the idea of getting Dale into trouble. They also intimated it might have been a sex game gone wrong."

"What?"

"That was their impression from Dale's remarks and her demeanor."

"That is some fucked-up shit."

"It happens. Some people have some messed-up proclivities. My officers brought him in, because she had marks on her and clearly looked to be innocent. Still, how many times did she drop the charges?"

"I thought she was the victim," Owen said, trying to wrap his brain around this new information. "All this time, it was some sick and twisted game they played together."

"Only one way to confirm it. Let's go ask Dale. This

time, let's listen to what he has to say with this new scenario in mind and see what rings true."

"You need to find Shannon and bring her in," Owen demanded.

"I will, but I thought maybe if we can confirm our suspicions you'd go out to her place and pay her a visit. See if you can't get her talking."

Owen understood. "You want me to lead her on, thinking I've had a change of heart, and see if she doesn't incriminate herself."

"A deputy and I will stick close to corroborate whatever she says to you."

"I'm in, but I want to hear Dale's side of all this first. I have a hard time believing she did all this because of some crush she's got on me."

"Not a crush, Owen. An obsession. If we don't stop her, she may decide to remove Claire from your life permanently."

"Don't talk that way. I can't imagine . . . I need to call Claire."

"Let's talk to Dale and confirm our suspicions. I'll send someone out to your place to protect Claire while we bring in Shannon."

"Claire's at her place, packing things up to move to my place."

"Okay, she's got the alarm system you put in her place. We know she's safe for now," Dylan reassured him.

Dale hadn't moved since they left him, except to down two cans of soda. His lawyer sat beside him, leaning in close and whispering.

"Mind if we speak to your client, counselor?" Dylan asked.

The lawyer glanced at Dale, who shrugged and gave a nod.

"Didn't get a whole lot to eat in jail, did you, man?" Owen asked to break the ice, keeping his voice light and nonconfrontational.

"I sure as hell missed a home-cooked meal. I did. But then, I ain't got no home to go to, thanks to you, asshole."

"Come on, man, you know Shannon wanted you out of that house for all the times you beat her senseless."

Dale laughed, and this time Owen didn't think it was to show off. Dale genuinely thought that description of events was laughable.

Dale smiled and leaned forward in a conspiratorial way. He dropped his voice and said, "She may look sweet and innocent, but that girl is a wildcat. Now, she don't want people knowing that about her. No way. She likes people to underestimate her, think she's weak and meek as a mouse. I'll tell you what, she hunted me down and wouldn't back down after she saw me shove this pushy woman outside a bar. That girl, she likes it rough. Orders up what she wants—'smack me hard on the ass'—like she's ordering a burger and fries. Wrap your hand around her throat, squeeze, and give her a little shake, and she's hot and wet and begging to be fucked hard. Now, most times I'm happy to oblige her demands, but sometimes she can be a mouthy bitch.

"I never used to hit women. I guess you could say, she taught me to hit her the way she likes it. The payoff is usually so fucking good I can't wait to smack her around just to see that wild side of her come to life. Lately, it's not enough to keep me in line by calling the cops because I'm too drunk to know my own strength. Though the make-up sex is damn good. Those are the times she's real sorry and does all the things I like."

"The last time you went to jail, you hurt her bad."

"I lost my temper. She wouldn't stop nagging me about the house and living a better life. I get she wanted better. Well, I wanted better, too. If she didn't call the cops all the time, I'd have kept all those jobs I lost. It's her damn fault, too. I didn't do anything she didn't want or ask for in the first place.

"Then, you stepped in and she fell for your good looks and charm. Now, all she wants is to be a lawyer's wife, live in that big house with you, and share your money and your bed. Watch out, I tell you, she'll turn you into me in no time."

"I'm not interested in her. Even if I was, I don't hit women."

Dale compressed his lips and shook his head. "You think that now, but I'm telling you, the first time you grab her ass just a little too tight and you hear her sigh and moan for more, you'll do it again. She'll ride you so hard and beg for you to do it again. You will, too, because she wants it and you want her."

"Believe me, Dale, if you have to hurt someone to get them off, that's not making love, and I can do without it."

"I thought that once, myself. Now, all I do is think about those times it all went right, and I was a happy man."

"Yeah, and look at you now. Shackled and chained and about to face some serious jail time for hurting Claire."

"I'm real sorry about that. I never meant for that to happen. The booze, you know. Still, when I told Shannon what happened, well, I think she came without me even touching her."

"When did this happen?"

"The morning after I hurt that lady. I saw Shannon that night, but she wouldn't let me in the door on account of my being drunk and acting stupid. But the next morning I sobered up and went back to see her to try to make things right. She got pissed off and shouted a lot, but she wouldn't take me back. Said I could rot in a cell for all she cared. She was going to have you and a better life and that was that. Pissed off and drunk, I followed you. Was going to get you good. Then, I saw you with the pretty blonde. You kissed her at her shop and later at her house after your dinner. I figured you really wanted her and not Shannon, which would piss her off, and she deserved it for ruining my life and making me want her even though I didn't want to. Well, I'll tell you what, I lit out of there. I didn't want to spend another day in jail for that bitch."

"And you haven't been back to town since?" Dylan asked.

"Not a once. If I hadn't gone to town and stayed out at my cousin's place, I'd still be there now. No reason to come back, and a whole lot of reasons to stay away. You get me."

"We get you, Dale," Owen confirmed. "Why didn't

you ever tell the cops she instigated the fights and wanted to get hit?"

"Shoot, I told the cops every time they came, but they just shook their heads and called me a drunk fool. Would you believe me if I told you she wanted it? One look at her and that sweet, young face and no one would believe me. Like I said, she got off on people thinking she was one way when she was really a freaky piece of ass."

"Shannon called the cops, said you'd been to her place, you two fought, and you bashed her head into the counter. She had a lump the size of a golf ball on her head and a nasty cut," Dylan said.

"Did she now?" Dale asked, a one-sided smile tilting his face. His eyes danced with laughter.

Dale leaned forward in the conspiratorial way, and Owen leaned in to hear what he had to say. "Sometimes, when a woman doesn't have a man around to take care of her needs, she's got to take matters into her own hands. One hand between her legs to take care of her pussy. The other she'd use to pinch and bruise the inside of her thighs and her titties."

The shock must have registered on Owen's face. Dale cackled and laughed and fell back into his seat.

"I told you. She's a wild one. Bashing her head like that must have set her off good. Ya see, when the cops showed up to arrest me, not all them bruises was from me. She done plenty of that on her own to get herself off."

Owen truly didn't need Dale to spell it out for him anymore. He got the picture and his stomach went tight, revolting from this new awareness about a client he'd thought needed protection, but turned out to need a psychiatrist.

"Sounds to me like Shannon's tried everything to get your attention. Did it work?" Dale asked, a mix of sadness and anger in his eyes.

Owen gave him the truth. It might make Dale feel better to know his suspicions had never proven true. "I never slept with Shannon. I've never been interested in her that way. I've tried to make that clear to her on numerous occasions."

"She won't listen," Dale commented with another shake of his head. "She'll wear you down until she gets what she wants."

"It won't work. I'm marrying Claire."

Dale's eyes went wide with surprise. "Well now, there's some news. If Shannon knows that, you'd best find your lady and protect her. Shannon can be a jealous bitch when she wants to be. In your case, I think she's proven that if she's been messing with your lady all this time."

"She doesn't know I'm marrying Claire."

"She might," Lynn interrupted from her seat across the room. "I saw her going into Claire's place earlier today as I was coming out. Believe me, if she saw Claire, she didn't miss the skating rink on her hand," she added, referring to the diamond ring Owen gave her this morning.

"You're sure?" Dylan asked.

"About her being at the shop and the ring," Lynn confirmed. "That ring was gorgeous. You did good," she told

Owen. "Your Claire makes the best blueberry muffins in town." Lynn held up the white bag with Claire's store logo on it.

"Shit. We need to find Claire."

"I'd do it fast," Dale suggested. "If she knows, she'll want your lady out of the way, maybe even for good if she's determined enough to have you."

"I'm going to have her behind bars before anything happens," Owen promised.

"Lock him up," Dylan called to his deputy.

"Yeah, you bring her here," Dale said, standing to go with the deputy to the holding cell. "I have a few things to say to her myself."

Alone except for the few remaining office staff, Owen turned to Dylan. "We need to get to Claire's place, make sure she's okay before we go after Shannon."

"We are not going after Shannon. This is a police matter, and I'll handle it with my deputies," Dylan said.

"The hell you will. Your plan will still work."

"Not if she knows you're marrying Claire."

"I'll convince her that we had a fight and broke things off. It could still work."

"You'd have to be hell of convincing."

"Then I will be. No matter what, that bitch is getting locked up for everything she did." Owen thought about Dale's admissions. "You know, most of the times Dale got arrested and convicted of domestic abuse are probably nothing more than foreplay gone wrong. She asked for it. Literally."

"It's like anything in this gray world. I'd rather err on

the side of morality. You do not hit women, even if they ask you to do it."

Owen opened his mouth to argue on Dale's behalf, though he wondered why he even bothered after what he'd done to Claire.

Dylan continued. "If things went wrong and she called the cops to get him to stop, I say she's got that right, like any woman who says no. No means no, and I don't care how far things have gone when she says it."

Owen had to admit, when seen that way, it made sense, even in this twisted scenario. Dale had to know after all the times he'd been with Shannon what crossed the line and what didn't. Maybe a slap across the face got her off, but a punch in the eye just pissed her off.

Ah hell, he didn't want to think about it anymore and turned to leave.

"Where the hell are you going?"

"I need to see Claire."

"Call her, then we'll go get Shannon."

"Not good enough. I need to see her and tell her what's going on."

"Owen—"

"I need to see her," he said again, shutting up Dylan's next protest.

"Okay, let's go see her. I'll drive. We'll pick up Shannon after and bring her back here."

"Whatever," Owen agreed, walking out the door and sliding into the cop car. "It's strange sitting in the front seat of one of these."

"If it makes you feel better, I can handcuff you and

shove you in the back." Dylan didn't break a smile, but Owen laughed all the same.

"No thanks. I'm good."

"Don't make me do it when we find Shannon. By the book, man. We'll lock her up for what she's done."

"By the book," Owen agreed, and hoped he could keep that promise.

Chapter Thirty-Nine

CLAIRE CLOSED THE box packed with the last of the living room decorations and grabbed the tape. She held the box closed and ran the tape over the lid, once, twice, and across for good measure since most of the items were breakable. She'd used the box to move here, and now she'd use it again to move to Owen's place. She couldn't wait to settle in with her things mixed with Owen's. They'd make a nice compliment to his guy stuff, adding a layer of elegance and whimsy to his classic, sparse surroundings.

Thoughts of moving in with Owen took her upstairs to her bedroom. She scanned the room she'd barely spent any time in over the last weeks. She'd start with her pretty bathroom. The pictures and decorations would complement Owen's master bath. She'd pack them up and take them over later tonight. It wouldn't take long to decorate the bathroom there, start making his place their place. The thought sent a thrill of excitement through her system.

An hour later, her bathroom bare, she took the two boxes she'd packed downstairs and straight out to her car. She put them in the backseat and went back inside to start on her room. First, she stripped the bed and tossed the bundle of sheets and blanket in the hall outside the bedroom door. She grabbed one of the boxes she'd left there earlier and the roll of padded wrap and packed up her pretty things.

By the time she put the third box from her bedroom and all the hanging pictures and antique mirrors in her car, she felt tired and dirty. She headed back into the house to take a shower and change before Owen arrived and they went to his place. She shut the front door, bolted it, and set the alarm, not that she really needed it with Dale in custody, but it had become a habit and made her feel safe.

She wondered about Owen and what was happening with Dale, but curbed the urge to call him and find out. He'd be here soon enough to give her the details. Finally, this would be over.

The pile of sheets and blankets still lay in the hallway. She'd have to take them down to the laundry room after her shower, along with her wet towel. She stepped over them and surveyed her near-empty room. Nothing but the furniture and her clothes left, she waited for the feelings of trepidation or anxiety to come. Nothing but overwhelming happiness and excitement fluttered in her gut. She couldn't wait to be Owen's wife, live with him full-time, and spend their lives together.

She pressed a hand to her belly and smiled. Soon, she'd get pregnant, and they'd have a child. She undressed and stepped into the shower, thinking of their child growing up with Owen's nieces and the baby Rain carried now and their cousin, Dylan's son, Will. She thought of family barbeques, birthday parties, and holidays together as one big family. The thoughts made her smile.

Dried off, the towel wrapped around her middle and secured at her breasts, she brushed out her wet hair and walked into the bedroom, pulling out clean underwear and a bra to wear. With a shimmy, she slid her underwear up her legs and over her hips. She pulled on the matching cream bra and secured it behind her back.

"Sexy, yet sweet," Shannon said, standing in the bedroom doorway, her hands casually behind her back. "Is that what Owen likes? Do you let your hair fall over your breasts to hide them, make him want to push it aside and see what you're hiding?"

"What are you doing here? How did you get in?" Claire asked, trying to sound casual and unafraid.

Scared still, she made herself take a breath to calm her racing heart. She needed to think. Something seemed off in Shannon. That sweet face disguised the cunning in her eyes. The soft way she spoke hid the ominous undercurrent laced in her words. It all came clear, the facts of the last months aligning and finally adding up.

Shannon. The crush on Owen that had turned to obsession and a need to be with him all the time. The trivial reasons for her dropping by to see him. The way she was always polite and cordial to Claire with just a hint of frost to her words.

He was supposed to be my future. Not Dale, but Owen, before Claire got in the way.

"Did you think an alarm system would keep me out? Easy enough to follow you home, wait for you to disarm the thing, then slip inside through the back door while you bustled around packing up this and that. Do you really think I'd let you move in with Owen and live happily ever after? That's my life you're stealing, bitch."

"I didn't steal anything from you."

"We had something going when you showed up. The beginning of a relationship is always the best part, don't you think? The flirting and getting-to-know-you phase. Well, I had to take things slow, let him want me, all the while I only hinted at how much I want him. Men. They so love the chase."

Claire grabbed a pair of black yoga pants and pulled them on, trying desperately not to break the tension in the room and set Shannon off.

"I know exactly what it's like to love someone and have another woman get in the way."

"Yes, your ex cheated on you, didn't he? That's why you left him." A smirk lit her face, changing everything about her. Claire saw the woman beneath the veil she wore to hide her true self from the world.

"He did. So, you see, I know how it feels to watch the man you love choose someone else. I know the pain and hurt you must have felt seeing me with Owen. But, Shannon, you and Owen do not have anything beyond a friendship based on a professional relationship. He is not and never was interested in being with you in a romantic way. He made that clear the first day we met and he's made it clear since then by word and action whenever you've injected yourself into his life."

Shannon shook her head. "Like with your ex, you just don't want to see what is so obvious. He wants me, but felt sorry for you after what happened with Dale."

"You don't believe that," Claire said. "If Owen fell for that BS, you'd have had him enamored with you after all the helpless, wounded-soul routine you put on for him."

"Some men like that shit."

"But not Dale, he liked something else about you." She guessed at the nature of their relationship and Shannon's true nature.

Shannon gave her another of those disturbing smiles. "Dale knows exactly what I like and how to please me."

"Yes, until it goes too far, right?"

"He wasn't quite the drunk he is now. He used to control himself."

"Right, because you get off on the danger. Will he take it too far? Will it sting or hurt, and how bad?"

"It's not easy to find someone willing to cross that civilized line. Dale learned to do things my way, but he's unpredictable."

"Adds another layer," Claire guessed. "But no matter the games you played with him, there is still a line that shouldn't be crossed. If you're hoping Owen will be your match, give you what you want, and not cross that line, you're wrong. He'd never hit a woman. For any reason," Claire added.

Shannon laughed and reached up, tracing her finger down the center of her chest and over her breast. "I can be very persuasive when I want to be."

"I'm sure you can, but that doesn't change who Owen is at the core."

"Dale has some of Owen's immense strength, but lacks Owen's control. Once he gets a taste of me, he'll be the perfect lover." Shannon licked her lips and took on this far-off look, fantasizing about Owen. It pissed Claire off.

"You're right about Owen's strength and control, but you're wrong about everything else. Underneath everything, Owen is an honorable man. What you want from him isn't inside him to give. He'd never hurt someone on purpose the way you want him to do. It's just not in him."

"That's what you think?"

"That's what I know. Don't forget, I've been with Owen for months."

"Well, that's about to change."

Claire had never really been in a fight in her life. As an only child, she'd never experienced wrestling and roughhousing, which put her at a serious disadvantage against a charging woman. Despite Claire's two-inch height advantage, Shannon's attack overwhelmed her. Shannon planted both hands on her shoulders and shoved her into the dresser. It caught her on the back, hitting and bruising her hips. Her shoulders hit the wall, stopping her from falling, but putting her off balance on her feet. Shannon had the advantage, held her hand back, and swung, slapping her across the face, cutting her lip on her teeth. Claire tasted blood and came out fighting. She grabbed

Shannon by the arms and shoved her back, gaining her feet again. Shannon wasn't deterred or slowed down. She planted her feet and pushed against Claire's grip. She tried to hold Shannon off, but she swung her hands up through Claire's arms and out, breaking Claire's hold. Stumbling forward, Shannon shifted and knocked Claire to the ground. Shannon landed on her back and grabbed her hair, pulling hard and lifting her head. The sting in her scalp brought tears to Claire's eyes.

Shannon leaned over and whispered in her ear. "He's mine, bitch. You can't have him."

"He loves me," Claire said, fighting with her words.

Enraged, Shannon tried to slam her head into the hardwood floor, but Claire got her hands under her and pushed off the floor, sending Shannon falling off her back. Claire rolled and kicked her away. Shannon didn't even slow down when her foot connected with her thigh. She jumped up and kicked Claire right in the ribs, taking all the air out of her. Claire wrapped an arm around her middle and tried to suck in a breath, but couldn't.

Shannon grabbed her by the hair and dragged her backward toward the bed. Claire had no choice but to scramble to keep up, crab-crawling to keep Shannon from pulling out her hair. One hand fisted in her hair, the other grabbing hold under her arm, Shannon dragged her onto the bed and landed on top of her, straddling her hips.

Claire planted her heels in the mattress and tried to buck Shannon off. She laughed and smiled and it only frustrated and pissed Claire off more.

"What's the matter, bitch, no one taught you how to fight?"

"Get off me. There's nothing you can do to stop me from marrying Owen."

"Wanna bet?"

Shannon closed her fist and swung. Claire raised her arms to block the blow, but Shannon kept on swinging and used her other hand to pull Claire's arms from her face. Shannon landed a punch to her temple and left eye, blurring her vision and stunning her.

Shannon grabbed her hand and tried to pull the ring off. Claire closed her fist to stop her, grabbing Shannon's wrist to pull it away. All she managed to do is rake her fingernails over Shannon's skin, tearing the flesh, but not stopping the determined bitch.

"Stop. You can't take my ring."

Shannon pinched the top of her breast and twisted hard. Claire screamed again and bucked her hips, trying to throw Shannon off again. She laughed and let out an aroused sigh, her eyes closed on a ragged exhale. Claire snatched the opportunity and threw a punch, hitting Shannon right in the jaw. She didn't stop, but hauled her arm back and punched again, hitting Shannon in the cheek and eye, sending her falling to the side on the bed. Damn, that hurt her hand. Claire scrambled up to her knees to make a run for it, but Shannon wasn't done and grabbed her shoulders and slammed her forehead into Claire's temple.

"Nighty-night, bitch."

Claire blacked out, falling backward onto the bed.

Shannon grabbed her face and shook her to make sure she was out.

"You've got some fight, bitch, but you need some practice."

Shannon touched a finger to her swelling eye and winced, even as the smile bloomed on her face and rush of heat shot through her system. She wiped the blood from Claire's split lip and cut eye off on Claire's exposed belly and pulled her legs out from under her, positioning her on the bed to look like she'd gone to sleep.

She pulled the ring from Claire's finger and slid it onto her own, holding the diamond up to catch the light from the bedside table lamp. Despite the smear of blood over the stone, it still sparkled like crazy, making Shannon smile.

"This is mine."

Shannon turned, fell on her butt, and bounced off the end of the bed. A distinct spring in her step, she closed the bedroom door behind her. She kicked the sheets in front of the door, took the lighter from her pocket, and lit the pile on fire. She waited for the blaze to catch, turned, and sprinted down the stairs to the living room. She grabbed one of the thick pillar candles on the coffee table and placed it on the table next to the couch. She lit the wick, leaned down, and blew softly on the flame until it caught the couch on fire. The fire grew quickly, thick smoke filling the air. Once the curtains caught, the flames quickly spread up and across the ceiling. With Claire's room overhead, it wouldn't be long before the bitch burned.

The smoke detector upstairs went off a split second

before the one downstairs. The alarm panel on the wall rang louder than both, creating a blaring sound that nearly made her deaf. The fire continued to spread and she coughed from the noxious smoke rising from the couch and area rug. She ran for the front door, unlocked the deadbolt and handle, and burst outside, quickly closing the door behind her. Two steps away, she turned back and opened the door just enough to reach in and lock the handle. Heat and smoke quickly billowed out. She slammed the door shut, confident the fire department would find everything as it should be. She used her shirt to wipe the already-warm door handle free of her prints and ran from the house.

Nearly eight o'clock, the sun had set and cast the yard in gray shadows that darkened with each passing minute. She'd left her car parked down the road, pulled into some bushes to hide it. When she reached the car, she jumped inside and gripped the steering wheel. She took several deep breaths to calm her racing heart, but only ended up coughing and hacking from the smoke and fumes she'd inhaled.

Her gaze fell on the ring and she spread her fingers wide, taking a better look. Much better than the tiny chip Dale gave her.

"Now that's more like it."

Hands on the wheel, she squeezed her eyes shut, and tried to think what came next. Her eyes stung. She flipped the mirror down and examined her face. Black eye, a knot on her forehead from head-butting Claire, some rake marks and bruises on her arms. Nothing major, but just enough to prove Dale went nuts again and attacked her. Then, he'd gone after Claire and killed her.

"Such a tragedy, Owen losing Claire that way. He'll need consoling. We'll bond over his grief and the pain and anguish Dale put us through."

She smiled, her heart filled with triumph. This time, she'd get what she wanted. What she deserved.

Chapter Forty

Owen dialed Claire's cell phone again. It rang four times before her voicemail picked up for the fourth time.

"Maybe she's in the shower."

"Something is wrong," Owen said again.

This time, his phone rang. He checked caller ID and the knot in his stomach turned to stone. Dread filled him so swiftly, he couldn't breathe, but managed to answer anyway.

"Owen."

"Mr. McBride, this is Fallbrook Security. We have a fire alarm at Ms. Walsh's residence. We've contacted the fire department. They are on the way, but our instructions indicate to notify you of any alarm to the property."

"I'm on my way there. Thank you for calling me." He hung up and glanced at Dylan. "The house is on fire."

"Shit." Dylan picked up the radio and called in the house fire to dispatch at the same time he stomped on the gas and the cruiser hit some dangerous speeds around the back-road corners.

Owen barely held on to the dash and his sanity.

"Hurry the fuck up."

"I'm going as fast as I can."

Owen grabbed his cell again and punched in Brody's number. "Are you at the ranch house?"

"Yes, why?"

"Do you see smoke coming from Claire's place?"

"Shit. Yeah. I see it."

"I'm on my way. She's there. Go get her."

Brody didn't need to be told twice. The line went dead in Owen's ear.

"We're about the same distance away," Dylan pointed out.

"I don't give a shit who gets there first, so long as she's okay."

"Maybe she got out and is fine. Her phone is still in the house, so she can't call you."

"Maybe," Owen said, not believing it. Everything inside of him said she was in that house and he needed to get there. Fast.

They pulled into the driveway just as Brody ran around to the back of the house. Claire's car sat parked in the driveway, the back end pointed at the front door. He leapt from the car, leaving Dylan talking on his radio, giving orders, and detailing the situation.

Owen rushed to look inside Claire's car, hoping to find her waiting inside. No Claire, just a bunch of boxes she'd packed to take to his place. The thought made his heart ache even more.

No use trying to go in through the front. The double doors were engulfed in flames, the glass broken out. He raced after Brody and found him behind the house dragging one of Claire's patio chairs underneath one of the upstairs windows.

"That's her bedroom."

"I saw her by the window," Brody said.

"Where is she?"

"I think she collapsed before she could get the window open."

"Fuck," Owen shouted.

"Only one way to do this." Brody handed him a rock, walked behind him, and stuck his head through Owen's legs, raising him up on his shoulders when Brody stood again. "Hold on. This chair isn't exactly built for our combined weight."

Owen tried to balance and move with Brody as he hoisted them up onto the chair. Brody braced one hand on the wall and the other on the drainpipe attached to the side of the house.

"Can you reach the window?" Brody asked.

"Not really."

"Up you go, man. I've got you."

Owen sucked in a deep breath, and knowing time was of the essence, he maneuvered himself up to stand on Brody's shoulders. Rock in hand, he bashed it into the glass, shattering it. Some rained down on Brody, but his brother didn't move. Owen tried not to move his feet too much on his brother's shoulders while he used the rock to knock all the glass from the frame. He tossed the rock away, planted his hands on the sill, ignored the bite as a leftover piece of glass pierced his skin, and hoisted himself up into the window frame. Claire lay sprawled on the floor, half-naked.

His shoulders barely fit through the sash window, but he managed to wedge them in so he could drag his legs up and through the window. Sirens sounded out front, giving him a momentary sense of relief. Help was on the way.

He fell to his knees and carefully rolled her onto her back. Her hair covered her face, so he traced a finger along her forehead, felt the large welt, sticky with blood, and pulled her hair away.

This was no accidental fire. Shannon had beat her, set the fire, and left her for dead.

Flames licked up the door from inside the house now that he'd opened the window and provided another oxygen source. He needed to get Claire out. Fast. He pulled his shirt up and over his nose, coughing from the smoke quickly filling the room and sinking to the floor. Claire didn't stir when he hoisted her over his shoulder and bent close to the window, gulping in fresh air. Several firemen stood below, raising a ladder. One came up. Reluctant to give up Claire, he did so for her benefit, helping the fireman slide her out the window and over his back, her long hair draped down his legs. He stepped down the ladder, ever mindful of the precious cargo he carried. Owen followed, staring up at the smoking hole, knowing everything in Claire's house was gone, but not her. He'd saved what's important.

Brody gave him a hearty slap on the back when he reached the bottom of the ladder. Firemen let loose with the water hose, shooting it at the flames licking out from beneath the roof eaves.

"They can't save it," Brody said, leading him behind the firemen who'd taken Claire to the front of the house on a stretcher. They set her on the ground out of the way of the firemen trying to contain the fire to the house and not let it spread across the dry grass to the couple of outbuildings.

A medic put an oxygen mask over Claire's face, slid a cuff onto her arm, and checked her blood pressure and used a stethoscope to listen to her heart. The frown made Owen's heart sink into his stomach. The guy pressed on her bruised ribs. The first sign of life sent him to his knees beside her. She flinched from the pressure to her battered side and coughed uncontrollably, trying to roll to her side, but the medic and Owen held her down.

"You're okay, sweetheart. I've got you. I'm here," Owen crooned, holding her hand to his cheek. She didn't open her eyes, but the coughing subsided when the medic gave her some water. He used an instrument to check her nose and throat.

"She's got clear airways, despite the irritation from the smoke," the medic reassured him. "I'm concerned about that head injury. She may have a concussion to go with her cracked ribs. I don't think they're broken, but we'll get X rays at the hospital. The ambulance should be here in the next couple of minutes."

"Thanks for taking care of her."

"You got her out fast and alive. That's what counts."

The medic covered her with a blanket. Owen held her hand and whispered he loved her into her ear. He hoped and prayed she heard him and held on until they got her to the hospital. Even he could hear how hard she labored for each breath. The longer she struggled, the more she squirmed and tried to shift to relieve the ache in her ribs. He hated every moment she hurt.

"Where the fuck is that ambulance?"

"Right there." The medic pointed to the driveway. The blue and red flashing lights momentarily confused him, but then his vision focused past the chaos of the firemen and police on scene to the car that pulled in behind the ambulance.

Shannon.

Owen felt the rage swell inside of him and fill him up, but he held it down, leaned over Claire, and kissed her on the lips, despite the nasty cut.

"I love you. I swear to you, no one will ever hurt you like this again."

The rage was only tempered by the squeeze of her hand in his. She'd heard him.

"I love you, sweetheart, but I have to leave you for a few minutes. I promise you, I'll be right back."

She held firm to his hand, letting him know without words she didn't want him to go.

"I need to finish this once and for all. I swear to you, I'll be right back. Brody is right here beside you."

Owen placed Claire's hand in his brothers. "Don't let go. Watch over her until I get back."

"I swear, no one gets by me," Brody assured him. "Go. Do what you have to do."

Owen touched his finger to her forehead and with a heavy heart left her in Brody's protection. Not that Shannon would get past him. Not this time. Not again.

Owen approached Dylan, who stood at the front of Shannon's car, waiting for her to get out.

"Ready?" Dylan asked, saying so much in that one short word.

"I've got this," he said, reining in his rage and the need to kill her the minute he saw her. Instead, he thought quickly, ordering his thoughts into a cohesive plan.

Shannon stepped out of the car and approached them. He hoped she saw grief on his face and not anger. He noted the black eye, the bruise on her jaw, and the gashes on her arms. Claire didn't go down easily. No, she went down fighting.

"Owen, are you okay? You look terrible," Shannon said, rushing up to him, putting her hands on his chest, and pressing close. He let her. She'd played games with his life, his turn to play games with hers.

"She's gone," he said, his voice gruff and raw, mostly thanks to the smoke he'd inhaled saving Claire, but it worked to his advantage now. Okay, maybe he played it up.

"What happened?" she asked, her voice filled with concern. He wondered how she did that so convincingly.

"I don't know how the fire started, but she must have been overcome from the smoke." He touched his finger to her eye, which probably hurt like hell. She didn't even flinch, but leaned into his touch. "What happened to you? Are you okay?" he asked, adding as much fake concern as he could to the question.

"Dale. He came back and did this to me. He threatened to finish it. I guess, maybe . . . Do you think he came here to kill Claire?"

So that's how she wanted to play this. Blame Dale again. Make him the scapegoat to her latest plan to get Claire out of the picture and somehow win his heart.

"When did you see Dale?" he asked, holding her by the shoulders.

"Just a little while ago. He found me at the house. We got into it when he refused to leave. I rushed out here, concerned he might have gone after you or Claire again."

"Why didn't you call the police? You know I can't stand it when he hurts you."

"Oh, Owen, everything is going to be okay. They'll find Dale and arrest him for all of this. Claire is gone, but you've got me to lean on. We'll get through this together."

"You think so?" he asked, squeezing her arms when she tried to pull back.

"Owen, you're hurting me."

He met her gaze and squeezed harder, seeing the excitement in her eyes. He dropped his voice and whispered, "You like it when it hurts just a little bit."

"Owen?"

He slid one hand up over her shoulder to the back of her neck and pulled her close. He cringed being this close, but sucked it up for Claire, and whispered in Shannon's ear. "You like it. You want me to make it hurt oh so good, because that's what excites you. That's what gets you off."

Her hand came up to hold on to his wrist. She smiled and her breath came out in short pants, excitement and anticipation rolling off her in waves.

"You understand me," she said. "Without her in the way, you'll see, we'll be so good together."

Owen traced his fingers across her neck, drawing away from her. He made a show of wiping his hand down his shirt, like wiping off something distasteful after touching her. He had to admit, as much as he wanted to wrap his fingers around her throat and choke the life out of her, he hated touching her.

Surprised and confused, she stared up at him, but didn't see the real danger in front of her.

"I have something to tell you."

"What? What is it?" she asked, a bundle of anticipation.

"Dale is locked up behind bars. He has been in custody for days and weeks before that."

Her eyes went wide. She stepped back, her butt hitting the front of her car. Nowhere to go, he took a menacing step closer and she leaned back, finally understanding the threat he posed.

"I know you hurt Claire. Over and over again, you terrorized her all in some sick attempt to get her out of my life. This has been nothing but your vain attempt to get my attention. Well, you have it."

She reached up and grasped his shirt in both hands. "Owen, please, I'm sorry."

"Sorry you got caught."

"I didn't do anything," she pleaded, her eyes filling with tears he ignored. Too good of an actress, he didn't believe a single tear that slid down her cheek.

"You smell like smoke. I'll bet we find your skin under Claire's nails. If that isn't enough, you're wearing her engagement ring." He pointed looked down at the hand fisted in his shirt. "That ring and everything it symbolizes belongs to Claire. I love her. I feel nothing but pity and contempt for you. I will do everything in my power to see you spend the maximum amount of time behind bars for doing this."

"Maybe, but you won't have her."

"Yes, I will." He turned just enough to give her the perfect view of them loading Claire into the ambulance, Brody beside her, holding her hand.

"No!" Shannon shoved past him, but he grabbed her wrist and held on, until she stopped trying to pull free.

He got right in her face. "I'll see you spend the rest of your miserable days behind bars. You like pain. I hope you find it every day for the rest of your life without ever feeling any of the pleasure you crave at another's expense."

Owen pulled Claire's ring free and shoved Shannon away, right into Dylan's hands. Stunned by the move, Dylan had her handcuffed before she knew what was happening. Dylan stuffed her into this patrol car. Pissed off and out of control, she kicked the seat and thrashed against the backrest.

"Stop, or I'll tase your ass," he threatened.

Both of them shook their heads when a spark of anticipation lit her eyes.

"There is something truly wrong with that woman," Dylan said, walking with him to the ambulance.

Brody switched places with him, and Owen sat on the small bench beside Claire, holding her hand. He slipped the ring onto her finger and kissed her palm.

Her eyes fluttered open, and he showed her the ring. "Shannon is on her way to jail. This belongs to you, and so do I. I love you."

Claire squeezed his hand. He let out a deep sigh and pressed her palm to his cheek as the paramedic watched over Claire and they drove to the hospital. He stayed by her side, and would for the rest of his days.

Epilogue

OWEN SAT BESIDE Claire's hospital bed, marveling that ten months after he'd sat beside her like this after the fire she held his baby boy in her arms. Tired after the birth, she still looked radiant when she smiled.

"He's beautiful," she said.

"You're amazing."

She laughed and reached up to stroke his cheek. "I'm tired, but I can't stop looking at him."

"I can't stop looking at both of you in wonder. I'm so happy, Claire, and so damn lucky to have both of you in my life." He took her hand and brought it to his mouth, kissing her knuckles above her wedding rings.

The first time he brought Claire home from the hospital, he'd surprised her with the few items that survived the fire that she'd packed in her car. He'd hung the black-and-white photos of Paris in their bedroom. The four sea scenes hung in the bathroom as she'd had them at her house. He put the pretty blue glass bottles on the sunken tub ledge. The other items he'd spread through the downstairs living room and kitchen so that any room she entered, there'd be a piece of her mixed with his.

She cried that day for all she'd lost, but soon wiped the tears and looked to their future and planning their wedding.

They got married two months after she got out of the hospital. A small ceremony in the backyard he'd had landscaped with a stone patio and path to complement the deck. Flowers and shrubs filled in the garden spaces. With the tall, old trees spreading their limbs over everything, the canopy shaded the yard and cocooned them in the quiet peacefulness they found out there together both day and night.

A knock sounded at the door. Brody pushed it open and allowed Dawn, Autumn, and Rain, carrying baby David, into the room before he followed.

Brody finally asked Rain to marry him the night before they moved into their new house. He married her in a quiet family ceremony a month after David arrived. Owen served as best man and Claire stood beside Rain as her matron of honor. Dawn and Autumn were beautiful flower girls at both weddings with little Will serving as the ring bearer.

"Hey, is it a good time for a visit?" Rain asked.

Owen stood and wrapped her in a hug. "Hey, beautiful. It's a great time to have family around."

Owen greeted his brother with a hug and a slap on the back. They stood side by side, looking down at their wives sitting next to each other with the two new McBride boys in their arms.

"If they're anything like us," Brody said, "We're in trouble."

Owen laughed and smiled at his wife. "I'm up for it. Are you?"

"Absolutely."

Another knock sounded and Dylan stuck his head in. "Mind if we come in?"

"Not at all," Claire called, showing off the baby to Dawn and Autumn, who stood close to the edge of the bed to get a better look.

Dylan had bought Claire's old place and built a new house. He and Will had settled in just a week ago. Dylan was busy buying furniture and keeping the peace in town.

Owen gave Will a tickle to the gut, snatched him from Dylan's arms, and settled him at the foot of the bed next to David under Rain's watchful eye. He turned back to Dylan and accepted the congratulatory hug. Sticking close, he whispered, "I heard about Mr. Thompson dying this morning."

"Yeah," was all Dylan said.

"Did you speak to Brian about Jessie?"

"No. Not yet, but I will. I just hope it's not too late to find out what really happened to her. If she didn't leave town on her own, I hope that bastard didn't take his secrets to the grave."

Owen hoped so, too. For Dylan's sake. He gave his cousin a squeeze on the shoulder and propelled him toward Brody to say hello and join the family. He settled on the bed next to Claire, his arm around her shoulders, their baby asleep on her chest.

"So, what's the newest McBride's name?" Brody asked.

Claire looked up at him and smiled, letting him say it. "He's our Sean Brody McBride."

"Oh, I love it," Rain said, tears glistening in her eyes. The girls shared her sentiment. Owen stared at his brother and they exchanged a silent moment of connection. He'd repaid Brody for doing the same. David Owen McBride wiggled at the end of the bed, trying to grab his cousin Will's fingers.

This is what they'd wanted. Family.

The door opened again and Claire's parents came in with balloons and flowers. Owen stood to take them and add them to the rest Brody and Dylan had sent earlier. He greeted his in-laws and everyone settled around the room, carrying on conversations and fussing over the babies and Claire. He settled next to her again on the bed, this time placing his sleeping son on his chest. He held him there with one hand, Claire tucked against his side.

A nurse came in to check on her. "Mrs. McBride, can I get you anything?"

Claire glanced around the room at everyone gathered to see her and the baby. She settled back into his side and hugged him and Sean close.

"No. I have everything I need."

Can't get enough of Jennifer Ryan's McBride men?
Good news, the sheriff of Fallbrook gets his turn next in

DYLAN'S REDEMPTION

Book Three: The McBrides
Coming August 2014

AFTER A HEATED fight with her father, Jessie Thompson fled Fallbrook, vowing never to return. But when her father dies, she reluctantly returns home for the funeral, only to find herself face-to-face with the man who shattered her heart. A man who, for eight years, believed she was dead.

Dylan McBride accepted the position as the new sheriff of Fallbrook, looking for a fresh start. He didn't expect it to include the woman he'd once loved and thought he'd lost forever.

Even though Dylan's heart has already grieved for Jessie, he can't deny the passion that still smolders between them. Can they heal their past and find a second chance at first love?

About the Author

JENNIFER RYAN writes romantic suspense and contemporary small-town romances featuring strong men and equally resilient women. Her stories are filled with love, friendship, and the happily-ever-after we all hope to find. Jennifer lives in the San Francisco Bay Area with her husband and three children. When she isn't writing a book, she's reading one.

Visit www.AuthorTracker.com for exclusive information on your favorite HarperCollins authors.

About the Author

JENNIFER RYAN writes romantic suspense and contemporary small town romances featuring strong men and equally resilient women. Her stories are filled with love, friendships, and the happily-ever-after we all hope to find. Jennifer lives in the San Francisco Bay Area with her husband and three children. When she isn't writing a book, she's reading one.

Visit www.AuthorTracker.com for exclusive information on your favorite HarperCollins authors.

Give in to your impulses . . .

Read on for a sneak peek at two brand-new e-book original tales of romance from Avon Books.

Available now wherever e-books are sold.

THE RETURN OF BRODY McBRIDE

Book One: The McBrides

By Jennifer Ryan

THE CUPCAKE DIARIES: SPRINKLED WITH KISSES

By Darlene Panzera

An Excerpt from

THE RETURN OF BRODY McBRIDE

Book One: The McBrides

by Jennifer Ryan

From *New York Times* bestselling author Jennifer Ryan comes an unforgettable new series about the sexy McBride men of Fallbrook, Colorado. Brody McBride left devastation in his wake when he ran away years ago. Can he return and win back the heart of Rain?

Brody woke with a start and gasped for breath, his hands pressed to his heaving chest, where the bullet had slammed into his bulletproof vest months ago, severely bruising his ribs. Used to sleeping in some of the most hostile places in the world, he took in his surroundings with a quick sweep of his gaze. All safe. Adrenaline racing through his veins, he checked his first instinct and stilled his hand, already reaching beneath the pillow for his gun. He wished he could shake off the nightmare and memories as quickly as he had sleep.

Alert, he now remembered arriving at the old cabin late last night. Clear Water Ranch. He and Owen should rename the place Mud. Nothing pristine about the blood running through his veins. His father had sullied it, along with the McBride name.

Just the thought of being on the ranch again set off a barrage of memories, most of him and Owen running wild. He couldn't pick one out, or grasp the prevailing feeling that went with them. A mixture of happy and sad times, frightening things better left forgotten but relived in Technicolor nightmares, and anger stored up over years, like a river cutting its path until a deep gorge separated the banks. Instead of spending the last eight years rebuilding bridges, he'd let the gap grow wider.

His stellar military career came with its own kind of horrors—right up until a roadside bomb took out three of his friends and left him wounded, ending his third tour in Afghanistan and his stint with the Army Rangers. He'd stowed them away with the other bad memories.

Two months of rehab under his belt, he'd returned home to pull the tattered pieces of his life together and mend them into something of a happy future. Hell, he'd settle for dull and normal.

He'd have exceptional if he won Rain back.

He'd blown it with her and let love slip through his fingers. Back then, he'd had nothing to offer her. Now, he was a different man, the man she'd always seen inside of him.

Her trail might be cold, but he'd track her, and before she knew it, he'd be hot on her tail. That was exactly where he planned to stay until he convinced her his days as a selfish prick were over. He wanted to put the past behind him, prove to himself and everyone else that he could be a different kind of man than his father was, and find that all-American dream he'd spent years protecting for others. So long as Rain was part of it, he'd find that elusive happiness.

Judging by the sunlight streaming in the windows, early morning was greeting him. A soft breeze filtered up to the loft from what could only be the open door downstairs. Papers rustled, then everything went quiet. Company. His brother had come calling. Time to face his past.

An Excerpt from

THE CUPCAKE DIARIES: SPRINKLED WITH KISSES

by Darlene Panzera

Fans of Debbie Macomber will adore the fifth installment in Darlene Panzera's sweet Cupcake Diaries series . . . a tale of sand, sun, and summer love!

"How much for the ice cream scoop?" the man beside her asked.

His voice was rich, smooth, with a deep timbre that struck a chord within her, and she cast a reflexive glance in his direction to see if he looked as attractive as he sounded.

Yes, *oh yes*. The man dressed in bathing trunks and a t-shirt standing less than an arm's reach away was definitely heart breaker material. His six-foot-four-inch height made her Amazonian five-foot-eleven feel normal. His sandy blond hair and aqua eyes replicated a Ken doll, while his muscular frame exuded the masculinity of a sculpted G.I. Joe.

Did he wear a wedding ring? Her gaze darted toward his left hand. *Nope!* She took a deep breath to steady her nerves. This guy could be a prime candidate to ask to accompany her to Kim's wedding if only she could summon the courage to ask him.

Wait, a minute. Not so fast. She needed to get to know him better first. She needed him to ask her on a date.

The handsome guy paid the yard sale owner the amount requested and turned toward her as if sensing her gaze. "The vintage scoop my grandfather gave me broke, and the new ones they make these days just aren't the same. See how the sides of this scoop dip down to form an elongated oval?"

Her skin prickled with self-awareness, and she wished she'd taken the time to brush her mousy rust-brown hair into at least an attempted semblance of order. Too late now. Her appearance was what it was. She'd just have to try to dazzle him with her personality instead.

No, she feared that wouldn't work either. But what if she tried to be smart like Andi?

"You must really love ice cream." *Oh no.* Did she really just say that? *Lame!* Incredibly *lame.*

"I do love ice cream," he replied. "My grandfather's homemade blackberry sherbet could make an ice cream enthusiast out of a heat-lovin' gecko."

Flirt like Rachel. She smiled—hopefully with nothing stuck in her teeth. "Now you're making *me* hungry."

"For ice cream or lizard?" he teased.

"I was referring to the ice cream. Lizard isn't on my favorite foods list."

Okay, good job. Would he take the hint and ask her to accompany him to an ice cream shop? Or a beach picnic? Anywhere but a formal restaurant. She hadn't dated much in the past but for some reason dinner dates at restaurants never fared well.

A handsome guy like him undoubtedly had a girlfriend. Or several. Maybe that was why he hadn't responded to her last comment. Maybe taking her out for food was off limits.

A pro when it came to taking precautions, she decided a backup plan was in order and grabbed the half-dozen peanut butter–and-cracker MREs she spotted in a box on the table beside them. The military surplus snack was a perfect fit for both her budget and her backpack.

In addition to the Meal, Ready-to-Eat find, she picked up a multi-tool knife, which also included folding mini scissors—as well as a screwdriver, bottle opener, file, and corkscrew.

"Great tool for camping," the ice cream lover said, still beside her.

She nodded. "A must-have for my backpack."

"I'm Dave Wright," he said, smiling.

"Stacey McIntyre."

"How many miles do you average?"

"Excuse me?"

"Hiking with your backpack," he clarified.

Did Dave think she was a nature lover like Kim? Or an adventurer like *Kate Jones,* the kick-butt heroine from the treasured action-adventure novels on her bookshelf? A surge of warm, wishful thinking filled her. If *only.*

beside them. The military surplus store was a perfect fit for both her budget and her backpack.

In addition to the Meal, Ready-to-Eat kind, she picked up a multi-tool knife, which also included folding mini scissors—as well as a screwdriver, bottle opener, file, and corkscrew.

"Great tool for camping," the [illegible] lover said, still beside her.

She nodded. "A must-have for my backpack."

"I'm Dave Wright," he said, smiling.

"Stacey McIntyre."

"How many miles do you average?"

"Excuse me?"

"Hiking with your backpack," he clarified.

Did Dave think she was a nature lover like him? Or an adventurer like Kate Jones, the kick-butt heroine from the treasured [illegible] adventure novels on her bookshelf? A nurse or warm, soulful [illegible] like [illegible].